## PRAISE FOR LAURA RESAU

### *The River Muse*

"As she did in *The Alchemy of Flowers*, Laura Resau has crafted another enthralling, transportive, and heartfelt story in *The River Muse*. Infused with subtle touches of magic and set against the sumptuous backdrop of Southern France, the story unfolds with the same lyrical dreaminess as La Chanson, the mystical river that draws Callie to its shores. The novel deals with the toll psychological domestic abuse takes on Callie and her young daughter, but that subject's weightiness is deftly balanced by the healing forces of the found family and friends Callie discovers at the mystical Chateau of the Lost. Secondary characters like a mercurial 'wine witch,' a restless young ghost, and the handsome but troubled Luc add richness to the story's layers as their pasts become entangled with Callie's present. At its core, this is a tale about healing and courage, about facing the demons that haunt you so that you can remember who you were always meant to be. *The River Muse* is as savory as a warm croissant, as rich and satisfying as a haunting melody or a perfectly paired wine."

—Suzanne Nelson, author of
*The Librarians of Lisbon*

"Lyrical and atmospheric, *The River Muse* transports you effortlessly to the South of France with a cast of characters who feel like old friends. And yet, this book is more than its rich setting. At its heart, this is a story of the power we all carry—sometimes a roar, and other times a quiet voice we must be bold enough to hear."

—Nicole Hackett, author of *Mom Brain*

"*The River Muse* is a lyrical story of loss, healing, and second chances. Resilience, forgiveness, and the courage to begin again are expertly interwoven with ghosts from the past and long-held secrets to create another page-turner for Resau."

—Elizabeth Bass Parman, author of *The Empress of Cooke County* and *Bees in June*

"Fans of Sarah Addison Allen's magical novels will rejoice over Laura Resau's *The River Muse*. This fanciful tale unfolds in the South of France as a woman escapes a dangerous relationship, intending to hide away in a charming cottage, but instead she rediscovers her own creativity and befriends a quirky cast of characters that inspire the courage to fight for a new life for herself and her daughter. At the Chateau of the Lost, a place where magic abounds in both music and nature, lost souls find their way and good things are still possible. Even the most unexpected second chances."

—Kimberly Brock, award-winning author of *The Fabled Earth*

"Laura Resau knows how to capture the heart as well as the senses, deftly balancing rich characters, lush settings, and a little bit of magic with the painful reality of leaving an abusive relationship. Evocative, unflinching, and emotionally generous, *The River Muse* brings readers deep into its world and offers a gift as powerful as the mythic carnyx: a resonant story of finding a path toward healing, finding a family, and finding one's voice."

—Amy Rossi, author of *The Cover Girl*

"*The River Muse* is brimming with gaiety and delight, in both plot and place, and yet this novel does not shy away from the very real dangers of escaping an unhealthy relationship. As the protagonist—and an entire community—gathers strength to stand up to dark forces, we see the power of resolve and resilience. To borrow a line from the book, this work is 'A song . . . A song beyond space and time.' It is a song, calling to us all: Be delighted by the world while simultaneously standing up for one another."

—Laura Pritchett, author of *Three Keys*

## *The Alchemy of Flowers*

"'An impossible marvel' . . . *The Alchemy of Flowers* by Laura Resau is a spellbinding journey of one woman's journey toward hope and healing, set amidst a garden of both promise and peril. Full of lush sensory detail, this tale is a vivid reminder that while the path to healing may be fraught with challenges, it is often through confronting the shadows that we find our true strength. A beautifully written, atmospheric novel that will leave readers both mesmerized and moved."

—Sarah Penner, *New York Times* bestselling author of *The Amalfi Curse*

"Set in a secret garden, *The Alchemy of Flowers* offers a lush blend of myth, magic, and mystery. Beautifully written and brimming with heartache, danger, and enchantment, this is a moving, memorable story about hope, healing, and starting over."

—Heather Webber, *USA TODAY* bestselling author of *Midnight at the Blackbird Café*

"Utterly captivating. This beautiful novel casts a whispery spell of dark enchantments, secrets, and myth."

—Evie Woods, bestselling author of *The Mysterious Bakery on Rue de Paris*

"For everyone who has dreamed of teleporting to the paradise of Provence, I have the book for you. *The Alchemy of Flowers* is a treat of transporting, incandescent storytelling, with a riveting undercurrent of suspense and mystery too. With tender, heartfelt prose and characters who will break your heart and then stitch it back together, Resau's adult debut feels like the modern French Provençal take on *Under the Tuscan Sun* we've all been jonesing for. Capturing the magic of beloved childhood reading experiences, while dealing with hard adult topics lovingly and achingly explored, the book is at once an enchanting journey and an unforgettable, page-turning read."

—Jaclyn Goldis, author of *The Chateau* and *The Safari*

"Laura Resau's *The Alchemy of Flowers* is an immersive, sensory experience. Resau treats bone-crushing-hard topics, like pregnancy loss, with love and sensitivity, all the while taking the reader on a mystical journey. Deftly crafted and imaginative; a rare treat of a book."

—Aimie K. Runyan, bestselling author of *The Memory of Lavender and Sage* and *The Wandering Season*

"*The Alchemy of Flowers* is a pure magical and sensory delight. Like roots in soil, though, the gift of this book goes deeper. Resau's novel offers an honest and compassionate portrait of the physical pain and health-related sorrows that go along with being human. So many of us can relate, and we can also relate to the wondrous alchemy and healing found in nature. This gorgeous novel captures both the heartbreak and the true healing at our disposal, if only we seek to turn difficulty into blooms."

—Laura Pritchett, author of *Three Keys*

"*The Alchemy of Flowers* captivates the senses as well as the imagination in a magical tale of healing and forgiveness. Yet this Paradise harbors its own dark mystery that threatens the tranquility of the gardens and the well-being of its inhabitants. Resau has written with great heart an eerie yet deeply touching story that keeps the pages turning until the very end."

—Melissa Payne, bestselling author of *In the Beautiful Dark* and *The Wild Road Home*

"A haunting, immersive tale set in prose as lush and magical as the garden itself."

—Kate Khavari, author of the
Saffron Everleigh mystery series

"Gorgeously written and threaded with herbal wisdom, floral intuition, and mythology of the feminine, *The Alchemy of Flowers* is a journey into how nature and friendship can deeply heal. Resau tangles sweetness and bitterness, tenderness and fierceness to offer a thrilling tale rich with emotion. A delight in every sense of the word."

—Bailey Cattrell, author of the
Enchanted Garden Mysteries

"This book made me want to sleep in a hammock in a treetop bungalow surrounded by the novel's lush, magic-steeped gardens. Eloise's journey to healing is poignant and tender—a testament to the strength of love, the power of tending to earth and growing things, and found family."

—Suzanne Nelson, author of
*The Librarians of Lisbon*

"I devoured this in one sitting! Immersive, enchanting, and packed with mystery, *The Alchemy of Flowers* drew me in from page one. I was rooting for the curious and brave heroine, Eloise, and her cryptic compatriots in the Jardins du Paradis, as each finds friendship and healing after their own separate heartbreaks. The dreamy Provençal walled garden is the perfect escapist setting. Fans of Sarah Addison Allen will love this charming, feel-good novel."

—Andrea Jo DeWerd, author of
*What We Sacrifice for Magic*

ALSO BY LAURA RESAU

*The Alchemy of Flowers*

# THE RIVER MUSE

*a novel*

LAURA RESAU

*The River Muse*



Published by Harper Muse, an imprint of HarperCollins Focus LLC, 501 Nelson Place, Nashville, TN 37214, USA.



ISBN 978-1-4003-4913-5 (ePub)
ISBN 978-1-4003-4914-2 (DA)
ISBN 978-1-4003-4912-8 (TP)



HarperCollins Publishers, Macken House, 39/40 Mayor Street Upper, Dublin 1, D01 C9W8, Ireland (https://www.harpercollins.com)

**Library of Congress Cataloging-in-Publication Data**

CIP data is available upon request.

*Printed in the United States of America*

26 27 28 29 30 LBC 5 4 3 2 1

*Art Direction: Halie Cotton*
*Cover Design: Lindy Kasler*
*Interior Design: Jackie Alvarado*

*To my husband, Ian, for love*
*To our son, Bran, for music*
*To our dog, Opal, for laughter*

We have fallen into the place
where everything is music.

—RUMI

# AUTHOR'S NOTE

Dear Reader,

If you'd like a heads-up about sensitive content, please read this note.

I want to let you know that this story is about healing and hope, but it does deal with issues of moving on after an emotionally abusive relationship. I've found that sharing our experiences in this realm can help us feel seen, heard, healed, and connected.

Warmly,
Laura

*La Chanson*
*Provence, France*

*You call me the Song, you humans do. You always have, in your ever-shifting languages, since long ago, before the Provençals and Gauls and Romans and Celts, back to the time before speech, when your sound for me was itself a song.*

*My waters rise from the source, deep in the earth, from secret caverns, hidden pockets of spirit. A rumble of bass moves through limestone tunnels, upward and onward, around curves, gathering chords, minor and major, until out flows a song, azure and cerulean, plucked from sunshine and moonbeam.*

*Some say my music echoes your soul, harmonizes with fears and longings, calls forth your own song, until it spills out in liquid jewels.*

*If, of course, you are worthy.*

*My waters sing of death too, a low drumbeat that rattles the bones.*

*There are those of you who bring out the river dragon in me.*

*And my gaping mouth swallows you whole.*

# 1

# ESCAPE

In morning sunshine, as her daughter slept, Callie cranked open the window of their attic nook, breathing in buttery scents of croissants from a nearby *boulangerie*.

*We are free.*

Peering at the cobbled street below, she tried out the thought. It felt like looking over a cliff, that mix of vertigo and awe, fear and joy, some muscles clenching, others relaxing, as her heart tried to make sense of it all.

One week ago, back in Colorado, she'd taken an axe to her prison, left behind heaps of splintered wood and glass, then flown away. Literally and figuratively on all counts. And now, bit by bit, she dared to open the window in her chest, a crack at first, then wider and wider still, letting birdsong and street music breeze in and out.

*We are free.*

Maybe if she thought it enough, she'd feel only the bright aspects of their escape and none of the dark ones.

For a moment, she allowed herself to sink into the coziness of her rental, tucked into the top floor of an eighteenth-century building. Sipping café au lait, she observed the street below, people walking tiny dogs, coming and going with baguettes. A waiter was setting up tables at the bistro, propping up a chalkboard sign with the *prix fixe* menu. An ancient fountain bubbled a low tune, drawing from underground springs—the namesake of this town, given by Romans two thousand years ago—Aix, meaning "waters." Aix-en-Provence.

Amid the bustle, one person remained still. A tall blond man, staring at the entrance to her apartment building.

As Callie scrutinized him, the back of her neck prickled. He wore a button-down shirt and linen pants that evoked her ex-partner's style—custom tailored and oozing wealth. But the resemblance ended there. This man looked a couple decades younger than Brett, closer to Callie's age, mid-thirties, his hair wavy and light, eyes hidden behind sunglasses.

She squinted, recognizing something about him. What was he doing? Waiting for someone?

It hit her like a throat punch. This was Brett's personal assistant from the Paris office. The sorcerer had tracked her down. Blood pounded in her ears. Would this man take them back? *Could* he?

A voice rose from the cave inside her. A voice she'd once thought was stolen forever. Low and thunderous and bold. An underwater whale sound that reverberated through her bones.

*No.*

She cranked the window shut, hoping the morning light would glare off the glass and hide her—but he'd probably already seen her. Tearing at a hangnail, she watched him glance between his phone and her building entrance.

For a fraction of a second, part of her wondered if she was just being paranoid, imagining things. But a bigger part knew that her uncertainty was a remnant of two years with Brett, years doubting her own eyes, her mind, her intuition.

Callie checked that the deadbolt was locked, then peeked at Eva, still asleep. Hopefully, her eight-year-old mind was dreaming of happy things—dogs and ice cream and freedom.

In swift, quiet movements, Callie cleaned and packed, forming a plan. How surreal, that her life had come to this. Also, how had Eva gotten sticky fingers over every single cabinet and table surface in just one week? And how had her shorts ended up on the windowsill and her sunscreen under the bed? The child was a whirlwind.

Twenty minutes later, Callie had packed their two carry-ons and backpacks, mostly removed the stickiness—jam? honey? fruit tart glaze?—and taped a note about a family emergency to the landlord's door. Luckily, she'd only paid for a week so far.

All the money she had in the world—three thousand crisp euros—was stashed in an envelope in her backpack. She thanked Past Callie for this secret gift, knowing she'd have to manage it very carefully. Brett had cut her off from friends and family—there was no one to ask for help. At times, the responsibility felt crushing.

From the window, she eyed the blond assistant, whose gaze hadn't strayed from the entrance. Should she call the police?

But there had been no tangible crime against them. Not here and not in Colorado. Brett had never physically hurt her or Eva, never directly threatened or harassed them. He'd only controlled in the subtlest of ways. And his assistant on the street below was doing nothing illegal.

By the time Eva woke up, Callie had breakfast spread on the table—*pain au chocolat* and yogurt and fresh apricots from the market.

Her daughter's first words upon waking: "We should really get a Pomeranian." As Eva ate and chattered about the benefits of the breed, Callie nodded along while her mind raced, emotions in turmoil. Her daughter was old enough to grasp the gravity of their situation, yet Callie didn't want to traumatize her even more.

"You can carry them in your purse. Or even in a baby carriage, Mom!" Eva had recently stopped calling her Mommy, which gave Callie a pang.

Eva scooped yogurt into her mouth, making a little white mustache. As she shook off grogginess, her chocolate-brown eyes sparked brighter, framed by thick lashes, both of which she'd gotten from her late father. "They're smart too. I could train one to do tricks."

"Hmm." Callie ached at the thought of uprooting her again. She watched her chatter, her skin a shade darker from the early June sunshine, her hair the deep mahogany of her dad's, but with Callie's wild curls. She was funny and lighthearted and quirky like he'd been, and just as gifted with languages.

"Pomeranians are perfect for small spaces, Mom. Like this apartment." Eva waved around her yogurt-coated spoon to emphasize the point.

"Hmm." God, her daughter was beautiful, especially when she was elated—but that was what all mothers thought about their children, of course. Eva was extra beautiful, though, since she was a talking, walking reminder of Nick—including the timbre of her voice, pleasantly resonant like his, even back when she was a toddler.

What would Callie's dead husband think about this situation she'd gotten their daughter into, these past two years of nightmare? Even though she'd never married Brett, he'd found ways to metaphorically handcuff her to him.

Back in Colorado, just last week, the final straw that made her break away had been so sudden. She'd had only days to plan, and so much going awry. She'd left the way you'd flee a tsunami, something huge enough to let her intuition burst through, to grab her daughter and go.

Callie took a deep breath. "Sweet pea, you up for another adventure? A new town?"

"What?" Alarm spread over Eva's face. "No! I want to stay and get a Pomeranian. Maybe two."

Callie bit her lip. "Hey, let's just do some exploring."

Eva was an expressive child, emotions clearly written on her face, not in shades of pink like Callie's but in wild movements of eyes and brows and mouth and chin and cheeks, which leapt around like little creatures. And now, realization dawned over her face, a vivid mix of sorrow and fear. "You think Brett found us," she whispered.

Callie steadied her voice, realizing Eva was more aware than she'd assumed. "We'll handle it, but he might have sent someone to watch us."

Eva widened her eyes, as if fully grasping the extent of his reach. "A spy? Really?"

A spy—Callie could work with that, make it feel like a game. Hand on her daughter's shoulder, she pointed out the window. "See that tall, blond guy in a suit?"

Eva nodded, furrowing her brow.

"He's Brett's assistant."

The man's gaze stayed eerily locked on their entrance. Callie remembered how she'd thought he'd looked like a suave Gumby when she'd met him. She forgot the man's name, but he'd delivered a package of antiquities to Brett's house last year—probably an illegal trade.

She kept her voice light. "Let's see how fast you can get ready, sweetie." On her laptop, she pressed repeat on a whimsical folk version of "You Are My Sunshine" that Eva loved. Gamification was in order. "Let's see if we can be ready to go before the third time the song plays."

In ten minutes, Eva was dressed, teeth brushed, hair somewhat tamed into a ponytail. With a stab in her chest, Callie took one last look at the sweet attic apartment, then shut the door behind them.

"Hold on to the handrail, sweetie," she said, struggling to carry their bags down the narrow stone staircase. When they'd arrived last week, it had felt like scaling the Rocky Mountains on a rainy day without hiking boots. Navigating ancient stairs must be one of those European life skills, like making meals last three hours.

At the bottom, she waited inside the cool shadows of the tiled foyer, going over her plan with Eva, amid locked bikes and strollers overflowing with blankets and outdoor toys. Callie carefully framed it as a spy game, drawing on a movie they'd watched a dozen times, with the premise of kids defeating an evil mastermind by using their wits and gadgets.

Once Eva had the plan down, she searched for potential spy gear among the toys, chattering about how, if only they had a bunch of dogs, she could throw the enemy off track by pretending she was a professional dog walker. She punctuated her reflections with, "Really, though, what do you think about getting a Pomeranian, Mom?"

Callie sensed Eva was choosing optimism over fear, but of course the fear was still there, layers deep. She detected it in her daughter's eyes, heard the slightest quaver in her voice, saw the set of her chin, her refusal to cower. A part of Eva was scared but was channeling that energy into joy, the way she'd transformed stage fright into charisma at her school's talent show.

Kissing the top of Eva's head, Callie drew her in for a hug, breathed in her citrus scent. "Hey, we got this, sweet pea."

"I know, Mom."

Twenty minutes later, when a couple with two children emerged from their first-floor apartment, Callie stayed inside the foyer while Eva followed them. Her brown curls were tucked under her cap, sunglasses hiding her eyes, backpack strapped on, wheelie bag bouncing behind her. Callie kept the door cracked, and with an ache in her chest, watched Eva strike up conversation with the family as they walked down the street, as if she were their kid. Marveling at her daughter's French skills, she gave a silent *merci* to the language immersion school back in Colorado.

Callie hated having her out of sight, but they'd agreed to meet at the nearest fountain, which spymaster Eva claimed was a perfect clandestine meeting point—*hidden in broad daylight* was the phrase she'd used.

Callie forced herself to wait another minute, watching the man through the cracked door, wondering if this was a stable-mother thing to do, by any stretch of the imagination, even if it was couched as *Minecraft* meets *Spy Kids*. She breathed out as she realized Brett's lackey hadn't moved from his spot—no alarm bells raised. The trick had worked.

Now, Callie's turn. With a twinge of guilt, she stashed her suitcase in the biggest stroller, covered it with a blanket, then stuck her backpack in the compartment underneath. She'd have to borrow it. Hands shaking, she put on her sunglasses and tucked stray, coppery tendrils into the silk scarf she'd wrapped around her head.

After a deep breath, she rolled her shoulders back and channeled a chic French *maman,* despite her decidedly unstylish shorts and tee. She headed outside, orienting the stroller away from the man and pushing it nonchalantly toward the fountain up the street, relieved to see Eva there. Her daughter was squirming and sitting on her hands, probably to resist waving.

Approaching, Callie whispered, "Hey, sweetie, let me go down this side street. Then count to thirty and follow me."

Of course, Eva speed-counted. Three seconds later, Callie heard the rattle of a wheelie on the cobbles behind her, and then Eva threw herself into her arms. Seeing no sign of the man, Callie ducked with her into a *pâtisserie* and let her order a *tarte aux fruits* to restickify her fingers.

Just when Callie was thinking she might have traumatized her child for life, Eva raised her hand for a high five. She met her hand, laughing, and prayed Eva would remember this time through fun, spy-colored glasses. "Next time, we'll have secret-agent gizmos."

"Yes, please! A jet pack, electroshock bubbles, an inflatable suit. Oh, and a Chihuahua we could stick inside a stroller, and she could jump out and fly at the evil mastermind because that's her superpower . . ."

Eva rambled on, stopping only to bite into her tart, aglow with adventure, just like her dad had been, always excited about the next archaeology trip or music tour. Although the speed and pitch of Eva's chatter bordered on maniacal, Callie couldn't detect any undercurrents of fear now.

When Eva finished her tart, she said, "Where to now, Mom?"

"Now we pick a super-secret, hidden place." A bone-deep exhaustion came over Callie—the weight of making these decisions alone. Brett had always hung that over her head, his conviction that she was a neglectful mother, that she needed him, Eva needed him. And it all came back to that one shameful day.

*Eva would have died if I hadn't been there,* he'd say over and over until the words left grooves inside Callie's mind. *Thank God I arrived when I did,* he'd say. He'd made sure the doctors at the hospital made note of it, that her therapist made note of it, that the Department of Child and Family Services made note of it, that her neglect was documented for perpetuity—and etched in bone inside her.

She shook herself. *An evil mastermind minion is on our tail.* Phrasing it this way helped her break out of self-doubt paralysis. On a napkin, she scribbled a note with their address and left it on the stroller, feeling guilty for having taken it, but assuming someone would return it.

*Merci mille fois for the use of your stroller. Kisses!*

Suitcases bumping over cobblestones, Callie and Eva hurried through the labyrinth of narrow streets, out to the wide, tree-lined boulevard of Le Cours Mirabeau, then around the huge Fontaine de la Rotonde, where they stopped at the bus station before a map of the bus routes.

The names of towns swam before Callie's eyes. She had no idea where to go, daunted without a phone for research, wishing for a travel guidebook from the days of yore. Of course, there were the well-known Provençal towns of Avignon and Arles—and the touristy villages of Gordes and Bonnieux. But she needed to find someplace off the beaten track.

"Hey, Mom, let's go here!" Eva pointed with a fingertip shiny with tart glaze.

From her daughter's wild enthusiasm—she was actually jumping up and down—Callie assumed there must be a dog in the name. Sainte-Marie-des-Poméraniens, or something along those lines. But then Eva said, "The song!"

"The song?" Callie's belly fluttered as she squinted at the map, and sure enough, there was a meandering blue line of river labeled *La Chanson* and a village of the same name on its banks. It looked to be a couple hours away. And sufficiently tiny. "Okay, let's do it, sweet pea."

Eva clapped and twirled in response. Her resilience astounded Callie. As for herself, Callie's entire body was thudding as she bought tickets and searched for the bus—scheduled to leave in five minutes—then ushered Eva onto it. In frantic movements, she arranged their bags, settled into a seat, then peered out the window. Her throat tightened when she saw the blond man darting around vehicles and people, glancing at the buses, approaching theirs.

She slid down in her seat, tugged Eva lower, and peeked around the seat back, down the aisle, at the open bus door.

"What's wrong, Mom?"

"Brett's assistant is out there," Callie said, forcing her voice to steady. "Let's stay down till the bus leaves."

He couldn't drag them off the bus with physical force—she'd yell for the police. But knowing Brett, he had a plan in place. He'd claim she was mentally unstable, had put a child in danger. Unfortunately, the damage and destruction she'd left in her wake suggested a woman who'd lost her grip. He had a plethora of evidence to use against her.

"We won't let him take us back to Brett." Eva's voice came out raspy, a mix of vulnerable and determined.

"We won't."

A minute after the doors whooshed shut, Callie craned her head over the seatbacks and looked around the bus. No tall blond man to be seen. Her pulse calmed a notch.

Once the bus moved out of the lot and into traffic, Eva sat up straight and peered out the window. It hurt Callie's chest to see her daughter's eyes blaze with tears, her lip quiver ever so slightly. Eva raised her chin and took a deep breath and declared, "*Allons-y!* To the Song!"

Callie squeezed her hand, guessing she'd be extra cuddly during her lullaby tonight, maybe even call her Mommy again—but for now, Callie was grateful for her courage. And she suspected that if push came to shove, Eva would simply dig in her heels and refuse to return to the castle prison—she could be stubborn, which, in this case, was a good thing. Motivation for Callie to do the same, no matter what.

Tucking her arm around her daughter's shoulders, she thought of the letters in the secret pouch of her suitcase on the shelf above. She felt an odd aversion to reading them, almost fear at the thought. They were reminders of all the weird, broken pieces of herself slowly coming together over the past few months. Evidence of how detached from reality she'd been for nearly two years. A horrific souvenir from her strange time sequestered with spider friends in the dank basement, writing letters to her own self.

Still, the act of writing had strengthened her. Every day, she'd written a letter, and little by little, her eyes and ears had opened, and she'd understood the looming danger. And taken action.

Slipping her hand into Eva's, not caring how sticky it was, Callie wondered what a village on the banks of the Song might hold and how well it might hide them. "We'll be okay, sweet pea."

Eva leaned her head onto Callie's shoulder, twirling her hair like she'd done for comfort as a preschooler. "I bet there are dogs in the Song, Mom." Her voice had smoothed out now, just the tiniest uncertainty rippling the surface. "I have a good feeling about it."

# NO

*Colorado, nine weeks before arrival in France*

Dear Callie,

Okay, I know I seem off my rocker writing a letter to *myself* and especially off my rocker since I'm hiding in the basement to do it, and that my scrawl is maniacal because the cameras think I'm in here washing clothes—well, the cameras don't think it, but if he's watching, I want him to think I'm doing laundry, which means I have fifteen minutes tops.

He's on a business trip, but who knows if he's checking the smart house monitors—or am I being paranoid? This is the only safe place, this little laundry room, even though it's dark and dingy, with raw cement and piles of musty rags and this flickering light and spiders galore.

A spider's actually crawling over my leg now, and I'm not even brushing it off because that's the least of my problems and it's kind of cute and not the bitey kind, I don't think. See how off my rocker I am?

I know what you're wondering, Callie. *Why start writing now? Why now after two years of imprisonment? Why did I finally hear your* no?

Your *no* was so forceful, like every ounce of your being was behind it, every last shred of power. And it came through last night when Brett and I were on the sofa, about to watch a movie, and Eva was in bed, and he put his arm around me and said, "Listen, cupcake." (Ugh, that nickname feels like a frosting-coated knife in my gut every single time.) "It's been two years since Nick died. And I've stepped in as Eva's dad. That's how everyone sees me now. I know you're hesitant to get married, but the reality is, we're already coparents."

Oh, Callie, I could see where this was heading and my blood froze and boiled at the same time and I felt a tsunami heading toward me.

He spoke in the same eerie calm tone he uses in antiquities deals when he makes it clear what he wants and that he always gets what he wants. Always. "I want to adopt Eva."

And Callie, that's when your *no* traveled up through the dark, twisting oceanic tunnels and made it all the way to me.

*No!*

Of course I didn't say it out loud. I only said, "Hmm. Okay, well, let's keeping thinking about it." My voice was dry and weak like a shriveled apple, but inside I've been hanging on to that word with everything I have left.

Most of the time, Callie, you feel far away, imprisoned in a deep cave, but sometimes I hear your voice, thin and distant and trying so very hard to reach me. And usually I can't make out your words, but yesterday I could. Like you're a blue whale and your voice is almost infrasonic, the sound waves huge and wide and traveling hundreds of miles through the waters of my psyche.

I feel like there's a fragile thread, silver, or maybe gold, and it's reaching from my hands down down down into the cave, deep deep deep into the darkness, where you're grasping the other end. For now, Callie, the best I can do is hold on to it and listen for echoes of your voice.

See how wacko I sound? I can see myself from the outside,

a thirty-five-year-old woman with red hair in a frizzy braid, dressed in black yoga loungewear, ghostly pale without makeup, huddled in the basement, writing furtively about whales and golden threads inside this enormous glass house perched on the edge of a cliff. This seven-million-dollar "cabin" in the Rocky Mountains. (Ha! Don't you love it when Brett refers to his "cabin"?)

But this is not a castle prison, and I'm not locked inside here, not literally. I could leave anytime, right? I could take Eva and leave.

That idea feels more impossible than waving a magic wand to remove a curse.

Still, your *no*—it offered hope.

Now I can hear that hope like a bright C major chord plucked on a tenor ukulele.

Callie, do you think it's strange I spend my days with rare editions of fairy tales? Do you know how alone I feel? No neighbors for a half mile, just snow-covered dirt roads and lodgepole pines, some dead from beetle kill, the others struggling beside patches of still-bare aspens, growth stunted from moose chomping on them. Sometimes, when Eva's at school, I have the urge to put on boots and follow deer and elk scat through the snow, just walk and walk. But he doesn't like me walking alone, so I can't even bond with the ungulates.

I could watch them through the thirty-foot-high windows, but instead I hole up in the library and read magical tales. Or, for a change of pace, come down to the dank basement. (The spider is now happily hanging out on my knee, probably considering a nest.)

Yesterday, I read that our namesake, Calliope, goddess of poetry and music, sang about Persephone, trapped in the underworld. And I think of you, Callie, in that watery cave, still singing, earnest and hopeful and determined . . .

Are these words reaching you? Honestly, it's hard to get them out—as soon as I write them, they feel lost, and I can't tell what makes sense. I'm shouting into a cave, no idea how far my voice will reach.

I have just another minute before I fold up this paper and zipper it into the secret compartment of that daisy-print carry-on that I used a lifetime ago. (Remember how whimsical life felt once upon a time?) Okay, Callie, I promise you, every day I'll come here and write you another letter. A string of letters, glinting silver and gold in darkness, reaching from me to you, our lifeline.

Maybe it was your infrasonic encouragement that helped me wean myself off the meds, and maybe that's why I could hear you yesterday—the fog is clearing. My ears feel less muffled, my brain sharper.

Why didn't I listen sooner?

Because he knows the skeleton in my closet. He witnessed it. And now he dangles it over my head, bones clacking, every chance he gets.

But now, knowing his intentions with Eva—*no*.

Callie, you're more than my *old* self. You're my self beyond space and time, the self that moves like a river beneath the surface and connects me to the rest of humanity.

You're my *true* self.

And I need you back.

Until tomorrow, Callie.

Love,
Callie

# 3

# FORMIDABLE

For the first hour of the bus ride, Callie gazed out the open window, watching the landscape of olive trees and lavender fields and vineyards, the limestone villages perched on hills, the red-roofed farmhouses, the occasional castle turrets. So much beauty, passing in a dreamlike blur, as if she were racing through a museum, glimpsing gold-framed paintings, trying to take it all in. Or as if the museum were racing around her.

Brett's antiquities collections existed static behind glass, and even though she'd lived in that "cabin" surrounded by millions of dollars' worth of ancient art, there was something stagnant and suffocating about it. She'd yearned for moving, living, breathing, singing, dancing beauty. On some level, she hadn't just wanted to shake up the snow globe but shatter the whole damn thing. Which she had done.

Eva was holding court across the aisle with new friends—a tow-headed preschooler and his small white dog whose fur looked like topiary art. Fairly glowing, she paused in her peekaboo game to lean toward his mother. "*J'adore* your *bichon frisé, madame!*"

Of course she knew the breed.

"*Merci.*" The woman smiled at Eva, then looked over her head at Callie. "Your daughter's so joyful. My son's having a blast with her."

*S'éclater* was the verb she used in French—exploding with joy—and that's exactly what Eva was doing, fairly shooting off sparks. Eva's mishmash, thrift-store outfit was quite the contrast to her companion's crisp white linen, but Callie loved seeing her daughter's unapologetic self shining through. Brett hadn't been a fan of Eva's chosen style of broken-in, worn-out, threadbare clothes.

"*Oui*," Callie agreed, and made small talk with the woman, her French returning surprisingly swiftly. She appreciated that this woman seemed unfazed by her disheveled state.

It wasn't just this morning that she'd left in a frantic rush—it was last week in Colorado too. She'd stuffed handfuls of her T-shirts and shorts and underwear into her suitcase, mostly concerned with Eva's comfort clothes, but she'd forgotten basics like anti-frizz serum, makeup, face cream, earrings, even a comb. With her shoestring budget, she couldn't justify buying anything beyond food, lodging, and transportation. At least she'd managed to keep their teeth brushed.

This woman struck Callie as a different species altogether, a confident young mother, with her subtle makeup, glowing skin, *à la mode* dress, delicate jewelry, breezy bangs framing her heart-shaped face. She seemed so put together, outside and in, secure with her place in this world. "I'm Nathalie."

"Callie." She was glad they weren't doing last names. Not worth the risk.

"What exuberance!" said Nathalie, still smiling at Eva.

Callie surged with pride, though she couldn't take credit. Eva's joy was largely *despite* her. Despite her decisions. Or, more to the point, lack of decisions, at least over the past two years. Because inaction was a decision too, wasn't it?

Still, Callie felt that her most recent decision was a solid one—the choice to come here. Although the Parisian assistant had somehow tracked them down, they'd successfully escaped. She *hoped*. Unable to see out the back of the bus, she suppressed the niggling fear that he could be following.

"Your son is adorable." Callie tried channeling a very normal mom. "*Très mignon*."

"Your French is wonderful," Nathalie said, volleying compliments. "You're American?"

"From Colorado. But I learned French here. Almost fifteen years ago. Study abroad." She didn't mention the summer she spent busking here after college. No need to bring up her own music in any way, shape, or form.

Nathalie gave a warm smile. "Amazing that you held on to the language after so long."

Callie flushed. Why did compliments give her the urge to apologize? "I read a lot of fairy tales in French. Originals from Madame d'Aulnoy and Charles Perrault." With a self-conscious smile, she added, "A bizarre *passe-temps*, I know."

She tried to sound lighthearted, but mentioning this "pastime" dropped a weight onto her chest, as heavy as a thousand books, leather-bound and gilded, from the library of the enormous, sleek glass-and-wood house perched on a cliff.

"So that's why your French sounds a bit seventeenth century!"

Callie smiled along.

"Here on vacation?" Nathalie asked.

"Something like that." Callie paused, searching for a less evasive response. "I'm hoping my daughter will pick up more French. She's been in a language immersion school, and she loves French books and movies."

"*Formidable!*"

Even though the meaning was "fantastic," Callie appreciated the idea that she was doing something daunting. Formidable indeed. Encouraged, she opened her mouth to offer more details, then closed it again. Her real reasons for being here weren't small talk material—she was escaping a sorcerer.

Or was she being melodramatic? She'd lost perspective. But in some way, dark fairy tales and myths had swirled together with her own strange reality, almost indistinguishable. Heat gathered in her cheeks. Being ghostly fair-skinned made it impossible to hide her feelings—she imagined her cheeks pink, bordering on magenta. Damn it. She was supposed to stay invisible.

Nathalie was looking at the children, though, grinning at their antics with the dog. "How long are you in the area?"

Callie considered how to respond. Their return tickets were for three months from now, the maximum length of a tourist stay—hopefully she could unravel the damage in that time frame. But would it be safe to take Eva back then? Her mother's intuition had been snipped two years ago. Since she'd be offline for the foreseeable future, she longed for an old-fashioned book: *The Dummy's Guide to Fleeing a Sorcerer.*

"For the summer." She injected confidence into her words. After all, Eva was more than okay—she was *exuberant.* Once they were in a new place, she'd make a solid plan.

"We should get together with the kids!" Nathalie reached for her phone. "Let's exchange numbers."

Another wave of doubt flustered her. She'd be the example in the chapter of what *not* to do when fleeing a sorcerer. "Oh, I, uh, lost my phone last week." She left it at that, remembering the strange moment she'd thrown it away in the Denver airport, hesitating with guilt, hand hovering over the trash and recycling bin options. The entire act had felt illicit.

Nathalie made a sound of sympathy, then retrieved a pen and receipt from her purse. "Here's my number." Lightly, she added, "Enjoy the phone break. Hope your new one comes soon."

Callie stuffed the paper into her purse, feeling a twinge of sadness that this friendship had no chance. Brett controlled her accounts, passwords, email, finances, nearly everything. He'd know exactly where a new phone would be delivered. And promptly come for her and Eva.

She considered telling this kind woman the truth. Why not? She was free now. Still, she hadn't told a soul that they'd escaped—or that they'd been in a situation that *required* escape. It would be a lot to dump onto a nice, normal stranger.

Callie glanced at the children—now Eva had the bichon frisé in her lap and was kissing its nose. She was a dog magnet, but when she was little, they'd traveled too much on music tours to have one. And Brett was decidedly not a dog person—turning up his nose at shedding fur and dirt and slobber and mess. Guaranteed, Eva would ask for a bichon frisé any minute now.

"Taking a day trip from Aix?" Nathalie asked. "That's what we're doing, visiting family."

"We're actually thinking about staying in La Chanson."

"Ah! Go to the cave at the river's source." She gave a sage nod. "One of the world's deepest springs." Noticing Eva trying to follow the conversation, Nathalie slowed down and winked. "Some say it's *magique*."

"*Magique?*" Eva echoed.

Nathalie nodded. "A sacred place for Celtic tribes. A couple thousand years ago, they left a magical instrument there. A carnyx."

Callie gave Eva context in English, drawing on the Mediterranean history class from her study abroad. She'd been surprised that Celts had lived in the South of France, intermingling with local tribes and later with the Roman invaders.

And the carnyx had fascinated her—a six-foot-long trumpet of sorts, with a dragon or bird or other creature at the bell end, used in ceremonies and battle, a sonic weapon. She could still hear echoes of its sound from a video—a single low note like the deepest indigo velvet, its tone musty and mysterious.

"You know," said Nathalie, tapping her finger on her chin, "the owner of the *cave à vins* has a place for rent."

Wine cave, literally, but most likely a wine shop. Still, Callie imagined deep caverns filled with thick, old bottles. "*Merci.*"

"Madame Lavigne is her name." Nathalie's expression shifted to wonder. "A true *magicienne du vin*."

A wine magician? Or wizard? This idiom was new to Callie.

Nathalie lowered her voice. "Of course, some say she's more of a *sorcière du vin*."

A wine witch? Callie wasn't quite sure what to make of this, but she nodded along. From context, she guessed that being a wine *magician* was a good thing, but a wine *witch* was a bad thing. The nuances evaded her.

Nathalie was growing animated. "The Château of the Lost, that's what they call her place."

A medieval castle? Or a mere mansion? Either way, it would be excessive. Not to mention, the idea of a witchy owner was disconcerting. "Well, a château would be way too big for us."

"Oh, I bet you could stay there, at least for tonight. So you have somewhere to go. Tell her I sent you."

"*Merci.*" Callie wondered about the name—Château of the Lost. Lost *what*? No, thank you. She'd find a modest hotel for tonight, then ask around for a simple, longer-term rental tomorrow.

"*Et voilà!*" said Nathalie, spreading her arm to the open window.

Just around the bend, the village of La Chanson appeared, bright in the late morning sunshine, a cluster of ancient buildings tucked into a lush valley, where a ribbon of river sparkled. Callie almost gasped at its otherworldly color, like emeralds and sapphires turned liquid.

Parasol pines lined the banks, and patches of forest and fields and wildflowers blanketed the hillsides. Here and there, limestone outcroppings rose like sculptures along the river. A hush fell over the bus, and Callie felt the air grow gentler, the poppies in the meadows more vibrant. Soon the driver pulled to the roadside, and Callie saw a narrow cobbled street leading down toward the river, beckoning, something from a fairy tale.

Not a fairy tale from Brett's collection.

Her own damn fairy tale.

She stood up, head spinning.

Eva, too, looked drenched in wonder. "*J'adore La Chanson!*"

Realizing the driver was waiting for them, Callie waved farewell, then grabbed their bags and ushered Eva off the bus as Nathalie called after them, wishing them luck. "*Bon courage!*"

Stretching her legs, Callie breathed in the scents of rosemary and lavender, warm stone and parasol pines. An ancient smell, something long forgotten. Through the birdsong and breezes, she heard light tenor notes of the river, bubbling like trills of a lyre. And the deeper bass lines, rumbling with vibrations of cello, and beneath it all, the bellow of a carnyx.

Her palm flew to her heart. This entire place was a song. A song beyond space and time.

For a stretched-out moment, she closed her eyes and listened. Somehow, the river itself was making chord progressions, leaping from minor to major keys, rising into crescendos and falling into diminuendos, moving from verse to chorus to bridge.

Her soul let out a sigh as her neck muscles relaxed and her throat opened, and for a moment she felt that a song was about to flow out. No song emerged, but her breaths felt easier, fuller, deeper, in a way they hadn't for two years.

Eva took her hand, and Callie squeezed it back. Their gazes met, and Callie could tell she felt it too—a feeling so deep and strange and melodic, she had no name for it.

"Ready, Mom?"

"Ready." Callie adjusted her backpack, and they wheeled their suitcases down the ancient road as the music rose and pulled them onward, closer.

Eva skipped along, giddy, and her usual chatter returned. "Know what this place reminds me of, Mom?"

"What, sweet pea?"

"The way you used to sing to me."

Callie blinked. "I still sing to you."

"Only sometimes. Only at night. Only softly. Only when he's not around."

"Well, he's not here. I can sing however I want. However you want."

"Loud and wild?"

Callie laughed, readjusting the strap of her backpack. "Bedtime songs are supposed to make you fall asleep. Not head bang and mosh." Of course, indie folk didn't lend itself to head banging and moshing, but it was an inside joke—Nick had liked playing heavy metal for his workouts, and Eva had loved going wild with him.

"Sing like a carnyx! Like a dragon roar!"

"Then my song would make you ready for battle. Not for bed."

Eva giggled. "You could sing now. Like, normal."

"I don't know if that would be normal. We don't want everyone in town thinking I'm the wacko American."

"But you could sing other times, Mom," she insisted. "Like you used to. When you're washing dishes or taking out trash or driving the car."

"We'll see."

"You think the wine lady's really a sorceress?" Eva asked after a moment.

"I think Nathalie meant *witch*." What was the difference between gaslighting your kid and strategically reframing? "A magical wine lady," Callie added, floundering. "In a good way. Probably."

"Think we'll find a dog here, Mom?"

"Maybe."

"Think we can keep it?"

"*Oh la la la la la LA*." Callie said this in the way her French host family had, in comic annoyance, accompanied by an exaggerated eye roll.

She listened to Eva's easy chatter about bichons frisés as they headed down the main street. Her daughter seemed to feel safe here too, for the moment, at least.

She glanced around, taking in this town's charm—ridiculously picturesque, impossibly sweet—lined with old stone buildings and clay pots of geraniums and tiny café tables, and at the far end, the sparkle of the river, its notes growing clearer and closer with each step.

*Too perfect.* She looked over her shoulder to make sure the tall Parisian hadn't tracked them here. No one suspicious. How had he found them in Aix? She'd been so careful, putting her laptop in airplane mode, leaving no digital money trail. And now, here in this off-the-beaten-track village, were they safe?

# 4

# PRECIOUS

*Colorado, eight weeks before arrival in France*

Dear Callie,

Well, I'm back in the basement. Or, as Brett's interior designer might spin it, the industrial-chic cellar launderette . . . ah, the life of luxury in a secluded, bespoke smart cabin in the Rockies.

Still, I like the basement better than the blindingly sunny great hall overlooking half-dead lodgepole pines and scat-spewing ungulates. (Well, I do love spotting baby moose.) Down here, I'm not being watched. Here, I can be alone and connect with you, Callie.

Calliope, Muse of Music.

Says the woman who hasn't composed a song or touched a guitar or sung above a whisper in two years. Who can barely even listen to music anymore, not even in sappy commercials.

Yesterday afternoon, I decided I was going to stop writing these letters—it seemed like too big of a risk . . . What if he finds them? What if they give me reckless courage? It would be easier to go along with the status quo, live the small, controlled life of a puppet.

And he was sweet at lunch, bought me my favorite leek-potato quiche and a new collection of fairy tales from the bookstore café—the illustrated one I'd admired last time we were there. He pays close attention to what I like, gives me lovely little gifts, kisses me tenderly on my lips and neck, tells me throughout the day he loves me, how lucky he is to have me.

And I echo, "I'm lucky to have you too."

Last year, I made a list on my laptop of pros and cons of Brett. There were hundreds of pros. Perfect dental hygiene. Knows precisely how to make me come. Picks out just-right presents. Looks like a magazine model in every outfit he owns. Always has clean boxer-briefs without holes. Deals with paperwork, mail, bills, and the general upkeep of modern life in society. Drives Eva to her practices. RSVPs to her friends' birthday parties. Makes generous donations to her school, speaks at her career day, brings her bouquets at dance recitals. Rubs my feet on the couch for a full hour without tiring, despite the rough callus-things.

Although now that I think about it, he does have his assistant schedule "deluxe" pedicures for me, which feels a little insulting, or at least overstepping. (The pedicurist just buffs for a long time, then shrugs and says, "As long as they don't bother you . . .") Is it a pro or con that his assistant makes those appointments? I don't know.

Anyway, I was too scared to write the cons. After forty-one pros, I left the con column blank and deleted the file, then emptied the trash folder.

Then checked three times to make sure it was gone.

Maybe that con alone outweighs all the pros.

So yesterday at sunset, Brett and I were having cocktails on the back porch—it was one of those sunny, weirdly warm Colorado winter-spring days between snowstorms. That's another pro—he mixes those smoky mezcal-hibiscus-lime drinks and always manages to have the ingredients on hand. (Probably thanks to his assistant, but still.)

Anyway, he kissed my forehead and said, "You make me so happy," and I thought, *That's it. No more sneaky, hidden letters. Things are tolerable, sometimes even good, sometimes downright great.*

But last night, while I was putting Eva to bed and Brett was downstairs in his office, I sang her "Fly, Fly Away," and I could see why it went viral. True, it's catchy, but there's more. It speaks from my soul to other souls—the gossamer threads and all that—I'd never say that aloud because: *vain much?* (That's Brett's voice I hear in my head.) It's strange to think I composed it a decade ago when I was a bird flying free, when I felt those spiderweb threads connecting us all.

Now there's just this one strand left, and it joins me to Eva.

After the last line of her lullaby, which I sang oh-so-softly, I leaned over to kiss her and felt her cheeks damp on my lips. "Keep singing, Mommy." Her voice quavered—a low, plucked violin string in A minor. She reached out to twirl one of my curls like a security blanket. "Keep singing."

So I sang her one more song, tears streaming down my cheeks.

Whenever my old song lyrics float into my head, I wonder if it's you, Callie, trying to send me a message. *Let's fly away, my love, fly away. Follow the water, follow the songs.*

Here's the thing: Every book I open is overflowing with stories of women and goddesses trapped by men who took their power. All it takes is one selfish man tricking her and stealing her skin—her *self*—controlling her, forcing her to stay.

Take the Celtic version: Once upon a time, a selkie swam to shore and shed her sea skin for a bit, just to see how it felt to be human. And in that moment of vulnerability, a human man stole her skin and took her as his wife. For years, she longed for her sea skin, her truest self, but finally resolved to accept life on land. Until one day, her daughter mentioned she'd found beautiful silky skin hidden away and showed it to her. The selkie slipped it on and returned to the sea, to her *self*.

In the myth, she bids farewell to her husband and child, but of course I would bring Eva with me.

It's not just that myth. It's all of them. I open a book and it smacks into me, this tidal wave of selkies, and their cousins, the Greek nymphs and Roman sirens and German nixies and Russian rusalki. All of them riding waves of flowing, sparkling, turquoise water and giving me looks that say, *Get out while you can!*

I miss that kind of water. The river is frozen now, and even when it thaws, it will be violent and frothing and rushing and frigid, a dark shade of brown-gray, and too cold to swim in at nine thousand feet.

Brett hasn't brought up the adoption thing again, but I feel it there, under the surface, a riptide that could get me at any time. Of course, Eva would be against an adoption, but Brett and his team of lawyers could easily reframe her resistance to the Child and Family Services team.

The real, true, weird reason I keep my songs to a whisper is this irrational belief: What if the sorcerer wants to capture my voice and use it to strengthen his own power? I mean, that's what he's been doing for two years. I know I sound completely and absolutely off my rocker, but just in case, I'm saving up the last remnants of my voice for the secret space of lullabies.

Callie, I'm so aware of time passing, Eva's childhood passing, a quarter of it under Brett's vulture gaze. Those two years from ages six to eight passed in my medicated fog. It makes me sick and sad. I have a few more years of lullaby singing to her, and I just want my songs, my voice, to last until then.

And I want her to get a damn dog. One day.

Brett left for a business trip this morning. I could fly away. I could take Eva and fly away. But he's on all my accounts and has my passwords and dual factor authentication access, and there's no way we could leave without a trail. And I see it now, Callie: Over the years, bit by bit, I've let him cut me off from family and friends, more golden threads snip-snip-snipped, and he's so, so close to snipping this thread to you.

You know he won't let me go. When he first called me that infernal nickname *precious*, I encouraged it—worlds less cringey than *cupcake*—until his confidence turned creepy and goblin-like.

And I imagine Brett like Gollum, monitoring us with the smart house app—it's connected to camera feeds in every room except bathrooms and here in the laundry room. Believe me, I've checked. I feel reasonably confident he won't find these letters in the secret compartment of my old daisy-print suitcase—it's conveniently stored on a shelf across from the washing machine. Not in the sightline of any cameras.

Last night, I asked him again if the cameras were really necessary. "Maybe we can only turn them on when we're out of the house," I suggested.

"Precious, when you get to a certain level of wealth, a smart house is a nonnegotiable." And he kept rubbing my feet, running his finger over the callus-things, as if to say, *See what I accept from you?* He added, "You know I only check the screens if there's an alert, right?"

"Of course. It just feels weird sometimes."

"Well, you have nothing to hide," he murmured, and kissed my lips, my cheek, my earlobe, sliding his hand up my bare leg. "And I want to keep you safe."

Now I feel it in the hairs on the back of my neck—he watches us—even as I wonder if I'm being paranoid.

I'll tuck this letter away, then walk back into the gaze of the cameras with a basket of clothes, and feel his hooded eyes watching me as I go back into my dark fairy-tale library and read for hours until it's time to pick Eva up from school, and I won't get out of the car and talk to the other parents like I used to.

"They're gossipy and cliquey," he tells me, even though he chats with them, knows them all by name, their jobs and hobbies. He's thoroughly charmed them, even the admins. "Jealous of you, that's all."

I suspect he's told them I'm fragile and mentally unstable and not safe around their children, so it's easiest for me to stay in the car line in silence. Remember how in the old days, waiting for nursery school pickup, I'd be rocking out in the car, checking my socials, responding to fans' comments, reposting videos from my shows, posting that clip of me playing guitar while Nick made tamales and Eva clapped her pudgy four-year-old hands? Remember how I felt all those silver-gold threads everywhere all the time?

Last night, I lay in bed, hearing Eva's words, "Keep singing, Mommy." And I decided to keep writing the letters.

Sometimes I want to do even more. I want to grab that axe—the ridiculously expensive one he keeps for show by the store-bought wood stack at the fireplace, as if he's a mountain man who chops wood himself. I want to grab that smooth, untouched wooden handle and bash each and every one of those cameras with the steel blade. I'd take Eva and fly, fly away.

Sometimes, Callie, sometimes I wonder if there's more darkness inside him—it's something I glimpse from the corner of my eye, a shadowy form beneath the water. I wonder if he's Bluebeard with a secret room of skeletons.

Until tomorrow.

Love,<br>
Callie

# 5

# THE SONG

When Callie reached the river, La Chanson, she paused to catch her breath beside Eva, peering over the wrought-iron railing. The water's deep blue-green felt unreal, something you'd expect in the Caribbean or in a fantastical realm. Its songs rose, spiraling and wisping, whirling with dragonflies.

Callie kept looking around, expecting something less-than perfect to emerge—the Parisian assistant could appear at any moment, or even Brett himself.

"Let's explore!" said Eva.

Shaking off her fear, Callie followed her through narrow side streets, as if wandering through a fairy tale—a light, gentle one. And oddly, the river was accompanying their conversation, echoing her mood, her thoughts—a kind of organic movie soundtrack, spontaneous and improvised moment to moment.

Here and there, they passed people who smiled at them with curiosity, offering *bonjours*. A mix of ages, the faces were kind and open and fully human—no elves or fairies or princesses in sight. And everyone seemed rooted in this century, but perhaps less glued to cell phones than the rest of the world.

Surely, someone could offer directions to a hotel if they couldn't find one on their own. Although, she had a growing worry this village might be too small for even a modest inn.

A huge church bell rang to mark noon as they passed, and the river playfully wove each strike into its music. Or was she imagining this? She'd always been tuned into soundscapes, but this was beyond anything she'd experienced before.

Her mouth watered as they walked by a *pâtisserie* giving off scents of warm butter and caramelized sugar. Farther along was a Moroccan *salon du thé*, smelling of mint tea and roasting almonds. Next, a *fromagerie* with its earthy smells of Brie and Camembert. A bistro with people sipping tiny cups of coffee served with a thumbnail-sized cookie on each saucer.

Eva, of course, begged to enter every shop and taste every treat—"*Mais j'adore la pâtisserie!*"—but Callie said, "We'll have snacks after we find a place to stay."

As her daughter made a running commentary on each shop, Callie searched for a motel, inn, hostel, anything.

"Look, Mom!" Eva yanked her hand and gestured with her chin to a patch of trimmed grass lined with plane trees and benches, where a throng of dogs was gathered—curly-haired, delightfully scruffy, medium-sized, with friendly faces.

"Dog paradise," Eva said in hushed awe.

Beside the dogs, on a rectangle of packed dirt—which Callie guessed was a *pétanque* court—stood a group of white-haired men sporting actual berets and holding small silver balls, looking as if they'd stepped out of another time. They nodded at Callie and Eva, offering *bonjours* and inquisitive looks.

Callie gave a polite smile back, prepared to keep searching for a hotel, but within seconds, Eva had abandoned her bags and was running maniacally toward the dogs, shouting, "*J'adore les chiens!*" Remembering the rule about asking permission first, she skidded to a stop, shot a hopeful grin at the men, then at their dogs, then back at them. "*Ça va?*" she asked, panting, and her desperate, deeper meaning was clear: *Can I pet your dogs? Please, please, please?*

They laughed and nodded, introducing their dogs.

With resignation, Callie took off her backpack, rubbing her shoulders, then gathered the bags by a bench. They could use a break, and these men might direct them to lodging. Although she had trust issues with men, this group of old-timers seemed as non-threatening as they came.

Eva's favorite dog was a russet female with buoyant energy. "What's her name?" she asked in French.

"Belle!" declared one of the men. "She's my *copine*!" He clutched his chest, as if lovestruck, and blew kisses to the furry creature as Callie translated *la copine* for Eva: "His girlfriend."

"*Oh*, Belle is *belle*." Eva sprawled beside the dogs, delighted.

As her daughter became thoroughly coated in canine saliva, Callie greeted the men with standard pleasantries, then chatted about Colorado and La Chanson and the dogs, who were truffle dogs—the Lagotto Romagnolo breed. Realizing these men could talk forever about their dogs, Callie directed the conversation to her mission. "*Messieurs*, is there a hotel here you'd recommend?"

At that, they burst out laughing, some even slapping their knees.

She took that for a no. "Or just a small inn?" Somehow, she remembered the word *auberge* from her ten-dollar-a-night youth hostel days.

Once they calmed down, Belle's owner wiped his eyes and said kindly, "Oh, forgive us. But, my dear, this village is far too small for a hotel. You might try the nearest town, a short bus ride down the road."

She bit her lip. She didn't want a bigger town. She wanted the Song. And it would be impossible to drag Eva away after all this dog bonding. Callie had to admit—it would be hard to drag her *own* self away after this river bonding.

Her mind turned to the château, her last resort, and she exhaled a breath. "Then could you point us toward the *cave à vins*? I need to find Madame Lavigne."

Smiles fled the men's faces. Laughter wrinkles faded into frown creases. Belle's owner had a particularly intense expression, almost pained.

*Mon Dieu*, was she dead? Or was she *not* a good witch? Clearly, there was something these men weren't telling her, something disturbing. An image came to her—a *sorcière* of wines, with grape vines for hair, hunched over a cauldron of dark red liquid, deep in a cave.

Finally, a man pointed down the road. "The *cave à vins* is just past the *boulangerie*, madame, next to the *salon du thé*."

Odd. She hadn't noticed a wine shop there. "*Merci beaucoup, messieurs*."

The men exchanged wary looks. "May I ask what business you have with her?" one asked.

"I'm thinking of renting her château."

Silence. "The Château of the Lost," another man said gravely.

"It's haunted," said another.

Fabulous. The only thing better than a witchy landlady was a haunted castle. Not creepy, not creepy at all.

Before Callie could follow up, the *pétanque* players turned to watch a younger man walking down the sidewalk. He looked about her age, with broad shoulders, a narrow waist, wavy chestnut hair, a blue T-shirt, jeans, and a waxed canvas bag slung over his shoulder. As he approached, she noticed him cradling a puppy in his muscular arm.

Oh, she'd never get Eva to leave now.

"Luc!" A jubilant chorus rose from the older men.

"*Salut!*" he called back, and instantly the atmosphere lightened, as if this man's—Luc's—presence was a balm. And yes, there was something peaceful in his stride, easy in his expression. His voice, too, exuded calm—a rich, low G major chord in a golden, mellow tone. *Everything will be okay*, was the sunshiny message he gave off.

For a moment, Callie felt her breathing slow into the soothing rhythm of a metronome.

Then, with a jolt, her muscles tensed. For a hundred charming pros, it only took one terrible con to spark a nightmare. His kindness could be a façade, one she wouldn't fall for. She'd seen how compassion could become a sword in the end. Instantly, she felt a shield go up, thick and cold.

At lightning speed, Eva ran toward him as he set down the puppy—a truffle dog by the look of it, about four months old, white with large black spots—and within seconds, she was rolling around as it licked her cheeks. "*J'adore* your Lagotto Romagnolo," she informed him.

"And evidently, Chouchou adores you."

Chouchou. My little cabbage. The classic French term of affection seemed perfect for this roly-poly creature. The man watched his pup play with Eva for a moment, looking amused, then offered Callie a friendly nod.

She made her reciprocal nod perfunctory—polite bordering on distant.

He kissed the older men's cheeks in greeting, chatted with them in fast, low French, peppered with jokes she couldn't catch, but which set off rounds of laughter. Soon he set down his bag and knelt down, beckoning a gray dog to him. Ever so gently, he pet it, then rolled it over to examine its belly, exposing a stitched-up gash under its rear leg.

"It's healing well," he told the dog's owner. "She'll be back to her usual crazy self in no time."

"Thanks to your handiwork, Luc. But she keeps messing with the stitches."

Luc offered a sideways grin. "Well, ask her nicely to stop . . . or the cone's coming." He pulled one from the bag, held it up to the dog.

The older man chuckled and rubbed his dog's ears. "My girlfriend will leave me if I ask her to wear that."

Waves of laughter followed, a cascade of jokes that came too fast for Callie to catch. She found herself laughing along but stopped and pressed her lips together when Luc glanced at her with a curious smile.

The older man clapped his back. "How much do I owe you, Doctor?"

"Nothing." Luc shook his head and sighed, as if this were an old, well-worn argument. "And I'm not a doctor."

"When will you let us pay you, Doctor?" said one with a wink.

"When he gets that vet certificate," said another.

"Which will be never," said another. "How many years has it been?"

Luc finally managed to get a word in edgewise. "Just pay me with a jar of honey from those talented bees of yours."

"Make that twelve jars," said the injured dog's owner. "A year's supply. Enough for bachelors like you and your papa."

"That's how much he eats in a month," Luc joked, elbowing the man in the beret. "Right, Papa?"

As Eva ran in circles with the dogs, the not-quite-a-vet turned to Callie. "Your daughter made friends with the best truffle dogs in town."

"In the world," corrected one of the men.

Luc laughed. "She has a magic touch with them, I can tell." He extended his hand. "I'm Luc Forêt."

"Callie," she said, feeling his hand, both rough and tender, and she understood why the injured dog trusted his touch. *Be careful*, she told herself, snatching her hand away and crossing her arms.

He paused, as if waiting for her last name. She considered using Balam—Eva's last name, taken from her dad. Nicolás Balam Flores. Nick had wanted to pass on his Mayan family name, meaning jaguar, which Eva embraced with pride. But Callie didn't owe Luc Forêt any last name, so she offered none.

"We should go," she said, bracing herself to disentangle Eva from her new besties.

With a theatrical pout, her daughter gave a dramatic goodbye to the dogs. "*Au revoir, mes amis!*" she said, spreading her arms.

The owners' eyes crinkled with amusement as they waved goodbye.

"I'm sure we'll see the dogs again," Callie assured Eva. For better or worse, she had the feeling they—and their human companions—were fixtures at the park.

The dogs followed Eva like an entourage, as the men shouted, "Our girlfriends! Come back!"

When the laughter faded and the dogs returned, one of the old men called out, "Be careful!"

Callie stopped in her tracks, wondering whether this was a warning about the wine witch or her haunted house. What was she getting them into? But she had no phone, no internet, no way of researching lodging options beyond word of mouth. Maybe just one night in a witch's haunted castle? Famous last words.

"Wait, madame!" said Belle's owner. "My son will help you with your bags." He gestured to Luc, who had tucked Chouchou against his chest in a sling.

"*Merci, monsieur,*" Eva said with delight.

Quickly, Callie interjected, "Oh, no thanks, we've got it."

Luc wavered, but his father insisted. "Take their bags, son!"

The would-be vet gave her an apologetic look. "Sorry, but I'll get in trouble with my father." His expression was empathetic, as if he noticed her discomfort and wanted to reassure her that he had no agenda. "Let me help? My dad's got his *pétanque* posse and their girlfriends to back him up."

Callie chewed on the inside of her cheek. She could give a firm no, and she had a feeling he'd respect that—but Eva would sulk about leaving the puppy. It occurred to her that Luc could give her details about the wine witch on the way. After a beat of deliberation, she said, "Well, we can't argue with a mob of truffle dogs."

He picked up their suitcases, one in each hand. Again, she fought the impulse to refuse his help but felt relieved the bags were no longer rolling noisily along the cobbles, getting stuck every few feet.

As they walked, Eva chattered about dogs, not-so-subtly eyeing the puppy. "I can carry Chouchou if you're tired."

"How about another time?" He glanced at the fluffball curled into his chest. "Look, she just fell asleep."

"Awwwww." Eva's face softened into a puddle.

Callie glanced at Luc, regretting her decision to let a man swoop in to save them.

"I'll take our bags now." She grabbed them from his hands and dragged them over the cobbles, now at a fraction of the pace.

"Oh, all right." His voice held an easy, if puzzled, calm.

She and Eva were on their own now, doing fine, thank you very much, and after two years with the vulture, she was on guard—even if this guy seemed more dove than vulture. Objectively, there wasn't a bird-of-prey feather on him. Maybe an African grey parrot—weren't they the altruistic ones with a sense of humor? Still, helpfulness was manipulation in disguise. Especially from good-looking, kind men.

He looked a little adrift now, his arms swinging awkwardly as he slowed his pace to match hers, but he didn't insist, perhaps sensing this was important to her. As they walked, people greeted Luc with friendly waves—women especially. Inside, she rolled her eyes. Brett had been a charmer too.

She just needed Luc to take her to the *cave à vins*. Then she and Eva would be on their own again. Her goal was to stay in control, which meant staying away from men—octogenarian *pétanque* players excluded—and take steps to rebuild a stable life.

Her gaze flickered around, alert for any sign of the lanky blond assistant, and more viscerally, for Brett's shaved head, the black and gray stubble on his jaw, the casually rolled-up sleeves revealing hair as thick as feathers. The shape-shifter wielding dark magic, moving seamlessly from charming prince to circling vulture.

But of course, that all came from the ancient, dark fairy tales she'd consumed while trapped in his lair filled with his collections.

Of which she was a part.

He was very possessive of his collections.

# 6

# I'LL TAKE CARE OF EVERYTHING

*Colorado, seven weeks before arrival in France*

Dear Callie,

Last night, Brett was rubbing my feet on the sofa and we were rewatching *Lost,* and on a commercial break, he muted the TV and said, "What's going on?"

I kept looking at the TV, feeling his stare like laser beams. Ever since he came home from his business trip, he's been watching me like this, like he can read my mind, and he sort of can. He's like a manipulative, malevolent psychologist, tinkering around in my psyche, in it for himself. He examines my every word and gesture, analyzes every vulnerability, every weakness, every flaw, every fear . . . with the goal of exploiting all of it.

"What do you mean?" I said evenly.

"Precious, I've been observing your behavior. And I'm concerned you're going to have another episode. Your mental health is shaky."

I closed my eyes and for a brief moment wondered, *Is my mental health shaky? Would I even know?* I just said, "I'm fine."

"I made an appointment with our doctor. He may need to adjust your meds."

"I'm okay." But my stomach clenched—bloodwork would

probably show no traces of the meds now. I managed to wean myself off the pills over months, without side effects, just increased clarity.

It dawned on me that the original pronouncement of my mental instability, two years ago, came from Brett's doctor, who functions as part of his "team," just like his personal trainer or house cleaner or landscaper or designer or stylist. Someone who does his bidding. His doctor is the one who prescribed my cocktail of meds in the first place. In retrospect, they probably should have been prescribed for just a few months—for situational depression and anxiety and insomnia.

"Don't worry about me, Brett," I said, more firmly.

"It's my job to worry about you, cupcake. I'm concerned for our daughter's safety." He paused to let that sink in, that dagger tip. "She almost died that day. The worst day of my life. If I hadn't been there—I can't even think about it."

Callie, when he says this, I feel like an unconscious patient on a surgical table, naked and powerless, and he's a surgeon with the sharpest scalpel, and he's marked me with a black pen, planning exactly where to slice, especially the place I can't even think about, much less write about.

Of course, I couldn't respond because every cell of my body was flooded with shame—his words are poison, some dark, toxic chemical that takes over and sucks away my voice. I just sat there and listened and stared at the muted TV like a child being chastised.

He kept going, even once the commercial break was over. "And I'm gone on business more these days, and you two are alone here. I'm thinking I'll hire some help. A nanny who can watch Eva. Do some light housework. Like laundry."

"I'm okay," I managed to whisper. I only had a tiny bit of breath, of life force, available.

"That's the thing," he said. He was staring at me intensely

in the light of the TV screen, and he moved my face toward his, made me look at him, and it felt like he could peer into my eyes and see everything, all my terrible thoughts and regrets and flaws and mistakes. "Precious, you're not the best judge of whether you're okay. We saw how that played out in the past."

And a little piece of me wondered, *What if he's right? What if I can't judge my mental state? What if I shouldn't have stopped the meds? What if I'm delusional?*

That's why it's impossible to *fly, fly away* . . . he examines my actions and speech in the way he'd examine an artifact through a magnifying glass, every scratch and chip. He makes me doubt myself over and over.

Callie, how did we let this happen?

I will write the facts, the elusive facts, how they might have been before Brett twisted them to fit his will. His version is that he generously rescued a widowed mother and child after tragedy struck.

And I believed that for a long time. But lately, I'm grasping more bits of the truth, like pieces of a shattered plate I'm fitting together little by little.

So here are the facts I've rediscovered and reassembled:

Nick and Brett went for a run on a remote trail in the Rockies. Nick slipped on loose rocks, fell down a steep slope. His head cracked against stone and he died instantly. A terrible accident. Brett stepped in to deal with police reports and funeral arrangements. I lay on the couch and cried, nearly comatose with grief.

After the friends and neighbors and Mom returned home, Brett stayed. He took Eva to and from school and lessons. "You rest, Callie. I'll take care of everything."

His business team kept things going in his offices around the world. His personal assistant arranged for extra assistants—the chef who dropped off meals to my modest little house after the casseroles were gone, and the landscaper who mowed my lawn. His personal doctor made an actual house call, and Brett administered the prescribed pills to me with diligence. "It's just temporary," he said, "to get you through this tough time."

And when I couldn't be a parent, he stepped in, even though at that time he was just a new-ish family friend. His personal lawyers managed the logistics of Nick's will and presented me with digital forms to sign through my medication mist. "I'll take care of everything," Brett said. "Just rest."

That's when I let you slip away, Callie.

At the time, I was grateful to have another parental figure responsible for Eva. Someone had to donate to Teacher Appreciation Day and transfer funds for field trips, and those tasks went to his personal assistant . . . who required my passwords, of course. I got further lost in the haze of grief and medicine, became an increasingly neglectful mother, until I became more than that.

Something happened.

It happened a couple months after Nick's death. And I can't write it here. It fills me with too much shame.

But after the hospital, at home, when Eva was bandaged and stitched up and sleeping down the hall in her little bedroom, Brett gave me the wake-up call in a low voice. "Callie, honey, you're a danger to your daughter."

I wrangled my slurred voice, forced out words from my depths. It felt like my whole life had turned into the hour after you get your wisdom teeth removed and you're disoriented, with your mouth hanging open in the surgical chair. I don't remember the exact conversation, but it went something like this:

Me: "But I love her so much. I—"

Brett: "Shh. You can't do this alone."

"But I think—"

"Oh, honey, move into my place with me. I can take care of you both there."

"I don't know. I—"

"Shh. When you're back on your feet, you can move back to your little place."

"Well, thanks, but maybe just for a couple months."

Only, he made sure I never got back on my feet. After a couple months, his lawyer had me sign forms to sell the little two-bedroom home Nick and I had bought. His assistant hired an estate and moving company to get rid of my cheap, garage-sale furniture, and to pack up boxes of sentimental belongings . . . and then I was in his glass castle.

It didn't take much convincing for me to pass along the rest of my passwords so that his assistant could keep up with my vehicle registration and insurance payments and the zillion other things required to keep the gears of life going. "Precious, this is too much for you to handle right now. Let me help you."

Brett gently encouraged me to shut down all my socials. "Focus on your mental health. Posting and pretending and scrolling will only make it worse." He composed emails to my manager and music label, explaining that I was taking a break because of my grief and my daughter. He and his assistant prepared a PR statement to disseminate. "I know you're too lost in grief to deal with this. Let me help."

And that's how, little by little, he gained access to every single password and account, every fear and flaw. That's how I became entirely dependent on him.

He'd even called the Department of Child and Family Services, "just so you can get support, cupcake," and I didn't question it, not realizing this was a nice-sounding euphemism for the department that dealt with child abuse and neglect.

Even through my pill haze, I registered him turning on his charm full force for the social worker, talking with her as though I were a child myself.

While I was on the sofa in my pj's, he was in the kitchen with the social worker, pouring her Perrier and saying in an intimate voice, "Callie's trying, but she's just not able to keep her daughter safe now. I'm just relieved I'm here, Kathy."

Kathy nodded her white-bobbed head and blinked in sympathy behind her bifocals. "She's lucky to have you," she said in a loud whisper, clearly dazzled by his wealth and charm and expensive cologne and seven-million-dollar "cabin," probably a world apart from most of her clients. No doubt about it, she felt fortunate to become a member of his "team."

Last night I had a nightmare. There aren't any words to describe it—there were no people or places or things exactly. Just this darkness that was burying me, and I couldn't move or speak, just silently scream and try to break through the walls of my psyche, but I couldn't get back to the real world. Not until I focused on your word *no*. And that led me back.

I wonder if this is how Sleeping Beauty felt in that forced slumber, that powerless state, imprisoned, motionless and voiceless in those brambles. But I'm the prince in this tale, blue tights and feathered hat and sword and all. I'm the one who needs to find you and wake you up, Callie. Or maybe you're the prince. Or screw a prince—maybe we're both our own heroines, working together to wake the hell up.

And I'm proud of us. I manage to sneak away and write every day, just like I promised. I haven't read any of these letters, and I don't think I will, because I might freak out seeing it all laid out before me, what I've let him do, what kind of person he really is, written in black and white. The truth. The truth that he can't twist. The facts that are sitting in the secret compartment of my suitcase. The truth protected from his brainwashing. I'm glad these letters exist, but I won't read them. The truth will terrify me.

I know this doesn't make sense. I know I sound nuts. Which is another reason I won't read them, ha ha ha. I'll realize how nuts I sound and stop writing, stop producing evidence of my nuttiness. Seriously though, I don't really remember what's in these letters—it's like the words leave me and find their way to you, so I'll just keep writing and strengthening this golden thread.

But, Callie, he knows I have secrets now. He's watching me closely. He's vigilant. He knows something is up. I have to be careful.

Love,
Callie

# 7

# THE WINE WITCH

"So," Callie said, walking beside Luc as Eva galloped ahead, "why exactly should I beware of this sorceress of wines?"

He sputtered a laugh, which she thought he'd follow with a witty retort, but instead, a shadow fell over his face. "My family—the Forêts—and her family, the Lavignes—we have an old *vendetta*. The village has taken sides."

The water music shifted to a minor key, a mournful, midnight-blue cello solo, as if the river itself cared about the squabbles of its mortal neighbors.

"What kind of vendetta?" Assuming this meant a family feud of sorts, Callie thought of *The Godfather*, even though she'd never actually seen it.

"Oh, it goes way back, many decades. An argument over the forest we share. It's rich with truffles. For years, they've claimed there's a deed to prove it's theirs." He shrugged. "Yet they've never produced the document."

A fungus feud? There was no alliteration in French—fungus being *champignon*—so she didn't say it out loud. Also, he seemed to take this quite seriously. Callie wasn't completely sure what a truffle even looked like beyond a hard, dark blob. And honestly, she might not be able to pick its taste from a lineup. The extent of her exposure was the truffle fries happy hour special at a place she and Nick used to go, and any fungal flavor was overpowered by grease and salt.

Luc paused, stroking the puppy's ears. "Of course, it goes deeper than that. And you're only hearing our side. They have theirs." He gave her a meaningful, almost sorrowful look. "Just know that we're not welcome on their property."

Callie blinked—it wasn't easy reading between the lines in another language. She interpreted this to mean they wouldn't be seeing each other again, at least not on purpose. A perfect excuse to stay away. Snip, snip. He'd already be out of her life as soon as he'd entered. "So you won't be swinging by with a welcome basket of truffles," she said.

He crinkled his eyes, shaking his head.

"Well, what's this about a haunted château? Sounds like a ride in French Disneyland," she added, lightening it up for Eva's benefit.

"They say there's a ghost." He looked at Eva, his expression playful. "A mischievous boy your age."

Delight swept over Eva's face—a mischievous kid was right up her alley.

Luc gave Callie a sidelong glance. "But you two probably don't believe in ghosts. It's just a small-town thing."

"I believe in ghosts." Eva stood taller, proud of her area of expertise. "My daddy's ghost talks to me."

Callie let out a long breath as understanding dawned on Luc's face. Yes, she was a widow. What an odd way for him to discover this, through ghost gossip. She felt her cheeks flush, imagining this news would spread fast throughout the village.

"I'll make friends with the ghost boy," Eva said, exuding confidence.

"Bet you're as good with ghosts as dogs," said Luc, to which Eva gave an emphatic nod.

Callie appreciated him keeping the lid on that can of worms. His kindness toward Eva made her think of how he treated the injured dog, expecting nothing in return. His hands not grasping, just holding. Still, Callie had proven herself a terrible judge of men's motives, so she kept up her shield.

"What about you?" He turned to her. "Believe in ghosts?"

"All kinds of strange things can happen in this world." After saying it in French, she whispered its echo in English. "All kinds of strange things."

Her intention had been to keep a cool distance, but she realized she'd just quoted a line from her own song. That happened sometimes, like Freudian slips, like a little cave swiftlet or swallow carrying out secret messages.

But she had to stay under the radar, utterly and completely. The stakes were high. If any fan discovered who she was, where she was, and posted it online, word would spread like wildfire. And Brett would be waiting. The instant he'd realized they'd fled, he would have made online alerts for Callie Byrd—her reason for wearing sunglasses and a wide-brimmed hat and containing her blazing red hair in a braid this past week.

At times, it had made her laugh, how she felt like a criminal on the run, even considered a wig or drugstore bleach. Yes, she had perspective on the ridiculousness of this situation she'd gotten herself into.

But it wasn't too far-fetched to be—*slightly*—concerned about being recognized. Nearly a decade had passed since her song went viral, and two years since she'd dropped off the map. Most likely, the world had forgotten her. She was just another indie singer with a random song that gathered some fans and a few albums that gained some momentum. And then she'd willingly taken the step over the cliff into oblivion, and maybe once in a long while someone might hear that song and wonder, *Whatever happened to Callie Byrd?* and then move on with their own lives, leaving it at that.

All she had to do now was keep her daughter safe. Create a small, careful world. No music, no tours, no albums.

For a moment, Luc gave her a searching look, as if holding a flashlight to the cave, peering inside. "Any chance we've met before?" His question was casual, gentle even, as if he'd sensed her reticence but his curiosity had won out. "It's just—something about you is so familiar, Callie. Your voice, especially in English. And your face and hair."

Crap. Why had she quoted her song? Her cave self was trying to sabotage her plan, her need to stay anonymous. Had Luc actually heard that song before? It wasn't even one of her hits, just an obscure one that even fans might not recognize. She had the urge to put her sunglasses back on, but they were in the depths of her bag.

"I spent time in Aix about fifteen years ago. A study abroad thing." She kept her voice casual, left out her summer of busking. "Maybe we crossed paths."

He nodded thoughtfully. "I might have been living in Aix then." He gave a shrug. "Maybe you just have an unforgettable face. And voice."

People said she had a singer's voice, resonant and raspy, a voice like an instrument that came through in everyday conversation. *Sultry* was the word an interviewer used in a *Rolling Stone* article, which Nick had joked about whenever she asked him to buy dishwasher soap or clean the toilet. "Ask me in your sultry voice," he'd say.

It hadn't occurred to her that her speaking voice might give her away, but this was a reminder that she couldn't sing in front of anyone else. If any loud and wild singing ensued, it would be just with Eva. And it would be best to avoid Luc altogether, given the possible whiff of recognition.

They passed the *boulangerie,* its scent of fresh baguettes making her mouth water—it was past lunchtime, her belly rumbling, and she guessed Eva was on the verge of asking for food. "I'll get you a snack from my bag in a minute," she preemptively told her.

"Hang on a second." Luc ducked into the bakery and moments later emerged with two *pains au chocolat.* "Figured you were hungry after your travels."

*"Oh, j'adore le pain au chocolat!"* Eva bit in, not wasting a moment.

Callie took a grateful bite of her pastry, then caught herself and reached for her bag with buttery hands. "How much do I owe you?"

"I owe you. You made my dad happy. None of the old guys can

roll around on the grass with their dogs anymore. They got a kick out of watching Eva."

The river music shifted into a hopeful major key, a bright, folksy E chord. Maybe Luc was simply offering them chocolate and delight, no strings attached. Or maybe not.

"I insist." She pulled a five-euro bill from her wallet and held it out until he took it and folded it into his pocket, his expression thoughtful. He seemed a bit torn—a kind person who realized his kindness was not wanted, which only made him want to be kinder.

Not her problem.

As Eva finished her pastry, she interrogated Luc about being a vet—apparently her new dream job—and he reiterated he wasn't certified and could only accept food trades for his services. "We have dinner dropped off every night of the week. People think that since my dad and I are bachelors, we starve." He lowered his voice conspiratorially. "But he's a great cook, as long as you like truffle-flavored everything."

Bachelors. *Célibataires.* Literally, celibates, but she guessed he meant single. How quaint that this thirty-something man lived with his father—sweet and small-town, European and timeless. And there seemed to be some story behind his non-vet status.

None of which concerned her.

The river music crescendoed in anticipation as he motioned to a sign just ahead: *La Cave à Vins Lavigne.* A narrow storefront with a closed, heavy wooden door—maybe why she'd missed it earlier.

"*Et voilà,*" he said.

"*Merci,*" said Eva, petting the sleeping puppy in his sling.

"Enjoy your time here," he said. "If you need anything, my dad's at the park every day."

Callie kept her voice noncommittal. "When Eva gets dog withdrawal, we know where to go."

"Or if you ever need truffles." His eyes sparked—an unusual shade of sea green.

"Got it." With sudden apprehension, she glanced at the storefront windows draped in lace curtains, too dark inside to see anything. "So the ghost and the witch aren't too scary?" *Le fantôme* and *la sorcière.* It sounded positively eerie in French, something from a Gothic tale.

She expected more banter, but he lowered his voice to a serious note, eyeing Eva—who was tossing her bakery bag into a trash can, out of earshot. "Honestly? Some people are scared of the Lavigne family. My dad and I aren't fans of her son. Watch out for him."

Callie raised a brow, wishing for any other lodging option.

"But don't worry," he said quickly. "Madame Lavigne has a soft spot for children and mothers. Just stay on her good side."

"I feel so much better."

He gave her a smile, warm and real and easy, and Callie had the sensation of something thawing, water dripping from the long mountain winter she carried with her. Just as quickly, something slammed shut inside her, sealed tightly as a freezer door.

He waved a hand in farewell, and she raised hers stiffly, watching him walk toward the river, calling over his shoulder, "*Bon courage.*"

In return, she offered a quick nod. *Boundaries.* She'd had none during her years with Brett, and now she would carve them in stone. Build a wall if it came to that.

Callie turned the old brass knob and pushed open the door, entering the dim *cave à vins.* Behind her, river music rushed toward something, as though at the cusp of a waterfall, a powerful force with no going back. She closed the door behind Eva with the tinkle of bells.

An elegant woman who looked about eighty was dusting bottles, an array of white, rosé, red, and Burgundy wines, while mid-century French music played on speakers. She wore a black velvet dress with a cream lace collar, a throwback to the Victorian era. It looked a bit too warm for the summery weather.

The shop was narrow, stretching back into shadows. It struck Callie as odd that the door wasn't propped open like the other shop doors, as if there were something clandestine about this place. The counter was built of walnut, carved and polished, with shelves behind it lined with thick, green glass bottles and spouted oak casks, evoking an apothecary from centuries ago—vaguely magical.

*"Bonjour, madame."* The woman's voice sounded as old-school sophisticated as her clothing. Her silver hair was swept like silk into a smooth chignon, her earrings black pearls. "And *mademoiselle,*" she added, her gaze landing on Eva, who was peering around the shop, all curiosity.

*"Bonjour, madame."* Callie hesitated. She could say she was just browsing, then drag Eva back to the bus stop. This place was, well, a little creepy.

And the woman herself looked a little creepy in her nineteenth-century-style dress—but in fairness, most of the creepiness came from the expectation set up by the truffle dog crowd. There was nothing overtly witchy about her, no black cape or cackling voice.

Still, there was something formidable in her presence, and Callie could understand why you wouldn't want to be on her bad side. The woman exuded strength, with her defined jaw and solid build, tall enough that Callie had to look up at her. "How may I help you, madame?"

Callie took a deep breath and went for it. "Nathalie recommended I talk to you. My daughter and I are looking for a place to rent."

A measured nod. "For how long?"

"We're not sure."

Madame Lavigne looked at her for a long moment, her eyes bewitching, light and clear, a rainwater shade. She took three wineglasses from beneath the counter, then a bottle of rosé from a refrigerator case, and poured two half glasses. And into the third glass, an Orangina.

"Oh," Callie said, "we're fine."

Madame Lavigne ignored her protest and nodded to three tall

stools by a small round table. Eva skidded from around a corner of stacked wine cases, eyes wide in delight. *"J'adore l'Orangina!"* She hopped onto a stool and sipped, eyes closed in bliss, legs swinging, entire body exuding satisfaction.

*"Bievenues."* Madame Lavigne clinked her glass against Callie's in a toast of welcome. "So, how did you find our little town?"

Considering how to respond, Callie sipped the rosé, then startled at its taste—deep and light at once, all gemstones and wildflowers. "Oh, this is perfect. Just what I needed."

Madame Lavigne nodded, her gaze piercing. "I match the wine to the person. And of course, the food to the wine. But the person is more interesting to me."

Averting her eyes, Callie took another sip, feeling it slide down her throat, leaving a trail of cool pink light, a sunrise that unspooled into her entire body. Was this Madame Lavigne's witchy power? If so, bring it on. Much better than poisoned apples.

"*Alors,* what brings you here?" the wine witch asked again, not letting her off the hook.

Callie breathed out. Why hadn't she rehearsed this? Of course, it would be the question she'd get again and again. *Escape* was the first word that came to mind. But that would open the door to so many questions. The fact was, Brett's abuse was so subtle, his form of control so nuanced, his powers of manipulation so polished that she couldn't explain it in French, much less English.

One day last year, she'd gone into incognito mode on her laptop, careful to hide her search history, and typed in "signs of an abusive partner"—but for every sign that sort of fit with Brett, she could envision his calm, cool, collected defense that would convince any objective observer. Which was why it had taken her so long to recognize it and do something about it. He was the slickest of con men. In the end, all she could do was hang onto that *no*.

Swallowing the word *escape*, she said simply, "La Chanson."

Madame Lavigne nodded. "The river's song carries far, to people who need it, even across the ocean."

Before Callie could respond, Eva finished the last drops of Orangina. "*Excusez-moi, madame.* Can we see the cave?"

"Oh, sweetie, there's no actual cave. It's just a wine shop," Callie began, when Madame Lavigne said, "Of course, *ma petite.* Follow me."

Madame Lavigne picked up her glass, still a third full, and headed to the back, with Eva bouncing at her heels.

Fantastic. They were allowing a sorceress to lure them to her underground lair. Callie took a resigned sip of the ethereal rosé, then, unable to part ways with it, picked up her glass and followed. Madame Lavigne led them down a centuries-old spiral stone staircase, the temperature dropping as they descended into darkness.

A cellar stretched before them, far bigger than the shop itself. Bare light bulbs cast a dim light over the ancient stone floor and walls, rows of bottles glinting beneath cobwebs and layers of dust. Wooden casks lined one wall, parting for a small workbench covered with labels, pens, and corks.

On a high shelf above was a row of small blue vintage bottles whose contents she could only guess at—yeast? Sugar? Tannins? Or maybe old-fashioned ink for the labels?

Eva jogged around, exploring the *cave* in bliss, while Madame Lavigne told Callie about the Roman origins of this cellar, which later transformed into a medieval church, then a prison during the Revolution, and eventually found its way into her ancestors' possession a couple of hundred years ago as a *cave à vins.*

Callie shivered, hoping Eva wasn't sensing any prisoner ghosts, and sipped her wine, hoping it wasn't drugged, and wondered how, despite warnings, she ended up in a millennia-old dungeon with a *sorcière.* She redirected the conversation. "So, you have a place for rent?"

"Yes, just outside of town. I no longer live there. I live in this building, on the top floors." She gestured with her chin toward the ceiling. "But I grew up in the château, as did my sons. My eldest is in Paris, but my youngest lives in a *petite maison* on the grounds. He's renovating the château. There's another *petite maison* where you may stay."

Callie assumed this was a cottage of sorts—much more appealing than a haunted castle—but the son gave her pause. He felt like a gamble.

As if reading her mind, Madame Lavigne said, "Julien won't bother you. He's very quiet."

Careful not to commit, Callie asked, "May we see the *petite maison*, madame?"

"*Bien sûr.*" The wine witch sipped her last drops of rosé. "Business is slow at this time of day. I'll take you there now." She called to Eva, who darted happily around a corner. Apparently, if there were ghosts here, they weren't tortured, eighteenth-century prisoners.

Madame Lavigne led her and Eva back upstairs into the relative warmth and light of the shop. Callie savored her last sip of rosé, then left her glass on the counter, feeling ever so slightly elated—not drugged, right?—and hoping that wouldn't impede any last shreds of judgment she had left. She could only imagine how Brett would spin her day-drinking with a witch.

Madame Lavigne grabbed a chocolate bonbon from a bowl by the register, dropped it into Eva's hand, then flipped the sign to *Fermé* and held open the door.

Back outside, Callie blinked in the sunshine as the river music greeted them with a whimsical dulcimer tune. Madame Lavigne led them along the cobbled street, with Eva darting back and forth like a puppy, bonbon chocolate smeared on her hands. She was now unencumbered by her suitcase, which Madame Lavigne insisted on taking, despite Callie's protests.

Leaving behind ancient buildings, they headed downstream along a river path cradled by rolling hills of lavender, vineyards, and olive groves. Limestone cliffs jutted high, as the oddly sea-green water flowed and sang through the valley. The color of Luc's irises. As soon as the thought occurred, she tamped it down.

Spotting the hillsides were stone Provençal country homes—*mas* was the word for them, Callie vaguely recalled. And in the distance, several centuries-old châteaux rose from the high banks along the river, larger and more stately than the *mas*.

Callie snuck a glance at the wine witch, who was surprisingly agile and hardy—a mountain ram in black velvet and lace and, beyond belief, low-heeled pumps. Still, Callie started carrying Eva's suitcase in her other hand when, twenty minutes into the walk, the trail veered upward and the dirt path became cobbled stone, with occasional stairs unfurling through oleander and rosemary, weaving among cypress, then leading down into a valley. Madame Lavigne seemed oddly at ease in her unseasonable apparel, while Callie was sweating and panting as they descended.

And then, Callie rounded a bend and found herself face-to-face with a house more evocative of a *mas* than a castle, and built into a hillside overlooking the river, as if part of the natural landscape itself, butter-colored stone walls and steps zigzagging around it.

"Welcome to the Château of the Lost," announced the wine witch, not even out of breath.

Callie couldn't help asking, a bit warily, "How did it get the name?"

"It attracts lost souls. Like yours."

# 8

# PEPITO

*Colorado, six weeks before arrival in France*

Dear Callie,

Okay, what should I do about Eva's talking-to-ghosts issue? What would a good mother do?

Yesterday, after Brett told her to have raw walnuts and raisins as a snack, she whispered to me, "Daddy's ghost says life is short and I should be allowed to eat *mucho chocolate. Mucho!*" It did sound like the kind of thing Nick would say, and I snuck her a caramel truffle.

A few days ago, Brett tried to give her a hug, like he sometimes does, and she slipped away, like she always does. And that night, putting her to bed, I whispered beneath my breath, using terminology from her school, "Brett never tries to do anything inappropriate with you, does he?"

"No. Not in that way. But I think it's inappropriate that he doesn't like dogs." She started ticking off his transgressions on her fingers. "He doesn't know any knock-knock jokes, doesn't let me have chocolate, wears stinky cologne, doesn't appreciate my thrift shop style." Her voice grew hard as steel on her last complaint: "And he made you stop singing."

I'd heard this litany before, of course, but this time she

added, "Daddy's ghost tells me that Brett lies. That he lies and you believe him. Because you're trapped somewhere."

I got that spine-chill feeling that horror movies give me, and I tried to form words that a responsible mother might say. Nothing came out.

Eva tried to reassure me (because beyond all comprehension, I've somehow managed to raise a compassionate child). "We'll get you back. Don't be scared. That's what he tells me."

I pressed my hand to her cheek and felt how soft and smooth it is, like a piano key, or a honey legato melody, and it grounded me into the now. "I'm here, sweetie. Right here." We hardly ever talk about Brett—it's like we've internalized the cameras everywhere. "Anything else?"

"Daddy says we'll get Pepito back too." She paused. "Where'd Pepito go, anyway?"

"I don't know, sweetie." I scanned my memory of the past two years—it felt like peering into a dense fog. When had I last seen our little Mayan statue? He was such a big part of our lives before Nick died—family heirloom meets good-luck charm meets comedy act meets ancient artifact. Remember how we loved him like a handheld pet or an elderly aunt? How did I let him slip through the cracks?

I can still hear Nick's *abuela* in Guatemala calling him a *diosito*—a cute little god. "A *diosito* of music," she explained, pointing her calloused finger to the turtle drum he held. "For you, since you're a *diosita* of music too, *mija*." She put the sculpture into my hands, patting them, and trilling out her sweet chipmunk laugh.

When did Nick and I start imagining Pepito's commentary on our everyday lives? Channeling his *abuela*'s endearingly nasal voice? *You're getting a cough—put on a scarf! Here, drink this garlic tea!* I miss that silliness and spontaneity and warmth, how Pepito somehow embodied it all.

Eva wouldn't let it go. Tears welled up. "But I *love* Pepito."

"Oh, sweetie, he must've gotten lost in the move." I spewed out platitudes. "But he lives in your heart. His spirit is with us."

After she fell asleep, I went down two flights of stairs and looked through the boxes labeled *Sentimental,* which are in camera range in the main part of the basement, and I knew Brett would ask me about it. So, afterward I sat on the sofa and waited for him to finish in his office, then preemptively asked, "Hey, any chance you know where that little Mayan music deity went?"

He took a long sip of his local craft IPA. "Listen, cupcake, you need to get over Nick. It hurts me when you pine over him. It's time to let go."

Now that the medication fog has cleared, it hits me how devoid of humor our relationship is, no silly jokes about Pepito, no jokes at all. I chose my words carefully. "It's not so much for me but for Eva."

"That's even worse. She's got this unhealthy belief in Nick's ghost." He took another sip and shook his head like he was delivering terrible medical news. "Your instability is affecting her. The last thing she needs is a Mayan god as an imaginary friend."

I kept my voice casual, even though inside I was screaming, *Where the hell is Pepito?* And I had a guess, but it seemed too insidious to contemplate. "I was thinking more as a connection to her heritage, not just Nick but her grandparents and great-grandparents."

He closed his eyes. I was sure he was rolling them beneath the lids, like I was a naive child and he was the authority on all things related to ghosts, artifacts, and child psychology. "Bad idea. Trust me, precious. She needs to move on. Take her back to that psychologist my doctor set her up with."

Oh, God. Eva hated that man, flatly refused to talk to him. Apparently, he'd sit on the floor with her and an array of creepy dolls and try to engage her in play. After the first session, she'd said with a shudder, "Daddy's ghost thinks he has bad breath, serious chronic halitosis. And it's true. The guy needs major mouthwash." After six sessions, I stopped taking her. Brett blamed her and me for the epic therapy fail, and for my part, I kept wondering where she'd picked up the term *chronic halitosis*.

"Never mind—the statue probably got lost in the move," I told Brett. "The estate company might have thought it was broken trash."

He gave me a measured look, like he suspected I didn't really believe it. "Well, you'd better get Eva's ghost under control. I'm her father now, and she needs to accept that."

I bit my tongue hard and thought, *Yes, dear, I'll just channel my inner ghostbuster.* And then I shoved the thought away, because sometimes I feel like he can read any snark in my mind.

Then I thought of your word. *No.*

I let it fill me, and if he could read that thought, *so be it.*

I've been rereading *The Goose Girl,* which is a weird name for it because geese don't have much to do with anything in the fairy tale. It's about a woman whose identity is stolen, and her voice is taken, and she's banished from the kingdom. As if that isn't enough, her beloved horse's head is chopped off. The horse was like her intuition, but his head lives on and tells her the truth of what happened. That decapitated head holds the truth.

Not as gross as it sounds, but not Disney material, not that any of these fairy tales and myths are, not by a long shot. I mean, Bluebeard has straight-up serial killer vibes.

Lately, when Eva talks about Nick's ghost, I can't help

thinking it's the horse's head speaking the truth of the situation, the truth of who we are . . . because yours truly has been a hollow husk filled with whatever lies Brett feeds me. No wonder she puts her faith in a ghost.

Probably I'm just an unstable mother obsessed with dark fairy tales and trying to rationalize why her kid talks to spirits, because yes, I feel ashamed that her mind has to fabricate a ghost in order to deal with this life I've made for us.

If I manage to get us away from Brett, I will never let a man save us again. I will never give a man my trust. And I will never let another man be a father to Eva. Nick is the only father she'll ever have, and if he's in the form of a ghost who encourages unhealthy snacks and jokes about chronic halitosis, so be it.

But damn it, I want Pepito back. The more I think about it, the more I realize that little statue is more than a good luck charm or family heirloom. Pepito holds light and love and hope and fun and laughter and wisdom. And I want him back.

Love,
Callie

# 9

# THE CHÂTEAU OF THE LOST

"A pool!" Eva shouted.

Callie's gaze landed on a modest, empty rectangle, tucked into a hillside terrace beside the château, surrounded by zigzagging stone walls and stairs.

The lack of water didn't dampen Eva's enthusiasm—she hopped from one foot to the other, fists tucked beneath her chin. "I always wanted a pool! Almost as much as a dog!"

"My son will be filling it later this summer," said Madame Lavigne. "You can swim in it if you stay long enough," she added, looking at Callie, as if offering a challenge.

Eva's eyes widened, her exuberance unbridled. Callie had to admit this pool held potential, worlds more appealing than the dank indoor one back in Colorado that smelled of mildew, where Eva had taken swim lessons.

Madame Lavigne kept her gaze fixed on Callie. "If you help upkeep the grounds and gardens, I'll reduce your rent. Put in enough work, I'll waive it altogether."

This felt too good to be true. The rent was already a tiny fraction of what they'd been paying for the apartment in Aix. Callie's three thousand euros—minus some change now—could go toward necessities for the next three months. She could find an under-the-table job to pay for a lawyer. Still, it was hard to shake off her deepest fear: Was this place hidden enough?

As if in response, the river sang a soothing tune, and if there had been lyrics, they might have said, *We've got this, Callie.*

While Eva skipped down the steps, Callie took in the château, thinking again that it seemed more elegant country manor than castle. Less than a hundred feet away from the château, two cottages sat side by side, both with the classic Provençal clay-tiled roofs and gray-blue shutters. Pink bougainvillea and white jasmine crawled up the stone walls, and in between, herb gardens of rosemary and sage spun out their fragrances.

Timeless, all of it, plucked from a storybook.

"The *petites maisons* have housed workers and guests over the years," Madame Lavigne said. "They're quite comfortable."

As Callie struggled to think of a sane way of asking whether the cottages were haunted too, Madame Lavigne led her and Eva to the one on the left, and ushered them into a small living room. Modest, just what they needed. White walls, thick oak beams, terracotta floors. Wavy glass windows draped with lace curtains. Simple wooden furnishings, worn linen spread over the love seats.

Eva's hand hovered over a mid-century dial phone. "May I touch?"

"Be my guest." Madame Lavigne spread her arms toward the vintage decor—mostly, curious farming-related antiques—wooden grain scoops, burlap sacks, rusted scales, and a scythe over the stone fireplace.

Eva ran her fingers along every surface in delight, asking questions as Madame Lavigne offered thoughtful answers sprinkled with anecdotes.

If Brett's "cabin" had an opposite, it would be this—a sweet cottage, nothing behind glass. Even the windows were wide open—a breath of fresh air after living in Brett's temperature-controlled house with its floor-to-ceiling blinds operated by a complicated phone app. And this cottage was a short, musical stroll into town, unlike the forty-five-minute drive from Brett's house to pretty much anywhere.

Madame Lavigne watched Eva exploring, fondness in her expression.

Despite Madame Lavigne's scary reputation, Callie had to admit the wine witch was downright grandmotherly with her daughter. Still, the woman never seemed to actually smile, no hint of curvature of the mouth and definitely no teeth showing. Laughter seemed in a different universe altogether for her.

Soon, she led them out the back door onto a private patio and garden by the river, whose melodies were floral now, tendriling around them with the scent of jasmine. Like a little real estate agent, Eva pointed out ripe apricots and cherries on the trees. "Healthy, free snacks, Mom. Now imagine teatime at this table . . ." And on and on she went, selling it hard.

Back inside, they climbed up the narrow staircase to the sloped space upstairs—a tiny bathroom and two bedrooms, each with its own balcony, one overlooking the aquamarine river, and the other, the empty pool. Eva plopped onto the quilted bedspread, claiming the pool side—so that she could "dream about dolphin-diving in there one day"—while Callie happily accepted the river side.

Standing on the balcony, the water flowing below, she felt as if she'd been dropped into a gilded book of fairy tales—not the dark ones from Brett's library but cozy, pastel-illustrated ones with an abundance of sparrows and flowers and happy endings. She felt *hope*. And for a moment, she let herself swim in it. Her throat opened and her lips parted, and once again she had the sensation that a song would pour out. Her body quivered like an instrument, ready and waiting.

"Would you like to see the château?" Madame Lavigne asked, watching her from the balcony doors.

"Is that where the ghost boy lives?" Eva asked—although, in fairness, her question came out more as: *Ghost boy live in big house?* She could understand French amazingly well, thanks to her immersion school. It was the reason Callie had chosen France for their escape, along with her good memories. She resisted correcting Eva's grammar, knowing from experience that fluency hinged on the confidence to risk speaking, despite the inevitable errors.

"He's there much of the time." Madame Lavigne's eyes misted over. "But he wanders the whole estate. I can't always see him, but my son can."

Callie's muscles tensed. Not because of the ghost but the son. So, their only neighbor was creepily quiet *and* consistently saw ghosts? The storybook illustration in her mind turned dark and spectral—of course this was all too good to be true. Just like Brett swooping in to save them two years ago, an act that had come with a staggering price.

Wary, she took Eva's hand as they went outside, walked a few dozen yards to the manor, then followed Madame Lavigne up the exterior stairs. The wine witch opened the carved wooden door, revealing an entryway and a large living room in the midst of renovation. The ceiling was high, the molding elegant, the windows tall and regal, the walls of the foyer covered in a mishmash of old paintings.

Somehow, it still felt homey, far from the cold atmosphere of Brett's place, and surprisingly not-spooky, even with the furniture covered in drop cloths, and tools and building materials and ladders scattered around.

"The first floor renovation should be done soon," Madame Lavigne said with satisfaction. She ushered them farther inside and opened a door that led to a stone staircase descending into darkness. "Of course, there's a cellar. It holds my most exquisite wines, the oldest and most special." She gave Callie a meaningful look. "I can help you select the right one for the right person and the right occasion."

Callie doubted they'd use this bizarre perk but nodded, as if it were all a normal part of a house tour.

Eva immediately took note of a knotted rope toy and chewed-on rawhide, glancing around hopefully. "Does this place come with a dog?"

"Of course," said Madame Lavigne. "My son's." She turned to Callie. "I grew up here, and my children spent their childhoods here too. Always with dogs."

Delighted, Eva entertained herself by peeking behind sofas and chairs, making soft beckoning sounds for a dog—and possibly for the ghost boy too.

Wandering back to the entry hall, Callie took in the standard framed landscapes and portraits with pets and flowers and fruit, but one stood out—a woman in a gold frock, pouring contents from a small bottle into a blue goblet, a black cat at her feet, a crimson shoe sticking out below her gown. There was something skeletal, even corpse-like about her, as she hunched over the goblet. Something witchy. Now, *this* painting was exactly the kind of thing a wine witch might have.

"This is Giulia Tofana," said Madame Lavigne, as if introducing Callie to an old friend. "In the seventeenth century, she helped women liberate themselves from abusive men."

Goose bumps sprang up on Callie's arms. "Oh."

The wine witch gave her an even look. "For many years, this place was a safe house. The women and children mostly came from Paris and other cities, but a network formed, and they found their way here."

*Château of the Lost.*

This was all hitting too close to home, and Madame Lavigne was giving her a look that said she knew it. Had Nathalie from the bus somehow known too? Callie stepped outside of herself for a moment, saw the bird's-eye view—a disheveled, desperate mother and child, clearly on the run. Callie felt embarrassment, followed by gratitude and a feeling that somehow the universe was looking out for them.

Madame Lavigne moved her gaze back to the portrait. "The first woman I helped gave this to me. A distant cousin from Nice. She and her children stayed here until she was back on her feet. After my husband died, I wanted to be of service. Over the years, dozens of women and children came. But my heart has hardened around men. Except for my own sons, of course."

A wave of empathy swept over Callie. To deal with the ache in her throat, she promptly changed the subject. "So, what's in the goblet?" She stepped closer and squinted at the print.

"Wine mixed with Tofana water. *Aqua Tofana*. A colorless, tasteless liquid containing arsenic, belladonna, and other secret ingredients. Her signature poison."

"She—she *killed* the men?"

Madame Lavigne gave an indignant shrug, as if to say, *They deserved it*. "It sickened the men for a week or so, mimicked symptoms of a natural illness. The women could tend to their husbands and appear devoted while slipping poison into their wine until they died, and no one would suspect what the wives had done."

"Huh." Of course Callie would never wish death by poisoning on anyone, but there were days when she wondered what it would be like if Brett died in a car crash on impact. *Poof*. He'd be out of her life. The biggest, deepest relief. Freedom. The world expanding, all the windows and doors opening, the roof flying away.

"We protect everyone who comes to the Château of the Lost."

Oddly, this tall, strong-boned eighty-something lady did make Callie feel safe. *Mess with me and my octogenarian bodyguard will destroy you*.

Callie gave a grateful nod and, hoping not to offend, asked, "Is this technically a château?"

Madame Lavigne lifted a shoulder. "It's just a *mas*," she said, "but people in town gave it the name. It creates an aura of reverence. Deters trespassers."

Callie wasn't sure what to make of this, but the woman had a point—a haunted castle owned by a witch felt more fearsome than a fancy farmhouse.

"Now, would you like the full tour?" Madame Lavigne asked.

"*Oui. Merci*." Callie called Eva over.

Her daughter looked triumphant, giddy and rosy-cheeked, with a sheen of sweat. "I was just playing with *le fantôme*!"

*The phantom*. After a moment of deliberation, Callie put him into the category of harmless imaginary playmate. "Sounds good, sweet pea."

Eva spun toward Madame Lavigne. "*J'adore* the phantom boy!"

"Well, dear, tell him *bonjour*." Madame Lavigne led them upstairs to the hallway, letting them peek inside bedrooms with ornate—if musty—furnishings. She paused before a built-in bookcase of leather and clothbound volumes. In a practiced movement, she pushed its side molding, and the bookcase swiveled to reveal a secret room. It was set up as a studio apartment with a kitchenette, a double bed, a basket of toys, and a tiny bathroom.

Callie blinked, searching for words. "Wow."

"The women and children mostly stayed in the bedrooms. But sometimes, they had to stay in here for a day or two." She gave Callie a meaningful look. "I still keep it stocked with supplies."

"I want to stay here!" Eva was already riffling through stuffed animals.

Callie said lightly, "Maybe you can play here sometime."

"*Bien sûr*," said Madame Lavigne with a nod.

The room touched a nerve in Callie, and as she left, her insides churned with emotions she couldn't quite pin down. They continued the tour, Eva darting and giggling—with the ghost boy, she assumed, noting that Madame Lavigne took it in stride. The guests she'd hosted here over the years must have come with all kinds of emotional idiosyncrasies. Eva's antics would be nothing new.

Madame Lavigne gave her a set of antique keys to the cottage and the main château. "Help yourselves to anything, including toys." She winked at Eva, whose ears immediately perked up at toys—*jouets*—one of the first words she'd mastered in French.

As Madame Lavigne led them back downstairs and outside into the sunshine, Callie considered whether it was a reasonable idea to stay. True, the wine witch had eerie edges, but the cottage was perfect, and the son, well, he was a wild card. And the fungus feud? As long as she avoided Luc and his father, that wouldn't be an issue.

*Do it,* sang the river, and Callie found herself counting out the first month's deposit from her wad of euros.

Madame Lavigne tucked the bills into her purse. "There's a landline in your *petite maison.* My number is on the notepad beside the phone."

So the old-fashioned phone in the cottage actually worked. Untraceable to her name. Just what she needed. A landline in case of emergency.

She considered calling her mother, a thought that stirred mild guilt. Her father had always been out of the picture, and her mom was, for all practical purposes, now out of the picture too. She was a retired expat in Ecuador, a serial monogamist who rarely visited Colorado, never liked kids much, but, in her own way, did her best.

No, Callie couldn't contact her. Brett would manipulate her into divulging Callie's whereabouts. Her mom always leapt to his defense, charmed by his confidence, his wealth, even his age, halfway between Callie's and hers. He'd just say, *Linda, listen, I'm worried about your daughter's mental health. What if another accident happens and I'm not there to save Eva next time?*

No, she couldn't call anyone. Not worth the risk.

When Madame Lavigne bade them *au revoir* by the pool patio, Callie insisted on walking her up the steep stairs on the hillside, lightly holding her elbow, hoping this wouldn't insult her. Hoping she'd *stay on her good side,* Callie thought, remembering Luc's words.

At the top of the hill, Madame Lavigne kissed her cheeks in the customary farewell, then pierced her with an intense gaze. "People say I'm a witch. They fear me. As they should."

Callie wondered if this was a bizarre warning to be a good renter—or a threat to the ex-partner who might come after her. Or something else altogether. Before Callie could formulate a response, Madame Lavigne plucked a bonbon from her purse, tossed it to Eva, and walked back along the path toward town.

Watching the wine witch leave, Eva popped the chocolate into her mouth and announced, "Madame Lavigne would be an awesome grandma."

From the bedroom doorway of the cottage, Callie observed Eva unpacking her favorite thrift shop clothes and arranging them in the wardrobe, which she'd checked for a door to Narnia. Eva seemed delighted, far from destabilized. And she was already making new friends—canine, human, and ghost.

Of course, she'd had cranky moments over the past week, hangry and tired at times. And irrational moments of stubborn insistence over one thing or another—limits around video game use and enforced bedtimes. And raw moments of barely-beneath-the-surface fear that Brett would find them.

It had pained Callie to see her daughter's vulnerability peek out beneath the jubilant façade—just a waver in her voice, an uncertainty in her eyes. Eva had always been an exuberant child, but like anyone, she had layers of worries and fears, even if they surfaced only occasionally, in the subtlest of ways.

Callie handed her three apricots she'd plucked from the tree. "You feeling okay, sweetie? It's all right if you feel scared or sad."

"I'm marvelous." Eva set the fruit on her bedside table beside her handheld gaming console, now charging. Then she continued hanging up shirts in a businesslike manner.

"I'm here whenever you need me, sweet pea."

"Got it."

Callie moved in for a hug, and Eva wriggled away. "Mom, I don't need a hug *now*. I'm arranging my vintage apparel."

"Okay."

"Oh, and before I forget, Daddy's ghost said that Luc is *muy buena gente*."

Callie translated the Spanish slang in her head—"a really good person." It was a turn of the phrase Nick had often used. How strange that Eva remembered it. Callie wanted to shut down any conversation about Luc, but clearly he'd made an impression on her daughter. "Want to talk about it?"

"Nope," Eva said matter-of-factly. "That's it. Just thought you should know." She slid a yellow polka-dotted top onto a hanger. "Mom, I'm kind of in the middle of something."

Callie released a breath. "Want some alone time?"

"Yes, please," Eva said with an eye roll. Understandable. Callie needed alone time too. "Oh," Eva added, picking up her gaming console, "what's the Wi-Fi password?"

"There's no Wi-Fi here."

Eva shot her a doubtful look. "There's Wi-Fi everywhere, Mom. The password's probably on a piece of paper somewhere, like in Aix."

Callie's chest froze. "Were you using Wi-Fi in Aix?"

"Just to play *Minecraft* with Olivia."

Callie rubbed her face, putting it all together. It hadn't occurred to her that Eva would be resourceful enough to get online, but of course a digital native kid would figure it out in two seconds flat. Brett had given her this console, and his IT guy would have been able to track it with ease, the moment she'd gotten online.

Hands shaking, Callie picked up the device, checked the settings, toggled on airplane mode, then double and triple checked there were no cell capabilities or GPS. She released a breath. Okay, he couldn't have tracked them after they'd left the apartment. Probably. Hopefully.

"Sweetie," Callie rasped, "if we get online, Brett could find us."

A pause, a quiver in Eva's lip. "Sorry, Mom. I didn't know." Her voice came out thin and quiet. "Is that how he found us?"

"Just keep it in airplane mode, okay?" Callie pulled her in for a hug, breathed in the lemony scent in her soft hair.

This time, Eva allowed the hug, pressing her face into Callie's shoulder, holding her tightly.

"In a few months, you can chat with your friends again. Once I get stuff settled."

"Everything would be easier if we just had a dog." Eva let out a long sigh. "Can we get a Lagotto Romagnolo? Or even something not so fancy? Any dog?"

"One day." This was Callie's usual response, but this time she added, on impulse, "One day I'll write a song for you, and that will be the catchy chorus: 'Can I get a dog? Any dog?'"

"Yes, please!"

Callie wondered how that had slipped out, the idea of writing a song again. Of course, she wasn't serious about a dog or a song.

"Let's make 'one day' this summer, Mom."

"Quiet time now." Callie gave her another kiss and left the room, letting her mind turn to more serious things. How else might Brett be tracking her?

She shut the door, leaning against it for a moment to do a mental scan of their possessions. No other electronic devices besides her laptop, which she'd been careful to keep offline. *We're safe now. We're safe.* Again and again she said it, as if she whispered it enough, she could wish it true.

As if one day in the future, she might, in fact, get them a dog. Or write a song.

Back in her own room, Callie set her suitcase on the bed, savoring the soft melody of La Chanson weaving with cicada hums through the open balcony doors.

She used to have hours of alone time every day when Nick was alive and Eva was in preschool and kindergarten. She'd compose and rehearse, and the hours would fly by. But with Brett, her alone time just made her lonely. She was no longer a musician, just a frizzy-haired lady in yoga pants, sequestered in a private library, her only friends being characters from ancient fairy tales.

Now, Callie tucked her practical T-shirts and shorts into drawers, and then, ever so carefully, unpeeled her bundled-up socks to reveal her tender treasure.

Pepito. She held him in her palms, so small to have sparked something so huge. She'd fought for him. Destroyed for him. She ran her fingers over his carved lines, smoothed over the centuries, his familiar face framed by ears of corn, his tiny turtle-shell drum at his side.

*Nice digs*, she imagined him saying in a lighthearted, nasal voice. She kissed his cool stone cheek, then put him on her bedside table.

How swiftly and strangely Brett had become taken with Pepito two and a half years earlier—and with her, his favorite additions to his music deity collection. At first, she hadn't understood the delight in his eyes when he'd learned her full name. She'd just given an uncomfortable laugh when he'd said with calculating awe, "Calliope, you are the living goddess of music."

In the beginning, when Nick was alive, she'd had only a vague sense of Brett's profession—an old guy who dealt in old stuff. After Nick died, she'd learned that Brett owned an antiquities business, inherited from his father, giving him access to artifacts bought before the cultural property laws made fifty years ago. And the further she'd fallen into their relationship, the more she'd grasped the extent of his wealth and connections—offices in Paris and Mexico City and Tokyo, employees around the world.

It had all made her cringe, but she hadn't realized until too late the *obsession* he felt for his most treasured collection—music deities from around the world, throughout time. He'd pounced, dug in his talons while she was lost in grief. He'd put her behind glass, cut her off from her friends, her family, her music, herself. Her bond with Eva was the only one he couldn't cut, although he'd tried, with beak and claw.

Now, safe for the moment in La Chanson, it was time to make a plan. For the past week, she'd existed in limbo, licking her wounds, savoring freedom. But Brett wouldn't let her go easily—his obsession felt almost supernatural.

She scoured her brain for ways to earn money for a lawyer. Music lessons? Easy but too risky. Babysitting? No, she'd need references, background checks. Some kind of farmwork? Harvesting? That might be safest—that way, Eva could be with her. Maybe Madame Lavigne could recommend her if she proved herself by cleaning up the grounds.

Once Callie had enough money, she'd find a lawyer to extricate her from the documents she'd signed in a drugged, grieving stupor. She'd report her own side of the story to the authorities, protect herself legally, then return to the States. Not to Colorado—she had to keep a distance from Brett. Ideally, she'd accomplish this by late August—three months from now, the length of her tourist visa.

Callie glanced at Pepito, feeling the love emanate. Then she stared at her nearly empty suitcase, the inner pocket bulging with letters—and with the three file folders she'd added just before the escape.

Folders that felt like unexploded bombs. She had the dramatic urge to burn them, but her future lawyer would need them. Still, at the moment, she couldn't bring herself to open them. She shut the suitcase and pushed it to the back of her armoire.

Sometimes, it felt like Brett had superpowers—to read her mind, control her actions, confuse her thoughts—although distance was breaking the spell. Here across the sea, the link was weakening. But he'd sent that man to Aix, which meant Brett wasn't letting them go.

She could almost hear Pepito's nasal voice: *He's no sorcerer, just a jerk.*

True, perhaps, but his obsessive nature felt sinister.

He did not like his collections dismantled.

Especially the most prized pieces.

# 10

# LIVING GODDESS IN PAJAMAS

*Colorado, five weeks before arrival in France*

Dear Callie,

I'm back in the laundry room, which feels like a dungeon but still a haven, away from cameras. I'm starting to like the musty smell and fluorescent light down here. A taste of freedom.

Yesterday, I brought up Pepito again. Brett and I were in the kitchen and he was making a protein smoothie after his trail run. He was on an endorphin high, and I thought it would be a good time to ask.

"Hey, Brett, I know we need to move on, but I really feel like the little Mayan deity is important for Eva." Of course, I couldn't call him Pepito in front of Brett—it might make him feel threatened. A reminder that Pepito is like a beloved pet. More than that. A reminder of the happy, warm, fun, whimsical family life Eva and I once had. I kept my voice neutral. "A part of her cultural heritage. A connection with Guatemala."

He leaned against the counter, sipping his green smoothie, watching me like I was a rambling child.

I took a breath but couldn't quite meet his gaze. "Can you maybe have your assistant call the moving company? Or estate company? Or whoever was in charge? They must have records. I mean—"

"Let it go, cupcake," he said. "I'm taking a shower." He rinsed his glass and put it into the dishwasher, then disappeared into the bathroom. Like Pepito meant nothing, less than nothing.

And at that moment, Callie, I knew. I knew he was lying to me.

Now I keep thinking, what if I'd never shown Pepito to Brett that day two and a half years ago? I wonder how life would be different if I'd somehow cut him off at our first real conversation.

But at first, Brett seemed harmless—just a professional acquaintance of Nick's—some rich old guy in a different generation and social class altogether. Someone to be vaguely polite to . . . a rando who'd read Nick's articles in *Archaeology Today* and reached out.

Remember how Nick joked about the old guy's "cabin" in the Rocky Mountains, his oh-so-casual mention of flying in from his flat in Paris, how weird it was that he'd chosen Nick as his Colorado buddy?

I wish he'd never been in Colorado when I was playing that festival in Lyons. I wish Nick had never given him our extra ticket. I wish the weather had been bad so he wouldn't have been charmed by the perfect blue sky, the sunshine sparkling off the Saint Vrain River, the red cliffs cradling us all, everyone dancing in peak-summer bliss, the bluegrass and folk tunes rising over the Rocky Mountains. I wish it had been windy and gray and stormy.

The day after that, Brett looked at me differently. Lately, I've been going over how it all unfolded, wishing I could rewind. That morning, he came over to get Nick for a trail run, and while Nick was getting ready, Brett sat at the kitchen table and said in a low voice, with weird reverence, "Calliope, Greek goddess, Leader of the Muses. You're a true, living goddess of music."

How did I respond? Probably an uncomfortable smile as I put Eva's cereal in front of her. We were tired and moving slowly from the late night—this was the absolute last conversation I wanted to have in my pajamas.

He was wearing those expensive running shorts and tank made of merino wool—at that time, I just saw him as a middle-aged guy with hairy legs and arms, although now I know how proud he is of his quads and biceps, his trim torso, the lack of belly pooch.

How did our conversation go anyway? I probably just rubbed sleep from my eyes and asked if he wanted coffee, to be polite.

I remember how he kept his gaze fixed on me for an oddly long time and then moved it to Pepito on the fridge next to a loaf of sourdough. "What's that?"

Why didn't I just say, "Oh, nothing," and usher him out of the kitchen and sit him down on the sofa and have him wait there?

Instead, I answered in a groggy (hopefully-not-sultry) voice, "A little Mayan statue. Nick's grandmother gave it to us."

"Why do you keep it on the fridge?" He looked horrified.

"Tradition. That's where his family keeps the *diositos* they find in their cornfield. To keep them away from little kids' hands. Although Eva's always gentle with Pepito, right, sweetie?" I kissed her forehead—she was in a groggy cereal stupor, uninterested in conversing—then I reached up and took Pepito and pressed him to her cheek for a kiss. Our beloved pet, a stand-in until our lives became more conducive to a dog.

"May I see?" asked Brett.

Why didn't I say no? Why didn't I find some excuse to extricate myself? Instead, I handed Pepito to him and said, "A god of corn and music. See him holding a turtle drum?"

I remember how Brett stared, transfixed, mesmerized, and yes, there was something creepy about it, and why didn't I register it? "Did you know," he said, "I have an extensive collection of music deities?"

I shrugged, although probably Nick had mentioned it at some point.

"Oh, you'll have to come over to my cabin and see them sometime." He stared into my eyes. "You're a living music deity, Calliope."

I looked away, wishing he would just leave and stop saying stuff like that. Sometimes people called me a goddess on social media, and that made me uncomfortable too, but I appreciated the intentions behind it. I always told them we were channeling music *together*, co-creating the experience, that our energy fed into each other's, which felt true to me.

But here was this weird, old rich guy, calling me a goddess in my own kitchen and looking at me like he was trying to look inside me. The intensity was too much. Did he think that because he was filthy rich he could do this? He wasn't hitting on me, not exactly—I didn't know how to describe his energy, how to categorize it.

Now I understand that he *wanted* me. Not just in a sexual way but a deeper way. Now I know that he coveted me. My essence. My power. Ironically, two years later, he now likes me weak and vulnerable.

Callie, I don't know what to do about his new obsession—becoming Eva's father. He keeps bringing it up, saying stuff like, "I'm ready for us to be a real family."

In his younger days, he fancied himself an Indiana Jones meets James Bond character, all about adventures and women around the world, pirate ship scuba dives in the Caribbean and spelunking in Africa, but now that he's in the second half of life, he wants a family, and here we are, ready-made and served on a platter. And I'm the cherry on top of his music deity collection.

The weird thing is, after he acquired me, he didn't want me performing anymore. He wanted my essence for himself, like those stories about the human husbands of selkies stealing their sea skin so they can't return to water, can't reclaim their power.

It started within a few months of Nick's death. Brett got in psychologist mode and said, "Listen, has it occurred to you that it might be selfish to get back onstage so soon?" He'd drop those little seeds of doubt that germinated inside me, and he watered and cultivated them. "Listen, precious, have you considered being a full-time mother to Eva? I can provide for you both."

And when I expressed my desire to perform, he'd say something like, "Well, you learned the hard way that you need to give Eva your full attention." Or "Think about how the stress of a music career could damage your mental health. Which is already precarious at best, dangerous at worst."

He always punctuated it with something like, "I'm only telling you this because I love you."

And more recently, once in a while, when I bring up the idea of getting back into music, he says, "Listen, I'm only saying this because I care about you, but you need a reality check—it's egotistical of you to want to abandon your daughter, after all she's been through. And for what? To get up onstage and shake your ass and expect everyone to adore you? I mean, I hate to say this, but this need you have to feed your ego? It makes you a megalomaniac."

Sometimes, I try to put my feelings into words, speak from

my heart, say something like, "But I feel like I'm channeling the music, like it's something bigger and deeper than me."

He always laughs and says something along the lines of, "Classic, cupcake. Listen to yourself. You don't think that's what a megalomaniac would say? You really think you're a goddess, don't you?" At some point, his voice turns serious, like he's giving a dire prognosis. "You're rationalizing your pathological behavior."

The conversations give me that fiery feeling of shame, burning up my voice and my songs and everything about me to ashes. Of course, now I'm seeing how he's full of contradictions, projecting onto me. But it's how he convinced me to part ways with my label and manager, to delete my socials, my website, my presence in the world.

And now I'm a husk of a person in a giant glass prison. No music, no song, no voice. The only golden thread left is for Eva. For under-my-breath bedtime songs. So very fragile.

Love,
Callie

# 11

# THE TRUFFLE FOREST

At the moment, the ripples of La Chanson made Callie think of the lighthearted Beatles tune "I Will." She found herself swaying as she sat across from Eva on the back patio, sipping orange blossom tea. Just hours after settling in, they were manifesting Eva's vision of a tea party, using vintage porcelain dishes, delicate and painted with blue and gold flowers.

Eva held her pinkie out as she sipped, looking so enchanted that Callie resisted the urge to make her hold the cup with both hands. This back patio offered a pastoral view of meadows, fields, the town center, scattered houses, a forest, and stone outcroppings—with the cerulean river meandering through it all.

As Callie sipped her tea, Eva stirred more lavender honey into hers, and said, "Keep humming, Mom."

Callie had indeed been humming, she realized, all through making and serving the tea. "Sadly, I can't hum and sip at the same time, sweet pea."

"I'm a really good hummer and sipper," Eva said, attempting the challenge and promptly drooling tea. She giggled and wiped her chin with a toile napkin. "I feel like we're inside a song, Mom."

"Me too, sweetie."

"Let's stay here forever."

"Forever, huh?"

"Brett can never find us here, can he?" Vulnerability snuck into her voice, a quaver that cracked Callie's heart a little.

Callie said nothing for a moment. A long pause, a *reste*, then the river music dropped to a low D minor. "You heard what Madame Lavigne said. We're safe here."

Eva gave an emphatic nod. "She's like a grandma and a bodyguard in one."

"Yup, she's got our backs." Callie wondered if the other women and children had felt this way when they'd arrived at this sanctuary, tucked into a cozy nook of music outside time and space, a pocket dimension of sorts. And if, in the depths of their minds, they still feared they'd need to use the secret room.

The tea and nuts felt nourishing, but she'd have to buy groceries soon. Shops might close early in small-town France. "Let's go food shopping, sweetie."

"Let's explore the forest first!"

Callie had only a vague sense of the property boundary, maybe a half mile into the forest. "Just a quick walk."

After washing the dishes, they headed along a short path through a meadow and into the woods—a cool refuge of dappled light, oaks and pines, beeches and maples. As they followed a game trail, the breeze blew through leaves like a flute, harmonizing with the river. It all evoked a fairy-tale forest just before something happened—a wolf, a witch, a bear, a silver apple, bandits, a prince, a sorcerer.

Ahead, the underbrush rustled. Callie's chest snapped shut and she grabbed Eva's hand. They weren't alone. It hit her, hard, the panic. She felt herself shrinking, throat closing, neck clenching.

A little dog barreled through the bushes. A bundle of scruffy, copper fur, heading straight for Eva. She dropped to her knees, kissing the dog. "Oh, Belle! You found me!"

Heart thudding, Callie glanced around just as Luc's dad appeared through the oaks, white hair poking out beneath his beret, framing rosy cheeks and a pink nose. Leaves and seedpods stuck to his sweater vest, and he held a walking stick made of a tree branch, channeling a gnome or elf.

"Belle!" His voice quivered with fear. "Belle!"

When he saw Callie and Eva, his face relaxed. "*Bonjour,*" he said, out of breath.

"*Bonjour.*" Callie's own muscles unclenched until she remembered the fungus feud. "Hope we're not trespassing." Her mind, infused with dark fairy tales, instantly went to the territoriality of gnomes.

"*Non, non, pas du tout.* I'm the one who's trespassing, madame. This is the Lavignes' side of the forest. Our side is over that wall."

Sure enough, a stone wall, three feet high and half hidden in foliage, cut through the forest. The other side of the forest looked the same—dappled light beneath a canopy of oaks and pines, patches of moss on north-facing trunks, a few wildflowers in lacy sunlight.

Her gaze landed on a fresh bouquet of daisies at the base of a particularly majestic oak. At first, the flowers struck her as a whimsical gesture, and next, as an offering of some sort. There was no indication of an actual grave, but something about the oak, so ancient and enormous, lent a mystical air, a sacred feel.

"Belle caught a whiff of your daughter," he said. "Her new best friend. She took off and found a little hole in the wall."

Two more dogs bounced through the underbrush and squeezed through the hole. Luc's spotted puppy and a caramel-colored dog.

"Jolie! Chouchou!" cried Eva, cuddling the dogs.

Of course her daughter remembered their names. Callie assumed Luc was nearby. *Muy buena gente,* according to Nick's ghost—or at least according to Eva. Callie still wasn't sure what to make of this spectral declaration that Luc was a *really good person.*

"Papa!" Sure enough, his voice rung out, edged with concern. "Papa!"

From the other side of the wall, Luc appeared through the trees in the same faded jeans with grass stains on the knees, chestnut hair that flopped over his forehead, flushed cheeks that made his irises stand out, the strange blue-green. With a surprised smile, he eyed the dogs and Eva, then nodded a warm greeting. "*Salut, Callie. Eva.*"

Callie arranged her face into a neutral expression and nodded.

In her peripherals, she noticed him climb over the wall, then lean toward his father. "Papa, what are you doing on this side?"

"Belle snuck through the wall to get to her new friend." Smiling at Eva, he pulled something from his pocket and handed it to her in the same way Madame Lavigne had casually handed her bonbons. "For you, *ma petite*."

Eva held it up to the sky, delighted—a cobalt-blue marble, old and scuffed, right up her alley. *"Merci!"*

Luc gave an amused smile, then quickly glanced around. "We should get going."

The copper dog let out a high bark, pawing at the ground. *"Belle, non!"* cried Monsieur Forêt as Luc ran over and grabbed the dog.

Callie furrowed her brow. "What's going on?"

"She found a truffle," said Luc.

Callie glanced at the earth, seeing only paw scratches. "And that is terrifying because . . . ?"

"If the Lavignes thought we were stealing truffles, things could get ugly." Monsieur Forêt tamped the dirt with his shoe, shoving forest debris overtop with his walking stick.

"Ugly how?"

"Certain members of that family did terrible things to ours. All in the name of protecting their territory and guarding their truffles. Including murder."

Callie sucked in a breath. Madame Lavigne did have a hard side. A scary side. *People say I'm a witch. They fear me. As they should.*

Still, Callie felt the need to defend her landlady. "Madame Lavigne has been kind to us."

"She used to be kind to me," said Monsieur Forêt. "Seven decades ago. Then she turned cruel. She's just like her son. And his father. Her true self was stolen, replaced by a coldhearted witch."

He took a breath to compose himself, and his tone softened a notch. "Perhaps your daughter brings forth remnants of the person she used to be."

Another dog appeared, the same truffle breed, but the color of vanilla pastry cream. Callie didn't remember seeing this one at the park. It sniffed the Forêts' dogs with cautious curiosity. "Not one of yours?"

Flustered, Monsieur Forêt shook his head and looked around in growing alarm.

"She belongs to the Lavigne son," Luc said under his breath.

Through the oaks, a man appeared, at least a decade or two older than Callie—around Brett's age, but without the slick polish. He was tall but stooped, as if trying to make himself smaller. Callie took in his loose T-shirt and old jeans, grease-stained fingernails, hair spotted with wood shavings, forearms flecked with paint. A scar at his left temple just beneath his white-blond hair. The outline of something rectangular in his shirt pocket—a tiny notebook?—and a pen poking out. The overall effect: nerdy-woodsman-meets-construction-worker.

Tension filled all three men's faces. There were no guns in sight, thankfully, just Monsieur Forêt's walking stick, which he clutched so hard his knuckles were white.

"*Bonjour,*" Callie said to the stranger, in damage control mode. "You're Madame Lavigne's son?"

No answer beyond a garbled "*euh*"—which she mentally translated to "uh." The wine witch had said he didn't talk much.

She cleared her throat. "I'm Callie and this is Eva."

"Julien," he rasped.

"We're renting the cottage from your mother." The brightness in her voice rang hollow. "We're neighbors now."

Another wordless grunt. "*Euh.*"

Okay, not the chatty type. As he returned his wary gaze to the Forêts, Callie wondered if he'd seen Belle pawing at the soil. Murder had been a past consequence.

"Fleur, come." Julien whistled, and his dog returned to his side.

Callie sensed this was the tip of the iceberg, decades of bitterness underneath. She turned to Julien and stumbled through an explanation in French. "The Forêts only came here to get their dogs. One of them smelled my daughter, crawled through a hole to say hi. That's all." She lightened her voice. "No truffles were taken."

Still, the men stayed silent.

Callie leaned over to Eva, who was busy petting Fleur, blessedly oblivious. "Time to go, sweetie."

"Aw, man." Eva stood up, still grinning at the dogs. "*J'adore* this forest."

Monsieur Forêt said, "I felt the same at your age. I still do." He gave Julien a long, hard look. "And I will never let it go."

"Okay, well, *au revoir*, everyone." Callie pulled Eva along, wondering if she could get out of the lease. She hadn't signed anything. And it would take less than an hour to pack up again and clean the kitchen, although her daughter would put up a fight, thanks to the sheer abundance of dogs in this town.

But the last thing Callie needed were men with egos. Never again.

On their way back to the cottage, the river roared and thundered like a Metallica-meets-Beethoven concert.

When Callie and Eva returned, their landlady was descending the outdoor stairs with two large totes, baguettes sticking out from the tops.

As Callie ran over to help, Madame Lavigne said, "I thought you'd be hungry. I brought groceries and leftovers from my fridge—ratatouille, a gratinée, a quiche Lorraine, a potage, a salad. Meals for tonight and tomorrow. And wine paired for each dish."

Callie's eyes filled. She felt cared for by this slightly scary lady. She rarely saw her own mother, and Brett had further estranged them. Even her maternal neighbors a half mile away had been off limits under his gaze. And her friends who used to do nurturing things for each other—they'd been cut off too. This touched a place she'd forgotten about.

"Oh, you didn't have to," she began. "How much do I owe you?"

Madame Lavigne waved away her words. "Don't be ridiculous." As they walked down the steps, she explained, "Now, the Chardonnay goes with the gratinée and the Syrah with the ratatouille, the Sauternes for the apéro." She winked. "And the Côte de Provence rosé is for sipping by the poolside with friends."

How much did she think Callie would be drinking, alone here with her eight-year-old? And did she really think they'd be eating multicourse meals together? Also, *what friends*? Still, Madame Lavigne had put a staggering amount of care into this gesture—Callie couldn't bring herself to break the lease.

Eva peeked her head inside the bag, pulled out a silver-wrapped candy. "*J'adore les bonbons!*"

The corner of Madame Lavigne's mouth turned up—she didn't seem to have actual smiles in her expression alphabet. Her age-spotted hand reached for Eva's curls.

Usually, Eva ducked away when people tried to touch her hair, which was, indeed, irresistible—such wild, delicious, dark spirals—but beyond belief, she allowed Madame Lavigne to stroke it, even leaning into her hand like an affectionate pup.

"I'll heat up the food," Callie said when they reached the patio. "Will you join us, madame?" Realizing her landlady might be sacrificing business to be here, she added, "Or do you need to get back to your shop?"

Madame Lavigne waved away her concern. "This is a special occasion."

Now Callie really couldn't back out of the rental. As Eva and the wine witch chatted by the pool, she walked a couple of dozen yards to the cottage and put away the groceries—welcome items like yogurt, olive oil, nuts—as well as a variety of pâtés—foie gras, duck pâté, pâté de campagne. How many pâtés did an eight-year-old need?

Peering out the kitchen window, she watched her daughter recap their forest outing, miming the dogs digging for truffles, which hopefully wouldn't lead to any new vengeful murders. Callie caught a glimpse of Julien trudging up the path from the forest, his lanky form hunched over, with Fleur trotting at his side.

He waved to Eva and let Fleur greet her with nose licks. After chatting with them—or at least nodding and grunting—he headed into the château.

Uncertain of the etiquette, Callie grabbed a fourth plate. She should get to know him. If he gave her a bad feeling, she'd just forfeit the deposit—although at this point, he was giving off vibes that were more Hunchback of Notre Dame than creepy killer neighbor.

She set toile linens on the round table on the front patio overlooking the empty pool and imagined it filled with sparkling turquoise water, the gardens and terraces cleaned up, the château renovated. This place could be magical. She dared to envision sipping rosé with a friend, an imaginary friend who was *not* the would-be vet. Another thirty-something mom would be just fine.

When she knocked on the château door, Julien answered, his expression nervous. "Would you like to join us?" she asked, using the formal *vous*.

"*Euhhh* . . ." He nodded, shuffling his feet. "Just need to put away tools. Wash my hands."

At his mother's request, he snipped fresh lavender with Eva's help and arranged it in a vase, his dog at their heels. He seemed kind enough, but was Callie the best judge of character? Oddly, she felt Eva's intuition was better. *What does Daddy's ghost think?* she imagined asking her. Which made her remember the matter-of-fact assessment of Luc. *A really good person.*

With a sigh, Callie sat down at the table. What a long, strange day. The sun was lowering toward the hills across the river, casting beams of honey-golden light. The river music calmed into a peaceful accompaniment to dinner, like a tuxedoed pianist sweeping fingers over a baby grand just for them.

Fleur settled herself between Julien's and Eva's feet. Callie reminded

Eva not to feed the dog, although she noticed Julien sneaking her bits of food under the table. Eyeing the surreptitious feeding, Eva asked him, "Is Fleur your *copine?*"

Callie smiled to herself—her daughter must have remembered the word *girlfriend* from earlier, in the canine context.

"*Oui,*" said Madame Lavigne, and it looked for a moment as though her hint of a smile might break into an actual laugh.

"More like my wife," Julien dead-panned. "We're very committed."

The other corner of his mother's mouth turned up.

Eva laughed with abandon, which made Callie laugh too.

They had an apéro of Sauternes, with cheese, *saucisson*, and salted nuts—Callie didn't want to risk any pâtés, assuming Eva would be horrified at blended-up goose liver. Madame Lavigne explained the sweet white wine was made with grapes desiccated from a fungus called noble rot, and as Callie sipped it, she remembered how the *sorcière* matched the wine to the person and wondered what it meant that this pairing did, indeed, feel so perfectly right.

She savored the flavors of honey, notes of ginger and lemon peel, hints of cinnamon and roasted peach, appreciating that it wouldn't exist without the fungus causing the sweetness to intensify. The Sauternes made her feel that yes, she could stay here after all.

Julien pulled a truffle from his front shirt pocket—mottled black and textured, the size of a plum—and shaved it over the *chèvre* as Eva peppered him with questions, and he answered in short, soft responses punctuated with *euhs*, teaching her fungus vocabulary.

Over the next couple of hours, following Madame Lavigne's instructions, Callie brought out course after course—lettuce with a dressing made of lemon juice, olive oil, and mustard; *potage aux légumes*; ratatouille; and baguettes with a cheese plate of Comté, Brie, and Roquefort. Fresh-picked apricots for dessert.

Callie had managed to get the wine pairings right, and yes, each one highlighted the food's flavors . . . and did something more, something intangible. Each one seemed to complement her *mood*, course by course. Or maybe the delicious buzziness of it all was just making her imagine things.

When twilight came, Julien pulled a box of matches from his pocket and lit the candle lanterns on the table, creating a glowing, gold little world wrapped in river music. Callie would have felt entirely blissed out if it weren't for the dark undercurrent of the vendetta. She needed to understand any violence lurking beneath the surface. After Brett, she wasn't taking chances.

Once the final course ended, Callie sipped a glass of brandy, then took a long breath. "We noticed the wall that divides the forest."

*"Ah, oui,"* said Madame Lavigne, a whole story in her sigh. "The wall."

"Did Julien mention we ran into him and the Forêts there?"

Madame Lavigne's eyebrows shot up and she glanced at her son. *"Non."* Tension thickened in the silence. "Stay on our side. An old boundary dispute caused problems in the past. Death and destruction. My late husband built the wall to end it."

Callie could sense Eva struggling to follow the conversation, so she gave her daughter a quick summary in English, leaving out the death part, hoping she didn't know that word—*la mort*. In response, Eva simply asked, *"Pourquoi?"*

Madame Lavigne swirled her brandy, as if musing over the bigger questions beneath Eva's *why?* "This forest holds the best truffles in the world. Monsieur Forêt"—her voice quavered as she said his name—"is the best truffle hunter in the world."

Eva's eyes widened. "Look what he gave me." She pulled the old blue marble from her pocket, set it on the table, rolled it around with her finger.

Madame Lavigne snuck in another pat on Eva's hair, then picked up the marble. "We played marbles together when we were your age. How tragic that sweet boy turned into a selfish man."

Callie tried steering the conversation toward facts. "Couldn't property records clear up this feud?"

"The originals and copies were either lost or burned in a fire in the local archives." Madame Lavigne let out a sigh. "There's no hope of ending the vendetta. My late husband accused Monsieur Forêt of stealing truffles. My husband grew enraged. Horrible things ensued. Heartless things."

Callie absorbed this, wondered if the husband had committed murder. And whether either of his sons took after him. What if she'd brought her daughter from one dangerous situation to another? She assessed Julien, whose gaze was lowered, cheeks pink, impossible to read.

When Eva asked for clarification in English, Callie gave her only broad strokes, but her daughter turned to Madame Lavigne, curious. "What did your husband do?"

Madame Lavigne and her son exchanged glances. She shook her head. "Let's just say he had a temper."

Callie let out a breath, hoping Eva would drop it, but her daughter, ever persistent, tilted her head and said in choppy yet understandable French, "But he's gone now. Why can't you all be friends?"

Madame Lavigne firmed her jaw. "There's no going back. Some things keep growing, out of control. The Forêts hate us. Monsieur Forêt has made that abundantly clear. He won't speak to me, even look at me." She dropped the marble onto the table like a burning coal.

Callie sensed pain in her voice—deep, old, aching pain, the kind that transforms into resentment, even cruelty. She suspected something tender and raw at the center of this feud, buried deeper than truffles.

Madame Lavigne raised her chin. "Everyone in town has taken sides. Since you live here, you're with us. Stay on this side of the wall."

Julien put his arm around his mother's shoulders. "I'll fix the hole soon, Maman."

Callie measured her words. "It's a small town—won't we run into the Forêts?"

"Keep your distance," snapped Madame Lavigne.

Callie left things there, sipping brandy as she studied Julien. He struck her as someone who wasn't happy inheriting a vendetta. She imagined he felt best alone in the woods with his dog.

Still, it was strange how little he spoke and how often he grunted. Callie wondered about the other son who'd been mentioned in passing, the Parisian son, whether he was stranger than this one, and she braced herself for when they'd inevitably cross paths. Because it seemed that, for better or worse, La Chanson was her new home.

# 12

# A RISKY BUSINESS

*Colorado, four weeks before arrival in France*

Callie, I can't get them out of my mind, those selkies who let a man take their sea skins . . . I've even been dreaming about them, searching and swimming, lost in watery caves. And I keep dreaming of Brett circling and swooping, a blur of black feathers hiding a beak and sharp claws, taking my voice, dropping it like nearly dead prey into his lair.

Callie, most of all, I can't stop thinking about Pepito. I feel like he's close by, the way Eva feels Nick's ghost here with us. I just can't imagine Brett letting Pepito slip through the cracks.

Before he died, Nick was annoyed at Brett's persistence. "The rich old guy's obsessed," he told me one day after their run. "He thinks he can get me to sell Pepito."

Apparently, Brett didn't have any Mayan artifacts in his music deity collection and desperately needed our *diosito* to complete it. Nick kept laughing it off and saying no, it's a family heirloom, worth nothing beyond sentimental value.

Then one day, after a run just weeks before the accident, Nick came home with his eyes bugging out. "Holy moly, Callie! The old dude offered me a half million bucks for Pepito!"

He pulled the statue off the top of the fridge and kissed his head.

"What did you tell him?" I asked.

"I said Pepito's not for sale. Not now, not ever."

"Good. The guy sounds seriously entitled."

I didn't know all the details of his antiquities business then, and even now I just glean things from overheard conversations, catch glimpses of the music deity collection in his office—not a *lair* per se, but off limits to me and Eva. Once in a while, he'll bring in clients and colleagues, but never us.

Still, even outside his office, over the past two years, I've witnessed how his dealings play out. He simply doesn't accept a *no*. A quality that, he says, came from his father and grandfather. Remember how, when he first told me about the family business, I actually felt sorry for him? How he spun the story with him as the underdog victim?

But of course, he's more than a spoiled child at heart. He's a deeply wounded child whose heart has warped and twisted to accommodate the pain. A child who developed strange obsessions, with an almost cultish fervor, to try to assemble some shadow of love, of family.

Yesterday was the twenty-year anniversary of his dad's death, which brings up all kinds of mixed feelings for him. And for me.

When he first confided in me about his tortured feelings about his father, I felt deeply for the little boy in him. And last night, I still felt an echo of sorrow when we talked after Eva went to bed, but then I wondered if this was his strategy, to make me feel sorry for him, to manipulate my emotions. I just sat on the couch and listened as he rehashed what I already knew, what had at one time made me cry for him, made us cry together.

"I was just devastated when my dad left," he said, rubbing his face. "I mean, you know I was barely twelve, a crappy time for a kid to learn his dad's a chronic cheater with families around the globe. So what did I do? I worked my butt off to convince him I was special, make me his favorite, get him to choose me to inherit the business."

Brett wiped a tear—or maybe there was no tear. "I hated and loved him at the same time. But in the end, I used his playbook to get my way."

He turned to me and cupped my face, and yes, there were real tears in his eyes, and he spoke with deep feeling. "I swore I wouldn't have a kid, a partner—I didn't want them to suffer like I had. Not just from his cheating but his abuse. But then I met you, precious."

I bit my tongue because of course I now suspect that his sudden desire for a family related more to him turning fifty than to me and Eva in particular. But when he told me this six months after Nick's death, I ate it up—that calculated mix of vulnerability and redemption and fate.

"You made me change my mind." He drew my face toward his, but this time I felt repelled by his monologue. The last thing I wanted to do was kiss this man. I pulled back, feeling nauseous.

He took that as a sign to keep talking. "My dad hit my mother, hit all his women, I later discovered. Sometimes his children too."

When Brett first admitted this a year and a half ago, I held him and he shook in my arms. I felt the old innocence in him, his insecurities and weaknesses, his longings and sorrows. I felt the person he once was, ages ago, maybe his long-buried true self. It made me want to comfort him. That night was the first time we made love.

But last night, as I held him, I realized he's carried on more than his father's business and collections—he's carried on his controlling nature too. The hidden violence.

Of course, he doesn't get his own hands dirty.

A few months ago, I overheard him on the phone, vying for

an artifact—a bronze statue of Saraswati, Goddess of Music. He took a trip to Bangkok, tried convincing his opponent to sell, wining and dining him. No luck.

Fast-forward to a few weeks ago, when I overheard another conversation with the opponent—it sounded like bribery, moving into blackmail territory. Months ago, I wouldn't have paid attention to it, half lost in a medication fog. This time, I did.

Still, the opponent wouldn't sell.

And then yesterday, his Tokyo assistant showed up here with the goddess statue from Thailand.

A sick feeling came over me. "How did you manage to get it?" I asked the man.

He exchanged looks with Brett and said after a moment, "It became available for auction."

"The guy just changed his mind?" I pushed.

The Tokyo assistant remained silent.

"Antiquities dealing is a risky business," Brett told me after a long pause, holding the statue with gloved hands. "Third-world countries, shady local dealers, remote no-man's-lands. Who knows what happened."

His Tokyo assistant nodded with grave authority.

In the beginning, two years ago, I ignored the phone conversations, believed the lines Brett fed me, fed to everyone. Not just in the area of business, but family. He was a noble man saving a vulnerable widow and child. That's the tale he tells to friends and colleagues. The tale he tells himself.

Yesterday, I couldn't shake the icy feeling in the pit of my stomach.

The medication fog has cleared, and I'm facing the truth.

Love,
Callie

# 13

# BOX OF SECRETS

After the Lavignes left around midnight, Callie opened the balcony doors as Eva yawned and settled into bed, covered in a light cotton quilt, her dark curls spread over a pillowcase with crocheted trim. Callie stroked Eva's cheek, the warm walnut color of her favorite old guitar—the one back in Colorado, the one she hadn't touched for two years. Even half asleep, Eva embodied the soul of the instrument, all brightness and sparkle.

In a sleepy voice, Eva mumbled, "Sing to me, Mom."

The river music echoed her request, impossible to refuse, so despite her exhaustion, Callie sang a song from her most recent album. Strangely enough, her voice rang out clear and smooth, like glassy water. Indie folk was the official categorization of her music, but to her, it felt more fluid, something deeper than boxes and labels.

"You can sing louder, Mom. Brett's not here."

For a moment, Callie bit her lip, paused in her singing, blinked back tears. Then she took a deep belly breath and sang, louder now, hearing her voice rising, oddly unfettered. She opened her throat, urged herself to follow the golden thread up and out from the cave. She wondered if one day her throat could fully open and her diaphragm completely fill, the way she used to sing for crowds of thousands, when her entire body would become an instrument.

For now, she kept her voice at a conversational volume and

sang more songs from her most recent album, released two and a half years ago, just before Nick's death. She didn't sing these often now—they felt too raw, reminded her of his accident, her grief.

After the third song, she kissed Eva's forehead. "Good night, sweet pea."

"One more? Please?"

Callie's exhaustion had faded, replaced with new energy, and when she opened her mouth for another, a brand-new tune emerged, as easily as a leaf floating downstream.

Strange. Was it the wine sparking this? Or La Chanson? She had the urge to record this melody, jot down lyrics, create harmonies, make it into a full-fledged song. Something she hadn't done for ages.

"I like it," Eva murmured. "Sing it again. Louder and wilder."

"Okay, but no moshing or head banging," Callie joked. Then she opened her throat, filled her core with air, and sang with abandon. The song wove together threads of folk, soul, roots, rock, and a dozen other styles into her own unique web—and the river added dewdrops of notes that shimmered.

She glanced at the bedside table, at the digital voice recorder she'd used years earlier for songwriting, which Eva now used as a diary. Once Eva was asleep, Callie grabbed a notebook and pen, and brought the device to her balcony. She recorded her tender new shoot of a song, then jotted down ideas on the chorus and verses and bridge. *Mon Dieu,* this felt good. Being in the flow. Pure magic.

Again, she let herself sing with a new freedom, let the moonlit air fill her body, let the song fly out. Tears streamed down her cheeks. God, she'd missed this. She thanked herself in the cave. Somehow the wine and river had found their way deep into shadows and removed the dark spell, long enough to compose this song.

For hours, she played with possibilities as the lyrics came to her in lapping waves: *Stay, stay, stay. Reste, reste, reste.*

In a patch of fragrant rosemary, spade in hand, Callie wiped sweat from her temple. It was ten in the morning and already the Mediterranean heat was setting in. Bees hummed as she weeded around Provençal herbs and lavender and peonies on the far side of the pool. She gazed at it longingly, wishing it were full. The melodies of La Chanson brought some relief, rippling on the breeze, refreshing her with cool, turquoise currents.

Eva had lasted about ten minutes helping her in the garden and was now playing near the cypresses—apparently with her ghost friend—and balancing on the limestone walls that meandered through the hillside estate. After three *be carefuls*, Callie gave up. Her child loved climbing things and wasn't fazed by occasional falls, just dusted off her knees and carried on.

Well, except for that one catastrophic fall in Colorado, but Callie pushed it from her mind. Losing herself in her task, she made her way deeper into the garden, now in the shade of olive trees and oleander bushes, the pool patio blocked from her view. She hummed along with songbirds and river tunes and cicada chirps, filling a bucket with limp weeds.

At some point, she realized she hadn't seen or heard Eva for a while . . . maybe ten minutes? Fifteen? With mild alarm, she hurried to the patio and looked around, removing the gloves, wiping sweat with the back of her hand. "Eva?"

No answer.

She called again and again, her voice growing shriller.

No answer.

Her mind felt chaotic, all fire and smoke, and she struggled to clear her thoughts. At the center of it all: Brett had always used Eva as leverage—seen her, too, as a possession.

Callie's insides clenched as she darted around the grounds, calling out, more frantic by the second, gasping for breath as she raced up and down the stairs, peeking behind trees. She ran to the cottage, throwing open the door, checking every room, calling out, fear escalating. Flames of panic roared in her head, spread through her arms, her entire body.

*He took my baby. Oh God, he took my baby.*

She skidded to a stop at the old-fashioned phone, grabbed the receiver with shaking hands, on the brink of dialing 112, when she heard Julien's quiet voice at the open cottage door. His hair was damp from a shower, and his clothes looked hastily thrown on.

"Looking for Eva?" he said, so softly she could barely hear.

"Have you seen her?"

He shook his head. Of course, he'd just heard Callie's terrified calls.

"I've searched the grounds. Nothing." She suppressed a sob, clutching the receiver with both hands. "I'm calling the police."

"Have you tried the château?"

Callie shook her head, put the receiver back, and raced outside. The château was a possibility. It fascinated Eva . . . and her mischievous ghost friend. Callie ran the few dozen yards to the château and climbed the exterior stone stairs two at a time. Yes, the door was unlocked. A shred of hope. She passed the wall of old paintings, screaming, "Eva!"

She held her breath. No answer.

Ahead, drop cloths covered the furniture, suddenly eerie. To her right, the kitchen was torn up, stove and refrigerator not yet installed, electrical wires exposed, spilling from the wall like guts.

And she heard it, a muffled call, nearly inaudible. "Mom? I'm right here."

Callie paused, tilting her head. "Where?" She darted upstairs, through the bedrooms and bathrooms.

"Mom, I'm in here playing."

With a start, Callie remembered the secret room. The bookcase that opened into the hidden space. With *toys*. She ran back into the hallway and pushed on the molding of the bookcase. Slowly, it creaked open.

And there Eva sat, cross-legged on the floor, surrounded by stuffed animals and puppets. "Hey, Mom! Check this out!"

Callie dropped to her knees, grabbed Eva, and hung on tightly.

"Ouch!" Eva said, wriggling away.

"Sweetie, you can't just disappear without telling me." She wiped her face on the inside neck of her T-shirt, all tears and sweat. "Okay?"

"The ghost boy led me here." Eva gestured toward a wicker chair in the corner. Then she paused, taking in Callie's red eyes, damp lashes. With a meek expression, she added, "Sorry, Mom. I forgot to tell you."

Callie felt disconcerted about the ghost, but mostly awash with relief. *Eva's safe. We're safe.* She sat on the floor, tucking her knees to her chin, catching her breath.

"Oh, and look what I found, Mom! It was hidden under the bed, behind this board." She held out a wooden wine crate, about a foot long and half a foot wide. A square piece of old paper was fastened to it with cracked, peeling tape. *Secrets,* it read.

Callie set the box on her lap. "How on earth did you find this?"

"The ghost boy showed me. It's got papers inside, but I can't read cursive. Especially weird cursive in French."

Callie opened the box and pulled out several sheets of old, yellowed graph paper, the kind used by students in France. She squinted in the dim light, deciphering the French script.

***My Secrets:***
*I'm supposed to hate M. Forêt but I wish he were my father.*
*I wish he would take me truffle hunting.*
*There's someone I like, named after a springtime flower.*
*I feel invisible. I always hide my real self.*
*Sometimes that makes me happy.*
*Sometimes sad.*
*Sometimes I think my real self might get hidden forever.*

*I know about the little blue bottles.*
*I know who killed Papa.*
*I'm glad he's dead.*
*There's someone else I hate. I wish he were dead.*
*I know who killed Marguerite.*
*I know more secrets too.*
*Secret kindness and secret poison.*

The back of Callie's neck prickled. Who had written this? It seemed decades old, written by an older child or a young teen—based on both the language and handwriting. The script was neat and deliberate, with flourishes that looked intentional, careful curlicues here and there.

She was surprised to see Monsieur Forêt's name there, then remembered what he'd said about murders in the truffle forest war. Callie's mind landed on the bouquet of daisies—*marguerites* in French—the offering in the forest. A shiver ran through her.

And the little blue bottles—where had she seen them in a neat row? Right, the *cave à vins*. Biting her lip, she shuffled to the next page.

*What would I do without my poems?*
*Here's one inspired by Verlaine.*

*The barks of the dogs*
*in winter forests*
*pierce my heart*
*with les pics à truffes,*
*the sharpest sorrows.*
*Who will find*
*the black diamond*
*hidden in my chest*
*waiting*
*and waiting?*

Callie felt emotion inside her own chest, the lonely secrets of this long-ago child. So much darkness in these admissions, this poetry. She imagined the "Papa" referred to could be Madame Lavigne's late husband. Had one of her sons written this? Or the ghost boy, whoever he was, when he was alive?

"What's it say, Mom?"

"Oh, it's stuff that a child wrote. A long time ago."

"Cool." Thankfully, Eva had no follow-up questions, now absorbed in tying a blue satin bow at the neck of a dog puppet.

Callie shuffled through more papers, landing on a packet held together with an old-fashioned clip. It looked archaic, sepia beige and torn at the edges, with a circular, official seal. It was handwritten in calligraphy cursive, most likely from before typewriters—maybe the early nineteenth or even eighteenth century. She struggled to read it, not just because of the ornate script but the historic French legalese.

The final page was a hand-drawn map of a château on a river, edged by a forest. A property deed? It had to be ancient, from before the cottages were even built.

She was just searching for a date when footsteps sounded in the hallway. She spun around and saw Julien at the open bookcase door. He grunted—a sound of relief? Or a simple greeting? Or a question?

*"Bonjour, Julien,"* Eva said with enthusiasm.

Callie lowered the papers, vaguely guilty to be caught reading the contents of a box labeled *Secrets*. "Eva wandered in here," she said apologetically.

*"Euh."*

Callie stood up and passed the box to him, careful to let only casual curiosity into her tone. "She found this. Know anything about it?"

Gingerly, he flipped through the papers. After a moment, he tucked them back inside the box and put it under his arm. With a shrug, he mumbled, *"Euh euh."*

Callie took that as either a *no* or *none of your business*. Still, she pushed. "It mentioned murders. And the forest. And truffles. And Monsieur Forêt. Think it has to do with the vendetta?"

"*Euhhhh.*" In a low voice, so low that Callie had to lean in to hear, he added, "We leave these things buried."

Goose bumps spread over her arms as she took a step back and turned to Eva. "Sweetie, let's clean up. We have errands to run." She gathered the toys and dropped them into a woven basket in the corner, with Eva reluctantly helping.

Julien muttered, "*Au revoir,*" then disappeared down the hallway.

Callie clutched Eva's hand as they left, minutes later, closing the bookcase behind them. "Sweet pea, listen, you're not allowed in the château without me."

"But Madame Lavigne said I could play here. And the ghost boy—"

"I'm telling you *no*."

Eva blinked and quieted.

Was all of this truly buried in the past? Or were there dangers stretching into the present? This living situation felt idyllic, except for these strange, dark shadows. And the ghost boy.

On the way out, Callie noticed Julien sitting at the kitchen table, hunched over the property deed. He held a matchbox, turning it over in his hands slowly, staring at the document.

She hurried past, pulling Eva along and reminding herself she was not part of this feud. Her only goal was to keep her daughter and herself safe.

# 14

# CREEPY COLLECTIONS

*Colorado, three weeks before arrival in France*

Dear Callie,

Yesterday, I ventured into Brett's weird, secret room in the attic, full of his childhood stuffed animals from the seventies. Musty museum meets abandoned toy store . . . with a dash of Chucky.

The animals are painstakingly arranged on shelves, according to species and color and size—bear, rabbit, horse, monkey, lion, dragon—dozens, maybe hundreds of them. He won't let Eva play with them, not even touch them, but he comes in here alone and locks the door for hours.

Remember when you first discovered this? It was about a year ago, I think, when you were still in your fog, when you heard sounds coming from the top floor. Remember how you knocked just once and he swung open the door? It was disconcerting, his expression when he stepped out and slammed the door behind him—he knew you'd glimpsed those toys. And he was vexed.

He wouldn't even talk about it till that night, and he spoke in such a strange, low, raw voice. "When I was little, I believed each stuffed animal had a special power. Once I owned them, I got that power for myself."

Callie, remember that icy feeling at the base of your spine? How slowly he spoke?

I can recall his words almost verbatim, even from the fog, because they were so unnerving. "I never let anyone else play with them," he said. "I was scared they'd take the powers. Brave, smart, funny, strong, good at games, good at music . . ."

He ticked off the powers on his fingers, as if they were memorized. His tone was uncanny, like on one level, he was reflecting on the odd things he believed as a child, and on a deeper level, maybe he still believed them. "I didn't have those talents myself. I got a B minus in piano class. I never won checkers. I couldn't even do three push-ups. So I needed the animals to give me their talents."

And Callie, now it's even clearer: As an adult, he *still* thinks that he lacks talents, that he can only gain them through possessions—objects or people. He'd never admit it, but I can tell by the strange, vulnerable look in his eyes.

Recently, whenever I peek in that stuffed-animal room, I feel more and more visceral fear. And last night, with my mind lucid, I could see beyond the spookiness to the engine that drives his life. That's why he guards all his collections so fiercely. He has no true sense of self—he needs the essences of things and people to compensate for his own lack.

He cares about his music deity collection more than anything. It was his dad's most prized collection too. On the guy's deathbed, Brett promised to continue it, build it into something extraordinary, something that would make him proud.

Callie, it's hard to wrap my head around it—even after his father's abuse and betrayals, Brett still craves his approval. And the guy's been dead for years! Brett stepped into his dad's shoes—he thinks that by taking his power, he can somehow repair the pain of his childhood.

Notice the pride that comes into his voice? "I'm keeping my dad alive through the gods of music. Giving him immortality." Like he believes it's the noblest of tasks. My take? The little abused boy is trying to turn his hurt into power, soaking in the essence of his dead father.

This morning, when Eva was getting dressed and I was loading the dishwasher, Brett said, "I can't wait to adopt Eva."

I just stopped mid-dish, trying to understand. I mean, what are his motives? He'd ignored her all through breakfast while she talked about dog training. He didn't ask her any questions, or even give any half-hearted responses, or even make eye contact. Not even a distracted *hmm*.

Before I could think better of it, my question slipped out: "Why do you want to be Eva's father?"

"I love her," he said automatically. "I love you." He kissed my head, and his voice dropped. "A family, my own family—it'll make me complete."

There might be truth to this, but it's strange, his obsession. I mean, Eva doesn't show him affection, they have no real connection, he doesn't enjoy her company, and she doesn't fit into his lifestyle. But as some kind of midlife crisis, he's glommed on to the *idea* of a family. He's never felt real, deep family love—his only framework for it is collection and possession. Owning the essences, taking the power, hiding the sea skin.

There's another motive he'd never admit: If he adopts her, he can use her to bind me to him forever. He can even use the threat of my supposed neglect as leverage to make me stay.

And yes, that scares me. But the even deeper motive that scares me most? He believes he needs our essence, our power. We are no more than artifacts behind glass. Stuffed animals in a secret room.

For him, it would be a matter of life or death if we left. He'd kill to keep us here. Immortalized in his collection.

Love,
Callie

# 15

# SONGS TO KEEP YOU UP AT NIGHT

"Let's go to the magic cave, Mom." Eva swung her arm, hand in hand with Callie, as they strolled along the river toward the town center. An hour had passed since the hidden room, and Callie had changed clothes and washed her face, trying to shake off the darkness of old secrets.

Now, on their walk to town, the Provençal sunshine edged out any last shadows. Callie simply resolved to refrain from entering the château and to keep her distance from the Forêts. No need to fuel the vendetta. She'd just savor the ridiculous beauty of their surroundings, these rippling melodies, the lemony morning light, the robin's-egg-blue sky. Nature was conspiring to make them fall in love with La Chanson, and she'd float right along.

"Magic cave! Magic cave!" Eva was chanting in rhythm to her footsteps.

*Magic cave? Oh, right.* Nathalie from the bus had mentioned it. The source of the river, sacred to the ancient Celts. The carnyx inside it. "Groceries first, magic later, sweet pea."

For better or worse, American kids craved snack foods beyond pâté. Ideally, cereal and Goldfish crackers, although Callie doubted the latter existed here. She needed more toiletries too—her skin demanded constant sunscreen—and she wanted a fresh notebook for songwriting.

A sudden movement to her right made her jump. A blur of fluff balls ran up from behind and hurled themselves into Eva's open arms.

The caramel-colored one and the spotted pup, Chouchou, panting and licking her face. The river music rose into a jaunty tune.

"It's Jolie!" shouted Eva. "And Chouchou!"

Callie looked over her shoulder and saw Luc jogging after his dogs. For the briefest of moments, she felt the window in her chest open, the softness of curtains rustling in a breeze. She slammed it shut.

He settled into a stride beside her as Eva skipped along with the dogs, tossing sticks for fetching. "May I join you?"

Callie gave a noncommittal shrug. With a guarded sweep of her gaze, she took in his jeans with grass and mud stains on the knees, maybe a permanent fixture from interactions with dogs, both his own and his patients. Instead of the vet bag, a cotton shopping bag labeled *Truffes de la Forêt* was looped over his shoulder.

Harmless small talk was in order. "No unofficial vet duties this morning?" she asked.

He shook his head and opened the bag for her to see. Heaps of dark, lumpy blobs. "On truffle duty today. Official family business."

"Just so you know, I'm staying neutral. About the truffle troubles, that is."

"An excellent decision," he said. "So you'll be here for a while?"

"In the cottage next to Julien's. Who is either creepy or just quiet?" Her voice turned up at the end, as if in a question.

After a beat, he nodded. "I heard singing last night."

Callie froze in her tracks. Had she been singing so wildly that it had carried to his house? How? She'd seen the red-tiled rooftop across the forest, what she'd assumed was the Forêt estate—it had to be a quarter mile away. Were the acoustics strange, bouncing off cliffs? Or had the river somehow carried her song downstream?

She tried untangling her emotions. Most prominent was a sense of betrayal—she'd thought she was alone last night, just her and the river and moon. It felt as if he'd been spying, seen her naked. But of course that was ridiculous. Her voice had invaded *his* space, not the other way around. Still, he could have gone inside, shut his windows and doors, respected her privacy.

*Seriously, Callie?* A wave of embarrassment rose inside her, a new fear, and it sounded like Brett's voice. Was she egotistical for making noise pollution? Being a rude American? She pressed her hand to her face, now hot and flushed. "Hope I didn't keep you awake."

"You did." He grinned. "In a good way. I didn't want it to stop."

She bit the inside of her cheek, wondering if she'd be able to sing again tonight, knowing she had an audience. She felt *exposed*. She glanced at Eva, who was playing with the dogs by the river's edge. She considered ending this conversation, grabbing her daughter, and distancing herself, once and for all, from this man and his dogs.

"The song was beautiful," he said. "You wrote it?"

"I, well, it's new and I didn't really—" She stumbled over her words, then took a breath. "La Chanson inspired it."

"Well, I'd put that song on a playlist." He paused, made a show of thinking. "A playlist called 'Songs to Keep You Up at Night.'"

She made a face. "More like 'Songs from Your New Weirdo Neighbor.'"

"Really, though." His aqua eyes turned sincere. "I'd call it 'Songs to Feel Alive Again.'"

She flicked her gaze away, knowing she should let this drop, but instead found herself asking, "What do you mean?"

"It gave me a feeling I haven't had for years," he said slowly, as if trying to find the words. "Back when I couldn't wait to be a vet, start my own practice. All hope and wonder." He was quiet for a beat. "But then life got in the way and all the hard stuff."

This hit a tender place inside Callie. People used to say those very words about how her songs made them feel. *L'espoir et la merveille.* Hope and wonder. She felt ashamed even thinking about this and heard Brett's voice: *Aren't you just feeding your giant ego?*

She used to believe that her songs bonded her to people, that her singing and their listening created something new together. Then Brett's voice intruded, as if shouting at top volume, drowning out the voices of hundreds of thousands of listeners. He hadn't just stolen her voice—he'd stolen all of their voices, or at least her ability to hear them. She didn't consciously *believe* his voice anymore, but she couldn't get rid of it, damn it.

"You should sing at the open mic soirée," Luc said. "It's every Saturday at the *salon du thé*."

Brett's words crashed and clanged in her head. *Strutting around the stage like you own it. Shaking your ass. Trying to seduce everyone. Pathetic.*

Finally, she spoke in a cool voice. "No, thank you."

He paused. "It's okay if you're shy onstage."

She let out a low laugh. Onstage was where she felt most herself. "That's not quite my problem."

"At least come and hear my dad. He plays accordion. Traditional French songs. And the kids do dances and skits. Think elementary school talent show meets old folks variety night." He hesitated, as if weighing his next words, then added, "That's how my friend describes it—the woman from Aix I'm dating. She comes every week, says it's small-town charm at its most charming."

*The woman he's dating.* Well, that changed things. Completely. Callie shifted her understanding of their interactions. He'd deliberately dropped this information, probably sensing she was wary around him, wanting to put her at ease. She imagined he'd use the same basic strategy with a particularly skittish, somewhat traumatized canine patient. *See, no need to be scared.*

She rearranged her assumptions. He was taken. And open mic night was not threatening. She watched Eva playing chase with the dogs—of course, her daughter would love an excuse to hop onstage. It might, in fact, be fun. But *too* fun, a place where she might let her guard down. The most important thing was to stay under the radar, far from any music venues.

"Maybe." To put an end to the topic, she added, "Where are you headed with all those truffles?"

He held up the bag. "The *épicerie*. We sell them there."

She took another peek inside at the truffles, ranging from the size of walnuts to clementines, their smells earthy and mysterious. They were ugly-beautiful—wasn't there a term for that in French? "*Jolie-laide*," she guessed, and must have gotten it right, because he said with an amused smile, "Exactly."

"Your dogs found all these?" She felt infinitely more relaxed now, knowing he had a girlfriend. Or at least, he was dating someone. She didn't quite grasp the subtleties in French language and culture.

"My dad and Belle have the magic touch. A sixth sense. I just run the boring parts of the business and distribute the goods."

"The town truffle runner?"

"I think of it as sidekick to truffle dog superheroes." He grinned. "It's a good father-son business, though. We manage a bit more than breaking even, enough to pay the bills. In the winter, we gather black truffles, pretty valuable. They keep us afloat—black diamonds, they're called. We make truffle oil and truffle honey too. You name it and we add truffles to it."

Despite herself, she was interested in this truffle lore. "Chocolate?"

A nod.

"Ice cream?"

Another nod.

"Cocktails?"

Another nod.

Callie stopped herself, wiping the smile from her face—this was moving dangerously close to flirting territory. And she was initiating it. She pulled back, injected polite-conversation vibes into her voice. "So that's why the forest is so valuable. The black diamonds."

He lifted a shoulder. "More than that, for us at least. We love that forest. We've been walking in it with our dogs for our whole lives. It's part of us."

*Us* meaning him and his father. Again, it struck her as odd that he lived with his dad. Still, this was a small town in rural France, so maybe a thirty-something guy living with a parent was normal here. And he did have his own cottage. And the woman in Aix. Maybe he stayed over at her place sometimes.

She thought of the old papers in the secret box, the admission of a child who wished Luc's father were his own. "Can you tell me about the murders? Related to the fungus feud? I have a right to know."

He pressed his lips together. "Officially, Madame Lavigne's husband, Tristan, died of drowning. He was fishing while drunk and sick. But rumors spread that my father killed him. Hit him on the head and forced him underwater."

"Because of the territory dispute?"

He paused. "Shortly before Tristan's death, someone murdered my dad's dog. My dad suspected Tristan. People say he killed Tristan in vengeance."

"Doesn't sound like your dad."

"Agreed. But apparently, he was really upset over the dog. Out of his mind. This was before I was born, before he married my mom. He loved that dog more than anything. She was the most important thing in his life. Marguerite."

The name settled inside Callie. Marguerite from the secret box. Someone—Julien?—knew who killed her and who killed Tristan. Was Marguerite buried beneath the daisies under the great oak?

She wanted to ask Luc a follow-up question but closed her mouth. Julien had said his family wanted to keep this buried. So be it—as long as fingers of the past didn't reach into the present. As long as there wasn't a murderer in her midst.

Eva galloped over with her canine entourage. "When can we go to the magic spring, Mom?"

With a sigh, Callie turned to Luc. "Can you give us directions?"

"Just follow the river upstream." He gestured with his chin. "It's about ten minutes ahead. I can take you there now."

"*Oui, oui, oui!*" Eva shouted, jumping up and down with fists beneath her chin.

Callie considered the offer, which would mean dropping her shield, allowing space for a friendship with Luc. Ahead, the river path did look enticing, turning to earth and gravel as it headed upward, through wildflowers and butterflies.

As she wavered, Luc filled the silence. "They say there's a carnyx deep in the source, left there by the ancient Celts." His expression turned mysterious, maybe for Eva's benefit. "A kind of trumpet, two meters long with a dragon mouth at the end."

"Let's swim there and find it," said Eva.

"Some divers have tried that over the years," Luc said, his tone grave. "It never ends well for them. The village has outlawed it. Too dangerous. You can swim in the river downstream but not in the cave."

Treasure divers. Callie could imagine the type—obsessives like Brett who lit up telling stories about diving for pirate treasure in his younger years. Supposedly, a few times, he'd barely made it out alive—likely an exaggeration, but he believed it gave him clout with his colleagues.

Eva tilted her head. "What's magical about the source anyway?"

Luc's mysterious expression returned, and he spoke slowly so Eva could understand. "They say it has the power to bring forth your truest, deepest music. And once in a while, when light shines on it just right, and if the river feels your intentions are true, you can glimpse the carnyx."

"Have you seen it?" asked Eva.

He shook his head. "I've only known a few people who have."

Not surprisingly, Eva responded with, "Let's try it, Mom!"

Callie considered this. Bring forth her truest, deepest music? Of course, if she hadn't already felt the river's magic, she would have assumed it was just a myth. But she wouldn't put it past La Chanson to make her spontaneously burst out in song. Which could be funny if the stakes weren't so high. She couldn't risk singing in front of anyone besides Eva. Period.

"Not today," Callie said finally. "The carnyx has been there for thousands of years. It's not going anywhere." She wasn't quite sure if this was an actual artifact or a mythical concept, but either way, she wouldn't risk going with Luc. "Maybe another time."

Seeing her daughter's face screw up in indignation, Callie added, "We have urgent errands. What would you do without cereal, sweet pea? You'd starve between meals."

Eva let out a dramatic sigh, as Luc said lightly, "Sure, another time."

Callie saw in his eyes that he understood the boundary she was making, the stones she was adding to her wall. He was perceptive and would honor her wishes, even if, here and there, some warmth snuck through her cracks.

# 16

# SECRET ACCOUNTS

*Colorado, two weeks before arrival in France*

Callie!!!

I think I might have buried a treasure for myself years ago—then forgotten about it! But all this writing is making me remember. Or maybe it's that the meds are finally out of my system. Anyway, I thought of it just now, opening this notebook . . . I might have an email account Brett doesn't know about! And a bank account!

Remember, Callie? Back when I first started putting music on streaming platforms, a few years before "Fly, Fly Away" went viral. I had that old email account in college, and the streaming distribution service on auto-renew—with direct deposit.

I forgot all about it since it made about twenty dollars a year. And then, when my song went viral, money started flowing in from other places, and my manager and label took over the distribution and payments for my new songs. And you know I've always been terrible at keeping track of finances. Anyway, this is like a secret, forgotten account. A buried chest of gold . . . gold that's been growing underground in the dark.

I think I remember the passwords—ha! That was back when I was using names of childhood pets. So if these accounts somehow haven't been hacked, maybe I can access them—I doubt I even had dual factor authentication set up.

And Brett knows nothing about it. I'll try it on incognito mode so I won't leave a trail.

Callie, this could be a key to the lock of our prison.

How much money is there?

How will I use it?

When will I use it?

Will he find out?

Here's the thing: That man can read my mind. He's been learning me like a book for two years. Remember how, in the early days, this felt kind of nice? He knew my favorite foods and TV shows and movies and jewelry taste and clothing style.

And when we started sleeping together, he studied my reaction to his every move, every word, and he knew which details made me respond. Remember how good this felt at first? In the beginning, I was grateful.

But over time, I felt more and more like a puppet, like he was pulling exactly the right strings. And now, he notices I'm not responding the way I used to, not hugging him the way I used to, not even looking at him the way I used to.

I see him notice. I see him threatened.

Callie, you tried warning me, but I tamped down your voice. I ignored you. I banished you. Yes, I did it as much as he did. I allowed it. I'm so sorry.

This money means we could fly away without leaving a trail. It would mean staying under the radar, keeping my music quiet, limiting myself to lullabies . . . which is all I can manage anyway.

Still, it would be a risk. If I fly away, how far will he go to get me back? He has a ruthless side when it comes to his prized possessions.

Okay, I'm going to grab my phone and try to get into those old accounts now. Dig up my treasure . . .

. . . My passwords worked!!! I had to try a dozen combinations of pet goldfish names, but I did it. And there's almost ten thousand freaking dollars sitting in that account!!! Like heaps of secret gold coins!!!

But it scares me. I can't use lack of money as an excuse to stay. And now more excuses are flooding in. How can I leave without my own private phone? Without a single friend for support? With the cameras always watching? I have to find a way.

XO,
Callie

# 17

# WHISPER WORDS

The village smelled of sun-soaked limestone and river currents and baking bread. Outside the *épicerie*, Callie's mouth watered at the artful arrangement of strawberries and raspberries, but she limited herself to her shopping list, aware of the finite bundle of euros in her envelope—the remainder of her buried treasure. Hopefully, payment from music-streaming platforms would keep trickling into that account, more gold coins here and there—but it wasn't something she could count on.

Inside the *épicerie*, Callie more or less abided by her list—shocker, there were no Goldfish crackers—while Luc dropped off the truffles to the shopkeeper at the front. Once they'd walked out together and parted ways on the sidewalk, when it was just her and Eva, she felt oddly exposed. As they strolled along, she looked over her shoulder, scanning passersby, even squinting through car windows, as if spies lurked everywhere.

*We are free*. She urged herself to actually believe it.

When they passed the *pâtisserie*, Callie let Eva drag her inside, unable to resist the scent of caramelized sugar. "You can pick out one thing, sweet pea." Paying for a lawyer would take priority over the rainbow array of macarons in the storefront window.

A tiny woman greeted them with an enthusiastic "Welcome!," immediately offering Eva a purple macaron and winning her heart. "I'm Violette."

She looked like a doll, evoking one of her pastries—a dulcet smile, a glittering dress in berry colors of blue, purple, and red, shimmery lipstick and eye shadow like fruit glaze. She could have been somewhere in her forties or fifties, but her sweetness and stature brought to mind a child playing dress-up. After exchanging pleasantries, she asked, almost shyly, "How's Julien?"

"Oh, he's fine." Callie was mildly surprised at the question. Word must have spread that they were neighbors.

"And his renovation?"

"*Incroyable!*" Eva answered, launching into the *incredible* plans to fill the pool.

Violette echoed her enthusiasm, sprinkling exclamations like powdered sugar over a cream puff. "How marvelous! How beautiful!"

Eva gave a knowing nod, a little bewildered to find a match for her own exuberance, and in an adult, at that.

Violette stuffed the paper bag with macarons and pastries—a welcome gift, she insisted—then waved goodbye. "Tell Julien I said hi!" she said, sparkling brighter than edible gold dust, savoring his name like an éclair.

*Très intéressant.* Callie left the shop smiling, getting the feeling that there was more to Julien than met the eye. On impulse, she turned back. "What do you think of him?"

Violette blushed and stammered out, "He's a magnificent poet and human."

"Glad to hear it." Callie felt a bit in awe of this woman's passion. "I assume you're on the Lavignes' side of the feud?"

"*Mais, bien sûr,*" she said without hesitation. "Poor Julien. Left fatherless as a kid. And no one to defend him against his horrible brother."

Callie gave a thoughtful nod and walked outside with another wave. Violette, she noted, had the name of a springtime flower. Callie thought back to the secrets in the box, more and more certain the person behind it must be Julien. *Julien the poet.* He'd said he was glad his father had died. He'd made no mention of a brother—unless the brother was the one he wished were dead too.

Despite the disconcerting confessions, Callie felt tenderness toward the lonely boy Julien once was. The lonely man he'd become. Because he did seem lonely, despite his closeness to his mother and dog. She recognized his loneliness and secrets and shame. She'd been there.

Next door, the *boulangerie* owner also knew that Callie was staying on the grounds of the Château of the Lost. "I'm Liliane Flamant, but my friends call me Lili, so you should too."

*"Enchantée, Lili."* In return, Callie offered only her own first name—she wasn't taking any chances. This woman looked about her age, in the demographic to have heard her viral song.

As Callie asked for two baguettes, Lili interrupted her, insisting she use the familiar form of *you*. Word spread fast in this village, but the welcome was swift and sincere too.

Lili's young son was arranging baguettes on the shelves, and Eva, of course, instantly volunteered to help. *"J'adore les baguettes,"* was her entrée into conversation, and it worked like a charm.

"Me too," he said softly. "You'd think I'd get tired of them, working here. But I never do, especially when they're warm and steaming."

He struck Callie as a miniature, thoughtful adult, the kind of kid who might have trouble relating to his peers. Her daughter could work with that.

At first glance, Lili appeared to be one of those gorgeously dressed French women with perfect, glowing skin and model cheekbones, impossible to relate to. Even her black canvas apron oozed style. But Lili was kind and generous too, tossing in extra croissants, chatting and laughing at Callie's attempted jokes.

The boy, Samuel, was Eva's age, although several inches shorter and about ten pounds skinnier. There was something frail and Victorian about him, not what you'd expect from a family that owned a *boulangerie*. But within ten minutes, Samuel and Eva were exchanging knock-knock jokes despite the language difference.

"Your daughter has a gift," Lili said, watching Eva with her son, her eyes shiny. "She brings out the best in people, doesn't she?"

"She's been through a lot," Callie admitted. "But she does."

"Well, that's why. She's wise beyond her years. So is my son."

Callie appreciated this woman deepening their small talk. By the time she'd paid, and briefly met Lili's husband—a rotund, cheery baker in the back kitchen—Eva had already invited Samuel and his mom to a poolside playdate.

"We'd love to have you," Callie added, "but full disclosure—the pool has no water."

Lili laughed, a bright, tinkling sound like bells. "They'll still have fun."

Callie wondered if errands would always be such a social event—she'd just made two new friends, and how strangely easy it had been. She found herself looking forward to a pool date, despite the nervousness of getting back into the world of socializing. Brett had cut her off from her friends, and she missed them. Even Luc, she had to admit, had tapped into this unconscious need.

She felt a sense of camaraderie with Lili, who had been through something too, something that kept her emotions close to the surface. This woman made her think of the limestone cave system beneath La Chanson, water seeping through pockets of stone, emerging as rivulets like tears. It was something about the way Lili had looked at her son interacting with Eva—with so much raw love it brought a lump to Callie's throat.

"So, whose side of the fungus feud are you on?" she asked Lili.

"The Forêts," Lili said without missing a beat. "I heard you met them yesterday. Luc's our unofficial vet. The absolute best." She lowered her voice. "I'm happily married, but he's *un vrai beau gosse*."

Callie processed the slang—a real good-looking guy, or something like that—and, well, she couldn't argue with it. Still, she kept her face neutral, refusing to nod along.

Lili waved her hand. "But don't worry. The Lavignes buy their baguettes here and I buy my wine there." She laughed and winked. "We're cordial enough that they'll probably let Samuel play in their empty pool."

"Good to know." Callie returned her smile and jotted down her landline number on a napkin. As Lili passed her a business card with her own cell number on it, Callie couldn't resist asking, "Why is Luc just your *unofficial* vet?"

Lili tossed up her hands, a bit theatrically. "Something happened to him. Some tragedy. Something to do with an old girlfriend. Apparently, she died. Afterward, he became an echo of his former self. Gave up on his dreams of being a vet, even after he finished vet school. He's just missing his license." Her voice dropped further. "He's seeing a woman from Aix now, a veterinarian, but he keeps it casual. If you ask me, he's scared to get close to a woman again."

"Well, I'm not interested. Definitely not."

Lili winked. "Of course you're not."

Back outside, tote bags brimming, Callie was ready for the trek home, when Eva cried, "Look, Mom! The *salon du thé*!"

Callie read the sign overhead, then the chalkboard easel announcing a *Soirée Scène-Ouverte*. Right, the open mic night. She took Eva's lead and peeked in the window.

Everything shone—sumptuous cushions threaded with gold, ceramic-tiled tables, ornate silver tea sets. Giant-leafed plants created the feel of a conservatory—an array of monstera, heart-leafed philodendron, dragon plants, fig trees.

Enticing, but then her gaze landed on a small stage, just a foot high, tucked in the corner between modest speakers. Her stomach flip-flopped and she stepped backward. This was the closest she'd been to a stage in two years.

"Let's go inside!" Eva pressed her face to the glass in a smear of condensation.

"No, sweetie." Callie's hand flew to her heart, which was somehow both leaping and sinking. "We can't."

She was just turning to go when Eva grabbed her arm. "Wait, Mom!"

Through the window, Callie saw a woman striding toward them, and before she could pull Eva away, the door opened. A toddler on her hip, the woman waved and propped open the door, flipping the sign to *Ouvert*. She wore a vibrant green silk and cotton tunic edged in gold. Draped around her dark hair, a cream scarf set off her warm skin tone and amber eyes. "*Bonjour, mes amies.*"

"*Bonjour, madame.*" Eva beamed at her. "*J'adore* your dress!"

The woman laughed. "Well, thank you, sweet girl. It's my *djellaba*." She spoke French with a light accent—Arabic?—and looked about Callie's age or a bit younger, maybe thirty, her face smooth, cheeks high and rosy. "*Entrez. Entrez.* I'll bring you mint tea."

"Oh, we're just looking." Callie shifted her bags, overcome with the need to stay far away from the stage. "We're new in town."

The woman's face lit up. "Oh, then you must come in! I'm Amira and this little one is Hamza."

Unable to articulate an excuse in French fast enough, Callie let Amira lead them inside, around tables and cushions, breezing through the open French doors onto the patio overlooking the river. At the center was a fountain, its water covered in rose petals and, around the perimeter, trellises of jasmine, and lemon trees hiding warblers and larks. The river harmonized with the spouting water, and despite herself, Callie sank into the melody, lush and whimsical and alive.

Back inside, Amira set down Hamza, who was at that cute phase of chubby-legged staggering around. Eva immediately took his pudgy hands, led him onto the low stage, and danced with him to soft Moroccan music. Callie braced herself against the magnetic pull of the stage, feeling her nails dig into her palms.

Amira didn't seem to notice her discomfort, just smiled at the kids, amused. "Business is slower during the week, mostly locals, but on weekends we're lively with tourists. They come to La Chanson for the river and swing by here for refreshments and entertainment."

Callie's muscles tensed further. She'd felt protected at the idea of living in a tiny village, a pocket dimension. But an influx of tourists every weekend? Maybe she'd just hole up in the cottage, wear a scarf and hat and sunglasses to go out.

And what about her voice, which Luc had almost recognized? Well, she'd just keep quiet, listen and nod and let Eva do the talking. It was unlikely anyone would recognize her . . . but it would take only one to destroy everything.

"Well, I should get this stuff in the fridge." Callie stepped away from the stage, motioning to her shopping bags. "Thanks for the tour." She grabbed Eva's hand and tugged her toward the door.

Amira followed them back outside, propping her son on her hip. "Come to the open mic soirée!" She gestured to the easel. "Eva and Hamza can dance all night long."

Callie breathed out, searching for an excuse. Eva was playing peekaboo with the toddler, who was giggling. Of course, she'd beg to come back. Stalling, Callie glanced at the three words on the chalkboard, oddly placed: *secret, earth,* and *taste.* "What's this?"

"Inspiration for the open mic soirée."

"Like a theme?" Callie wasn't sure how to say *prompt* in French.

"More than that. A breath of inspiration to sing a long-forgotten song." Amira gave a peaceful smile. "Or to create a new one. The whisper words change every week. We hear them on the breeze from the river's source."

Once Callie summarized this abstract concept in English, Eva raised her brow. "Like fluffy seeds!"

"Exactly," said Amira. "Come, and you'll see."

Callie could already feel an undercurrent inside herself composing a song with *secret, earth,* and *taste.* La Chanson was humming along, sending curious rivulets through her. She shook herself. *No performing.*

"People love it," Amira added, kissing Hamza's wispy curls. "That's what we have to thank for our five-star reviews."

Brett always looked up the highest rated restaurant in a new place. If he did track down Callie and Eva, he'd come here first, to get the lay of the land. He'd manipulate the locals, find out where she was staying, and show up unannounced.

She had to get ahead of this. Before she could change her mind, she jotted down her landline number on a receipt from her purse and handed it to Amira. She spoke quickly, glancing at Eva, who was now running up and down the sidewalk, out of earshot. "Listen, an American man might come looking for us. Silver-black hair, shaved close, pale skin, in his fifties, expensive clothes. Or he might send another man. Parisian, tall, blond, thirties." She ran her hand through her hair, flustered. "If anyone comes, please don't tell them we're here. And call me right away."

A soft expression came over Amira's face, then she reached out and hugged her, wrapping her in the scent of toasted almonds. After a moment of astonishment, Callie sank into the embrace. This woman *cared.*

Amira found Callie's eyes. "How dangerous is he?"

"I—I don't know."

But she did know, didn't she? The dangers were written in the folders zippered into Callie's suitcase, files she was scared to touch. She'd only glimpsed the contents but had seen enough to know: They held the truth in black and white. She'd bring them to the lawyer appointment, once she saved enough money, and then together they'd read the documents, untangle the mess, assess the danger.

"*Merci,*" Callie whispered, then turned to go, as Amira called out, "*Bon courage.*"

For the whole walk home, Callie kept scanning their surroundings and half listening to Eva's ideas for a dog-themed open mic skit.

For now, Callie would lay low. Limit their time in town.

And if Brett came, she'd hide. There was that secret room in the château. She'd hole up with Eva until he left. If she stayed hidden, they'd be safe.

When Callie and Eva returned from errands, a guitar was leaning outside their cottage door like an unexpected guest, an old friend who'd popped in for a visit. It had been carefully propped against the doorframe beneath the overhang, and an old case lay beside it.

In awe, Eva brushed her fingers over the frets. "Mom, this is just like yours."

Callie stared. Acoustic, made of a nut-brown wood, maybe walnut, with a mother of pearl inlay—yes, it was vintage, like her own favorite one. Brett had turned it into decoration, hanging by its neck in a guest room, along with her lyre and ukelele and mandolin and a dozen other instruments. She'd stopped going into that room—it chilled her to see her best friends lifeless in their nooses, like Bluebeard's secret victims.

Now, hot tears came to her eyes as she reached for the guitar, felt the smooth wood, ran her fingertips over the steel strings. Taking a breath, she wiped her cheeks, then plucked a few tentative notes.

A full, rich sound. Someone must have recently strung and tuned it. She peeked inside the case, saw a packet of strings and a few small tools resting on the blue velvet—but no clues to its origin.

"Where did it come from?" Eva asked, eyes wide.

"Who knows," Callie said, but her first strange thought was this: La Chanson had delivered it to her doorstep—the river was in cahoots to get her to perform at the open mic soirée. Then logic took over and she wondered if Madame Lavigne had dropped it off. But Callie had never mentioned her musical past to her. Would Luc have brought it? Or his dad? No, they seemed terrified of stepping onto Lavigne property.

Julien, then? Of course, he would have heard her singing last night. Well, if it had been him, she appreciated his anonymity. No questions, no need for explanation. Or was this his payment for her silence? He'd seen her reading the secret papers, discovering things about him and his past. And the murders.

"Well, I think the ghost boy brought it," Eva said.

"Why is that?"

Eva gestured to the olive tree, its silver leaves rustling. "He's watching us. He wants you to play it."

Callie squinted at the spot, seeing only dancing shadows. "Well, I can't argue with the ghost boy."

For the rest of the afternoon, she sat on the sofa and played the guitar, as if reunited with an old lover, stroking its contours and whispering sweetness. She took breaks whenever her fingertips grew sore and pink—she'd lost her calluses entirely—but joy flooded out any twinges of pain.

Meanwhile, swaying to the music, Eva drew pictures of Lagotto Romagnolos with colored pencils on a sketch pad from a desk drawer. When Eva announced she was starving, Callie reluctantly stopped playing to heat up ratatouille for dinner.

That night, cradling the guitar, Callie sang to Eva, older songs from her first album. Eva struggled to keep her eyelids open to watch Callie's fingers fly over the strings, barely visible by moonlight through the open balcony doors.

After the third song, Eva stared at the balcony, eyes widening. "The ghost boy. He's over there."

"What?" She followed Eva's gaze but saw only shifting shadows of foliage.

"He likes how you play. You're cheering him up. He gets lonely."

Callie swallowed, unsure whether to keep encouraging her. "What does he look like?"

"Old-fashioned clothes. A hat like the one the old men in the park wear."

"A beret?"

"Yeah." Eva kept staring at the spot. "A white shirt with a collar.

Short sleeves. The kind that buttons up. A gray sweater vest. Shorts. Sandals. And a feather stuck in his beret."

Oddly specific details. "He's not scary?"

"No. But he gets sad sometimes. He feels trapped here. Like he doesn't belong anymore." She paused, tilted her head. "He wants you to sing another song, Mom."

Callie hesitated, nerve endings alert, as though her body could perceive a presence, even if her mind couldn't. "Okay, one more, sweet pea."

After the first verse, Eva said with a drowsy giggle, "Now he's waving the feather around like a conductor."

Once Eva fell asleep, Callie sat on the balcony with the guitar, wondering if the ghost boy was here, watching and listening, secretly conducting music. Searching the shadows, she could almost see traces of movement like stardust trails. She felt an odd sense of camaraderie with the ghost, watching life from the edges.

The river flowed below, opalescent in the darkness, whispering breezes and breaths. *Secret. Earth. Taste.* Of their own accord, her fingers plucked out a melody, and La Chanson harmonized like a skilled session musician, shifting from cello to keys to sax to conga. Rhythms wove together with water and air and moonlight. Lyrics flowed out from her into the sky. She felt herself soaring and diving, tasting earth and secrets, touching the carnyx.

Vaguely, she remembered her resolve to sing quietly. Luc could be listening across the forest, soaking in her song, feeling *alive* again. And no, she shouldn't encourage their invisible bond—but her voice had its own volition. The self in the cave was making her way out.

And, *mon Dieu,* how Callie had missed her.

# 18

# BLUEBEARD

*Colorado, one week before arrival in France*

Dear Callie,

I have to get the hell away.

Something happened. Something in the realm of Bluebeard. I've been rereading that fairy tale, Perrault's *La Barbe-Bleue*, and I keep picturing a seventeenth-century version of Brett, his stubble grown into a midnight-blue beard.

In the story, Bluebeard gives his new wife keys to every room in the castle but tells her never to use the smallest key. One day he goes away on business, and shocker, she uses the smallest key to open a room . . . full of the dead bodies of his previous wives.

The illustrations look so much like Brett, they actually made me gasp the first time I saw them—the long line of his nose, the thick eyebrows, but most of all the way he's looking down at his new wife on her knees, exerting complete control, dangling keys before her.

The drawing that really chills my bones shows his victims' decapitated heads, hanging by their hair. The one on the right has a curl behind her ear just where I do, the same damn curl, and her eyes are closed. I imagine her hair ginger and her skin pale, and I can almost hear her ghost thinking, *Why didn't I open my eyes and get the hell away?*

Yesterday, I entered Bluebeard's room. Brett's been on a business trip in Cairo, coming back next week. Eva was at school and I was alone in the house. Can you tell my hands are still shaking? I don't even know where to start.

Okay, so I was washing dishes when I got an alert on my phone saying the hallway camera wasn't working. Which meant I could try opening the door to his office without him knowing—he likes privacy for his shady deals, so he doesn't have cameras there. I dried my hands and headed down the hallway. I paused outside his office door, put my hand on the knob. And it turned.

I glanced behind my shoulder, hoping the camera was truly broken. Callie, I really thought my heart would explode—the pounding was filling my ears. I pushed the door open a crack. There was a keypad lock, but he must feel so confident in my obedience that he left it open.

You know those elephants from old circuses? The trainers would tie the baby elephant to a metal hook in the ground, and it learned its limits. They'd keep that same rope as the elephant grew into a massive, five-ton adult. When it was fully grown, the elephant could easily tear away the rope, but it had learned not to. It assumed its strength still had those limits.

I stood on the threshold of Brett's office with the door cracked open, feeling like the elephant tugging at the fraying rope, scared to exert its power. I pushed the door wide open and walked inside. For a moment, I breathed in traces of expensive cologne, took in his large desk with its locking drawers, the ceiling-to-floor shelved cases, his most precious collections behind glass.

Other parts of the house have a rotating display of antiquities for guests to admire. In theory. People hardly ever come over. Once in a while, members of his team stay here, like the Tokyo and Paris assistants, but that's it.

I scanned the corners of the room to make sure there weren't hidden cameras, then my gaze landed on his collection of music deities. And right next to the new goddess from Thailand, I saw Pepito. He was just sitting there, staring at me, and I imagined him saying in his nasal voice: *It's about time!*

Realization swept over me like dominoes tipping:

Brett wanted this *diosito*.

Nick refused to sell it.

Nick died in an "accident."

Brett was there.

And Brett got the *diosito*.

My hands were shaking so much I could barely open the glass case. I took out Pepito, cradled him in my hands, felt his smooth, worn stone, gave him a light kiss.

Brett must have found him when he was overseeing the estate company emptying my little house. He'd taken my *diosito* for himself. And I'd let him.

I put Pepito back and wiped my fingerprints from the glass with my shirt sleeve. Then I surveyed the desk. Brett's monitors and keyboard were there, but he'd taken his laptop to Cairo. Not that I'd be able to access it anyway—I didn't know his passwords, while he had full access to mine. I knelt down and tried the drawers. Locked.

A shiver passed through me. Bluebeard's secrets. Brett's secrets. The fact that he'd taken Pepito emboldened me. What else had he taken? I took a paper clip from the container on his desk, poked around in the lock mechanism. No luck.

I rocked back onto my heels and looked around the room. The key must be hidden somewhere here. It would be tiny, and I didn't remember seeing him with a tiny key. He was minimalist, no key chain, used his phone to start his Tesla, tapped in codes for the house door locks.

It occurred to me that it was around ten p.m. in Cairo and he might be relaxing in his hotel room for the night, watching the house camera feeds on his phone or laptop. He would have gotten the alert about the malfunctioning camera. And he'd notice I'd disappeared in the hallway. But the powder room was also accessed in this hallway. That would be my excuse. I calculated that after fifteen minutes, he'd get suspicious about why I was in the powder room so long. Ten minutes had passed, which meant I'd need to be quick.

I exhaled. I'd lived with this man for two years, and even if most of it was in a haze, I still knew his patterns and preferences.

The Indiana Jones in him loved the mysteries that came with treasure hunting. I stared at the statues lining the shelves, sweeping my gaze from the music deity collection to the opposite wall of Greek goddesses, and lingered on an ancient brown-and-black vase featuring Hecate, holding a key.

The key to the gates of hell, the underworld. But it was also the key to the entire cosmos. To freedom. Hecate, goddess of boundaries and crossroads. Of magic and moonlight.

I walked over, opened the glass case, and carefully lifted the vase. Beneath was a tiny, thin key. I kissed her in thanks, then knelt back down beside the desk drawers and—

# 19

# SECRET EARTH TASTE

The next morning, Callie hummed while getting dressed, as if the river music had seeped into her cells overnight. She'd slept deeply and woken up refreshed. The castle prison in Colorado was fading from her mind, only lightning flashes coming at strange moments. She wanted to put it all behind her, but part of herself warned: *Do not forget.*

Between birdsong, a memory struck her—the terrifying moment when Brett returned early from his Cairo business trip while she was in the basement writing the letter about finding Pepito. And more. She shivered now, recalling how she'd stuffed the letter back into the suitcase in a panic. And recalling what else she'd found in his office.

*Do not forget.*

Gingerly, she pulled the daisy suitcase from the armoire, unzipped the files, and held them, feeling their power. Power *against* her, from what she could tell . . . but she could change that, couldn't she?

Here in La Chanson, she was connecting with friends and music. True, she hadn't found a lawyer yet, but she could already feel Brett's power diminishing. He was not a sorcerer. He was an abusive, delusional human.

She tucked the file folders back inside the suitcase and pushed it to the back of the wardrobe. Soon, soon she might gather the courage to open them.

After checking on Eva—who was still sleeping despite morning light pouring through the French doors—Callie padded downstairs, savoring the feel of the old, worn wood beneath her bare feet. Through the kitchen window, she watched Julien make his way from the forest toward the château with his faithful dog, Fleur, at his side. They must have taken an early morning walk. Callie let herself be drawn back fully into the present, the angled light, silver olive leaves, harpsicord ripples.

On impulse, she stepped outside in her pajamas, and after an exchange of polite *bon matins*, she said, "I didn't realize this cottage came with a magical guitar."

"*Euh*." He shrugged, avoiding her eyes. "Guess the river brought it."

"My thought exactly."

He gave a small smile. "I restrung it for you."

"That's kind," she said, scratching Fleur's ears. "Where did it come from?"

"*Euh*, just something from the château. There for decades."

She sensed there was more but left it there.

For a brief moment, he met her eyes. "Your music." His voice emerged in a whisper, "It makes me feel something. Something lost. From childhood. Hope. Or freedom. The feeling of when my father left on business trips."

"You didn't get along?" Callie said after a pause, rubbing Fleur's belly.

"He was crushed. From the war. Algerian war. His heart, that is. His heart was crushed."

"I'm sorry." Callie smoothed the dog's fur, trying to follow. "When did he pass away?"

"I was twelve. By then, he'd crushed me too." Almost absently, Julien ran a fingertip over the scar at his temple. "I hid. Became small. So small I vanished. My body kept growing. Taller and taller. A tree bent beneath a ceiling. He stole the truest part of me."

Callie felt for this lanky, stooped, middle-aged man who spoke in cryptic poetry and tended to his renovations and his dog and his mother. Why was he telling her this? She had the feeling he rarely opened up to humans. It must be because he knew she'd read his childhood confessions, his poetry. And he seemed almost relieved to speak to her about it.

Callie's gaze landed on his scar, and she asked the question she wished her friends and mother had asked her about Brett. If they'd spoken it, maybe she could have admitted it. "He was abusive toward you?"

Surprise passed over his face, and then resignation. He grunted with a nod. "Whenever I defended my mother."

Her chest ached for young-boy Julien. It made sense that his mother would have felt inspired to run a safe house for survivors of domestic violence. She imagined how it would feel to see your husband hurt your child. Brett had never physically hurt Eva or her, but her daughter had witnessed how he'd controlled her, silenced her. A different kind of pain.

"Did anyone know?" Callie asked.

"No one outside our family."

She sighed, understanding how this could be hidden, especially if friends and neighbors looked the other way.

"My mother was brave in the end. She started the safe house. Women and children came. But I felt shame. A piece of my father inside me. Waiting to come out. I shriveled. A dried fig."

Callie wanted to hug him. "I'm so sorry."

A grunt of acknowledgment. "But your music. It brings hope. The boy is still here. Underground and waiting. A truffle of sorts."

"A black diamond," she said, thinking of the poetry.

Words from the secret box echoed in her head: *I know who killed Papa. I'm glad he's dead.* On impulse, she asked, "Julien, do you still think someone killed your father? Who?"

Silence. His eyes filled, and he looked away.

Had this quiet man somehow drowned his father himself? He would have been a child. No, impossible. "What about Marguerite? Who do you think killed the dog?"

He winced. "My father. Went out before dawn. To the forest. With rat poison. Left sausages. I followed him. Gathered the sausages. Missed one." He hung his head, a look of utter defeat.

"I'm so sorry, Julien."

"She's buried in the forest. Just beyond the wall. I visit her grave at dawn. From a distance."

Callie nodded, encouraging him to continue, imagining him peering at the daisy bouquets beneath the oak, paying solemn respect.

"Then my father died. A week or so later. My brother accused Monsieur Forêt of drowning him." Anger and sorrow and shame roiled over his face in red blotches. His lips pressed together, eyes squeezed shut. "A lie."

Silence for a long moment, only sounds of cicada songs swelling with the heat setting in, the river music, now churning and rushing. How odd that this guarded man was opening up to her, barely knowing her. But she was a stranger, and sometimes strangers were best for confiding secrets.

And she'd asked. Maybe no one had asked before.

Searching for some way to lessen his pain, she landed on another secret from the box: *There's someone I like, named after a springtime flower.* "Oh," she said, her voice light, "Violette from the *pâtisserie* says hi."

At that, Julien turned pink to the tips of his ears, then turned and fled into the château.

An hour later, on the back patio, amid the chatter of chickadees, Callie sipped café au lait and Eva gulped *chocolat chaud,* content before the remains of their breakfast spread—croissants, *pain au chocolat,* yogurt, apricots and cherries from their trees. Callie was reflecting on her chat with Julien while trying her best to engage in an endless stream of knock-knock jokes, when Chouchou darted through olive trees and straight onto Eva's lap.

As Eva squealed in delight, Callie felt her heart lurch—where there was this pup, there might be her owner—though, he'd probably use the term *companion*. She looked around but saw no sign of him.

Eva leapt up. "Let's bring her back to Luc!"

After a beat of hesitation, Callie said, "Okay, but first, toothbrushing."

Eva raced to the bathroom, carrying the pup, and was done in two seconds flat, but Callie did a more thorough job, washing her face too, applying sunscreen followed by tinted lip balm that she also used as blush—a perfectly normal thing to do when leaving the house.

*He has a girlfriend.* Each word a stone in the wall.

Soon, she and Eva were heading toward the woods, Chouchou bounding beside them.

Callie figured it would take less than fifteen minutes to walk to the Forêts' place. The forest was all dappled light and fresh earth and pine smells, and she breathed it in as she strode along, legs loose and free, aware of the vast difference between her frozen, static life in Colorado and her life here, a song full of tempo changes and dynamic shifts, allegro con spirito.

When they reached the wall, Eva scrambled over, and after a moment's hesitation, Callie followed, carrying the pup, who must have gone through the same hole—which meant Julien hadn't patched it yet. A subtle act of resistance? His words came to her: *I'm supposed to hate Monsieur Forêt, but I wish he were my father. I wish he would take me truffle hunting.*

As Eva dropped to her knees to smooth her fingers over a patch of moss, Callie's gaze landed on the bouquet of daisies beneath the massive oak, and she felt herself drawn toward them. Up close, she noticed this must be a new bouquet, freshly picked this morning, the petals firm and white, the leaves full, the stem cuts sharp. *Marguerites.*

She reached to touch the flowers when a rustle sounded nearby, and she jumped. Belle and Jolie bounded through the trees, tails wagging, nuzzling Chouchou in greeting, followed by Luc, cotton bag slung over his shoulder, jogging toward them. Despite herself, Callie felt her muscles soften.

Monsieur Forêt brought up the rear at a quick pace with his walking stick. He took in the situation and let out a chuckle. "The pup can't stay away from you, Eva."

Callie met the old man's cheeks for kisses of greeting, and then, because it would have been weird not to do the same with Luc, she leaned in to kiss him too.

*He has a girlfriend.*

Perfect. She could use a casual acquaintance with no strings attached.

His cheek was rough against hers, and he took her hand briefly as they kissed. The moment seemed to slow down, lento, lento. There was the warmth emanating from his chest, the bulk of his shoulder grazing hers, the muscles moving beneath his T-shirt, the forearms rippling. His scent—sun-drenched countryside, a mix of rosemary and oregano and thyme.

She forced herself to step back and cross her arms, then took another step back for good measure. She'd tapped into something, a longing she hadn't realized she'd had. The need for a body she trusted. A safe, strong, warm, good-smelling body. And it astonished her, this raw need rising to the surface of its own accord.

"Chouchou ran all the way to our house!" Eva's eyes blazed with excitement. "She jumped on my lap!"

Luc rubbed his face, glanced at Callie. "Sorry about that. We'll keep her closer next time."

"Please don't!" said Eva.

Monsieur Forêt laughed. "Want to watch the dogs find truffles?" He used the verb *caver*—to go caving—as if these dogs were spelunkers, off to explore.

Eva put her fists beneath her chin and jumped up and down. *"Oui!"*

Monsieur Forêt gave a command to the dogs, who raced around trees, sniffing with vigor, until Belle started pawing at the ground.

Luc jogged over and pulled something from his bag—a sharp little shovel, like a pointy spade.

*"Un pic à truffes,"* he told Eva.

Ah, the term from the poem. The barks of dogs piercing one's heart with *les pics à truffes* . . . A truffle pick, she mentally translated.

Luc slipped into truffle-teacher mode with Eva, walking her through step-by-step, as his dad held back the eager dog. Dropping to his knees, Luc dug around gently with his *pic à truffes*, then pointed to a truffle, fresh dirt on his hands and stained jeans. "Go ahead, Eva, take it."

The surface was black, a bit smaller than Eva's fist, and the uneven texture brought to mind a little brain. Over the moon, Eva passed it around. Monsieur Forêt breathed in the truffle's scent, let out an *ahhhhh* of approval, and handed it to Callie. She took a sniff—earthy and mysterious. She let out an echo of his *ahhhhh*, assuming this was part of the ritual of *le cavage*, literally, *caving* in the soil for truffles.

Luc dropped the truffle into his bag and patted back the soil as the dogs bounded off in search of the next one. Monsieur Forêt took the *pic à truffes*, forged ahead with Eva at his side, leaving Callie unexpectedly alone with Luc. He pushed his hair from his eyes and gave her a sidelong glance. "You kept me up again last night."

Mortification flooded her. Of course he would have heard—she'd sung with even more abandon than the previous night. "I'll get you ear plugs."

"Please don't. My ears would protest. They were happily surprised at the guitar."

"Well, it just showed up at my door."

"As guitars do." He raised a brow. "At least in La Chanson." He gave her a thoughtful look. "When you were singing, I kept thinking about my vet license."

"The one you never got?"

*"Tout à fait." Exactly*. He exhaled in a soft laugh.

"Why haven't you gotten it?" she asked. Lili had mentioned a tragedy.

He grazed his hand over oak leaves. "The part of me that dreamed of being a vet—it disappeared. For three years. But last night, it came back."

She observed his face, so exposed, layers of hope and regret and fear like an excavated mountainside. "So, you'll get your license?"

"Maybe."

She felt an urge to help, even though bureaucratic forms weren't her forté. She just knew how emotional limbo felt, starting to reconnect with yourself yet unable to move forward. She'd wished for a friend to take her hand and say, *Hey, let's do this.* In fact, she wished someone would take her hand now and say, *Let's open those files and make that lawyer appointment and fix everything together.*

But she'd have to do that herself. Which was fine. Soon, she'd go to Aix and deal with it all. She just needed to stay away for a couple more weeks in case the Parisian assistant was still there. And she'd feel better with a part-time job to pay the lawyer's fees.

Eva bounded up with a truffle in her palm. "Mom, look what me and Chouchou found!"

Callie admired it. "Very brainy texture." She sniffed it deeply and channeled Monsieur Forêt. "*Ahhh.* Smells like leather and acorns."

As she dropped it into Luc's palm, their hands brushed. He pulled a folding knife from his pocket—old-fashioned with a wooden handle—and nicked the truffle's surface, exposing the pale tan interior.

He crouched to Eva's level, explained that its summer truffle taste was subtler than the black diamonds of winter, which had dark interiors and a more intense flavor. He inhaled the scent. "Notes of oak and olive, undercurrents of hazelnut and mushroom," he said, passing it back to Eva.

"Well, I think it smells like vanilla ice cream," she declared.

"Keep it," said Monsieur Forêt. "It's yours."

"Oh no, it's not necessary." Callie would feel strange letting an eight-year-old walk around with something so expensive, even if it was a glorified mushroom.

He waved away her words. "I insist. Grate it over your eggs or into salad dressing with olive oil and lemon juice." He winked. "And think of us."

Stroking his chin, Monsieur Forêt stared over the wall. "The Lavignes no longer truffle hunt. All those truffles are going to waste. When I was a child and there was no wall, we'd all truffle hunt together." His eyes shone with tears. "It hurts my heart, knowing everything buried here."

Callie wasn't sure whether to nod or shake her head, so she did a mix of both, feeling for this old man, and staring at the forest floor that hid truffles, memories, a beloved dog, and who knew what else.

"We were the best of friends—Sophie, Tristan, and me. The Three Musketeers."

It took Callie a moment to remember that Sophia was Madame Lavigne's first name, and Tristan, her late husband's.

He continued, staring at the wall. "She hates me, thinks I'm a murderer, can't bear to look at me or talk to me. It's been decades since she's spoken a single word. When someone treats you with so much cruelty, a wall builds around your heart."

Luc slung an arm over his father's shoulder, just as Callie realized she hadn't seen the dogs or Eva for a few minutes. Panic seized her.

She was about to call out, when noises cut through the sparrow songs—men's voices from behind the oaks on the Lavigne side. And there was Eva, walking along the wall, waving and shouting, "*Salut*, Julien!"

He waved back, his lanky form approaching with a man in his late fifties in a pastel linen shirt and pants and leather briefcase—a city slicker styled for a day in the Mediterranean countryside.

Julien's stained work clothes and boots provided a jarring contrast. The man must have interrupted his renovation work—he hadn't said anything about expecting guests. Julien gave her an apologetic look. "*Euhhhh.*"

"Julien!" Eva called out. "Look at the truffle I found with Chouchou!"

Quickly, Callie clarified, "It came from the Forêts' side."

Eva hopped down, puppy tucked beneath her arm, and handed the truffle to Julien, who turned it over in his hand, then smelled it, offering an *ahh* of admiration. "Nice, Eva." He handed it back, adding, "Grate it over omelets."

"That's what Monsieur Forêt said!" Thankfully, Eva seemed oblivious to the uneasy atmosphere. She crouched down to greet Fleur, letting the dogs rub noses and sniff each other.

Meanwhile, tension grew among the men—chests puffing, eyes narrowing, jaws clenching. Callie looked expectantly at them, waiting for an introduction, but alas, Julien was too socially awkward.

"You must be my mother's new renters," the stranger said, his voice deep and polished. "I'm Hugo." He leaned over the wall, as if expecting some cheek kissing.

Instead, Callie extended her hand, drawing back with the rest of her body. Something about him made her raise the shield. Or maybe it was just that she'd been wary of meeting this son from Paris. "I'm Calliope." It felt like an extra layer of protection, using her full name, which only her biggest fans knew. She should have used this name, or a completely fake one, with everyone in France, but she'd wanted to keep things normal for Eva.

Luc and his father had stepped back from the wall, putting more distance between them and the other men. If it weren't for Eva holding their pup, the Forêts would probably have walked away.

"A document has come to light." Hugo gave a smug grin, like someone who'd just won a poker match, like Brett when he'd secured a tricky antiquities deal. "It proves that this entire forest is ours." He made a cluck of false sympathy, then reached into his briefcase, extracted a pack of papers, and held them up just out of the Forêts' reach. "This is your last morning here."

Callie's chest tightened as she recognized the property deed from the secret box. *She* was the one who'd brought this to light, given it to Julien. She'd last seen it on the kitchen table of the château.

Hugo narrowed his eyes at the Forêts. "Now, *s'il vous plaît,* get the hell off our property."

# LAUNDRY AND LIES

*Colorado, six days before arrival in France*

Dear Callie,

I'm back in my dungeon haven. The past twenty-four hours have been torturous. Brett's been watching me like a vulture, and it's felt nearly impossible to slip away. He's on a run now, so I have a little time.

Okay, to pick up where I left off, he came home early from his trip—no text, no warning, like he wanted to catch me in the act, like he *knew*. I was here in the basement, writing, when I heard the door open. My heart was about to explode—I felt like a squirrel in front of an oncoming truck.

I stashed my letter in the suitcase and grabbed a basket of laundry and climbed upstairs. Then I paused at the basement door and took a long breath, composing myself. He's like a biofeedback machine, observing my breathing rate, pulse, heartbeat, the color in my cheeks—and of course, my emotions scream out in red blotches.

"Callie?" he called.

I released one more breath, opened the door, and stepped into the hallway.

"Oh, hey, Brett!" My voice hurt my ears—of course he'd notice the high-pitched false cheer. I clutched the basket, kept it in front of me so we couldn't hug. "What are you doing home?"

"I wanted to surprise you." He left his suitcase at the door and walked toward me, arms open.

"Oh. Great!" I set down the basket and forced my feet to move, suddenly scared I'd left the door to his office open, or hadn't cleaned my prints from the glass, or hadn't locked the drawers, or hadn't tucked the tiny key back under the Hecate vase.

I gave him a stiff hug and tried to hide my revulsion. His cologne, his smell of money, his secrets. It had only been a day since I'd opened the drawer and found what he'd been hiding—I thought I'd have all week to go through the papers, to make a plan, to take Eva and run . . .

But there he was, sensing my heart pounding and feeling the heat on my skin and seeing the flush on my cheeks and hearing my breathing as fast as a terrified squirrel's. He pulled back and studied me. "What's going on, cupcake?"

I swallowed. "I was just doing laundry and—well, you scared me. I thought it was an intruder."

He kept studying me. I'm such a bad liar.

Finally, he raised a thick, groomed eyebrow. "No one can break into our smart house. You know that." He spoke to me as if I were a child. "That's why we have these cameras and codes and locks. To keep you and Eva safe."

"Right. I know. I just—I wasn't being rational."

His gaze lingered, then he kissed me as I tried not to gag at his tongue slipping in. He pulled back, glanced at the laundry, then back at me. "That's dirty. Why are you bringing it up?"

"Oh." I avoided his eyes. "I don't know. I guess I just freaked out."

"If you thought it was an intruder, why would you bring up laundry?"

I sputtered a laugh. "I don't know what to tell you." Then I stole a glance over his shoulder and saw that yes, I'd closed his office door. "I think I'm sick."

"Sick?"

"A stomach bug." That would explain my flushing and sweatiness and strangeness. "I spent a while in the bathroom yesterday," I added, nodding toward the powder room.

A long pause. "Why didn't you tell me this on the phone?"

I breathed out, scrambled for a lie. "Oh, it seems like a twenty-four-hour bug. I didn't want you to worry."

He gave me a measured look. "You know I don't like you keeping things from me, cupcake. Remember, you need my reality checks. You need to stay mentally healthy for Eva."

"Right. Sorry."

This morning, his handyman fixed the hallway camera, so I won't go back into his office. And I bet he's monitoring the feed on his phone, so I can't stay down here any longer. Ten minutes for laundry, tops. If only I had anything to iron as an excuse. But his stuff gets dry-cleaned, and my wardrobe is all loungewear. Okay, next time I'll tell you what I found in his office.

Love,
Callie

# 21

# THE DEED

Callie watched in horror as Hugo waved the ancient deed before the Forêts, who made no move to leave.

Blood rose to Monsieur Forêt's face, turning it burgundy. "You have no right." He pounded his walking stick into the dirt. "This is ours to share."

Luc gently took his father's arm, but Monsieur Forêt tore it away and gestured to the wall, shouting, "Our families made an agreement!"

Hugo looked at him as if he were a doddering old fool. "This wall was never legally binding. Just a temporary fix to keep us from killing each other until my family could find the deed."

Monsieur Forêt's jaw clenched as Luc whispered to him, probably hoping his dad wouldn't have a heart attack. Callie was concerned too and moved closer to Monsieur Forêt, prepared to steady him if needed.

Luc stepped forward to examine the deed. "Where did you get this?"

"It was waiting for me on the kitchen table." Hugo's voice brimmed with smug satisfaction. "My brother found it in the château after all these years."

Julien glanced at Callie as if he wanted to shrink and disappear. Softly, he mumbled, "My brother found it before . . ."

His voice faded, but she filled in the blanks. Before he could burn it? Did he *want* the Forêts to have half the forest? Had he hidden this document all these years to protect them? She suspected he loved this forest as much as his sworn enemies did, like a member of his own family. He probably knew every tree and mushroom and nest and bird. As did the Forêts. Julien had more in common with them than with his own brother. *I wish Monsieur Forêt were my father.*

She didn't want to care about this—she had other things to worry about—but she'd found herself in the middle of this fungus feud, like it or not. And, she admitted to herself with a pang, her snooping had unearthed the deed that had sparked this.

When Monsieur Forêt began cursing, Luc told him in soothing tones, "Let's go home for now, Papa," and shot a look at Hugo, as if to say, *How could you do this to an old man?* "Send us a copy of that deed. We'll get our own lawyer and fight this."

Callie grasped the pain in his expression. Their truffle business brought in just enough to pay the bills. They couldn't afford a lawyer any more than she could.

"Keep out of this forest," said Hugo. As much as he tried to project the image of a slick professional, his glee was unrestrained, like a bratty kid winning through cheating. "That means no truffles, no business, no income. I can only assume you'll be selling your house as a next step. As a real estate lawyer, I can connect you with buyers." He offered a business card, which the Forêts made no move to take.

"Why are you being so cruel?" Luc's voice broke as he held his father's arm.

Hugo bored his eyes into Monsieur Forêt, his hatred old but raw. "This man murdered my father. He deserves much worse."

Callie glanced at Julien, who remained quiet, stooped, staring at his feet, shutting down in the midst of confrontation. If he knew who the true killer was, why wouldn't he say something? He liked Monsieur Forêt, always had. Why wouldn't he defend him? But of course, this silence could be the result of trauma, of domestic violence as a child.

"Lies." Monsieur Forêt stepped closer to Hugo, clutching the *pic à truffes* like a dagger.

Callie felt it in her bones, darkness spiraling. She felt the old man's righteous anger, Luc's ache, Hugo's vengefulness, Julien's helplessness. And as a newcomer, she had no say in the situation. She was just about to tell Eva to return Chouchou to the Forêts, and head home, when she heard the crunch of footsteps from the Lavigne side.

Callie's first thought was, *Brett.*

The ultimate bully, cut from the same cloth as Hugo. She might not be in a position to stand up to Hugo, but Brett was a different story. This time, she felt no urge to hide.

Instead, she grabbed the truffle pick from Monsieur Forêt, her knuckles white.

It was not Brett who stepped through the trees but Madame Lavigne. Still, Callie kept hold of the sharp tool. Given all the rage in the air, it was a matter of time before the *pic à truffes* became a weapon in someone else's hands.

Callie stared at her landlady, a strange forest apparition in her long black dress, white hair in a chignon falling loose and tangled with twigs, cheeks like pink apples, steely eyes blazing. As hardy as she was, her low heels weren't the best choice for forest walking. Yet it seemed she'd flown here like a true witch, defying age and other limitations, collecting leaves in her hair on the way.

Julien and Hugo rushed to her side, both exclaiming, "Maman!"

She kissed her sons, then approached and planted two big kisses on Eva's cheeks and, on cue, examined her truffle, breathing in its scent. *"Ahhh."*

She ignored the Forêts, as if they were unremarkable flora, nondescript mushrooms.

Luc said politely, "*Bonjour, madame.* Is this true? Are you forcing us out?"

Without eye contact, she puffed air from her cheeks, then gestured to Hugo. "My son just left me a voicemail, said he found a property deed." She glanced at Julien. "Apparently, it was lost for many years. So I suppose we do own the forest." Madame Lavigne's voice didn't hold the same glee as her son's—rather, something akin to resignation.

"Is it what you want?" asked Monsieur Forêt, barely containing a storm of emotion.

After a beat, Madame Lavigne's gaze flickered to him, and her energy changed too, thrumming now with resentment but also undercurrents of something else—hurt? Just as quickly, she looked away. "That's none of your business."

"You still own the estate," he pushed. "Not your sons."

"Doesn't matter." She flicked her eyes away, feigning indifference, but her entire body was shaking. "Our children inherit our estates. It's a matter of time."

Her deference to Hugo seemed out of character—but she did have a soft spot for children, maybe including her own grown ones. Maybe Hugo was an echo of Tristan, controlling his mother the way his father once controlled her. Even a strong woman could cower, especially if the manipulation was custom tailored to her vulnerabilities.

*"Tout à fait,"* said Hugo. *Exactly*. He leveled his gaze at Monsieur Forêt, slung an arm around his mother. "My mother is too old to enjoy the forest anyway."

At that, Madame Lavigne harrumphed.

Amusement flashed across Monsieur Forêt's face. An unguarded, spontaneous response that he swiftly quelled.

*"Excusez-moi,"* Eva said, earnestly looking at Madame Lavigne. She seemed to be vaguely following the conversation, at least its emotional core. "You'll still let us truffle hunt together, right? Monsieur Forêt and Luc are teaching me. It's my new dream job."

Madame Lavigne gave Eva a long look, playing with one of her curls. Finally, she said, *"Oui, ma petite."*

*"Merci!"* Eva threw her arms around Madame Lavigne's waist, then turned to Callie. "How do you say *Grammy* in French?"

When Callie paused, trying to remember, Luc answered with surprising tenderness. "Mamie Sophie."

Monsieur Forêt echoed, "Mamie Sophie," his voice hitching.

"What the hell's going on here?" Hugo's face was turning red—the situation was spinning out of his control, and clearly he did not like it.

Ignoring him, Eva hugged Madame Lavigne more tightly. *"Merci, Mamie Sophie."*

Madame Lavigne beamed—still no actual smile, but her eyes shone and her apple cheeks lifted. "I will allow the Forêts access to the entire forest to teach Eva *le cavage*. They may divide the truffles they find with her."

Losing any semblance of control, Hugo boomed his voice so loudly that Callie jumped and she found herself gripping the truffle pick anew. "But Maman, the man killed—"

His mother raised a hand, glancing at Eva. "The Forêts have one month to pass along their skills to Eva. Until the end of June. In that time, they may make arrangements for another form of income. Which, in all likelihood, will involve leaving La Chanson."

Hugo gaped—clearly, he wasn't used to her standing up to him.

"Listen," said Madame Lavigne, her expression defiant. "I want Eva to enjoy this forest—like I did when I was a girl." She looked everywhere but at Monsieur Forêt. "When I could be my deepest self. Before the cruelty of the world came in. The betrayals of those closest to me."

Monsieur Forêt found her eyes, and for a moment their gazes locked. Now, in both their expressions, something eclipsed the anger, something akin to heartbreak.

Madame Lavigne took a long breath, collecting herself. "Would you like to get the pool ready, dear?" she asked Eva. "So you can invite friends over?"

"*Oui, Mamie Sophie!* Samuel from the *boulangerie* is coming over."

"Ah, *oui*, what a sweet boy. And he's been through so much. Let's go."

Eva kissed the dogs goodbye and waved to Luc and his father, holding up the truffle and shouting, "*Merci! A bientôt!*" *See you soon!*

And she and her mamie Sophie headed back to the house, hand in hand.

---

Callie found herself alone with the men in the awkward aftermath. Keeping Eva in sight, she wordlessly handed Luc the *pic à truffes*, then leaned in for quick farewell kisses. "*Au revoir*," she said quietly, giving them time to regroup. And giving herself time.

As she walked away, she breathed in the scent of pine and earth. One month of forest tromping and truffle hunting. Then the Forêts—or at least Luc—would have to find a new source of income. There weren't many jobs in La Chanson, just family-owned businesses, and the Forêts had no seed money. Luc would have to leave town. Aix would be the likely destination—where his girlfriend lived.

Leaving the dappled light of the forest for the open meadow path, Callie listened to the river's mournful tune, almost funereal, deep indigo cello notes. Then, she heard footsteps behind her and glanced back to see the Lavigne men approaching, falling into step beside her. She leaned over to pet Fleur, whose tongue was hanging out and tail wagging.

Having composed himself, Hugo turned to Callie and said smoothly, "They're taking advantage of my mother. And you and your daughter."

Callie ignored him, letting the breeze take his words.

But Julien responded, softly, "That's not true."

Hugo raised his brow, shocked, perhaps, at his brother contradicting him. "Then they're taking advantage of you too. Human interaction isn't your strong suit."

Callie assumed this was all part of Hugo's manipulation strategy.

Witnessing this man bully his family gave her a new perspective on Brett's behaviors. Pull back the curtain on a sorcerer and there's just a pathetic man.

After a pause, Julien said, "For generations, we've shared the forest. Why should a paper change that?"

Callie was impressed. Not a single grunt.

Hugo shook his head in a mocking gesture. "You were hiding that deed, weren't you? Well, thank God I found it. You've always been a pushover."

"*Au contraire.*" Callie couldn't hold back. "Julien is a kind son, a helpful neighbor, a strong worker. Your mother is lucky to have him."

Hugo was silent for a moment, and then his voice slid out. "I like you, Calliope, and that's why I'll give you a heads-up. I'm selling the château as soon as the renovation is done."

"What?" Julien sputtered. "Our mother wouldn't—"

"Our mother is getting senile. She'll be easy to convince." He turned to Callie. "I'll send you listings of my clients' vacation rentals in the region. Mention my name and they'll give you a discount. My gift to you. Just give me your number."

She stared at him, thoroughly understanding what kind of person he was. This, she'd learned from Brett. The surface layer of amiability, but only for his own purposes. The assumption that everyone would bend to his will. The secret schemes. The indifference to the wishes and feelings of those close to him.

"No," she said simply.

He shot her a challenging look—which she matched—then he branched off from the path toward his red Alfa Romeo in the driveway.

Once he was gone, Julien said, "*Merci*, Callie."

"I was just telling the truth." Which actually, for her, was a big step. Listening to her intuition, trusting herself, speaking up to a cruel man who positioned himself as a hero.

"For more than that," Julien said softly. "You being here, your music, and Eva, and that box you found. It brings out something lost in me. The poet. The boy who loves this forest. Who stands up for it." He spoke in his usual stops and starts but without a single *euh*. "*Merci.*"

"Hugo's the one," she guessed. "The one you wished dead." As soon as the words were out of her mouth, she pressed her lips together, realizing how callous she sounded.

But Julien seemed relieved to have these words out of the box. "Yes, he is."

Julien was full of potential, Callie realized, like a source in a blocked cave, churning with secrets and poems and keys. Why, she wondered, did she care so deeply about this feud and these people?

She tried untangling her feelings. For one, she didn't want to leave the château. She'd just gotten settled in with Eva. And she didn't want the Forêts to leave. She didn't want bullies, past or present, to crush their power.

Here was what she wanted: to stand up for this forest and the people who loved it. To stand up in a way she hadn't been able to do for herself until very recently. Maybe if she could practice standing up enough, she'd stand up to Brett if he came for her. And maybe her new friends would do the same.

# 22

# BIRD OF PREY

*Colorado, five days before arrival in France*

Dear Callie,

Okay, I'll try to calmly write about what I found in Brett's office, figure out how to get out of this hell. Because that's what Hecate's key unlocked—a door to the underworld I've been living in without knowing. I'll write these facts so that if he tries to spin the truth, I'll have it here in black and white.

The locked drawer held Bluebeard's skeletons.

Oh, Callie, I don't even know how to write this.

First, I found a file labeled CALLIOPE. And it's full of detailed documentation of all my shortcomings as a mother, handwritten and dated and time-stamped. It's mostly from that first year after Nick died, when I was grief-stricken and on high doses of the pills from Brett's doctor.

The notes are in Brett's handwriting, painful reminders of what a terrible mother I was: *Callie on the couch from 10 a.m. to 6 p.m. watching sitcoms. She didn't make food for Eva. I covered breakfast, lunch, and dinner. She hasn't showered for five days. She doesn't engage in play with Eva.*

And on and on, day after day after day, the file thick with these notes. Humiliating and shameful to read. My rawest wound, my deepest fear. That I'm a bad mother. And he knows this. This is what his scalpel hovers over when I lie there, vulnerable and exposed. This is the key to him pulling my strings, controlling me. This is it.

So I looked at more recent entries, dating from just a few weeks ago. *Callie bailed on Eva's parent-teacher conference, so I had to go alone at the last minute. Lack of engagement in her school life.*

Rage shot through me. *This. Is. Not. True!* He asked me to stay home and watch the five-hour roast he decided we needed for dinner. I wanted to go, but he insisted I should relax, that he wanted to be an involved dad. Those were his words, *involved dad*. He's been doing that more and more lately, calling himself Eva's dad. Introducing himself that way. I haven't said anything. And Eva tenses whenever he says it. She's never called him dad. Not once.

His notes about the conference are lies.

And what if his other notes are lies too?

It hit me: He's been gathering "evidence" to hold over me. In case I ever try to leave with Eva. There were those visits he arranged with the Department of Child and Family Services, the social worker he charmed. All that documentation.

This is the kind of thing he does with adversaries in the antiquities business. Collects material for blackmail. Just in case. Just in case they ever stand between him and what he wants.

My hands shook as I picked up Eva's file.

I opened it.

A neck punch.

My breath left, my throat closed.

Callie, it's full of adoption paperwork in various stages of completion. He isn't just *talking* about adopting her; he's already taken steps to do it. I know his strategy from business deals. He does all the behind-the-scenes work, sweet-talks or bribes the right people, then presents the deal, nearly done, ready to sign on the highlighted lines, with blackmail ready and waiting. And if that doesn't work, well . . .

He gets his way. He always does.

Of course, he'd need my permission, but I can imagine him explaining his rationale to the social worker. That we're already common-law spouses, that he can ensure a stable life for Eva and be a loving father figure whenever I'm neglectful and unstable. Kathy would lap it up. And the documentation of my shortcomings—he can hold that over my head if I don't go along with his plan.

He's using Eva to bond me to him forever. He's making us a permanent part of his collection. I had the urge to tear up the files, burn them, anything, but of course his lawyers would have digital versions and copies. Oh, Callie, I don't know what to do, but I have to do something, and fast.

And there's more. Something maybe even more chilling.

When I returned the CALLIOPE and EVA files to the drawer, I noticed another file, labeled NICK.

It felt like a bucket of ice water thrown at me, chills moving through my body. I held my hand over the file, too scared to take it. I'd been in the office for a half hour, and I knew Brett could be watching the camera feeds from overseas, wondering what I was doing so long in the powder room, maybe suspecting I'd snuck into his office. After a moment, I closed and locked the drawer and put the key back under Hecate.

The goddess of crossroads stared at me, telling me to take a new path—but I have to think it through first, not make any mistakes. When I leave with Eva, it has to be planned out perfectly. I decided that the next day, I'd mentally prepare myself, then come back to read the NICK file.

Before I left, I looked at Pepito behind the glass. The facts clashed and clanged together in my head. Brett wanted this statue. He'd gotten it. Brett wanted me. He'd gotten me. Brett was with Nick when he died. Brett's lawyers dealt with the police. Brett got his way. Over and over, these facts are ringing out, loud and distinct as cymbals. In a clear pattern.

Callie, I wasn't brave enough to face the truth, and maybe that's why I left the NICK file in that drawer. So I just steeled myself and thought of plans to escape.

But the next day, Brett returned from his trip early, caught me with the dirty laundry. And now, the camera is fixed.

Every moment since, it's been gnawing at me, what might be in that file.

And every moment since, he's been looming, a sharp-eyed bird of prey.

More soon,
Callie

# INSIDE THE FILES

That evening in the cottage, after tucking in Eva, Callie pulled the packet of letters and three file folders from the suitcase, labeled CALLIOPE, EVA, and NICK, then dropped them onto her bed. They seemed glowing, red-hot, as if they might burn her.

*Look inside*, a part of her said.

Her hand hovered over the file labeled NICK, the only one she hadn't opened.

*Open it.*

She pulled her hand back, wrapped her arms around herself. Better to forget about it all, keep it zippered away in the dark.

She regarded his file like Pandora's clay jar. The early versions of the myth featured not a box but a Greek *pithos*—a giant cask used for wine or olive oil . . . or sometimes, human remains. Brett kept a six-foot-tall, two-thousand-year-old *pithos* in the entry hall of his "cabin," and it always gave her a little shiver, thinking of the possible dead bodies and misery once contained within it.

That was what she'd thought of back in Colorado after she'd glimpsed the NICK file, unopened.

She'd read enough versions of the myth to imagine the metaphorical suffering contained in that jar. When she'd finally managed to take his file, she couldn't find the courage to open it. Reading its contents would mean stepping into the wide world, with its clear and present dangers.

Now, she was about to stash everything back into the suitcase, when a voice inside her said, *Hope.*

In some versions, Pandora's giant clay jar also held hope. She felt Pepito's eyes on her. *It's about time*, she imagined him saying. Through the open balcony doors, the river flowed by, her moonlit ally, giving her courage.

Easing into it, as if stepping into cold water, Callie first picked up the letters she'd written to herself. She flipped back to what she now realized were red flags. It was chilling to read her letters, revisit how naked she'd felt under the constant gaze of cameras.

And she saw the facts laid before her. She saw Past Callie's mind clearing, remembering things from the haze of grief and meds, things that made more sense as she'd written them down. Things that made even more sense now, as she read about Brett's abuse. Things that she hadn't fully admitted to herself.

With a deep breath, she picked up the folder labeled CALLIOPE and forced herself to read through every last paper inside, but instead of humiliation and fear, she felt indignation. How dare he accuse her of being a negligent mother? She was a damn good mother. And he *lied*.

But the last page of the CALLIOPE file wasn't just more documentation of her incompetence. No, it was a notarized document, signed by her, giving power of attorney to Brett. Her heart thudded as if a wild predator were looming, a mountain lion watching and waiting for its moment to pounce.

With trepidation, she opened the EVA file, forcing herself to read through the adoption forms, which sickened her stomach. She'd never read through its entirety—before, even the thought of it had flooded her with dread and fear. Fear of seeing, in black and white, the staggering power she'd given this man.

Now, she made herself read every last paper, and saw with a start at the back of the EVA folder, documents she hadn't noticed before. Documents with notary seals and her shaky signature. She remembered, in strange and sudden flashes of memory, like bits of a nightmare, signing these papers for Brett's lawyer, in the deepest depths of her medicated fog.

A will, granting Brett custody of Eva if anything happened to her.

And oh, God—a notarized letter, giving Brett permission to travel across international borders with Eva.

*No, no, no.*

For a moment, she had a shred of hope that he was powerless—she'd taken the documents. But no, of course his lawyers would have their own notarized copies of everything.

She would undo this. First thing tomorrow, she'd make an appointment with a lawyer.

A knot tightened in her belly as she picked up the NICK file and set it on the cotton quilt. This folder, she'd kept shut, as if the contents might explode like unstable dynamite and rock her world to its core. She took another long breath and opened it.

She shuffled through police and law documents until her eyes landed on the words: "Cannot rule out foul play."

It knocked the wind out of her.

*Cannot rule out foul play.*

She caught her breath, forced herself to read the sentence, over and over, etch it into her mind. Then she flipped through the legal documents, realizing Brett's lawyers must have gotten involved and cleared his name. They'd been present at the interrogations, successfully argued there was insufficient evidence to charge Brett.

Lack of motive.

But there was a motive, wasn't there?

Callie and Eva and Pepito were motives.

And Brett was a killer.

In her bones, she'd known all along. The question was, what to do now?

A wave of urgency swept over her. First thing tomorrow, she'd go to the *salon du thé*, borrow Amira's laptop, research bilingual lawyers in Aix, then make an appointment. She'd figure out a payment plan if she didn't have enough money.

And she wouldn't allow Brett to intimidate her. He'd taken her husband from her. He'd taken two years from her. She wouldn't allow him to take anything else.

Brett would come for her, somehow, sometime.

And she would stand up to him.

"Want to see the pool? Want an apricot from our tree? Want to meet the ghost boy?" Eva was an enthusiastic hostess, taking Monsieur Forêt by the hand, sweeping her other hand over the grounds of the Château of the Lost.

Several days had passed since the confrontation between the Lavignes and the Forêts in the woods. Callie and Eva had been here barely a week, and already Eva was utterly and completely at home, as if she'd lived here all her life.

"Let's start with the pool," he said, setting down his accordion case.

It was the evening of the open mic soirée, and the sunlight was gently angled, the heat easing, crickets replacing cicada songs. Amused, Callie stood beside Luc, watching Eva's animated gestures as she explained the steps involved in prepping the pool to be filled.

"Now watch me and the ghost boy!" Eva said, running fifty feet to the low, ancient landscaping wall, then climbing atop it and prancing along as if it were a tightrope.

As the adults watched Eva, Monsieur Forêt sat down at the patio table and played a tune on his accordion. Callie admired the vintage instrument—lightweight and compact, which meant it had limited bass buttons but looked easier to wield than a full-size one.

A dreamy look swept over his face. "I came here as a boy to swim with Sophie. Her parents owned this place."

Ever since Madame Lavigne had permitted the Forêts to access the entire forest, he'd been talking about her with less bitterness, more ache. Luc was quiet, listening to his father, expression curious.

"When did she stop talking to you?" Callie asked.

"When Tristan—her husband—came home from the Algerian war. He'd left as an innocent twenty-year-old boy. He returned a year later as a traumatized man. We all opposed the war—it was France's last gasp at colonial power. Nothing noble about it. But he was drafted at the tail end of it, in the early sixties. And he proposed to Sophie soon after his return. She said yes."

He paused, overcome with emotion, took a moment to compose himself. "After that, she refused to look at me, speak to me. Even after he died. She believed the lies he told her. And then, she believed the lies her son told her. We were best friends growing up, and her rejection hurt more than anything. It still does."

Luc patted his father's shoulder, sharing his pain.

"Maybe she's changing," Callie said gently. "She looked at you in the forest."

"Only because of you and Eva." Monsieur Forêt sniffed, wiped his nose with his handkerchief. "You bring out her old self. She actually smiles around you two."

With perfect timing, Eva leapt down from the wall, her orange-flowered sundress and red-fringed shawl flouncing. She bowed as the adults applauded, then darted back over and announced to Monsieur Forêt, "Time for a tour!" She took his hand and led him along a stone path toward the cypresses.

Left alone on the pool patio with Luc, Callie couldn't help noticing his subtle scent of sandalwood and pine. And she couldn't avoid looking at him. He'd shaved and put on a button-down, shortsleeved shirt, his hair damp from a shower. She eyed the knees of his pants. "No grass stains."

"I'm pulling out all the stops tonight," he said. "No dog hair on my shirt either." He grinned. "I lint-rolled."

*Peluches* meant both lint and stuffed animals, and she had to smile, imagining him in a pile of teddy bears. Not the creepy ones of Brett's collection—just fun, sweet toys. Again, the contrast between the two men struck her.

She felt reluctant to admit it, but over the past week, she'd come to look forward to seeing Luc every morning in the forest—he seemed genuinely fun and spontaneous and lighthearted. Their interactions brimmed with warmth and humor, something Callie hadn't felt with a man since Nick. There'd been such ease with Nick too, the playful whimsy in their dynamic with Eva.

The truth struck her: Luc was a good man. A man to be trusted. A man she could allow in.

And this evening, she'd meet his girlfriend.

When Eva and Monsieur Forêt approached after a meticulous tour of the grounds, Callie was reluctant to end her conversation with Luc—nothing profound, just *fun*.

"The ghost boy came with us," Eva said. "He likes Papi's accordion."

"Hmm," Callie said, eyeing Monsieur Forêt, who patted his accordion case, unfazed.

Luc clapped his hands. "We should snag a table before they're filled. Ready to go?"

All week, Callie had been wavering about the open mic soirée. As much as possible, she'd pushed it to the back of her mind. She'd fallen into a daily rhythm with Eva—cleaning up the grounds, lending a hand with the renovation, wandering the forest, collecting truffles under the Forêts' tutelage, walking by the river, hanging with the *pétanque* players and their dogs in the park, running errands in town.

Still, throughout the days, people casually dropped reminders—Lili at the *boulangerie,* Violette at the *pâtisserie,* Amira at the *salon du thé*—and most of all, the water music itself, urging her onward with crescendos played fortissimo. Every night on the balcony, their duets grew stronger and smoother.

She'd distracted herself with other things, important things. For one, after borrowing Amira's laptop and Wi-Fi for research, she'd made an appointment with a lawyer, a step that brought her a mix of relief, excitement, and fear. The lawyer was bilingual, based in Aix, but she'd gone to college in California and had a background in criminal, family, and immigration law. The perfect fit.

Unfortunately, the lawyer would be on vacation for several weeks, so the soonest appointment Callie could get was in late July. Still, she was proud she'd gotten it on the calendar—now she'd have a month and a half to save up for the lawyer fees. Eva contributed some of her income from selling truffles to the *épicerie* owner—while setting aside enough money to support her macaron habit.

"Ready, Mom?" Eva chimed in, grabbing her hand.

Callie felt the river music flowing at her back, nudging her forward. "I'm ready."

As soon as she said the words, Brett's voice cut in, resounding inside her. *Egotistical. Shaking your ass onstage. Shameless.*

And then, that *no* rose inside her, a thunderous wave, a song that roared, inside and outside of her. She had the power here. She had the music and La Chanson and the warmth of friendship.

As their little group strolled toward town, the river sang in rhythm to her footsteps. *You did it, you did it!* The farther she got, the less likely she'd turn back. One step of fear, two steps of courage, forward and onward.

When Eva pointed out a silver trout flashing below the water's surface, that joke look came over Monsieur Forêt's face, and somehow, his nose grew pinker. "Why do fish swim in groups?"

Eva made some good guesses, including one about going to school, only to learn that the French say a *bank* of fish, and finally blew air from her cheeks in classic French style. "I give up. Why?"

"Because they don't feel like walking."

Eva shrieked in laughter. "Another, Papi, another!"

When she called him Grandpa, he couldn't refuse her anything. As he peppered her with jokes, Callie turned to Luc. "How can your dad remember all these? I know about three jokes."

"He says he has a twelve-set joke encyclopedia in his head."

"Which, in kid speak, translates to a hundred gigabytes of jokes."

"Exactly." He laughed. "I'm glad you decided to come tonight."

She smoothed her cotton sundress, which somehow made her braver—a Madame Lavigne hand-me-down from the seventies, and a bit musty, even after a wash. When her landlady had realized Callie only had a few sets of shorts and tees, she'd gifted her a pile of her own vintage clothes—and about half of them were actually wearable, even stylish again.

Callie had spent time defrizzing her hair, smoothing her curls with argan oil, putting on light makeup she'd bought at the pharmacy. She felt pretty, and more importantly, *strong*, as if channeling something from Madame Lavigne, from the days when she was running the safe house, wearing this same sundress, not taking flak from any men who might track down their wives.

Vaguely, Callie wondered if she'd taken an effort at her appearance because she'd be meeting Luc's girlfriend tonight. No, she decided, she just didn't want to be a sidelined ghost in life. She wanted to *live* her life.

She listened now to the encouraging voices of friends in her head, a chorus drowning out Brett's until his became a faint cartoonish squeak in the background. A part of her worried that something would possess her—that she'd hop onstage, a megalomaniac gone wild. Whenever Brett's voice snuck into her consciousness again, she imagined tossing it, squeaking and flailing, downstream.

Eva bounced along beside her papi, giddy with excitement—apparently, she and her friends had choreographed a surprise dance, which would "drop your jaw," as she put it. While Callie had been running errands in town this week, Eva had met with her new friends in the park to rehearse, under the amused gaze of Monsieur Forêt and the *pétanque* players. Her daughter's confidence astounded her.

Callie looked at Luc, feeling she should ask about his own legal situation with the forest. It wasn't lighthearted conversational material, but the deadline was looming over him and his dad. In three weeks, the Truffes de la Forêt business would close unless they figured out a way to save it.

"So, what did your lawyer say?" she asked, remembering he'd had an appointment in Aix earlier today.

"The property deed is valid." His voice dropped to a rasp. "The Lavignes have a right to keep us out of the forest."

"I'm so sorry." Her insides sank, especially knowing she'd played an unwitting role in this drama. She'd admitted this to the Forêts a few days earlier, and they hadn't held it against her—still, she felt responsible. "Any luck finding a job?"

He shook his head. "There's not much here in La Chanson. I'm looking in Aix."

"You can't just get your vet license?"

His expression closed, as if a door had slammed shut. "It's complicated."

She hesitated, aware she'd touched a nerve. "So what's your plan?"

"We'll see."

She sensed he was just as paralyzed as she'd been the past two years, disconnected from her own creative passion. She had the urge to grab his hand, take out a notebook and pen, sit down, and map out a way forward.

But no, that was not the responsibility of the new neighbor.

That was the job of a girlfriend.

As Callie entered the sumptuous, candlelit interior of the *salon du thé* with her little group, she glanced across the room and saw Lili, looking elegant in a burgundy slip dress, and beside her, Violette, in a sparkling blue top and flowy skirt. They waved with so much enthusiasm, Callie had to laugh.

The café was already crowded, the tables filled, people sitting on extra cushions and low chairs and stools, some standing along the walls. Callie smiled at familiar faces—the *pétanque* players, the *fromagerie* and *épicerie* owners, families from the park—she knew half the room. The other half probably came from nearby towns.

Amira approached with a man carrying a tray of small gilded glasses, a long-stemmed teapot, bowls of walnuts, dried dates, olives, olive oil, and a plate of still-warm Moroccan khubz bread. The scent of mint and green tea enveloped them as she kissed Callie's cheeks. "Meet my husband, Beni," she said, resting her hand on his shoulder.

"Welcome to La Chanson." His earnest brown eyes exuded kindness. He shone from the inside, just like his wife, and from the outside too—the silver trim on his white tunic complemented her shimmery *djellaba*. Sometimes, Callie felt a pang seeing two people fit together like puzzle pieces. A memory, a wish.

Weaving around tables, she spotted Julien, his mother at his side in a signature black dress, but now with a mauve scarf knotted at her neck. An unexpected splash of color. Madame Lavigne waved them over.

Callie hesitated, unsure whether the Forêts were welcome. As she and Luc exchanged glances, Eva tugged on her papi's hand and pulled him over to the Lavigne table. "Let's sit together!"

Callie could practically feel everyone's muscles tensing. She was shocked when Julien broke the silence in a clear, firm voice. "Please join us."

This was significant—she could feel it in her bones. The room's gazes followed them as the Forêts sat down. This was probably the first time these two families had shared a table in more than sixty years.

"Mamie Sophie," Eva said, "why do snails drool?" Too excited to wait for an answer, she said, "Because they always forget their handkerchiefs!"

The wine witch cracked a smile and released a puff of air that might qualify as laughter.

Callie laughed too, and then Julien and Luc joined in, as if it were contagious.

"My papi taught it to me," Eva said with pride.

"He's been telling the same jokes since he was your age," Madame Lavigne said. "Snail drool. An image that stays with you over the decades. Unfortunately." She wasn't exactly talking to Monsieur Forêt, but at least she'd acknowledged him.

He nodded in appreciation, not meeting her eyes.

Beni came around with his tray of tea, filling their tiny filigree glasses with a flourish, raising the silver pot high and creating a bubbling waterfall that sparked Eva to applaud. Beside him, Amira lifted a brow, looking back and forth between the sworn enemies at the same table.

From the corner of her eye, Callie noted a woman her age walk through the door—not a local. The stranger scanned the room, her caramel-blond hair in a wavy bob, fringe bangs, a spaghetti-strap top that showed off toned arms and a giant moth tattoo. Spotting Luc, she waved and headed toward their table.

Callie bit the inside of her cheek, willing herself to act natural.

When he stood up, the woman exchanged cheek kisses with him, then stayed close to his side, snaking her arm around his waist. She leaned over to kiss Monsieur Forêt's cheeks and gave a polite nod to the others at the table.

Callie felt her cheeks flush, damn it, but before she had to suffer through introductions, Amira climbed onstage and announced, "Welcome, my friends! Let's take our seats and get started."

Since there was no more room at the table, Luc joined the woman on cushions against the wall. Callie stared at her glass of tea, battling a hot chaos of emotion, hoping her face wasn't betraying her. From her peripherals, she saw Luc and the woman talking, heads close. Lili hadn't mentioned she was drop-dead gorgeous, only that she was a veterinarian. The vet must have lint-rolled too—there was not a trace of fur on her black silk top.

The first number was flamenco, and the performers invited the audience to dance on the floor in front of the stage. Callie noted the vet tugging at Luc's arm, but he shook his head. At least she wouldn't have to watch their hips gyrate together.

After the flamenco number, the crowd went wild with Monsieur Forêt's accordion act. And was it Callie's imagination, or did his gaze land on Madame Lavigne's? And was her landlady's face glowing from the general atmosphere or because he seemed to be playing just for her?

As Eva was twirling to old French tunes with Hamza and Samuel, Callie blinked back tears. This was the kind of childhood she'd dreamed of for her daughter. Despite two years of watching Callie dim her light around Brett, Eva was shining whenever and wherever she wanted, even inspiring other kids. Callie had made mistakes, but she deserved at least a little credit for this magnificent child.

After Monsieur Forêt bowed—to a roar of applause—and left the stage, Eva and her kid friends climbed on, shoulder to shoulder. She'd done a dress rehearsal with them at the park yesterday, guided by the *pétanque* players, while Callie ran errands.

Eva nodded to a boy who held her digital audio recorder, the one she used as her journal. He lifted the device to the mic and pressed play.

Callie recognized the music after just three notes.

It was *her song*.

The new one she'd composed for this week's whisper words. *Secret, earth, taste*. The one she'd been singing to Eva all week. First came the intro on guitar—G, C, and F chords—then her voice came in, tender and soft, a mix of English and French. Eva must have recorded it in secret at bedtime.

Fear flashed through her, but then she reasoned with herself. The audience didn't know it was Callie Byrd—and this was a new song, and the recording was low quality. She resolved to let herself sink into the moment and enjoy the interpretive dance. Here and there, Eva shot her a cautious look, and in return Callie gave her a resigned smile that said, *It's okay, sweet pea.*

Julien and Luc both glanced at Callie, recognizing the song—after all, they'd heard her singing it from the balcony. And she suspected Madame Lavigne and Monsieur Forêt knew as well—they both reached over to pat her hands.

Callie kept a polite expression pasted onto her face, and from the edges of her vision, noticed people's responses. They held hands, put arms around each other, leaned heads against shoulders, brushed cheeks, kissed lips. Violette pulled Julien onto the floor in front of the stage and danced with him, her tiny, elfish form cradled in his tall, lanky frame—and he loosened up in a way Callie had never seen before.

Callie tried not to look as the vet yanked Luc up. "Let's dance."

This time, he gave in, and as he passed Callie, his eyes flicked to hers, searching, and she forced a smile of approval. Interesting that he'd made a point to catch her gaze. Apologizing? Or asking her permission? Implying that Callie was his first choice? No, of course not. This wasn't even wishful thinking, because she was not, in fact, wishing for it.

Watching people dance, she remembered the effect her music used to have on audiences. And she saw it now—her songs weren't selfish tools of manipulation that fed her ego, as Brett claimed. She witnessed only wonder and hope filling the room. *L'espoir et la merveille.*

When the song ended, applause exploded. The kids bowed and beamed. People questioned Eva as she walked toward Callie. *What song was that? Who sings it?*

Eva gave a secret smile and locked eyes with Callie.

"That was magnificent, sweet pea." Callie pulled her into a hug.

"You're not mad?"

"*Au contraire.*"

From the corner of her eye, Callie looked at Luc and the vet woman, lingering on the dance floor, in close conversation, drawn together by the hope and wonder of her own music.

After the performances, past midnight, Callie stood on the patio between Madame Lavigne and Monsieur Forêt, as Eva and her friends splashed their hands in the petal-flecked fountain. Julien was chatting with Violette, engaged in shy flirtation, as if they were teenagers again. It felt otherworldly, staying up so late in this tiny village in the South of France as La Chanson flowed peacefully below, gleaming like an opal in the moonlight.

Until the river music shifted to a tense minor second. Callie glanced up, saw Luc and the vet approach. She braced herself for introductions.

The vet—named Mireille—was polite, perfunctory, and down to business. She spoke in an almost aloof voice, as if she were still in professional doctor mode. Her skin didn't touch Callie's as they went through the motions of air kisses and *enchantées*.

Mireille turned to Monsieur Forêt. "Sorry to hear about your truffle business closing, but we have good news. I offered Luc a job as my assistant. No license necessary. Just organizational office skills and ease with animals." She emanated satisfaction, as if she'd solved a puzzle. "He can start in three weeks."

Gravely, Monsieur Forêt looked at his son. "You'd move to Aix?"

Luc nodded with a smile that didn't quite reach his eyes. "Into Mireille's apartment."

"Workmates and roommates." Mireille took his hand.

Of course, they'd be more than roommates, Callie understood.

They'd be partners, in all senses of the word, sharing their lives, fully and completely. The sharp pain in her chest caught her off guard.

Monsieur Forêt patted Luc on the shoulder, already looking lonely at the prospect. "Have you accepted the offer?"

"I wanted to run it by you first, Papa." His eyes flickered to Callie. "But how could I refuse?"

"Congratulations," Callie said, mustering up enthusiasm and turning to Monsieur Forêt. "Eva and I will visit you and Belle every day. Promise."

He reached to take her hand, eyes shiny, smile warm. "Thank you, my dear."

From the corner of her eye, Callie noted Madame Lavigne staring at him, tears brimming. Despite her bravado, the wine witch *cared*.

# 24

# GET THE HELL AWAY

*Colorado, four days before arrival in France*

Callie, it's been so hard to get away from Brett, for even a minute. He questions my every move, even if I'm in the bathroom for more than five minutes with the door closed. He knows something is up, and he's determined to figure it out. I even had to secretly replace the pills in my prescription bottles with vitamin D, since he actually watches me taking them.

And last night, he did something that makes me wonder just how cruel he is, and not only to his enemies in the antiquities business. So, there was a fire in the fireplace, and we'd just finished an episode of *Pushing Daisies*, and he stood up to poke the logs. And he stared at that framed photo of me and Nick and Eva on the mantel.

That spontaneous one from the Rockygrass festival, with Nick sprawled on a picnic blanket, balancing toddler Eva on his feet and holding her hands and letting her pretend to fly. And me laughing, my head tossed back, guitar in my lap, blue Colorado sky behind us, and red rocks and flowing river and green grass. It captures the laughter and love and music of that day, of our life as a family.

Brett pulled the photo from the frame in a strange, violent

movement. "These reminders of Nick are holding you and Eva back. You can't move on." His face looked eerie and dangerous in the shifting shadows of firelight. "You're living in the past. It's not healthy."

I jumped up to stop him, but he'd already tossed it into the fire. It curled and burned, and inside I burned too. I bit back hot tears, tasted blood on my tongue. Of course the picture's backed up on the Cloud, but Brett could delete photos there too. He could destroy them all.

Then he put his arms around me and pulled me in, as if he hadn't just caused my anguish. As if I were a child, upset about something he'd done for my own good.

He stroked my hair and kept talking, and every word felt like a blowtorch. "Eva keeps me at arm's length because of Nick. Without him, we can be a real family. That could be us in the picture. We could take photos like that."

*No, we couldn't,* I wanted to scream, because Brett has none of the warmth and fun and spontaneity of Nick. None of the real, deep love. He could pose us like a family, but the photo would be as stiff and cold and lifeless as the statues in his collections.

He smoothed my curls, and I winced and watched over his shoulder as the photo vanished into flames. I bit my tongue even harder, gnawed on the inside of my cheek, secretly tearing myself up, tasting iron and fury. I can't show him I care or he'll destroy every other memento of life with Nick.

And for the past three days, even though he's tried to get me to stop thinking about Nick, the photo-burning has only made me think about him more. From before we even had Eva, back when we were in our early twenties and so innocent, so undamaged by life.

Remember the café where Nick and I met? I had that awful waitress job, and every customer just ordered a cup of coffee and kept asking for refills, and after they were whacked-out on caffeine, asked for glasses of water and sugar packets and lemon wedges and made their own lemonade, and five hours later paid two dollars for the coffee and a quarter for a tip.

And it was fun, wasn't it, how we bumbled through post-college life, and Nick and our friends clapped like wild at every open mic night, and how we drank beer and smoked weed and sang and played guitar at bonfires in scraggly backyards and wrote music on the spot . . . how we recorded in friends' bedroom studios in exchange for bottles of cheap wine, and how here and there, on a whim, I'd put a song on the streaming platforms . . . how spontaneous and wild it all felt.

And there was the strange July when "Fly, Fly Away" went viral.

And the whirlwind of how, by New Year's, I was recording in a real studio and putting out an album with a label, and within a year, I was on tour at big music festivals and venues, and it was all so surreal.

And Nick, thank God for Nick, keeping me grounded, always reminding me who I was and why I was making music, and just looking into my eyes and laughing with me at the strangeness of it all, like it was our secret. How he came along with me whenever he wasn't away on a dig. How bizarre it felt to be slightly famous, at least in the indie singer-songwriter crowd, having money to pay back student loans and quit that crappy café job.

And that sunny, cold day Nick and I got married in Colorado, and another celebration weeks later, that rainy, warm day in his Guatemalan village, and how I sang along with a local band and danced amid hundreds of balloons and tamales.

And how, after Eva came, we did those outdoor festivals, and how Nick danced with her while I was performing, and yes, of course it ended up being harder than it sounded—diapers and snack time and naptime and colds and changes of clothes, and watching an adventurous toddler and childproofing everything everywhere we went on every tour—but we made it work.

Remember how he'd bring her to shows and she'd sit on his shoulders and clap? And I'd look into the audience and see them and feel how much we three loved each other, and I'd sing and play guitar and dance and talk to the audience between songs, and I felt those silver-gold threads running through me and every person listening, all of us weaving this blanket of music and love.

And people would message and post about how they felt this too, how they decided to get married after my show, or reached out to an estranged sibling or a long-lost friend. Dozens, then hundreds, then thousands of these messages about how my music connected people. *Our* music, I'd think as I read them.

God, I loved being onstage, loved feeling the music flow from an underground spring and feeling it sparkling, moving through me, through the crowd, lifting us up, letting us all fly, fly away.

I wonder if I'll get the courage to fly away with Eva.

If I'll ever feel that way about music again.

And more secretly, if I'll ever feel that way about a man again. If I'll ever have a family again.

Mom called yesterday, three months late, to wish me a happy birthday. Brett answered, put her on speaker phone, like he always does. He's like a dictator that way—discouraging private conversations where mutiny might occur. Stamping out secret alliances before they even start.

He listened to her go on and on about the expat dramas in her Ecuadorian town, acting riveted and monitoring my shallow interactions with her. "Oh, Brett, you're the best," Mom said, winding up the conversation after ten minutes. "Callie's lucky to have you. Now you give her a big birthday hug for me!"

Afterward, as always, he diagnosed her flaws: narcissistic, selfish, flighty, senile, and on and on. As if to say: *Why would you want to confide anything in this unstable woman?* The same tactic he'd used with all my friends, I realize now.

All day, I've had the usual empty feeling that lingers after conversations with her. The feeling of longing, wishing I'd grown up in a real family with caring parents. Involved grandparents. Maybe siblings or at least cousins or even close family friends to provide some sense of continuity.

But there were none—we moved every few years, according to Mom's whims. Her traveling nursing jobs in random, out-of-the-way places. A different man every few years. There was never abuse or neglect, but she was always distant, wrapped in her own dramas.

You learned to exist quietly, Callie, to be what she needed. Remember how relieved she seemed when you left for college on that music scholarship? It felt like she was dusting off her hands, done with her parental duties, free to be as flaky as she desired.

Still, she loves you, of course she does. Why did it take until your thirties to find a truce with her? A way to be that felt good enough? But then, Brett stuck a wrench in that fragile bond. It was too easy for him to break it. She's a threat to him. Anyone who loves me is.

He knows how deeply I've craved a real family for Eva. And for myself. How I'd treasured it with Nick. He uses it against me, trying to convince me to marry him, to somehow force Eva to love him like a father.

"You know I'm your only chance for a family at this point," he told me last night when we were getting ready for bed. "What sane man would want a washed-up singer and her weird daughter?" He said it in a light, joking way, but of course it was a scalpel, slicing around my fears and longings.

He pulled me onto the bed and kissed me.

I flinched and my mind filled with thoughts of leaving him.

Of how life outside this castle prison could be.

A whole world out there.

Callie, I'm burning and blazing with determination.

The words looped through me all night: *Get the hell away.*

And weirdly, this morning, when Brett was on a trail run, Eva echoed this. She looked up from her yogurt snack and said matter-of-factly: "Daddy's ghost says it's time to leave. Like, yesterday."

A chill passed over me. Eva's always telling me how Nick chitchats with her, mostly saying funny things like, *Ooh! I love your outfit,* mi vida. *The pink stripes go great with the green hearts and orange cat print.* Or, *Oh,* mija, *you should definitely get a dog! Today!*

She's funny and lighthearted and quirky, just like Nick was. And already brilliant at languages too. Of course, he had an advantage with Spanish and Mayan, growing up in Guatemala, but then his brain just absorbed English when he moved to Colorado on scholarship. And he picked up French and Portuguese through pure osmosis in his archaeology work.

Eva says his ghost speaks in a mix of Spanish and English and sometimes even French. *¡Cómprate un perrito, mijita!*

*Achète-toi un petit chien, ma petite! Buy yourself a little dog, my little daughter!*

But this morning, there was no silly ghost talk. She licked the last of the yogurt from her spoon and gave me a long look. "Daddy says we have to get the heck away."

So, let's get the heck away, Callie.

Love,
Callie

# DRAGON

Of course, word got out that it was Callie's song at the open mic soirée—one of the kids must have told a parent, and it had spread from there. By the next afternoon, during her errands in town, nearly everyone in La Chanson was asking her to perform—the shopkeepers, the parents at the park, the *pétanque* players, the river itself. Luc and his father were exceptions. They hadn't brought it up during the morning truffle hunt, perhaps sensing her secrecy.

Neither had Julien, who was on cloud nine about Violette, stretched so tall he was floating. Callie couldn't help mentioning his transformation to her at the *pâtisserie*. In response, Violette dropped extra macarons into the paper bag with silver tongs. "Your song brought us together," she declared. "After four decades!"

It was just the two of them in the shop—Eva was at the park—but even so, Violette leaned in. "I fell in love with him because of his poetry. We were thirteen. Once, he shared it in class, and it was the most beautiful thing I'd ever heard. Poems about simple things—forests and dogs and the river, but it touched my soul. He started reciting his poems to me as we walked home from school."

*There's someone I like, named after a springtime flower.* Callie thought of the tiny notebook in Julien's shirt pocket—a pocketful of poems—the pen sticking out earnestly as he headed into the woods early every morning with Fleur. "Why did you wait so long, Violette?"

A shadow passed over her face. "In junior high school, his brother stole his notebook and read his poems out loud. Hugo acted like he was bragging about his brother, but I could tell he was making fun of him. Hugo pretends to be nice while he's secretly plunging a knife. Julien was mortified. After that, he locked away the poet in him."

"That's horrible."

Violette nodded. "After school that day, Hugo tossed the notebook back to Julien and called him a loser. They didn't see me watching. Then Julien threw it into the river and ran home. I rescued it. I put it in the sun on a clothesline, kept moving the pages so that each one dried. I still have it."

She reached beneath the counter, pulled out a warped, yellowed notebook. "I like to read it when there's a pause between customers. One day I'll return it."

Callie peered at the handwriting on the graph paper, the same curlicue flourishes as the writing in the secret box. "That day has come, *mon amie*." She locked eyes with Violette. "Let your selves shine."

"Maybe." Violette gave a flustered smile. "Listen, will you sing at the open mic soirée? I want to dance with him again." She dropped another pink macaron in the bag, folded the top.

Callie eyed it. "Is this a bribe?"

"And there's more where that came from," Violette whispered with a laugh.

Hours later, back home, Callie reclined in a lounge chair with her guitar, watching Eva skim a long net over the pool's surface, freshly filled with turquoise water, glittering in the sunlight. Julien supervised her, helping her aim the net for fallen leaves and bugs, offering her an encouraging "*euh*" here and there.

Every so often, both Eva and Julien would glance at a spot by the silver-leafed olive tree in the garden. Eva had claimed that Julien saw the ghost boy too, that when she'd asked him about it, "he grunted in the way that means yes."

"You understand his different grunts?" Callie had asked.

"*Euh* means yes. *Euh euh* means no. *Eughhhhh* means maybe."

Now, on impulse, Callie waved him over. As he approached, she noticed the tiny poetry notebook in his pocket. How many of those had he secretly filled over the decades?

"Hey, Julien," she ventured, "why not ask Violette over for dinner sometime?"

He pinkened. "Think I should?"

"And read her your poetry," she added, motioning to his pocket. "Show her who you really are."

He blinked, tilted his head, put his palm over his chest, and for a moment Callie feared she'd overstepped.

A smile spread across his face. *"Euh."*

Which, according to Eva's Julien glossary, meant *oui*.

Days passed in a blur of forest wandering and truffle hunting and flower gardening. Callie had every intention of singing for Julien and Violette at the open mic soirée—really, she did. It would be a short, sweet song with the new whisper words—*lemon, moon,* and *petal*.

But at the last minute, she found herself bowing out, claiming exhaustion from an afternoon of cutting lavender and picking cherries.

The Forêts tried hiding their disappointment as they took Eva without her. Callie felt a pang, missing out on the highlight of the week, but she rationalized that it was too risky to mix tourists and music and a stage. And maybe, at the heart of it, she dreaded seeing Luc and Mireille dancing together again.

On Sunday, the day after the open mic, a buoyant energy filled Callie—the long-awaited playdate with Samuel and Lili had arrived. The heat was sweltering, the sky cloudless, perfect pool weather. Reclined beside Lili on their lounge chairs, Callie watched Eva do a cannonball off the edge, letting out a whoop in the air before the huge splash.

Samuel did the same, his mouth wide open with the thrill of it.

Lili let out a little shriek as cold water sprinkled her legs. She and Callie were fairly drenched on the sidelines, watching joy spew out everywhere in tiny, magical droplets. Lili's face lit up, fully and completely, as she observed her son.

She'd canceled Samuel's playdate a couple times over the past week, but now they were finally making it happen. He hadn't been feeling well, she'd explained, her eyes shiny as she slid baguettes into paper sleeves. To which Eva had reassured her, "The good thing is, we'll have water to play in then."

And now, Lili's eyes shone again. "I'm so happy he's happy."

Callie reached over, put her hand on Lili's, surprising herself with this gesture, and Lili smiled in appreciation.

They were sipping chilled rosé, which Madame Lavigne had picked out specifically for this pool date, "to bond with your new friend, dear." And the rosé was, indeed, smoothing out any new-friend-date awkwardness like peachy-pink silk—not from the alcohol content, but from something more ethereal.

"Your landlady is a true wine wizard," Lili announced, tilting her glass.

"Indeed." Callie took another sip of hers, savoring it.

They went on to exchange observations about their kids in the endlessly fascinated way that mothers do—how Samuel had a gentleness about him, a contrast to Eva's boldness, but how they played to each other's strengths.

He shared his mesh bag full of pool toys and goggles and flippers, and they dove for coins until, after a half hour, Lili cupped her hands around her mouth and called, "Time for a break!"

After Lili wrapped Samuel in a towel, he and Eva settled into playing Papillon with warped cards—from what Callie could tell, a Go Fish–style game involving beetles, grasshoppers, and little butterflies. When Samuel raised his arms and shouted, "Butterfly," his towel fell away, and this close, Callie noticed a long, pink vertical scar from just below his neck to his sternum. Open-heart surgery, she guessed, or something equally invasive.

When his lips went from purple back to pink after a half hour, Lili said he could go back into the pool. With renewed energy, Eva whooped and dunked him—a little too aggressively, Callie thought. She leapt up, ready to say something, but Lili put a hand on her arm. "Let them play. The kids in town treat him like he's made of glass. He's had five surgeries so far—we're hoping the one from March will be his last, that he'll have a normal childhood from now on."

"I get it," Callie whispered.

It was strange to see Lili outside the context of the *boulangerie*, and not just because she was showing Callie the tender parts of her life. Instead of the usual black apron, she wore a gorgeous, bold white bikini with a gauzy ivory wrap that showed off her golden legs—her natural skin color, Callie thought a bit wistfully, the kind that wouldn't burn in two seconds flat. Lili's hair, always tied back in the shop, now tumbled in shades of chestnut over her shoulders.

Callie, of all things, was wearing a hand-me-down swimsuit from Madame Lavigne, a one-piece, black with diagonal stripes of fluorescent pink, green, and yellow. It screamed 1980s and fit surprisingly well. Decades ago, Madame Lavigne had worn this, maybe with permed hair and jelly sandals, although Callie really couldn't imagine that. Had she ever lounged at the pool with the mothers and children who were taking refuge here?

"My last swimsuit," Madame Lavigne had said with a sigh. "By the nineties, there were enough women's shelters that my services were no longer needed. A good thing, of course. Just one or two women came with their children every year. I opened my wine shop, but the château stayed empty and the pool went dry. And seeing it full again—I'm *aux anges*."

*With the angels, over the moon*. Which is how Callie felt now, with her new mom friend.

"Love your suit," Lili said with genuine enthusiasm. "So vintage."

"*Merci*. It's Madame Lavigne's."

Lili widened her eyes, sputtered a laugh. "I never would've guessed!"

"Right? I didn't bring my own suit. We left in a hurry."

Lili gave a sympathetic smile, as if she could imagine, somehow, the long story beneath those words. "Well, good for you for leaving."

Unspoken emotion passed between her and Callie. Someday, Callie decided, she'd dive into it all with Lili, but for now, this acknowledgment—*good for you*—was enough.

Lili leaned back in the lounge chair, tucking her arms behind her head. "Well, I'm always clearing out my closet. An excuse to shop. I'll bring you more clothes."

"*Merci*," said Callie, for more than the clothes—for this new level of friendship. "I'd love a wardrobe from this millennium."

"My pleasure." Lili closed her eyes and turned her face to the sun. "I used to adore dressing up and going out. Before Samuel was born, we lived in Aix, went to shows all the time—we had a busy bakery there—and our lives were so . . . *lively*."

"Life is pretty lively now," Callie said, watching the kids dolphin dive. It struck her how precious this all was, this *liveliness*—her friends, the château, the cottage, the pool, the dogs, the river.

Would Hugo really convince his mother to sell this place when the renovation was done? Already, in the two weeks Callie had been here, Julien had made impressive progress, refusing to slow down under the threat of his brother selling the place. Although she couldn't shake off worries about the estate being sold, his work ethic impressed her.

Thanks to her gardening, the grounds were looking sumptuous, something from a full-color real estate listing. She guessed the interior work might be done within a month—at least on the ground floor. She wasn't sure how plans might unfold for a second floor renovation, but she hoped Madame Lavigne would insist on keeping the château, come what may. Callie was feeling more and more invested in her new home every day.

She raised her glass of rosé to the blue sky. "To liveliness."

"To liveliness." Lili clinked her glass and took a long sip. "Samuel was born with a heart condition. Complex and major. My whole life became Samuel and hospitals. My husband kept our *boulangerie* going in Aix, just barely. Five years ago, we moved here, for country air for Samuel. La Chanson helps his heart—both the community and the river—I swear it syncs to his rhythms."

"I believe it." Callie listened to the burbling melodies now, a sunshiny soundtrack.

"He's doing so well now. He gets tired sometimes, but he's feeling good."

"That's great," said Callie, watching him go along with Eva's somewhat bossy instructions for their synchronized swimming routine. Earlier, she'd overheard her telling Samuel that the ghost boy was applauding from the sidelines. Samuel had nodded along.

Lili made a sound between a sigh and a laugh. "Now that we could actually leave him with a friend and go out, I can't find the person I used to be."

"She's still in there." Callie tilted her head. "Maybe an even better version."

After an amusing synchronized swimming performance, Eva climbed out of the pool and dried off, teeth chattering, with Samuel following. "Can I show him the secret room?" She leaned close to Callie, wrapping her cold arms around her neck. In a stage whisper in English, she added, "The ghost boy wants me to take him there."

Callie wondered vaguely if Lili had caught the word *ghost* in English, but she didn't see a reason why the kids shouldn't play there. Eva had no toys of her own in the cottage, and that secret room held the motherlode. They wouldn't be bothering Julien—he was in town picking up a *tarte aux fruits* from Violette at the *pâtisserie*. He'd had quite the sweet tooth lately.

"Okay, sweet pea, but wear flip-flops, and don't touch any construction stuff, got it?"

"Got it, Mom."

Once the kids disappeared into the château, Lili poured more rosé, then lowered her voice. "Now, speaking of the people we used to be, everyone's noticed the old Luc coming back. Since you arrived."

Callie took her own long sip of rosé. "We're just friends." She steadied her voice. "His girlfriend offered him a job. Asked him to move in with her."

Lili waved the words away. "Of course, he should refuse. His feelings for you are clear."

Callie swallowed. "What do you mean?"

"When you're with Luc, there's fun and laughter and connection. But with Mireille, things are cold and heavy and practical. I mean, she's perfectly nice, but there's no spark between them. No real warmth."

Callie leaned back in the lounge chair and sipped her rosé, cool and floral, trying to tame her emotions. "Well, he needs a job and a place to live in Aix. Within two weeks. That's when the Forêts have to close their business. No more truffle hunting in the forest."

Lili propped her head on her hand. "Why, exactly?"

"Hugo found a deed that proves the Lavignes own the forest. He's kicking them out. He wants to sell this place."

Lili shook her head in confusion. "But his mother owns the estate."

"Seems like she defers to him for most things."

"Well, tell her not to."

Callie raised her brow, surprised at Lili's vehemence. "He's her son."

"So is Julien." Lili's voice rose with indignance. "And he loves this place."

"It's out of my hands."

Lili harrumphed. "You and your daughter, you're already changing people in this town. In a good way." She leaned in, a conspiratorial gesture. "Convince Madame Lavigne to let the Forêts keep using half the forest. Convince her not to sell. *Et voilà*, problem solved. Problems *plural*. The Forêts keep their business. Luc stays. *Adieu*, Mireille."

Callie sputtered a laugh. "It's not that simple."

"Heart surgery isn't simple. Escaping abuse isn't simple. Ending an old feud isn't simple." Lili raised a brow. "But it's all possible, isn't it?"

Callie was starting to feel a spark of possibility, when she heard Eva shriek, "Mom!"

Alarmed, she shot up and saw her daughter racing out of the château, Samuel at her heels. Breathing hard, Eva held out a small tin box, its lid painted with fluffy brown puppies—maybe from the early-mid 1900s, judging by the style and font, the rusted edges and hinges. "Look inside, Mom!"

A bit wary, Callie opened it, her gaze landing on a tiny metal figurine of a white dog—a terrier?—and another figurine of a boy in a blue sweater with orange-blond hair comically sticking up.

Samuel pointed triumphantly to the boy and dog. "Tintin and Milou! Right, Maman?"

"*Oui*." Lili picked up the two figurines. "The secret agent boy and his loyal dog. From the classic comic." Then she picked up another one, a man with a feather in his cap. "One of the Three Musketeers?"

"I think so," said Callie, her mind spinning. Monsieur Forêt had mentioned that he and Madame Lavigne and Tristan—her late husband—had played the Three Musketeers as children in the forest. But there was only one musketeer in this box.

At the bottom of the box was a sepia-toned photo. She picked it up carefully and studied the three children posed by a river. La Chanson. She knew the exact spot, the shape of limestone outcroppings in the background. A girl was flanked by two boys, all about Eva's age. Hands on hips, chins raised high. The boy on the left had a child-sized accordion strung around his neck. The boy on the right held a guitar.

She squinted, recognizing the guitar that Julien had loaned her, the one she played for hours daily. Her gaze lingered on the boy holding it. He wore a beret with a feather in it, channeling a musketeer.

A breeze blew through the garden, rustling the olive leaves, and sweeping up something else inside the box—a white feather that landed right in Eva's lap.

Eva picked it up, waving it around, jumping up and down, unable to contain her excitement. She pointed to the spot beneath the olive tree. "That's him in the picture, Mom! The ghost boy! This is his box!"

Cicada songs swelled as Callie walked by the river on the way to town in the freshness of morning. It was a few days after the pool date, and she still felt full of the warmth of friendship, of the camaraderie of another mom, joined by their love of their kids, who had both been through their own traumas. Eva's imagination surrounding the ghost boy astounded Callie, but part of her wondered if he was, somehow, the childhood version of Julien's father, a restless spirit, a long-lost little boy.

The mystery of the latest secret box intrigued her too, and she turned over possible paths ahead in her mind—should they ask Julien about it? Or go straight to Madame Lavigne? Or even Monsieur Forêt?

Maybe, just maybe, it could be a pathway toward reuniting the two old friends. If that succeeded, maybe Madame Lavigne would reconsider kicking out the Forêts. Maybe Luc wouldn't have to take the job and leave. Maybe some version of Lili's advice could actually work.

Callie felt hope, too, from the sweet romance of Julien and Violette. She loved seeing it play out before her eyes, witnessing their true selves bond, their young-at-heart, poetry-loving souls, like jewels unearthed and finally held to the light.

Eva was truffle hunting with her papi, and Callie felt clear-minded, elated even, with time alone to reflect on next steps. The open mic soirée was coming up. The whisper words were *key, honey, stars,* and she'd been singing the song they inspired all week, every evening. She regretted missing last week, wished her fears hadn't held her back. Should she venture onstage this time?

She whispered it aloud to the river, as if asking an oracle: "Will I perform?"

When she reached the turnoff for town, she found herself passing it by, continuing uphill along the river, amid rosemary and lavender, toward the source of La Chanson.

At the cave entrance, tucked into a limestone cliff, she paused, breathless, leaning against the rough stone. Then, gathering courage, she peered inside at the dark, deep water far below, flowing through secret caverns.

She heard a rumble—the carnyx? The powerful bass note was filling her, gathering force, transforming into a roar, maybe the very roar the Celts had used during battles. And now it was scaring off her own enemies—any last remnants of Brett's voice in her head fleeing downstream like defeated cartoon soldiers.

She gazed, mesmerized, at the water, unknowable in the shadows, until a sunbeam found its way in, at just the right angle, and reached into the depths with a flash of blue-green. Light reflected off bronze, and she glimpsed the carnyx. It was *real,* this instrument.

She heard her voice emerge like a dragon's. And she felt her selves join. Singer and listener became one and the same.

Here was her answer.

*Yes.*

Yes, she would get back onstage.

Yes, she would share her voice.

Yes, she would enter the world.

*Yes.*

# 26

## DANGEROUS

*Colorado, three days before arrival in France*

BRETT IS DANGEROUS, CALLIE.

Don't forget it.

Don't let him convince you otherwise.

Don't let wishful thinking blind you.

You've been very good at sweeping this danger under the rug, making excuses, conveniently pushing it from your mind, tamping it down, giving him second chances.

Don't do it again.

He is dangerous and you need to get away somewhere he can never find you. If you leave, it has to be for good. If he discovers where you are, he will stop at nothing to get you back.

LEAVE AND STAY HIDDEN!

Okay, enough pep-talking. Here's the deal: Brett's been so suspicious, he's fast-tracking his plans. Which means I need to fast-track mine.

Last night, after I put Eva to bed, I sat on the couch beside him, ready to watch a show, when he brought out a bottle of champagne and two flutes.

"What's this for?" I asked, feeling dread.

"I'm going to be Eva's father."

My throat went dry. "What?"

"My lawyers are expediting the adoption paperwork. You just have a few things to sign and we'll have the social worker appointment. Kathy's on board. They'll process things on their end, and soon enough, I'll be Eva's dad."

I swallowed and jumped at the cork pop and watched him pour the champagne. Of course, I knew this was coming, but hearing him say the words with such finality chilled me.

He handed me the glass and clinked his against mine and took a sip.

I didn't drink mine. "That's so sweet of you," I began, my hand shaking, a little tsunami brewing in the wine flute. "But she still thinks of Nick as her dad. She's not ready."

"It's been two years." His voice was authoritative, bordering on exasperated. "She needs to move on."

"I know, but I don't want to force her."

"Let's face it. I'm already her dad. I go to her parent-teacher conferences, I pay for everything, I feed her, I drive her everywhere." He put an arm around me, rubbed my back.

I tried not to flinch. I knew I had to get out, to take Eva and run. Use money from that secret account.

"Kathy's doing the home visit. She'll help us finish the paperwork. She already knows the situation, so she'll make it all breeze through."

Kathy. The social worker he'd charmed and fed lies to—under the guise of being concerned for my mental health and Eva's well-being.

"My best lawyer will be here too. He's already taken care of my background check and other details. Just a few more hoops."

I nodded numbly. This wasn't a question or suggestion. This was a done deal. And if I didn't agree, he had enough documentation to get Child and Family Services involved. If I refused, was my so-called incompetence enough to have Eva taken away from me? I had no idea. But I wouldn't put it past him to go a step beyond exaggerating to inventing negligence.

"When are they coming?" I asked, keeping my voice steady.

"Thursday at two."

Which means I have two days to figure out how to fly away.

And I swear I won't ignore it this time.

BRETT IS DANGEROUS.

Be brave,
Callie

# THE TOURISTS

Several days after Callie's glimpse of the carnyx, its dragon roar still reverberated inside her, a deep hum, as she got ready for the open mic soirée. She brushed on light makeup and smoothed her hair, letting it tumble loose over her shoulders. With a sigh, she studied her reflection in the vintage, slightly wavy mirror, feeling a zing of excitement at the slip dress Lili had given her, the deep teal of La Chanson at twilight.

This morning, Lili had dropped off a bag of gorgeous clothes culled from her closet—silks and linen and cashmere, made in Paris. Like nothing Callie had worn the past two years, or ever, really. Back when she'd been performing, her fashion-guru drummer helped her pick out clothes for shows, in tune with little details, like how sequins could add magic, or which colors would set Callie's hair ablaze in the spotlights.

When Callie had tried on the dress, Lili had gasped with drama, then waxed poetic about how it accentuated her eyes, contrasted with her hair—which made Callie think fondly of her drummer. Having new friends was making her miss her old, estranged ones. She'd have to do something about that.

When the Forêts arrived, Callie grabbed her bag and her freshly restrung guitar in its case, and stepped outside, leaning in for cheek kisses.

"My dear," said Monsieur Forêt in his grandfatherly voice, "you look *ravissante*." *Enchanting*.

Luc stared and stumbled over his *bonsoir,* then echoed his father. "*Ravissante.*"

Callie felt her cheeks pinkening and was grateful when Monsieur Forêt turned to Eva. "And you look even more *ravissante* than usual, *ma petite.*"

Lili had gifted her a pile of silk scarves, one of which Eva wore now, a cherry-red one, tied artfully at her neck.

"And Chouchou looks *ravissante* too," said Eva.

The puppy wore a pink bow, ready to perform with her and her papi in a truffle-hunting skit, with accordion to set the mood. They'd been practicing all week, and the skit became more elaborate with every rehearsal—they'd even managed to incorporate the Emile Zola line, "*J'accuse!*" with the pup pointing her paw at the villain, and Eva acting as ventriloquist. Somehow, it worked.

As they walked along the river, Eva and her papi meandered off the path, following the pup, and leaving Callie alone with Luc. She pretended not to notice the glances he kept sneaking at her.

"Your lint-rolling was *ravissant* tonight," she said playfully. "Simply enchanting."

"Well, I still have grass stains on these pants," he pointed out.

"Brings out the grass-stain green in your eyes." Catching herself moving into flirtation territory, she cooled her voice. "So, have you officially accepted the job?" She didn't ask her unspoken question: *Will you move in with your girlfriend?*

"Not yet. I just—it doesn't feel right. There has to be another way."

Callie wanted to ask again, *How about getting your vet license?* He could set up a practice here—he already had clientele. But last time, that question had shut him down. Instead, she pulled the little tin box from her purse and handed it to him. She'd shown it to Julien this morning, and he'd cautioned against showing it to his mother, worried it could set her off. He'd told Eva and Callie they could keep it.

Now, Callie held it out to Luc. "Eva found this in the château."

He examined the figurines, then lingered on the photo, wonder in his expression. "This must be my dad and Tristan and Madame Lavigne. They called themselves the Three Musketeers. And they played Tintin together—joked that my dad looked like him. He even named his truffle dog Milou."

"Think we should show it to them?"

Luc rubbed his face, considering. "There's a reason all this has stayed buried, Callie. It might just bring up bad feelings."

"Or good ones," Callie pointed out. "If they become friends again, maybe Madame Lavigne will let you keep access to the forest."

"We'd have to do it carefully. They both have decades of anger."

The river music fiddled a wistful tune. "Heartache," said Callie.

Luc handed her back the box, and then, as if he'd rehearsed it, said, "Mireille isn't coming tonight."

Callie tucked the box back into her handbag, trying not to show her relief. "Oh, okay."

"She was upset I didn't say yes right away. To the job or living together." He ran a hand through his hair. "She's frustrated I won't move forward. So I suggested we take a break, figure things out."

"Hmm." Callie's heart lifted as La Chanson crescendoed in a flurry of strings.

When they reached the turnoff to town, Eva and Monsieur Forêt and Chouchou joined them again. Callie breathed out, glad for the distraction—she had no idea how to respond to Luc's admission. A show of sympathy would be ingenuine, but encouraging him to make the breakup with the vet permanent would be unethical. Not to mention, Callie wasn't exactly making herself available.

The sun was setting in smears of gold and apricot when they reached the *salon du thé*. When they stepped inside, Julien and Violette waved them over, sitting close together, hand in hand. Once again, Madame Lavigne allowed the Forêts to sit at the table, although she and Monsieur Forêt made only indirect eye contact through their adopted granddaughter. Luc ended up sitting next to Callie, as if the universe—or at least others at the table—had orchestrated it.

Eva's and her papi's performance was a hit—raucous laughter and cheers all around as the pup sniffed for truffles that the "villain" had hidden under cushions and behind plants, to the comical accordion soundtrack. Madame Lavigne, looking oddly colorful in a blue scarf and purple belt over her black dress, kept sneaking surreptitious glances at Monsieur Forêt.

Callie felt her own gaze returning to Luc—his blue linen shirt, his tan forearms, sun-kissed cheeks, genuine grin as he watched the performers. And the endearing details: his slightly overlapping front left tooth, the tiny mole on the right side of his neck, the way his left eyebrow was a bit unruly. When he found something extra funny, he'd toss back his head and squeeze his eyes shut, then shake his head appreciatively.

According to the lineup on the chalkboard, Callie's performance would be the last of the evening, and the wings in her belly fluttered the closer it came. When her turn arrived, the room erupted with shouts of "Callie, Callie, Callie!"

For a moment, she sat frozen, hearing her heart thud in her ears in rhythm to their clapping. She willed her legs to move. There would be no going back after this. She would be opening herself to La Chanson, which would open her to the world, which would make her vulnerable in so many ways.

Eva stood up and took her hand. "Ready, Mom?"

Callie met her eyes, then glanced at Luc, who gave her an encouraging nod. Eva led her onstage, spread her arms, and announced with theatrical flair, "*Bonsoir, mesdames et messieurs*. This is my mom!"

"Thanks, sweet pea." Callie kissed her daughter's head, then looped the guitar strap over her shoulder and checked the tuning. She listened to the river through the open patio doors, took in everyone's quiet anticipation, the clinks of glasses, the muffled whispers.

And she drew in a deep, opening breath, the way she did every night on the balcony. Here and now, her friends were the firmament, lifting her up. "*Merci* for welcoming us into your lives, *mes amis*."

She plucked out the first notes, and then she sang. Her voice flowed up and out like La Chanson itself, full and resonant, and she felt all parts of herself together, united, incandescent as a swirling galaxy. Over-the-top, maybe, but after two years of hiding, she deserved over-the-top. As she sang about honey and keys and stars, the river swelled, and her chest expanded and body swayed and foot tapped, and it all felt so *right*. And yes, maybe she did shake her ass a bit.

The children started dancing first, led by Eva, and then adults pulled one another onto the impromptu dance floor in front of the stage. The song lasted both forever and a split second, and afterward there was silence, breaths held, and then an explosion of applause. Everyone who wasn't already dancing stood up, shouting for an encore. "*Une autre!*"

"*Merci*." Callie tried to return to her seat, but like a river, her friends swept her back onstage. She stood before the mic, mentally shuffling through new songs she'd composed over the past weeks. But her true voice was now taking the driver's seat. And her true voice was neither modest nor shy. Her true voice wanted to perform *the song*.

The song that went viral a decade ago.

The song that launched her career.

The song that still played in stores, restaurants, bars.

The song that went global.

With the wildest abandon, Callie sang "Fly, Fly Away."

Afterward, Callie slipped outside to the back patio of the *salon du thé*, feeling the urge to be near the moonlit river. Under her breath, she whispered thanks to it for having her back. She had sung in public. And the world was still spinning.

Friends approached her, asking her to perform again next week, thanking her for the music, sharing how it made them feel. Hope and wonder was the refrain. *Espoir* and *merveille*. Hugging and hand-clasping, Callie kept one eye on Eva, who was inside, riding a natural high with her friends, giddy to be awake at midnight.

Once people started trickling out, Callie found herself alone with Luc. "*Merci*," he said simply, his voice quivering with emotion.

She turned to face him fully. Beside them, the river music rose, passionate now, with an undercurrent of *wink-wink* and *finally!* She moved toward him, and he cupped her face and stroked his finger down her cheek, giving her a frisson of pleasure. She stepped closer and wrapped her arms around him with the same abandon she'd felt performing "Fly, Fly Away." He drew her face to his and leaned in.

And they kissed, lips warm against the cool night air. The kiss was a key, unlocking something soft and honeyed, earthy and foresty, starlit and sunlit. They pulled each other closer still, and she clasped the back of his neck as his hand pressed against the small of her back. Just the two of them in this secret pocket of the universe.

After a long moment—with reluctant awareness that they were not, in fact, alone—Callie drew back and murmured, "To be continued."

"There's nothing I want more," he whispered, and pulled her in for one more quick kiss.

Arm in arm, they walked inside. Callie picked up her guitar, which she'd tucked into its case and left beside the stage. And that's when she noticed the tourists.

A couple in their twenties, a man and woman who looked like backpackers, their cargo shorts and college T-shirts and hair disheveled. She recognized the little dance they did, pretending not to stare at her, whispering and suppressing smiles, gathering courage to come closer.

An echo of life during those years after her song went viral. Back then, she'd chat for a couple of minutes with her fans and pose for a photo. It had been harder when Eva was a baby, when Callie had just wanted to get through grocery shopping and change her daughter's diaper and put her down for a nap.

Now she felt unable to move or speak. She felt her cheeks grow red-hot as she heard their words in American English: "Callie Byrd."

The young woman was holding up her phone, aimed straight at her like the barrel of a gun. Callie hid her face behind her hair. Her thoughts scrambled in growing panic. Should she talk to them? Ask them not to post anything? Or just hope they wouldn't?

Her insides sank. They'd probably video-recorded her performance. Maybe even photographed her and Luc kissing outside.

At least no one else seemed to have recognized her, no one from La Chanson thankfully, but all it took were these two tourists to post a video or a photo . . . and her entire life here would crash and burn.

"I have to go," she heard herself tell Luc, thrusting the guitar case at him with shaking hands. "Can you and your dad bring Eva home? And take this?"

"Wait, Callie, what's going on?"

She turned away, letting curls fall over her face like a funeral veil, then hurried out the door, down the street, onto the river path. La Chanson tried to comfort her with a soothing tune, but no, she couldn't do this, couldn't sing again, not even on the cottage balcony. She couldn't be out in the world at all.

When she was halfway home, Luc's voice rang out from behind. "Callie!"

She forced herself to slow down until he caught up.

"Hey, Callie, what's wrong?"

She glanced around. "Where's Eva?"

"With my dad. Your guitar too."

Steeling herself, Callie whispered, "I can't do this."

His brow furrowed. "Do what?"

"I can't—be myself." An anchor weighted down her chest. Nowhere would be safe. She had to send herself into hiding again.

"Tell me what's really going on, Callie. Please."

She stared at the river, forced the words out. "I brought Eva here to escape my partner. Ex-partner. He's powerful, rich, has resources." She looked back at Luc. "That's why I stay under the radar."

Understanding dawned over his face. "Oh, Callie."

She kept going, her chin trembling. "He tracked us to Aix, then we took refuge here. Those tourists—they took pictures, videos."

Luc pulled her close, wrapped his arms around her, and for a moment she sank into his warmth, letting him hold her. Then she made herself pull away, cross her arms across her chest, form a barrier. She would not let a man try to save her. Never again.

He raked his hand through his hair. "Callie, I get your fear, but listen, those tourists might not post it. And even with AI and image recognition—it's unlikely he'd come across it."

She hugged herself. Luc would have been right if Brett hadn't set up an online alert for her name. If her fans hadn't made a web page he was surely checking.

Yet if she told Luc this, he'd see her differently, as would the rest of the village. She'd grown fond of her small, safe life in La Chanson, and if word got out, it could break this cozy world wide open.

"You're safe here," he said. "We're all looking out for you. Hey, let's talk to Julien and his mom. Make a plan in case your ex comes." He paused. "And if you're worried, you can stay with my dad. The house is too big for him, and he'd be happy to have you. The dogs bark at strangers. And—"

She raised her palm to cut him off. This was sounding way too much like someone trying to rescue her. "Luc, thank you, but I might have to leave. Soon."

She heard Eva's voice chattering in the distance and turned to see her shining a flashlight, heading up the path with Monsieur Forêt, who carried the accordion case in one hand and the guitar case in the other.

Eva ran into her arms. "Mom! I'm so proud of you!"

Callie hugged her tightly.

"You're singing again next week, right?"

"We'll see." And in that moment, Callie resolved to give herself one week to make the bigger decision—stay or leave. Which, she realized, was also the Forêts' deadline. In one week, there would be no more truffle hunting. Luc would, in all likelihood, be living and working out of town, if not for the vet, then for another business.

Unless his father and Madame Lavigne repaired things. But Callie didn't have time or energy to worry about the Forêts' problems—she'd have to clean and pack and have everything ready to go at a moment's notice.

Now that the threat of Brett coming for her felt imminent, her resolve to stand up to him was weakening. If he found her, she'd take Eva and flee to another village, even tinier, even more hidden. And she'd never sing again.

# A PLAN

*Colorado, two days before arrival in France*

Okay, Callie. Here's what I'll do: I'll suggest a beach trip to Mexico, tell Brett that's why I've been acting strange. That I need a vacation. I'll tell him I need the passports to enter the numbers on the flight reservation, since of course, they're in his office.

Then I'll tell him I'm going shopping in Denver tomorrow for the trip, to try on swimsuits. In secret, I'll go to the bank to figure out how to buy Air France tickets for an overnight flight (digitally, since the Denver airport doesn't take cash for tix), and then I'll take out the rest of my money in cash for lodging and food.

Then the next day, Thursday, while he's at his haircut before the social worker appointment, I'll grab the packed suitcases, hop into the car, pick up Eva early from school, and we'll go straight to the airport. I'll abandon the car in the airport lot. And the next day, we'll be safely settled in Provence.

That's where we'll go. The South of France. My favorite place in the world. Memories of music and good food, feeling carefree and full of possibility.

There are so many little pieces, so much to go wrong. What will he do if he finds the packed suitcases? Or the envelope of cash hidden there?

He will be livid.

# 29

# BLUE BOTTLES

After a morning of gardening, Callie sat in a lounge chair on the patio, beneath the dappled shade of the olive tree, sipping chilled mint tea, watching Eva dive for coins, and flipping through an illustrated book on Provence that she'd found in the cottage. She tried, unsuccessfully, to relax.

For several days, she'd holed up, lying low, cooking, gardening, deep-cleaning, intending to leave the cottage pristine if they needed to flee. Her clothes were already packed, and all she'd have to do was stuff Eva's clothes into the other suitcase. She'd been studying the maps in the book, keeping a mental list of other villages that might be smaller, more remote, more hidden.

She hadn't been singing. It was taking great effort not to touch the guitar. Not to open her mouth on the balcony at night. Not to think about the next whisper words. *Dragon, spirit, fight.*

Something moved in the underbrush on the hillside slope, and she jumped, feeling her heart race. She bolted upright, craned her head, in fight-or-flight mode. Another rustle, and she jumped again, ready to grab Eva and run to the secret room.

A bird flew out, a little gray one, a warbler maybe. After a moment, Callie's pulse calmed and her muscles untensed, but she kept thinking she saw Brett out of the corner of her eye, everywhere.

She slammed the book shut. *That's it. I can't live like this.*

She'd have to go deeper into hiding. To a place where no one knew them, then stay away from people, refrain from singing again. Not even at night alone. Not even to her child, who could be recording her in secret. Her mouth would remain sealed. Her voice would return to the cave. She would cut the string to keep them safe.

Eva climbed out of the pool, dripping and shivering, and galloped over to the lounge chair. Callie wrapped her in a towel and pulled her close, warming her, the two of them against the world.

"Sweet pea," she began, "how would you feel about a new adventure?"

"What?" Eva's teeth chattered theatrically.

"Let's leave La Chanson, explore somewhere else."

"Nooooo!" Eva's voice pierced the afternoon air like a knife.

Julien popped his head out from the château door, holding a sledgehammer tight in his fist. He looked around, locked eyes with Callie, then descended the steps and walked toward her across the patio. "Everything okay?"

He was here for them. This fact brought a lump to her throat, but at the same time, she didn't want any man saving her, not even this timid, stooped, middle-aged poet with his belly pooch.

"Thank you, Julien," she said with a weak smile. "We're okay."

"My mom says we have to leave!" Eva ran to him, throwing her arms around his waist, hanging on like a stubborn burr. She'd never hugged him before—he didn't come across as the huggable type. But Eva stayed beside him, shivering in her wet towel, as if Callie were the enemy.

He looked at Callie, eyes alarmed, and awkwardly patted Eva's shaking shoulder.

Callie stood up and rubbed her face. "Hey, sweetie, why don't you change into dry clothes and get a snack?"

Eva eyed them both, making no sign of obeying.

"You can have the *pain au chocolat* on the counter," Callie said, not above bribery.

"Fine," said Eva, heading to the cottage. "But I'm not leaving La Chanson."

"Fleur will make you feel better," said Julien softly, and gave his dog a command.

Once Eva ushered Fleur inside, Callie turned to him, running her hand through her hair. "Got a minute?"

"*Euh.*" Nodding, he sat down on the lounge chair next to hers.

Sitting back down, she forced herself to come clean about Brett, even the deepest, darkest parts—that most likely, he'd killed Nick. That he'd sooner kill her than lose her.

Julien, it turned out, had already pieced together the basics. He had so much experience with women and children hiding here—he nodded with surprisingly un-awkward empathy as she spilled out everything. His response was kind yet matter-of-fact. "If your ex comes, stay in the secret room. We'll contact the police. Make a restraining order. Keep you safe."

Callie nodded, grateful he'd made it sound so simple, but Brett was manipulative, not just with her—with anyone who stood between him and what he wanted.

"I hope you stay," Julien said. "I asked out Violette. Thanks to you."

"That's great." She felt wistful she might not witness the next stages of courtship.

He studied her. "Know the reason I waited so long?"

"Why?"

He lowered his eyes, ran his finger across the scar on his temple, over and over. "I worried my father's violence was inside me. Waiting to come out. I couldn't put any women at risk. Or children. Or dogs."

"Julien, there's not a speck of violence in you. You have the heart of a poet. That shines through."

He flushed. "That's what Violette says."

"Oh," Callie said, digging around in the tote bag beside her. "I wanted to give you this before I leave." She pulled out the tin of old treasures. "I know you said you didn't want it, but maybe you could reconsider giving it to your mom. See if it taps into nostalgia about

Monsieur Forêt. Maybe she'll let him stay. The deadline's coming up in a few days."

Looking doubtful, Julien took the tin box, puffing air from his cheeks. "She's heard too many lies. From my father. From Hugo. She believes Monsieur Forêt abandoned her. Rejected her. Hated her. So much he couldn't look at her. Or speak to her."

Callie sighed. "You really think a truce is impossible?"

He paused. "When this was a safe house, we'd find gifts. Every Sunday morning. Bags of food and supplies in our shed. Even money. From neighbors, my mother thought. But I've always woken up early. And sometimes I saw him, Monsieur Forêt, dropping off presents. He didn't want her to know. So I never told her. She wouldn't have believed me. Or she would've refused the gifts. And we needed them."

Callie absorbed this, the *secret kindness*. "Why don't you tell her now?"

Running his hand over the tin box, he considered. "Maybe I should."

"Maybe so," she said.

"I want the Forêts to stay. I don't want the château sold. I dream it could be a retreat. For poets and musicians."

Callie could envision it easily—warm gatherings by the pool and river, creativity flowing. "You do have power here. Speak up."

He nodded thoughtfully. "That's what Violette says."

Callie had a pang that she might not see this plan play out if she left. The plan felt stronger now, more than tapping into nostalgia. It was about revealing facts that could shine a light on the past, change hearts in the present. At least, she hoped so.

Julien fixed his gaze on her face. "There's something you should know. Something that might make you feel safer here."

"What?"

He hesitated. "Or, more scared."

"Tell me, Julien."

He chose his words carefully. "My mother kept tiny blue bottles.

Hidden high on the kitchen shelf. If a woman's husband tracked her down, my mother gave her a blue bottle. To mix into her husband's wine."

Callie's mind went to the portrait of Giulia Tofana, the eighteenth-century poisoner of abusive men. "Are you saying your mother—she—?"

"My mother keeps women and children safe. That's all." He paused, then added, "And dogs."

With a shiver, Callie thought of the wooden box of secrets. *I know who killed my father.* Tristan's death had occurred soon after Marguerite was killed. Had that been the tipping point for Madame Lavigne? Her husband's death had been ruled an accidental drowning while intoxicated. But did Julien think his father's wine had been laced with poison? By his own mother?

Callie's horror was eclipsed by empathy for Julien. He'd been keeping this secret since he was just a little older than Eva. *I'm glad my father's dead.* Of course he was glad the violence had ended. And perhaps there was a secret he hadn't dared to write: He was glad his mother did it.

Reeling, Callie tried to untangle the consequences of a secret of this magnitude. No wonder he sympathized with Monsieur Forêt, the victim of false rumors, the man secretly supporting his mother all those years. She felt the poet boy's angst, the pressure to stay loyal to his family while knowing the truth. Or at least, what he'd guessed was the truth.

She reminded herself that this was all speculation. As far as she knew, there was no proof of poisoning. Not in Tristan's case. But what about in the cases of the women who took refuge here? Had they ever resorted to the little blue bottles to deal with their abusers?

Of course, Callie wouldn't touch any little blue bottles. Never. And who knew if they really did contain poison? She'd stick with her plan of running and hiding. Still, she'd never look at her landlady in quite the same way again.

A couple of days later, in morning sunshine, Callie ventured with Eva into the woods, where the Forêts and their dogs were overjoyed to see them after nearly a week apart.

As she kissed Luc's cheeks in greeting, she warmed, flashing back to their moment at the open mic soirée, but resisting the urge to move her lips to his. If she left, she'd be cutting off the possibility of more kissing with him. Of more *anything* with him.

Brow furrowed, Luc launched into how worried he'd been. "I called every day, but no answer."

"I was scared it was my ex," Callie said simply.

Luc's gaze lingered on her face. "Are you okay?"

She lifted a shoulder, tried to formulate a response, but came up with nothing.

"Listen, I'm heading to town." He kept his voice deliberately casual. "Want to come? My dad can hang out with Eva."

"Sure." She tried matching his light tone. "I've got errands too."

Not surprisingly, Eva was thrilled to stay with Monsieur Forêt and the dogs, who were also thrilled to have her company after nearly a week apart. Callie appreciated the break. Eva had been exhausting, constantly pleading to see the dogs while Callie had tried to make a rational decision.

Alone with Luc now, Callie headed out of the forest and back into the open sunshine. "Thanks for being there, Luc." On impulse, she slipped her hand into his, feeling the rough warmth. "After the open mic soirée, that is. And I'm sorry I worried you."

"I get it—but you're not leaving, are you?"

"We're mostly packed up and ready to go. But I gave myself till tomorrow to decide for sure."

"Our last day in the forest," he said. "The end of June."

"And your deadline for the job offer."

He slowed his pace. "Callie, I already told her no. No to everything."

A long pause. "Why?"

"It didn't feel right. But being with you does. I can be myself with you."

Heat gathered in Callie's chest, spreading like warm nectar. "Me too," she whispered, not daring to look at him. This development complicated things even more. She kept her hand interlaced with his as they headed upstream, the river's melody carefree, weaving with lark songs.

When they reached the turnoff for town, he squeezed her hand, electricity flowing between their skin, zinging through her body. "Want to go to the source?" he asked.

She hesitated, remembering how free and open she'd felt alone at the source. It might be strange to have another person there with her. Even Luc. Especially Luc.

She opened her mouth to decline, when she heard her voice say, quite firmly, "*Oui*."

*Well, okay then.*

As they walked uphill, along the river, the music rose to sunny G major scales, fresh and hopeful. They stayed close, bare arms touching, shoulders grazing, and she was very aware of the ripples in his forearms, the calluses on his palms, the stubble on his jawline, the feel of his hand in hers.

They climbed up through scents of rosemary and lavender, chirps of sparrows and cicadas, and a sense of clarity came over her. She had to tell Luc what he might be getting into. She took a deep breath and spoke as he listened intently. First, she painted a picture of Brett in broad strokes, then zoomed in to the darkest parts, speaking in stops and starts. "He's dangerous, Luc."

Luc steeled his jaw. "It would be him against the entire village."

She thought of the wine witch, hiding her little blue bottles. She thought of this last, terrible resort. "It's not just the threat of physical violence. He manipulates people. Taps into our weaknesses."

"How so?"

She shuffled through a thousand examples and settled on one that still felt tender. "Well, he convinced me to give up singing. Said I'm a megalomaniac."

Looking bewildered, Luc raised his brows. "*Une mégalomane?* If *mégalomane* had an opposite, that's what you'd be."

"*Une anti-mégalomane?*" She appreciated how silliness dispersed shame.

"Exactly."

She forced herself to verbalize the worst thing, the jugular vein of her psyche. "He said I was a bad mother."

Luc stopped in his tracks, faced her, gently gripped her shoulders. "You don't believe any of that, do you?"

"There's a kernel of truth. When my husband died, I fell into a depression. I *was* a bad mother for a while." She swallowed hard. "Something happened—Eva could have died because of my neglect."

Luc trailed his fingers down her arms and held her hands. "It's natural you'd be depressed—that's why family and friends would help you parent during that time."

When he put it that way, it felt simple. *It takes a village*. "Brett said he'd take care of us, so I let him. Once I got out of the depression, he kept saying I was an unstable mother. And I kept believing it."

"You, Callie, are the best mother I know." Luc kissed her hands, studied her face. "You always put Eva first. And even on the run, you've surrounded her with people who care about her."

Hearing him say it so clearly loosened something inside her. Forgiveness for herself. A new perspective.

"And as far as you being onstage," said Luc, "it's an act of generosity. Your songs brought together Julien and Violette." His voice softened. "And you and me."

Maybe one day, she would tell him who she was—a former,

slightly famous, indie singer-songwriter. She'd swear him to secrecy, of course. She trusted he'd honor her wishes.

Feeling light and free, she pulled him along, toward the source of La Chanson, which was calling to them. As their strides synchronized, she glanced at the river, braids of aquamarine and sapphire and emerald, like Luc's irises. She snuck a sideways look at them, refracting and reflecting the water's light.

As they approached the limestone cliffs that hid the source, he broke the pocket of silence. "You channel something when you sing. Something bigger than yourself."

She took this in, looking up at the towering white stone, a natural temple, then glanced toward the cavern beside them, with its deep pool of water far below in the shadows.

"Like an underground spring," he said.

She met his gaze, etched his words into her mind, engraved them into her heart. He *understood* her. She was just leaning toward his lips, when she heard a rumbling from the depths. The carnyx.

She peered into the darkness, the cool damp contrasting with Luc's warmth at her side. Just as before, a beam of light entered the cave, illuminating, for a split second, the carnyx.

Luc gaped. "Did you see that?"

"*Oui.*" She straightened up and turned back to face him. "I saw it the other time I was here too."

He looked at her in wonder. "This is a once-in-a-lifetime thing, Callie . . . and you're two for two?"

She felt the music coming from inside and outside and everywhere. All at once. If she opened her mouth, a song might pour out. On impulse, she grabbed Luc by the collar, pulled him close. Their kiss was a duet, soft and feathery at first, then growing more intense. Their music intermingled from a hidden source, and the river music swelled, rich and deep.

At some point, breathless, she pressed her forehead against Luc's and laughed, a sound of wonderment.

He laughed too. "I wish we'd come here sooner."

"So do I."

He raised an eyebrow. "I think La Chanson wants you to stay."

"You think?"

From the depths came another roar, straight from a dragon's mouth.

"Are you hearing this, Callie?"

She nodded, wondering if this, *this* was the music she could call on to face the danger around the bend. Because she was leaning, very heavily, toward staying in La Chanson, come what may.

As Callie and Luc walked into town, the river's soundtrack evoked romantic mid-century songs, so over-the-top she had to laugh. They stayed hand in hand as they ran errands, and from the corner of her eyes, she noticed passersby—neighbors and friends and shopkeepers—nodding in approval, all secret smiles and whispers and winks.

"Hey," she said. "Did you know your dad used to leave supplies for Madame Lavigne?"

"What?" Luc did a double take.

"For years. Julien told me."

"I thought my dad resented her. Why would he . . . ?" Luc's voice faded into bewilderment.

"We need to get them talking again." Callie was about to suggest some strategies, when she noticed a little blue Renault pass, slowly, the windows down. The driver was a blond man in his thirties, his head grazing the car's ceiling, his eyes hidden by shades. His head moved back and forth, apparently scanning the sidewalks. When he saw Callie, he latched his gaze onto her.

She quickly looked away, shielding her face, heart thudding. Was it the Parisian assistant? Part of her wanted to run and hide, but she forced herself to keep walking. The car was at the end of the street now, turning right. Crap. What if he circled back?

Luc seemed so caught up in the revelation about his father, he didn't notice her shift in mood. "Let's talk to my dad about it. And you and Julien can talk to his mom. We have one day left until the deadline—there's still hope." He looked uplifted, almost floating at the possibilities. "Want to grab some tea?"

She scanned the street, but the car hadn't reappeared. Maybe she was being paranoid. She turned to Luc, lightened her voice. "Tea sounds good, but you don't think your dad would mind spending more time with Eva? She's probably on her ninety-seventh *toc-toc* joke at this point."

"And he's probably on his ninety-eighth. And enjoying every single one."

"Okay, then." Outside the *salon du thé,* she snuck him a kiss, seeing no blue car in her peripherals.

When they walked inside, she froze. The song playing on the speakers was her viral song, "Fly, Fly Away." Halfway through the second verse.

Callie glanced at Luc, and he returned her gaze with a resigned expression.

*Mon Dieu, he knows.*

Amira spotted them across the room and hurried over, glancing at her husband behind her shoulder, making a desperate motion for him to turn off the music.

*They know too.*

Callie couldn't find words, just let Amira kiss her cheeks and lead them to a table. The music stopped. Silence.

Sitting on the cushion, Callie asked tensely, "How long have you all known?"

Amira sat beside her as Beni prepared the tea. "Since the last open mic," she said. "Well, the morning after."

Luc rubbed his chin. "At first, we thought you were just doing an incredible cover. Then, before bed, I looked up the album art, saw your photo. The next morning, Amira texted me about it."

"Out of concern," Amira clarified. "We care about you."

Callie put her head in her hands. "Who else knows?"

There was a long pause as Beni came over and poured their tea, placed tiny bowls of almonds and dates on the table.

"Who else knows?" she repeated, voice quaking.

Luc reached for her hand. "Everyone."

She snatched it away. "The whole town?"

Amira said quickly, "But we're keeping it a secret. We know you're concerned about your ex. Don't worry, our lips are sealed."

Callie felt the walls closing in, her head growing prickly, fear creeping over her, as if she were back in the basement laundry room. Her gaze flickered to the entrance, where she half expected to see the tall blond man blocking the doorway. No one was there, for now.

"La Chanson is good at secrets," said Beni. "You're safe here."

She looked at Luc. "How could you not say anything?"

"We thought you'd tell us when you were ready."

Dismay filled her. This felt like another form of manipulation and control, hiding the truth.

"I'm sorry," Amira said, pressing her hand to her forehead. "I shouldn't have been playing your song. It's just—it's so good."

Luc seemed to hold his breath, watching Callie carefully.

She pressed her lips together, overwhelmed by this betrayal. She'd trusted them. And they'd been talking behind her back. *For days.* Making decisions about her life as if she were a child. It was a flashback to her time with Brett, how he'd kept her in the dark.

"We'll help you stay hidden," said Amira.

"It might be too late." Distress edged Callie's voice. "Let me see your phone, Luc."

She held it in her palms, and with trepidation did an online search for her name for the past week. At the results, her stomach dropped.

She was all over social media. A video of her singing, a photo of her and Luc kissing. Hundreds, maybe thousands of posts.

With growing dread, Callie went to the page run by her fans. The video and photo had been posted, followed by a string of comments with an abundance of exclamation points. The original post read:

> OMG, we were just in this tiny town in Provence and we heard this amazing cover of that Callie Byrd song and we were wondering what happened to her anyway, it was like she dropped off the face of the planet. And we realized this wasn't just an amazing cover but CALLIE BYRD HERSELF!!! And we're not telling the name of the town because she might want privacy for her and her cute little girl, but all we'll say is that the name of the town is very fitting.

A sick feeling spread over Callie as she scrolled through the comments. Of course, in no time, someone had guessed the town. Her gaze rested on the words *La Chanson*. And the name of the venue, Salon du Thé La Chanson, complete with photos from the website.

Her throat closed up, chest tightened. She felt suffocated, like trapped prey. She glanced at the door. That Parisian assistant could be spying on her. Brett could even be watching her now.

She saw how this would play out. He'd find her and manipulate the situation to get her back. It would be all sugary love at first, maybe some apologizing. He'd infiltrate her friends here, feed them lies with kernels of truth.

The next battle phase would be threatening to take Eva away. He'd lain the groundwork back in Colorado. Money and power went a long way.

It occurred to her now: What if he'd found the château already, found Eva?

Adrenaline shot through her, shook her out of freeze mode and into flight. She stood up. "I have to get Eva."

# SHATTER AND CRASH

*Over the Atlantic Ocean, nine hours before arrival in France*

Callie!

I'm writing this on the plane and Eva has just fallen asleep against my shoulder and I'm sipping Styrofoam-flavored tea . . . and we did it! And yes, I'm scared Brett might find us, but I'll worry about that later, because for now at least, we're free!

And it's terrifying.

Okay, I'll tell you what happened. Things did not go as planned. Not at all.

When I asked him about the passports, he said, "Oh, precious, that's why I have a PA." When I tried pushing back, he said firmly that his assistant would deal with trip logistics. And he stared at me with hooded lids, almost challenging me.

It was like he knew.

And when I said, as casually as possible, that I was heading to Denver to buy a new swimsuit, he said, "Oh, cupcake, this is your chance to try out your stylist."

When I said I preferred doing it myself, he said, "Just focus on your mental health," and he opened my email account and brought up that message from the stylist—which I'd ignored—and he looked over my shoulder as I typed in my measurements and described my taste and asked her to select a wardrobe for me for a week on the Mayan Riviera. And the entire time, my muscles were clenched and my mind racing, trying to come up with alternate plans.

The adoption appointment loomed on Thursday afternoon, that point of no return.

Yesterday morning, five minutes after he left for his appointment in north Denver, I hopped into the other car and headed to south Denver, to the bank where I have that old account.

I glanced at the exterior house cameras in the rearview, knew he'd be tracing my path. The car is connected to an app on his phone that reports its location. I was very trackable. He'd know exactly how long I was gone and where I'd left the car. So I parked at the Cherry Creek shopping center and turned off the find-my-phone app, hoping he wouldn't check it. I walked a half mile to the bank and withdrew four thousand dollars, leaving the other five thousand in the account for expensive, last-minute plane tickets to Marseille.

I made a furtive dash into a surf-style shop, bought a flowered bikini, and raced back to the car. My heart was pounding the entire time, and my mind looped through my plan and everything else that could go wrong. But I heard your voice saying, *No.* I heard it, and it kept me strong, Callie.

I got home an hour before he did, and by then I had to pee, and hammed it up for the cameras, dropping the shopping bag, but keeping my purse over my shoulder as I ran to the bathroom. Inside, away from cameras, I peed, then tucked the envelope of money into the laundry hamper under a tangle of used towels.

I took deep breaths, then walked out of the bathroom into the hallway and calmly put the bikini in the bedroom, drank a glass of water in the kitchen, then brought the laundry hamper downstairs and slid the money into the suitcase.

When he came home, I immediately told him I wasn't happy with the stylist, so I'd made an impulsive decision to go to Denver to pick out my own suit.

He looked at me with suspicion. "Why didn't you text me about it? Or just come to Denver with me?"

"It was last minute. And I didn't want to bother you."

He knew something was up. I could tell by the way he looked at me through those bird-of-prey eyes.

Still, by this morning, I had everything ready in the suitcases—money, clothes, and toiletries, all of it snuck down in laundry baskets.

He had a haircut appointment on his calendar, just before the two o'clock adoption meeting. My plan was to use that hour to bring the suitcases to the car, then drive to Eva's school, take her out of class, and head to the airport.

A surprise trip to France, I'd tell her, and explain later. We'd always talked about a trip one day, a reward for how well she was doing in her French immersion school. This wouldn't be coming totally out of the blue.

The problem was the passports. I decided I'd go into his office and grab them right before I left. I'd just have to risk him seeing me on the hallway camera feed.

But this morning, he came up behind me as I was brushing my teeth and slipped his arms around my waist. "Hey, cupcake, I canceled my haircut to spend time with you. Before the big appointment."

He stared at my reaction in the mirror, as I kept brushing, trying to hide my despair. "We're growing distant," he said. "Can you feel it?"

*Damn it.* I spit out my toothpaste, leaned over to rinse my mouth.

"Let's go on a hike on Coyote Hill," he said.

I extricated myself from his grasp to wipe my mouth on

a towel, wanting to scream into it. Leaving the bathroom, I forced myself to say, "Sure."

An hour later, finding no other way out, I said, "You know, I have a headache. Go ahead without me."

He stared at me for a long moment, then found a bottle of ibuprofen. "Take some," he said, placing a glass of water before me.

After an hour, I claimed it didn't work, and he had me take two more. I could see him restless—he liked a trail run every morning and he'd skipped it today since we'd be hiking together. I had the urge to grab the suitcases and run out of the house, but I needed the passports. And he was in his office, where he kept them.

At noon, he reached his threshold of restlessness. "I'm going for a quick run before lunch. Then I'll shower and get ready."

I kissed him goodbye and watched him through the window as he disappeared down the path. I forced myself to wait ten minutes, just in case he was checking the camera feed through his phone app. If he saw what I was up to, he'd run home at top speed.

After ten minutes, I leapt into action. I put the suitcases in the car, then hurried to his office for the passports.

I rattled the knob. *Crap.* He'd locked it with the keypad. He knew I was up to something. He didn't trust that the cameras were enough deterrent. I was no longer the deluded circus elephant.

I rubbed my face, thinking, thinking. The exterior wall side of his office was mostly windows, but none that opened, and anyway, there was no deck access to them, just rocky cliffs. I hunched over, pressed my forehead to the door, my body deflating. My plan was impossible. This was a prison.

And I heard your voice, Callie. *No.*

It sounded more powerful this time. A low battle cry, rising from the depths.

So I ran to the giant stone fireplace and stopped in front of the axe. Brett had gotten it for show—his assistant arranged for deliveries of chopped wood. I brushed my fingers over the surprisingly sharp blade, then grabbed the axe by the handle and ran back into the hallway.

I paused before his office and let the roar fill me. I raised the axe and smashed its blade into the door. It split the wood with a satisfying *crack*. It took five minutes of bashing to make a hole big enough to walk through. The whole thing left my shoulders and back throbbing, but I'd done it.

Inside, I grabbed the key from beneath the Hecate vase and met her knowing gaze for a moment. Crossroads. I was taking my own path now.

My fingers were trembling as I unlocked the drawer and found the file labeled PASSPORTS—I'd remembered seeing it there last time. I took mine and Eva's, and then impulsively, grabbed the files with our names. Brett's lawyers probably had copies of everything, but still. Maybe one day I could scrounge together money for my own lawyer and deal with this.

My hand rested on the file labeled NICK. I was terrified to see what might be inside and considered leaving it. But then, in what felt like a spontaneous act of courage, I took it too.

I glanced at Pepito behind the glass, watching me with his cheery expression. I tried sliding open the glass like I did last time, but now it was locked. I tried Hecate's key, but no luck. The clock was ticking and my heart thudding.

I felt a low drumbeat thunder through me. I raised the axe. I brought its blade crashing through the glass, shutting my eyes and turning my face away. It cracked like a spider web. After another few whacks, safety glass fell away in tiny, glistening chunks.

Music deities tumbled onto the Persian carpet, but none seemed damaged. Pepito remained on the shelf, his expression as playful as ever. I grabbed him, then headed out through the broken door. I shot a bold look at the hallway camera, held up Pepito, and kissed him.

*Nice job, Byrdie,* his nasal voice seemed to say. *Now get me the hell out of here.*

Leaving shattered glass and splintered wood behind, I ran past the giant Greek urn and out the front door. I hopped into the car and sped down the driveway, onto the network of mountain roads, and then the main road to Eva's school.

I probably had a wild look in my eyes as I said to the admin, "There's been an emergency. I need to get Eva."

She looked at me in concern, a gossipy woman who was friendly with Brett, and who'd surely heard rumors about me—the school was small enough. She gave a furtive glance toward the interior window of the principal's office—thankfully, she was in a meeting.

I fought the urge to run straight to Eva's classroom and grab her. Instead, I located the sign-out form on the counter and entered the date and time and Eva's name and my signature. "She might not be back for a while," I added, "so she should bring her backpack."

"I hope everything's okay," the admin said slowly, and then, "Is her dad aware of what's going on?"

"Brett's not her dad." I pressed my lips shut. I was still Eva's mother, despite what this lady might have heard about my incompetence, and I had a legal right to take her out of school. "I can go get her myself," I said, moving toward the hallway.

"Just have a seat, please." After a long moment, the admin called Eva's classroom through the loudspeaker, instructing her to come to the office with her backpack.

My heart was racing as I shifted in the chair, bouncing my

foot, one eye out for Eva and one watching to make sure this lady didn't call Brett next. Could she do that? Probably. He was an emergency contact.

Minutes later, Eva appeared with her backpack down the hallway just as the admin picked up the phone and dialed. Eva ran into my arms, hugging me.

In a low voice, the woman said, "Sorry to bother you, Brett. Listen, this is—"

"Let's go," I whispered to Eva. "Now."

I hurried her out the door, to the car, and the second her seat belt clicked in the back seat, I sped out of the parking lot. "Okay, sweet pea, we're going on a surprise trip. To France."

"France?" Confusion eclipsed her delight. "Without Brett?"

I nodded. After a stretched-out pause, she whooped with joy, and for the moment I let go of worries that I was an unstable mother messing up my child. This was exactly what she needed. To *fly, fly away* with me.

On I-470, I forced myself to drive only five miles over the limit so I wouldn't get pulled over. After the chat with the admin, Brett had probably hopped in his car, started tracking mine, maybe even called the police. I glanced at my phone on the seat beside me, silenced and in airplane mode, and imagined the furious texts he must be sending.

I stared back ahead and answered Eva's questions and chatted with her about France, keeping my voice light. Nearing the airport, we passed the giant, creepy sculpture of the blue horse with glowing red eyes. A piece of this icon had fallen onto its sculptor, killing him. I stepped on the gas, raced toward the parking area, feeling like we were barely escaping being crushed too. Something huge and heavy was falling and I was pulling us out of its path at the last second.

Beneath the white peaks of the airport, I left the car in the garage—and as we went through Security I kept glancing over my shoulder. He couldn't have reached the airport this fast, could he? Once he got here, he'd buy a ticket somewhere just so he could get through Security and hunt me down, but of course he wouldn't know our terminal or where we were going. And the airport is enormous.

Still, to be safe, Eva and I sat at the back of a crowded pub, hidden for three hours until just before our plane boarded. She seemed surprisingly content reading her book and munching on bacon-cheddar potato wedges, followed by a vanilla milkshake.

I kept my phone in airplane mode with the find-my-phone app disabled until just before we boarded, when I took the SIM card out, broke it in half, and dropped it with the phone into the trash. I didn't feel safe until the plane doors closed. And to fully reassure myself, I walked up and down the aisle, looking at each passenger's face to make sure none was his.

And here I am now, sipping tea in a middle seat, with Eva sleeping by the window. I know more things could go wrong. But I'll be paying for our lodging and ground transportation in cash, and my laptop is in airplane mode. There's no reason to think he'll find us.

Still, he's rich and powerful. And angry. His prized pieces are gone—including Pepito, tucked into socks in my carry-on—and Brett will stop at nothing to get us back. The second I slip up, he'll be on it, in full, ruthless force.

Which is why we'll stay under the radar. Live a small, safe, hidden life. I'll wear big sunglasses, braid and tuck my hair beneath a hat, keep to myself, remain offline, stay far away from musical instruments, and most of all, never sing in public.

# 31

# THE THREE MUSKETEERS

Abandoning her shopping bags in the *salon du thé*, Callie ran outside, down the street, along the river path, toward the forest. The water music swelled like a Beethoven symphony. The carnyx thundered. She ran as if the blond man were following her, chasing her with long strides. As if Brett himself were after her. She looked over her shoulder, saw no one, but ran as if he were right on her heels.

She stumbled into the shade of the forest. "Eva! Eva!"

No answer. No dogs.

She raced to Monsieur Forêt's house, panic growing.

And there was Eva, on the patio, sipping lemonade with him.

Panting, Callie dropped to her knees, wrapped her arms around her daughter.

"Ow, Mom. You're strangling me."

"Sorry." She loosened her grip.

"What's wrong?" asked Eva. "Where's Luc?"

Callie pressed her lips together, turned to Monsieur Forêt. "We have to go."

"Why?" Eva said, indignant. "I'm not done with my *limonade*."

Concern etched Monsieur Forêt's face. "Is everything all right, dear?"

"Luc will explain." Callie took her daughter's hand and pulled her away, hurrying toward the forest.

"Why are you going so fast?" Eva's self-righteousness was shifting to fear. "Why are you acting weird, Mom?"

Callie took a long breath. "Brett knows where we are."

Eva blinked, stopped in her tracks.

"Come on," Callie said, tugging at her. "We have to pack up. We'll take the bus first thing tomorrow."

But Eva was rooted now, tears slipping out. "Where to?"

Callie leaned over to hug her, wipe her cheeks. "I don't know."

"What about the secret room?" Eva buried her wet face into Callie's shoulder. "We can hide there. I can play with those toys."

Callie paused to consider. "Maybe for tonight. But then we have to leave."

"No."

Callie bit her lip. Now was not the time to argue with a stubborn eight-year-old. After another hug, she said, "We'll talk about it at home," and pulled Eva through the forest.

At the cottage, Eva doubled down. "I'm not leaving." She slammed her bedroom door in an exclamation point.

Cursing under her breath, Callie tucked the last of her clothes and toiletries into her bags—which had been mostly packed already—and folded Lili's hand-me-downs beneath a note. *Please return to Lili.* Anyway, the clothes were too glamorous, too "look at me."

Callie considered the next steps. Should they stay in the secret room tonight? Or was that an overreaction? And how long would it take Eva to forgive her?

She gave herself a moment to sit on the bed beside her suitcase, to breathe. On impulse, she unzippered the packet of letters, reread the dangers she'd written to herself in black and white. And as she read, she felt struck by Past Callie's determination to connect with herself, save herself, save Eva, save the possibility of a shimmery future of family and friends.

And she'd done it. She'd done it, damn it.

But what if Brett kept following her? What if, despite a clear mind and determined heart, she *still* couldn't create a safe, happy life?

As she was stuffing the letters back into the suitcase, the landline rang. She didn't answer, in case Brett or his assistant had found the number. And if it wasn't them, it was probably Luc or Amira, and she wouldn't give them the chance to try to change her mind. She locked the windows and doors, shutting out the river, whose music was also urging her to stay.

At the heart of it, if she stayed, she'd be putting everyone in danger—not just her and Eva but Luc and Julien too. And anyone who stood in Brett's way. Look what had happened to Nick.

Hours later, Callie eyed the suitcase just inside the cottage door as she made a dinner of leftover courgette and tomato gratinée. She was sweating in the closed-up cottage air, hot and stagnant.

When a knock sounded, her muscles tensed. There was no peephole and all the curtains were drawn.

Luc's voice came through, muffled. "Callie? We need to talk."

Seeing him would only make it harder to leave. He was the one in the greatest danger. If Brett had seen the photo of them together, he'd be enraged. Another man had stolen his prized possession.

Eva's footsteps pattered downstairs.

"Sweetie, don't—"

But her daughter had already opened the door.

Callie took a long breath, wiped her forehead, then stepped outside to face him. Only it wasn't just Luc, but also his father, and Julien and his mother, faces earnest. And of course, the four dogs, tongues hanging out, tails wagging. Eva dropped to her knees to kiss each one.

Luc set down the grocery bags—rescued from the café—then glanced at the suitcase. "Callie, I'm so sorry."

His father spoke in an oddly formal voice. "We're here on behalf of the town of La Chanson."

"We'd like you to stay," said Madame Lavigne, raising her chin in a no-nonsense gesture.

Luc's voice broke as he said, "We're here for you."

Callie let herself meet his eyes. "Even if it could put you in danger?"

He gave a vehement nod.

It occurred to her that this unified front had taken coordination between sworn enemies. This gesture made it clear—they cared about her and Eva more than the vendetta. Warm, golden honey spread through her veins as she watched Eva hug her de facto grandparents.

Instead of her usual black, Madame Lavigne wore a linen-silk dress, the pale pink-peach of a glass of rosé in sunlight. Still, beneath the surface, Callie glimpsed the shadows that had shaped who she now was, dark emotions running deep. Callie's gaze moved to Monsieur Forêt, this gentle man who'd helped his enemy in secret, expression raw beneath his beret.

Eva's grandparents gripped her hands. They'd both be devastated if their *petite-fille* left—that was written all over their faces. And Callie saw their tenderness flowing into Eva, wanting to flow into each other but blocked by a dam of old pain.

As La Chanson's music swelled into sweeping arpeggios, it struck her: *This is an opportunity*. Before she left town, she could carry out the tentative plan—to help heal the old wounds, to let the Forêts keep access to the forest. The deadline was tomorrow. "Let's all sit down," she said, leading them to the patio table by the pool.

Over Eva's head, Madame Lavigne and Monsieur Forêt glanced at each other warily. But they took seats at the table, their sons beside them.

"Hey sweet pea," said Callie, "why don't you pick some apricots and cherries?"

"Will do!" Eva grabbed a basket from the garden, elated at this turn of events.

"But stay close, okay?" Callie watched Eva run toward the fruit trees, then gave their landlady a long look. "Madame, would you select a bottle of wine? Something just for us. Something to bring forth courage and love and our bravest selves."

After a beat, Madame Lavigne gave a curt nod and headed toward the château.

Callie's eyes briefly met Luc's, then Julien's, both of whom gave slight smiles, guessing what she was up to.

Ten minutes later, Eva returned with a basket of stone fruit as Madame Lavigne was placing stemmed crystal glasses on the table. Almost reverently, the wine witch dusted off a bottle of sparkling white wine that looked positively ancient—thick, old glass and a yellowed, peeling label, handwritten in calligraphy: *Aux Anges*. Over the moon, with the angels. A wave of vulnerability passed over her face. "I've been saving this for many years."

Monsieur Forêt stared at the bottle. "Value increases with age."

"As does wisdom," said Madame Lavigne. They weren't looking at each other, but this was something akin to a conversation. Baby steps.

Julien and Luc seemed to be holding their breaths as they watched this play out.

The wine witch pointed the cork toward the garden, trying to nudge it loose after decades.

"May I help?" asked Monsieur Forêt.

"*Non*," Madame Lavigne snapped.

Looking hurt, Monsieur Forêt closed his mouth.

Callie breathed out. Okay, so two steps forward, one step back.

After a moment, the cork popped and flew toward the olive tree, eliciting laughter that loosened the tension. Soon, the glasses were poured, Eva's with Orangina. She gulped hers down as the adults swirled and sniffed theirs. Its scent was sumptuous—hazelnut and crème brulée, with an undercurrent of deep, mysterious sweetness, like those old-fashioned candies from vintage tins that melt in your mouth.

"To courage," said Callie.

"And love," said Luc.

"And finding lost selves," said Julien.

"And family," said Eva, refilling her Orangina. "Including dogs," she clarified, giving each of her devoted entourage a pat on the head.

Madame Lavigne and Monsieur Forêt watched her with fondness, and as everyone's glasses clinked, theirs paused against each other's for an extra moment.

Callie sipped, feeling the cool, bubbly wine over her tongue, the inside of her cheeks, the taste morphing in each spot. Childhood summers, swimming in turquoise water, wandering in dappled light, climbing oak trees. Pure effervescence.

She savored it, letting Eva take a sniff. Her daughter had developed a refined sense of smell from truffle hunting, and closed her eyes as she breathed in the scent. It must have sparked something in her—out of the blue, Eva bolted for the château, returning moments later with the little tin box, which Julien had been keeping on the kitchen table as he'd wavered over whether to show it to his mother.

Ceremoniously, Eva placed the box on the patio table. For better or worse, she'd made the decision for him.

Callie sucked in a breath, exchanging glances with Luc and Julien. This could be the catalyst they needed. She watched nervously as recognition passed over the grandparents' faces.

Then, as if mirrors of each other, their expressions shifted—and not into any happy, nostalgic reflections of good times past. This was *pain*. And the consequences would be anyone's guess.

"Hey, sweet pea," Callie said to Eva in English. "Why don't you change into your swimsuit? Practice your dolphin dives. And maybe after the grown-ups are done talking, you can do a routine for us."

"Magnificent idea," Eva said, running inside, ever the performer.

Callie exhaled, then looked cautiously at the grandparents, who sipped their wine and eyed the box as if it were a bomb. She thought of Pandora's box, the *pithos* of secrets. This could go several directions. Disaster was one. Hope was another. She reached over and opened the lid.

Even the river seemed to hold its breath . . . a long pause . . . a rest.

Madame Lavigne picked up Tintin, turned him over in her age-spotted, crepey hands. "You still look like him, Philippe."

Monsieur Forêt took off his beret, and sure enough, a white cowlick appeared. He smoothed it down and it popped back up.

Madame Lavigne suppressed a laugh.

He picked up the white dog figurine, let it prance in the air. "Reminds me of my own Milou."

"Such a faithful dog." Madame Lavigne found the feather, brushed it against her cheek.

Callie glanced at Julien and Luc, eyes wide—this was going well.

From the bottom of the box, Monsieur Forêt pulled out the photo, stared at it with deep emotion, then, with shaking hands, dropped it onto the table. "Why did you stop talking to me, Sophie?" His expression shifted to bitterness, resentment. "Looking at me? How could you treat me with such cruelty?"

His words hung in the air for an uncertain moment.

"How dare you!" Madame Lavigne's voice erupted like a fiery volcano. "You're the one who ignored me. Rejected me. Betrayed me." She waved her arm in a wild gesture, and her glass crashed on the stone.

Everyone froze.

The woman's face was growing so furious that Callie was filled with instant, deep regret. Her plan was terrible; she saw it now. The wine witch herself had warned her the first day they'd met. *People fear me. As they should.*

Monsieur Forêt firmed his jaw and stood up, grabbed his walking stick. "I'm going home."

Madame Lavigne picked up the half-full bottle of ancient wine, raised it over her head, and smashed it to the ground, glass and liquid flying, bubbles pouring out, seeping into cracks between limestone.

Callie's chest hurt, first from the shock of the explosion, then from the feeling of waste. That magical wine, decades in the making, the courage and love it embodied, not to mention its value, not even quantifiable. So much beautiful potential destroyed.

Monsieur Forêt paused, hand on his walking stick.

Madame's voice rang out. "Coward! You're ignoring me all over again. You're the cruel one. Tristan told me how angry you were. That you regretted letting me go. That you took it out on him and me. That you were jealous of my marriage to him. And you've held it against me for our entire lives."

Monsieur Forêt turned around, wearing an expression of the deepest sorrow. "Not angry." His words were barely audible. "Heart-broken." He let out a long breath. "Tristan told me you wanted me to leave you alone, let you live life with him, leave our friendship behind with our childhoods."

Her rage eased just a bit. "And you believed him?"

"You believed him too." He searched her face. "Remember that summer before he returned? All that time we spent together? Sophie, I was going to ask—I thought . . ."

For a long moment, Madame Lavigne looked speechless, and finally her voice emerged, soft and bewildered. "When Tristan came back, he said you gave him your blessing to propose to me. That you only thought of me as a childhood friend, nothing serious."

Monsieur Forêt gaped. "What?"

"He said you were interested in the jeweler's daughter. The pretty one." Madame Lavigne's voice wavered, her pain still raw. Yet as she spoke, her anger leaked out, bit by bit, like air from a tire. "And yes, you visited her in secret."

Monsieur Forêt pressed his lips together, tears brimming. "I went to the jeweler's for a different reason. Tristan knew why. I'd written him letters about it. I wanted him to be my best man if—if you said yes to me. It didn't seem right to propose with him gone. I didn't want him to feel left out."

And then, in the most tender of voices, Monsieur Forêt whispered, "I loved you, Sophie."

Madame Lavigne's eyes fell, as if looking away from a too-bright sun. For a long moment, she stared at the broken glass, the wasted wine. The wasted everything. "He lied to us both, Philippe. And we believed him. At first, I didn't understand how much he'd changed in the war. I didn't suspect."

"Neither did I."

Slowly, Madame Lavigne returned her gaze to her old friend, as if it took staggering effort. "I needed you, Philippe. I needed my best friend. More than anything." She firmed her chin, blinked back tears. "Tristan abused me and my sons."

Monsieur Forêt stepped back as if he'd been hit. He steadied himself with his stick, then walked toward her. "What?"

"We kept it a secret," she whispered.

"I'm so sorry." He sank down in his chair, confusion scrawled over his face. "If you'd told me—"

"You abandoned me," she said fiercely, tears spilling over.

Julien spoke. "Maman, he's the one who left the supplies every Sunday."

A long silence. "It was you?"

Monsieur Forêt pulled out his neatly folded handkerchief and handed it to her, watching her wipe her cheeks. "I never stopped caring about you, Sophie."

She pressed her face into the cloth, then looked up at him. "And I you." She steadied the tremble in her voice. "I fell in love with you that summer. I loved you, Philippe. And that part of me, the truest part, never stopped."

Callie felt the ache in her own throat, hot tears forming. Realizing the old friends needed a moment alone, she glanced at Julien and Luc, motioning her chin toward the cottage. She whispered with them in disbelief as she found cleaning supplies, then intercepted Eva, who was in her swimsuit, looking mildly alarmed. "What's going on, Mom?"

"Go put on flip-flops, sweet pea," Callie said. "Some glass broke."

Back on the patio, she swept up the glass, giving the old friends their space. Moments later, Eva ran outside in flip-flops and looked curiously at her grandparents, who were studying each other in silence. Eva approached and took the musketeer out from the tin. "Where are the other two musketeers?"

Slowly, Monsieur Forêt brought his hand to his pants pocket and pulled out a musketeer.

And in response, Madame Lavigne took a musketeer from her own pocket.

Callie exchanged looks of wonder with the others. Had their parents really kept these with them for decades? Mementos? Or security blankets? Or maybe, like Pepito, they held warmth and laughter and hope.

"I knew it!" said Eva. "Sometimes, when you think no one's looking, you hold the musketeers. You each get a sad look on your face. I'm a spy, so I notice this stuff."

"Long ago," said her papi, "we swore we'd always be the Three Musketeers."

"That we would carry these around everywhere, forever," added her mamie Sophie.

They arranged their two musketeers beside the third, as Eva looked at the spot beneath the olive tree and said, "The ghost boy is smiling."

# BLACK DIAMOND

As the sun dipped low in the sky, many dolphin dives and knock-knock jokes later, when everyone was leaving and Eva had gone inside to change out of her swimsuit, Madame Lavigne stepped forward and offered Monsieur Forêt cheek kisses. Afterward, she looked into his eyes, clasped his hands. And there they stood, together after more than six decades. Touching each other. Seeing each other.

As they drew apart, Luc said tentatively, "Madame, tomorrow is the deadline you gave us."

Julien spoke. "Maman, they should keep their rights to the forest."

"*Oui!*" said Eva.

Madame Lavigne sighed, released Monsieur Forêt's hand, and told him, "Of course I want you to stay."

His eyes shone at her words.

"I always have, Philippe. Despite everything. I thought I'd destroyed all copies of the property deed decades ago, so that you and your family could stay forever."

Callie exchanged looks with the sons, absorbing this. Both of their parents had been helping each other in secret.

Madame Lavigne sighed. "But somehow Hugo found the original."

Julien spoke. "Actually, my father found it. When I was eleven. We were cleaning the attic. He was so excited. Said he was going to kick out the Forêts. Drank cognac to celebrate. Passed out in a drunk stupor. I took the deed and hid it."

Callie raised her brows in astonishment. Julien, too, had been helping out in secret. "A month ago, Eva and I found it in the secret room," she said. "We showed it to Julien."

Julien rubbed his face. "I was going to burn it. But Hugo made a surprise visit. Found it on the table. I felt terrible."

"There's nothing we can do now." Madame Lavigne tossed up her hands. "Hugo is determined. He'll never let this go."

"Why not stand up to him?" Callie asked quietly.

"Guilt," Madame Lavigne admitted after a pause. "He was in a violent home his entire childhood. And into his teen years. I suppose I want to make life easy for him now. Make up for it."

Callie was about to ask why Hugo would defend his father after his death, but closed her mouth again. Brett, too, had always longed for his own abusive father's approval, in a thoroughly irrational way.

"Let's stand up to him." Julien took his mother's hand. "All of us. It's time."

Madame Lavigne looked at Monsieur Forêt and nodded.

"It's time," Callie echoed. That wine had worked enough of its magic before the bottle was smashed. What if she and Eva no longer hid? No longer ran? What if they stayed here in their new home? Lived lively lives with their new friends? What if, together, they faced Brett?

She was the one with the power—the friends, the music, the love.

"Let's all stay," she said.

That night, she stood on her balcony, blood thrumming with courage and love and the sparkle of ancient wine. The river music crescendoed, a thundering symphony with a full orchestra, like "Ode to Joy" on steroids. In the moonlight, feeling the power of La Chanson roil through her, she composed a new piece, using this week's words, which the river was roaring—*dragon* and *spirit* and *fight*—the most formidable song she'd ever written, and she belted it out, preparing for battle.

The next evening, Callie walked into the *salon du thé* in a flowy sundress, white and sleeveless, courtesy of Lili. Steeling herself, she carried her guitar like a weapon—the open mic soirée would begin in twenty minutes.

On the walk over, as Eva and her papi had gone ahead, tossing jokes back and forth, Luc had read comments from her fan page on his phone. "We danced to Callie's songs at my wedding . . . After my mom died, I listened to Callie's songs on repeat to get me through it . . . Callie's show inspired me to follow my dream of writing a book—it was just published."

Now, unwavering, she crossed the room and sat down beside Madame Lavigne, already settled next to Monsieur Forêt. Her landlady patted her hand and leaned close. "I talked to the police. They're ready if needed."

"*Merci,*" Callie said, feeling touched that her landlady had her back.

"Well, I'm *aux anges* you're not hiding anymore." *Over the moon, with the angels.*

Callie squeezed her hand, then flicked her gaze to the chalkboard with the lineup. Someone had written CALLIE BYRD as the final act. Tonight meant more to her than headlining for a crowd of ten thousand at Red Rocks.

As the evening progressed, she let herself enjoy mint tea and *bistilla*—a savory-sweet concoction of phyllo and chicken and cinnamon and almonds. She sank into the fun of magic tricks and a puppet show and a comedy skit, applauding and whooping and whistling. Eva had somehow become the de facto MC, not just introducing performers but giving pep talks to the younger kids she ushered onstage.

After the penultimate act, faces turned to Callie. She floated onstage, where Eva introduced her simply as "*ma maman*"—but her full name rippled through the crowd. Callie scanned the audience for Brett. Or the blond assistant. Or anyone suspicious. But no, all the faces were warm and expectant. She snipped any last threads of fear and focused on these faces.

"*Bonsoir.* I'm Callie Byrd." And she belted out her new song, love thrumming through this space, and oh, how she'd missed it. She locked eyes with Eva and saw that she felt it too. People swayed and danced and held hands, stars and planets forming their own constellations.

After the last note and the applause that followed, she played an encore, a song she'd composed while pregnant. "This goes out to my daughter."

And together, she and La Chanson created a nest of hope and wonder, woven with shimmery, silken fibers. Pound for pound, silk was stronger than steel, a fabric of family, light and resilient and powerful enough to face the flimsy husk of a wannabe sorcerer.

Strangely enough, Brett didn't come for them—at least, not right away.

In the early July days that followed, Callie stayed alert, aware of every movement in her peripherals as she talked with the *pétanque* players in the park and the shopkeepers in town and the Forêts in the woods. Even with friends, at home on the château grounds, Callie kept one eye on Eva playing in the pool, her other eye skimming the gardens. One ear was taking in Lili's and Violette's and Amira's animated chatter, while the other was listening for a car rolling over the gravel driveway.

Whenever Callie could grab a moment alone, she'd swim in the cool turquoise waters of La Chanson, like a selkie getting comfortable again in her skin, reclaiming her freedom. Still, from time to time, she glanced over her shoulder, tuning in to the river music, trusting it would alert her to danger. Song after song was reviving, restoring, rejuvenating, bright trills of major chords. No ominous minor drops, no dangerous dissonance, no uneasy tritones.

Even Hugo was no longer a lurking threat. Madame Lavigne and Julien had called him in Paris, put him on speakerphone, and announced they would give the Forêts free access to the forest. Hugo had shown surprise at the mutiny but said he had more important business going on at the moment. And he'd let it drop.

Suspiciously easily, in Callie's opinion, but then again, she'd only met the man once. She decided to accept it as a victory. Madame Lavigne and Julien still hadn't broached the topic of turning the château into a poets' and musicians' residency with Hugo. One thing at a time.

By the end of the week, Callie was truly relaxing, letting down her guard.

By the end of the week, her new friendships were stronger than ever.

And, by the end of the week, she'd gotten very good at sneaking in kisses with Luc.

One morning, they were walking by the river while Eva was truffle hunting with her papi. Checking to see that no one was around, Callie threw her arms around Luc's neck and pulled him close. "Want me to be your girlfriend?" she whispered playfully. "Not to displace your canine one, of course."

He drew back, looking torn.

"Kidding, of course," she said quickly, flushing and feeling . . . *bewildered.*

"Callie, I'm not boyfriend material. At least, I'm scared I'm not." He paused, struggling for words. "Especially not in a case like yours."

A heaviness came over her. Of course, she couldn't expect him to accept the baggage of her ex hunting her down. He had every right to back away from this relationship. "I get it. That's fine."

"My last girlfriend died. It was my fault."

Callie blinked, remembering hints of a tragedy. But how was it *his fault?* Maybe a car accident and he was driving? But he would have emerged completely unscathed, not a scar in sight. She tried imagining other scenarios but only came up with a big, terrifying blank. "You can talk to me, Luc."

"I care about you and Eva, I really do." He squeezed her hand, glanced at the river, then back at her. It was strange hearing him speak in a tone devoid of any humor. "But Callie, I failed in the past. If Brett came and I couldn't save you, I couldn't live with myself. I don't even trust myself to save animals. How can I be responsible for two humans?"

"I don't want you to save us. That's the last thing I want."

"But if he came, I couldn't stand by and watch." He raked his hair, creases deepening in his forehead.

"You're not responsible for us," Callie said firmly. "Listen, we'll have fun and play with dogs and truffle hunt and take river walks and go to open mic soirées. You have zero obligation to us beyond laughing at Eva's *toc-toc* jokes." She reached out her hand toward his. "Deal?"

He met her hand, looking confused. "What exactly am I agreeing to?"

"That no one is responsible for anyone here." Callie heard the river flow by in a velvety D minor, a bit sweet, a bit foreboding.

He wrapped his arms around her, buried his face in her hair. "You know the strange thing?"

"What?"

"My girlfriend loved your music. She had every album of yours on her playlist. She'd play them in the car, at home while we made dinner. That's why you were so familiar to me. When I heard your voice that first day, it already sounded like . . . love."

This moved Callie, unexpectedly, and she tamped down her questions, secure in their deal for now. She kissed him, long and deep and tender.

When their lips parted, Luc said, "Callie, I'm just asking you to be patient with me."

"Got it," she said, and meant it. Or thought she did. This was for the best, moving slowly, waiting to see how things panned out. "I'll be your casual girlfriend."

But as she said it, she thought of his ex–casual girlfriend, Mireille the vet, and her valid frustration. She thought of her mom's string of casual boyfriends, and how, as a child, she promised herself she'd never do that. She'd sworn she'd create a stable life of real family love for her own kid.

So what the hell was she doing now?

Two weeks passed in mid-July bliss. More new songs. More open mic soirées. More duty-free kisses with Luc, whenever Eva was off with her papi and the dogs, or playing with Hamza at the café, or helping her mamie Sophie dust bottles of wine, or hanging with Samuel at the *boulangerie*, or in the park with friends. More and more, Callie felt comfortable letting her social butterfly daughter go off and deepen her bonds, trusting the village would keep her safe.

Which meant more opportunities for kissing. *Casual* kissing. Three times now, Callie had asked Luc, ever so gingerly, for details about the girlfriend's death, but each time, he'd said it wasn't the right moment or place, not at the pool or café or forest. "I'll turn into a blubbery heap," he'd said at first. "Things could get ugly." Then: "It's a long story. Like, *The Three Musketeers* long. Seven hundred pages, give or take." Then, simply: "Another time? Rain check?"

The conversation was swept under a rug. Still, she didn't feel ready to go beyond kissing if he wasn't able to talk about this shadow from his past. Not even the woman's name. Callie tried not to care, but she *did*.

In the three weeks since she'd announced her name onstage, there had been a global resurgence of interest in her music. On a girls' night out at the bistro, Amira showed her the Callie Byrd hashtag on social media, pointed out her streaming numbers bursting through the roof. Violette's squeals and Lili's air punches and Callie's surprise were tempered with the understanding: This had to be on Brett's radar too.

"Maybe he won't come after all," said Amira.

"Maybe he'll let you go without a fight," said Violette.

"Maybe you could reach out to him," said Lili. "Tie up loose ends."

Callie considered this. Maybe she could go back to Colorado to pick up sentimental things like her wedding album and her favorite instruments and Eva's preschool drawings. Maybe Brett would be okay with it. Maybe she'd been paranoid, imagining the worst. Maybe he was a reasonable guy after all.

Or was that what he wanted her to think?

Over these past few weeks, truffle hunting with the Forêts every morning was a highlight. Luc and his dad would hide a truffle behind a tree, cover it with leaves and soil, and then Eva would encourage Chouchou to find it, nose it, and sit in exchange for a dog treat. A comically choreographed dance with laughter and applause.

"My new career goal is world-class dog trainer," Eva now told anyone who'd listen. "With a specialty of *le cavage*," she'd add with pride, using the local word for truffle caving. She trained Chouchou to sit, stay, stand, shake, wait, speak, dance, high-five, and—most importantly for Monsieur Forêt—to wait for permission before eating any food she encountered.

One morning, Chouchou got especially excited, pawing at the ground near the great oak tree, on the opposite side of the trunk from Marguerite's grave. The older dogs knew they weren't supposed to dig in that area and gave the tree a wide berth. But Chouchou's enthusiasm could not be contained. Dirt flew, and Eva came to the puppy's side, as Callie watched curiously.

"Maybe it's a black diamond!" said Eva. She'd heard about those truffles, worth hundreds of dollars apiece.

"Good guess, but it's a few months too early for that," Luc said.

Monsieur Forêt said nothing, only watched the hole with a strange intensity.

Eva reached into the loose soil and pulled something out. Only it wasn't a truffle, but a small silver box, hinged and small enough to fit in her palm. Callie helped her open it. Inside was a ring.

"A black diamond!" Eva said in wonder.

It was simple, a dark teardrop gem in a gold band, tucked into creamy velvet.

Her papi reached out to take it, and after a long moment his voice emerged in a rasp. "I buried this the day Sophie accepted Tristan's marriage proposal."

He sniffed, wiped his nose with his handkerchief. "This was my grandmother's ring, and I knew it would be perfect. A black diamond. We always loved our truffles, especially those."

He let out a long sigh. "I did some detective work to figure out Sophie's ring size. Brought this ring to the jeweler to make it fit. Like Cinderella's slipper. I wanted everything ready for when Tristan returned and the Three Musketeers were back together. Then I could propose to her, and Tristan could be my best man." He paused. "It turned out, he had his own plans."

Eva picked up the ring, slid it on her finger, where it hung loose. "It's beautiful," she said with awe. "What will you do with it now, Papi?"

He returned it to the silver case and stuck it in his pocket. "We'll see. Who knows if it would fit after all these years." He paused. "If our hearts would fit."

One sweltering day in the third week of July, after their forest walk and truffle hunting, Callie and Eva were at home making lunch when there was a knock on the door. Callie assumed it was Julien, maybe inviting them to an *apéro* with Violette later, or bringing them left-over *daube* from his mother, or asking Eva to help him clean leaves from the pool—she loved wielding the net.

Callie open the door and there he was.

Brett.

# 33

# FACE-OFF

Callie stepped outside and closed the door behind her, praying Eva would stay in the kitchen. Hearing the deep hum of La Chanson, she straightened up, threw her shoulders back, widened her stance. She swelled like a river in springtime.

She imagined flying upward, seeing this play out from a bird's-eye view. For two years, Brett's powers had seemed invincible, those of a sorcerer. Now, she knew the truth. Beneath the façade was a hurt little boy, fueled by hurt and fear.

She assessed him as she would a stranger—a fifty-something man, black hair flecked with gray, shaved to a short buzz to disguise the thinning. Trim and toned in a tailored button-down shirt and leather flip-flops that said casual rich. Objectively, he didn't *look* threatening or underhanded or controlling. Actually, he looked older and tired, bags beneath his eyes, deepening wrinkles, cheeks sagging, a gray pallor under the tan.

Behind him, in the background, she noticed Hugo, carrying his briefcase, looking official. They were cut from the same cloth, and somehow, she wasn't surprised they'd found each other. Roughly the same age, the same MO in the world. They charmed people, tapping into others' weaknesses. Damaged boys turned into manipulative men.

Brett was smiling at her, searching her eyes. "Hey, cupcake."

She met his gaze, lifting her chin, staying on the stoop to look down at him.

"I missed you." His voice was weirdly civilized. "How's Eva?"

Callie said nothing, silently willing Eva to stay inside. She stood firmly in the doorway, ready to block her. Channeling a military strategist, she thought through next steps. Get rid of Brett, call her friends. If needed, call the police.

"Go away," she said in English, channeling the wine witch's iron voice. She glared over his shoulder at Hugo and translated to French. "*Allez-vous-en.*"

The men exchanged looks but held their ground.

"We're done, Brett." Apparently, Callie would have to make this crystal clear. She drilled her eyes into his. "Back in Colorado, I let you steal my voice. And here, I've found it. Now it's stronger than ever."

He gave her a measured look, revealing nothing.

She felt herself shaking, not from fear or weakness, but with the force of her words. "Eva and I belong here. With our friends. I'm telling you to stay away from us. Now and forever."

Dramatic, perhaps, but she needed her words to get through to him. Brett listened with a cordial expression, but Callie knew him well enough to sense the shock and confusion and anger beneath it.

Finally, he said, "Inspiring little speech, cupcake." He forced a smile, glancing at Hugo. This wasn't going according to his plan, she could tell, but he'd managed to pivot.

"We'll just explain why we're here," Brett said with a nod to Hugo.

"Good morning, madame, we have come on a business matter," Hugo said, stepping forward and speaking in heavily accented English for the sake of Brett.

Julien must have heard their voices—he ran out of his cottage and planted himself between her and the other men. "What's going on?"

Callie answered, her voice heavy. "This is Brett."

Julien clearly recognized the name from their chats about him. His jaw firmed and he turned to Hugo. "Why did you bring him here?"

"He's a potential buyer for the château." Hugo's voice oozed condescension. "He won't even make you leave your *petites maisons*. He'll rent to you. And he'll hire a company to finish the renovation. Then he'll move in. You and our mother just need to sign a few forms. Then you can occupy yourself with your little poems. I'll handle it all."

"*Non.*" Julien's voice brimmed with exasperation. "Our mother has already told you no. She has no intention of selling. And she's still the owner."

"Not for long," said Hugo. "She'll be easy to convince. Anyway, she has dementia."

Julien shot him a look of steel. "We'll discuss this later. With our mother. Whose mind is perfectly clear." He turned to Brett and said slowly, in French, "You are not welcome here."

Brett looked away as if he had nothing to do with the situation, as if it were just a brothers' spat.

Hugo, for his part, couldn't hide his shock at the transformation in Julien, who hadn't mumbled a single *euhhh. Au contraire,* his words held hurricane force. After composing himself, Hugo tried staring his brother down, but Julien wasn't playing games. He wrapped his hand around the hammer in his tool belt.

Noting this, Brett took a step back—perhaps wishing he'd brought a bodyguard—while Hugo said, "I can bring this to court. I have inheritance rights to half this place. I'll easily buy out your part once our mother is declared incompetent."

"We'll never accept," said Julien, tightening his grip on the hammer.

Hugo laughed again. "I'm a real estate lawyer. And you're no one. You have nothing. I'm doing you a favor."

Julien shook his head at his brother, a gesture of disdain, then turned to Callie. "Can we talk?"

She ushered him inside her cottage, telling the other men over her shoulder, "Wait outside." She locked the door and led Julien to the kitchen table, where Eva sat before two plates of freshly made sandwiches, looking anxious—she must have heard the heated discussion outside.

"What's going on, Mom?"

Callie drew in a breath. "Brett's here." Seeing the look of horror on Eva's face, she quickly added, "You don't have to see him. We'll make him leave."

Eva dove into her arms and kept a tight hold, positioning herself in Callie's lap like a toddler.

Meanwhile, Julien stood by the fridge, on alert. "What do you want me to do? Call the police?"

"I don't think the police could do much at this point," she said with a sigh. "There's no obvious crime or threat." She considered the options. Most of all, she wanted Brett gone, once and for all. She needed him to understand that buying the château would be pointless. "I'll talk to him," she said finally, "and make him understand there's no hope of getting me and Eva back."

She stood up, and her gaze landed on the scythe hanging over the mantel, vintage farming decor. She walked over to it, unhooked it from the wall.

Julien raised his brows.

"I won't use it." She ran her fingertip over the dull blade. "But he doesn't know that." She gave Julien a wry smile. "Just like he didn't know you wouldn't bash him with your hammer."

Julien grinned. "It does send a message."

"Listen, Julien, can you tell him I'll talk in twenty minutes? At the table by the pool. And will you be with me?"

"Of course. And I'll be ready to call the cops. Just say the word."

Callie watched him walk outside, then listened to the voices through the open window. Julien's voice, firm and low and terse. The gruff, annoyed voice of Hugo. The falsely mellow voice of Brett, playing the concerned parent and partner.

She picked up the landline phone and dialed Luc's number. "Brett's here," she said, without preface. "Julien's with me. Can you take Eva?"

"Oh, Callie. I'll be there in fifteen minutes."

"Just take her to the park, okay?"

"Of course. My dad's there now. You all right? Want me to call the cops?"

She turned the scythe over in her lap. "Just comfort Eva. I'll handle Brett."

"*D'accord*. I'm leaving now."

After she hung up, she hugged Eva, who'd been listening and watching in rare silence. "Luc's coming," said Callie. "You'll hang out with him and Papi, okay?"

Eva nodded and latched onto her like a baby monkey. Over her daughter's shoulder, Callie looked out the window and saw Brett and Hugo strutting around the gardens, pointing at plants, as if discussing new landscaping. She felt a hot wave of indignation. This was so *Brett*, exuding a sense of ownership in her safe place.

Callie was relieved when the men disappeared inside the château. Julien remained outside her door, like a bodyguard, while Callie comforted Eva.

Ten minutes later, a knock sounded. "It's me." Luc's familiar voice filled her with relief.

When she opened the door, he pulled her into a hug—he was panting, as if he'd run all the way here at top speed. Meanwhile, Eva greeted Jolie and Chouchou, then slipped her dog-saliva-coated hand into Luc's.

As Callie stood with Luc on the cottage stoop, filling him in, she noticed Eva take a quick peek at Brett, who was just exiting the château. From a couple dozen yards away, Brett smiled and waved, his exterior carefully composed as he descended the steps.

Eva turned away, put her other hand around Luc's, hanging on to it like a life rope.

Luc glanced at Brett as if dismissing him, then gave Eva a comforting smile.

With a controlled expression, Brett walked to the patio and watched Luc lead Eva away. As Julien and Callie approached him, she noted what a good poker face he had, like any sociopath.

Once Eva and Luc and the dogs had left, Callie gestured for the men to sit at the table by the pool. She stood above Brett, holding the scythe, running her hands over the steel.

The river music rose, her true friend and trusty bandmate. The sound of the carnyx rumbled in her bones, a force ancient and mystical. Her throat opened, her breath flowed, her torso filled with power. "Brett," she said, "we're done."

He blinked, quiet for a moment, as if maybe her words were finally sinking in. But then he rearranged his face into that of a loving partner who'd been treated unfairly, his gaze now soft and imploring. "Listen, honey, you don't know how much I've missed you and—"

"Your old tricks won't work. Not anymore. Go home." She sat across from him, next to Julien, and placed the scythe on the table, her hand firmly around its handle.

"Oh, precious," he said, voice dripping. "I love you and I'll wait for you, whatever you're going through. I love Eva. I'm her father now."

"You might wish you were. But you need to accept that you're not. Never were, never will be."

A pause, and then his voice emerged with a new hardness. "Reality check. You're uprooting our daughter. You have no money, no stability. Your depression will return. Debilitating." He pronounced it like a curse. "You need me to take care of you and Eva. You're being shamefully irresponsible. I know you better than you know yourself . . ."

She turned the scythe over in her hands and tuned him out. There was no point in talking. He was clinging to the same tactics. But now, she trusted herself. And she was not alone. In her head, the voices of her friends drowned his out, and most of all, her own voice did.

*You're a damn good mother.*

She cut him off. "Your lies and manipulation don't work anymore. I'm back. My self is back. My voice is back. And hear me now, Brett. I want you gone."

He assessed her as if she were an opponent in negotiations for a coveted antiquity, his tone shifting, tactics changing once again.

"I've already spoken with my friends in the Department of Child and Family Services. And I filed a police report in Colorado. I expressed my concerns about your instability. Fleeing the country with our daughter. Kathy saw the property damage with her own eyes. As did my lawyer. As did the police. Destruction from a madwoman. The point is, we're all concerned about Eva's welfare."

Callie's voice emerged in the low staccato of a mother lion's growl. "I'm protecting my child from *you*. And the police here see *you* as the danger. As does the entire town. Your lies won't work here. Now leave."

He paused, recalculating his strategy once again. She recognized this moment, when getting his way became a point of pride, when he was willing to spend energy and time and money to get something just to prove he could. Finally, he spoke. "You'll come to your senses. And I'll be here when you do."

She understood that he wouldn't be giving up—he would just retreat to make a new plan. He reached for her hand across the table, and she snatched it away, held the scythe with both hands. Being with him felt draining, but she would recharge and stand firm, no matter what else he threw her way. She stood up and gestured toward his car, indicating the conversation was over.

Brett gave Hugo a sidelong glance, face reddening in a rare show of humiliation.

Hugo stood up, looking a bit bewildered, in over his head. This must have been more than he'd bargained for. Of course, Brett would have framed the situation with lies.

Within seconds, he'd gotten his embarrassment under control. Standing up, he said, "Sometime, when you're out of the house, Hugo will give me a tour of the cottages. He has extra keys." Brett gave a smile that didn't reach his eyes. "Oh, and I enjoyed the secret room in the château."

*Damn him*. The secret room had felt like a safety net. Which, of course, he'd guessed.

"We'll be putting together an offer soon," he said, dropping any pretenses. "No matter if you think you want me out of your life. That won't happen. Soon I'll own this place. And your cozy cottage."

She worked her jaw, gripped the scythe. "You can play your games, Brett. But you won't get your way. Not with La Chanson. And not with me."

Julien stood to face him, shoulders back. It was strange seeing him not slumping—on the contrary, he was using his lanky frame to stretch himself bigger. "Time for you to leave."

"Get the hell out of here," she told Brett, in case he didn't catch Julien's French.

"We'll be back," Hugo said after a tense moment, then walked away with a "*Bonne journée, madame.*"

Brett lingered, stroking his chin. "I'll be staying in the area for a while. Such a beautiful town. Hugo told me about great places to dive. I even brought my scuba gear. And this château is charming. I've always wanted one in the South of France. And now I'll have it."

Callie rolled her eyes and shook her head, done with the conversation. Reasoning with him was impossible. "You're being absurd, Brett."

In a threatening tone, he murmured, "I don't know who that man holding Eva's hand was, but he won't get in my way." He stared at her for a moment longer, watching his words land. "Nick didn't."

A chill gripped her as she watched him walk to the car. His meaning was clear. The *truth* was clear. She'd been with her husband's murderer for two years. Yet she had no proof. And her lawyer appointment was still ten days away. As Callie watched him stride off, she grasped the situation with grave certainty.

She had put Luc in danger.

# 34

# GHOST BOY

Fifteen minutes later, Callie was still reeling when Julien came onto the patio holding a tray with a pot of orange blossom tea, lavender honey, and two teacups. "*Merci*, Julien," she said, truly grateful.

He poured the tea into her cup first. "When this was a safe house, I encountered all kinds of men. Men who tracked down their wives. Some were openly violent. Some hid a secret violence. The most dangerous. The coiled vipers." He paused. "Callie, that's what I see in Brett."

She took this in. It was somehow validating, knowing her instincts were right. But also horrifying. "Julien, listen . . ." She forced herself to say the words out loud. "Brett implied that he killed my husband. And that he'd kill Luc too."

Julien listened to her, *believing* her, as she kept going, processing the encounter with Brett. When she finished, he said, "We're here for you, Callie. All of us. I'll talk to my mom. Make sure she refuses to sell. Now, what else do you need?"

"No blue bottles yet." She was mostly joking. "How about a deadbolt? A new lock."

"Want me to do that now?"

She nodded. She didn't want Brett to taint her safe cottage with his presence. "Thanks, Julien."

He headed toward the path to town, then turned to look back. "You stood up to him. With guts and a farm tool. Be proud of yourself."

She gave a weary smile. "Be proud of yourself too, Julien."

Once he left for the hardware store, she went upstairs to take a shower, feeling the urge to wash herself of Brett's presence. As she undressed, she eyed Pepito and, this time, heard him speak in Nick's actual voice, not the funny nasal version but Nick's voice in the rare moments he'd been serious.

*Protect Luc.*

Callie half jogged along the river toward the town center, passing shops and friends with a brief wave of her hand, making a beeline for the park, where she spotted Eva playing with Samuel. She paused, catching her breath, feeling a wave of relief that despite everything, her daughter was content.

Luc caught her eye and ran over, as his dad and the older men stayed near the children, in guard mode, holding their *pétanque* balls like grenades. She imagined that if Brett came close, these men would form an impassible military line between him and Eva.

Luc wrapped her in his arms for a long moment. "What happened, Callie?"

She gathered her thoughts, aware Brett could be watching. Or Hugo. Or the Parisian assistant. Aware that every minute she spent with Luc could increase the danger. She filled him in as he pressed a fist to his mouth. Finally, she forced herself to say the most important thing. "Luc, he saw how much you mean to us. You're in real danger."

"Listen, Callie, I'm willing—"

"Luc, I think he killed my husband."

He blinked, stepped backward in shock.

She forced herself to keep going. "Brett was with my husband when he fell off a cliff. Died from the head wound. The police couldn't rule out foul play. They didn't know Brett had motives. His lawyers got him out of it."

Luc pulled her toward him and held her, kissed her hair. "I'm here for you. No matter what, Callie."

"It's too dangerous, Luc." She pulled away and slowly shook her head. "We need to stay away from each other, as long as he's here."

Luc's eyes grew shiny. "There has to be another way, Callie."

She braced herself, pushed down tears. "Listen, after what happened to Nick—I could never forgive myself if anything happened to you."

He rubbed his face and shook his head but didn't try to argue. She thought of the tragedy with his girlfriend, wondered if this gave them a point of connection. The circumstances of her death remained obscured, but something vulnerable in his expression made Callie think he could understand the stakes—and the ensuing guilt.

He reached out to hold her again, but she took a step back. "I'm so sorry, Luc." Biting her lip, she turned away and hurried toward Eva, who had just spotted her. Chouchou followed at her daughter's heels, like an imprinted duckling.

After a long hug, Eva asked, "Is Brett gone?"

Callie chose her words, tempering the truth. "For now. I told him we'd left him. Forever."

"Good."

Carefully, Callie added, "But he wants to buy the château."

"No," Eva said firmly. "Absolutely not." She buried her face into Chouchou's neck as Callie patted her back and whispered, "We won't let him."

Soon Monsieur Forêt approached with Belle and Jolie. "My son filled me in," he said, embracing Callie. "Listen, Luc and I would like Chouchou to stay with you."

Eva planted a kiss on the pup's head. *"Merci!"*

Her papi winked at her. "If that man comes by, she'll rip his fancy pants legs right off. No match for sharp puppy teeth."

"Ha!" Eva gave a smug smile.

Monsieur Forêt had made it sound lighthearted but looked at Callie from the corner of his eye. His meaning was clear—she and Eva weren't alone. He and Luc *cared*. And yes, it might be reassuring to have a dog to alert them if Brett trespassed.

"*Merci.*" Callie measured her words. "We'd love to have Chouchou over to visit for a few days."

"A few weeks," corrected Eva. "Or months. Or years!"

On the walk home, Monsieur Forêt kept his arm around Callie, joking about how he'd use his *pétanque* balls as weapons, how Brett would cower before them. Luc kept his distance, as requested, trailing a few dozen paces behind.

"You know," Monsieur Forêt said to Eva, "Chouchou was the runt of the litter. Her breeder didn't think she'd make it. So he said Luc could have her if he could keep her alive. She was just the size of a rat back then." He laughed. "But Luc brought her everywhere in that sling, fed her with bottles through days and nights. And look at her now!"

"A miracle," Eva said solemnly.

"Chouchou went through scary times, but she's stronger for it now." He gave Eva a meaningful look.

"Good thing she had Luc," said Eva.

Her papi nodded. "And Belle stepped in to be a mother, and Jolie became an aunt, and all the dogs at the park are like brothers and sisters."

Eva nodded. "But Luc saved her."

Callie remembered their first meeting with him, the puppy in the sling. She'd had no idea he'd just nursed it back from near-death. And now he was offering this resilient creature to her daughter, to make her feel safe and loved.

From time to time, Callie looked back at him as the river played a viola tune, deep and rich and wistful.

In the château, Callie chopped courgettes while Madame Lavigne chopped aubergines, and Eva played with Chouchou amid scents of onions and garlic sautéing in olive oil. The kitchen, now renovated, was a gorgeous mix of vintage and modern. Julien had moved his tools and equipment to the second floor to begin work there.

Several days had passed since Brett's appearance. And during that time, the wine witch had been spending less time at her apartment above the *cave à vins* and more time at the château. She'd welcomed Callie and Eva into the sparkling kitchen to cook dinners together, teaching them how to make Provençal dishes. Yesterday was grilled lamb with rosemary and thyme, and tonight was ratatouille, her specialty.

Callie sensed that the real reason Madame Lavigne was here every night was to keep a close eye on things, now that Brett had shown up. Callie didn't mind—she enjoyed the older woman's company and appreciated the excuse to spend time in the château. When she'd first stepped inside the renovated ground floor, she'd gasped. The drop cloths in the living room had been removed, revealing a velvet sofa in muted rose, silver-blue jacquard chairs, polished wood tables, antique Persian carpets, silky curtains, light pouring through tall windows, paintings and prints enlivening the walls—and it all felt sumptuous.

As she chopped, Callie imagined the women and children who'd come to this refuge decades earlier, feeling enchanted after all they'd been through. Then, her mind slipped to a darker place. She imagined a younger Madame Lavigne standing on a chair and reaching for a high shelf, taking a hidden blue bottle, dropping its contents into Tristan's wine, watching him weaken by the day, priming him for an "accident." How desperate she would have been.

Callie shook herself. There was no proof that Madame Lavigne had poisoned her husband, only the decades-old assumptions of a twelve-year-old boy. Not to mention Callie's own assumptions. Officially, the man had died from drowning while drunk and sick. There was no evidence of foul play. There was no evidence, either, that Madame Lavigne had given blue bottles of poison to women to feed to their abusers. Or that the bottles even contained poison. This had all been filtered through the eyes of an imaginative child. And her own mind.

Anyway, that was all long ago, and things were different nowadays. She'd let the police handle Brett if he kept pushing. The two officers at the station—a young woman and middle-aged man—had been kind and helpful when she'd stopped by to talk to them, grasping the gravity of the situation. They told her to call the moment she felt threatened. Same for Luc. Madame Lavigne hadn't had these resources back then, and neither had the women she supposedly handed blue bottles to.

Callie glanced now at Madame Lavigne chopping tomatoes with a serrated knife. She was an enigma, a bundle of contradictions. To the woman's credit, when she'd found out about Hugo's plan, she reiterated her refusal to sell. But he'd replied that he'd already made a verbal deal with Brett, that he couldn't go back on it or Brett would ruin him. Callie could, indeed, imagine Brett putting pressure on him, making subtle threats to destroy his reputation.

Madame Lavigne was standing her ground, but she was worried about legal uncertainties and tactics Hugo might try—and when it came down to it, she was reluctant to hurt her son or his business. Of course, Hugo was manipulating her, which Julien kept pointing out, growing more vocal by the day.

Julien's work continued on the second floor now—an occasional hammering sound came from above, and Callie appreciated him putting his heart into it. Violette had been coming over often, trailing her scent of caramelized sugar and berries.

Over the past few days, Callie had felt reassured knowing that Chouchou was present and alert everywhere they went. She was diligent about locking the deadbolts at night and whenever they left the cottage. The balcony door had a flimsy lock, but it was twelve feet off the ground, harder to access. Tending to these details distracted her from missing Luc's arms around her, his lips on hers, his thumb stroking hers in that subtle, sensual way.

Now, Madame Lavigne wiped tomato pulp from her hands and poured herself and Callie glasses of rosé—"To sip as we cook, dear." She looked quintessentially Provençal in her yellow cotton apron with a cicada print. She'd entirely abandoned her heavy black dresses, exchanging them for lighter shades with pops of color.

As they cooked, Eva was wandering around, engaged in imaginary play involving dogs and dancing. She paused in the kitchen, staring at a chair that Chouchou was intently sniffing. "The ghost boy is here."

Madame Lavigne nodded, chopping once again, beads of sweat shining on her forehead.

"He doesn't usually hang out in the kitchen," Eva said, looking puzzled.

Her mamie Sophie gave a sad smile. "Tristan loves ratatouille."

"Too bad he can't eat it," said Eva.

"Poor thing." Madame Lavigne gave a resigned nod. "He's ready to move on."

Eva nodded, then announced, "Chouchou wants to play hide-and-seek," and ran out of the kitchen with the pup, waving a hand behind her at the empty chair.

It was strange, observing this interaction. Clearly, Tristan's ghost was as real to Madame Lavigne as it was to Eva. Callie lowered her voice. "Have you always sensed his ghost?"

Madame Lavigne nodded. "His ghost showed up a few weeks after he died. Always Tristan as a little boy. The version of him I loved most."

Callie whispered, "I get it. I get how you can love the little boy in a damaged man."

The wine witch met her eyes—a look of wistfulness and sorrow. She set down the knife, wiped her hands on her apron, and motioned for Callie to follow. She paused in the entryway before the wall of prints and paintings, and pointed to the photo from the tin box, now framed.

Madame Lavigne ran her fingertip over Tristan's image. "He was ready to leave this life. A few days before he passed, when he was weak and sick, he finally opened up to me. He told me that during the atrocities of war, he felt the boy in him leaving. The piece of him that was playful, innocent, loving. The truest piece."

She wiped a tear with the heel of her palm, nodded at the empty chair. "That was the piece left behind when the violent man left this earth. The little boy Tristan, searching for what he'd lost."

Callie patted her shoulder as Madame Lavigne drew in a breath and continued. "When he came back from the war, the river played dark music around him. The dogs wouldn't come near him. And when he died, the lost little boy became a ghost."

Swallowing the ache in her throat, Callie drew her in for a hug.

After a moment, the wine witch pulled away. "Behind every cruel man is a lost little boy." She walked back into the kitchen and began slicing more tomatoes, juices and seeds spurting out.

Just when Callie thought the conversation was over, Madame Lavigne glanced at the empty chair. "I wish he could find his way to the other side. Philippe shares my wish. We've moved past our heartache and hurt. Now, if only we could let Tristan go."

# GONE

Later that evening, at dusk, the ratatouille steamed in its ceramic dish on the patio table. Julien and Violette sat across from Callie and Eva, with the dogs by their feet. According to Eva, Tristan's ghost had followed the ratatouille outside and now stood beneath the olive tree at the garden's edge, breathing in scents of *herbes de Provence*.

Candlelight flickered as Madame Lavigne served the ratatouille with a wooden spoon, heaping it over couscous on each plate. Eva had wanted to invite the Forêts over, but Callie had simply said, "Not tonight, sweet pea."

Despite the Forêts' glaring absence, dinner was lively, laughter increasing with each course. Julien and Violette's joy was music itself, an exquisite duet, a ballad decades in the making. Eva and Chouchou, too, exuded love, like the *bachatas* that Nick's family danced to in Guatemala. Eva's dream was coming true—a family and dog of her own—even though Callie gently reminded her that the Chouchou situation was temporary.

At one point, Violette dished the gossip that Brett was still hanging around La Chanson, staying in a fancy hotel in the next town over. He'd rented a flashy black electric Peugeot sports car, which people had sighted all over town. When he'd tried entering the *pâtisserie,* Violette told him they were temporarily closed. Lili at the *boulangerie* simply said he wasn't welcome and pierced him with an ice-pick stare. Even sweet Amira and Beni wouldn't let him step a foot inside the *salon du thé*. "La Chanson does not want you here," Amira had told him, shutting the door in his face.

Even as Callie smiled, grateful the town had her back, she felt unsettled that Brett hadn't left. Part of her had hoped that he'd processed her conversation with him, acted in a rational way, and given up. But he was a man who did not admit defeat. And this had become a battle.

Once the final course was done—a cherry clafoutis—Eva fell asleep on a pool lounge chair, cuddled with Chouchou and Fleur, while Violette and Julien insisted on doing the dishes. The river played a dreamy nocturne, a minor key with strings plucked like stars.

Alone now with Madame Lavigne, Callie sipped her tiny glass of port, its mysterious sweetness drawing them close. "So, have you had any Brett sightings?" she asked lightly.

"Actually," said Madame Lavigne, after a long pause, "for the past few days, Brett has been coming in daily to buy a bottle of Burgundy."

"What?" Callie set down her port with a splash. "You let him in your shop?"

"Someone needs to keep a close eye on him." Madame Lavigne gave a wry grin. "He thinks he's winning me over. Thinks he's so smart using that translation app on his phone. He thinks everything will be simpler if I just give Hugo my blessing to sell."

Callie's stomach tightened. "I don't think it's a good idea to interact with him at all."

"Don't worry, dear." Madame Lavigne waved away her concerns like smoke. "He thinks he's using me, but I'm using him. I'm playing to his ego while secretly learning his plans and motives."

"It's a dangerous game."

"I've met dozens of men like him. I know what I'm doing."

"Please be careful." But that wasn't enough, Callie realized. The best way to inoculate Madame Lavigne against Brett would be to open up to her.

With some trepidation, she recapped how he'd manipulated parents at Eva's school, making Callie appear fragile and unstable, nipping any mom friendships in the bud. On and on and on she went, spilling one secret after another, the trickle becoming a deluge. It felt good.

When Callie paused to catch her breath, Madame Lavigne clucked in sympathy. "Oh, I've seen all that before. I don't believe him for a second."

Callie breathed out. "Let's hope he'll just give up." But she knew how difficult that would be. A whiff of defeat would only fuel his obsession to get what he wanted.

And he'd enlisted Hugo, whether through threats or bribes or a blend of both. Hugo was probably the one who'd given Callie's number to Brett. Three times over the past week, Brett had called the landline. Callie had decided to answer, in case it was a friend. She was determined not to let him get in the way of her friendships, not anymore—which meant she simply hung up the moment she heard his oily voice.

"Hey, cupcake, I need to—" *Click.*

"Listen, precious. I really—" *Click.*

"Callie, don't hang—" *Click.*

Now, Madame Lavigne drained her last drop of port. "So, will you sing at the open mic soirée?"

"I'm not sure. I mean, with everything going on . . ." Callie's voice drifted off.

With unexpected ferocity, Madame Lavigne said, "Stand up to that man."

Callie met her gaze and reached for her hands. "Stand up to your son."

Madame Lavigne squeezed her hands and smiled, something bright and sad, strong and tender.

Callie matched her smile in a secret pact.

On her sofa, Callie sipped chilled linden blossom tea, guitar on her lap, river music floating through the open window. It was only late morning, but the heat was setting in, and she appreciated the breeze over her skin. A few days had passed since her heart-to-heart chat with Madame Lavigne, and her resolve—to stand up to Brett, to sing her heart out, to freely live her life—had only grown.

From time to time, she looked outside to see Eva playing truffle hide-and-seek in the gardens with the dogs. And she caught occasional glimpses of Luc, who'd volunteered to help Julien with some heavy lifting in the château.

Luc and Julien were forming a true friendship, as were their parents. Lately, Monsieur Forêt had been coming over to sit in the château kitchen as Madame Lavigne cooked, reminiscing about their childhood and joking together as the ghost boy basked in the scents of rosemary and garlic and lemon.

Now, as Callie sang and played her new song, with the river accompanying her in a catchy bass rhythm, she realized that she had a full album. *Whisper Words,* she'd call it. She mentally shuffled the songs, experimenting with the order. It gave her an expansive feeling to imagine performing on a big stage again.

The river music made a sudden shift to something dissonant and unsettling. She set down her guitar and stood up, trying to make sense of it. Then the dogs started barking—not in a playful way, or an *I found a truffle* way, but in alarm.

Something was wrong.

She opened the door, scanning the grounds for Eva. Her last glimpse of her daughter had been just minutes ago—Eva had been laughing and leaping over one of the walls that edged the hillside terraces. Now, Callie didn't see her. And the dogs' barking was growing frantic, transforming into growls.

Her insides froze. Even peaceful Fleur, who rarely barked, was raising an alarm.

The barking was coming from different spots on the estate, bouncing off the hillside and limestone cliffs, playing tricks on her ears.

"Eva!" Callie shouted.

No answer.

"Eva!" she called, louder now.

She homed in on Chouchou's higher-pitched puppy barks, coming from halfway up the hillside. As she ran up the steps, she registered Julien and Luc in her peripherals, now at the château doors, coated in plaster dust. She heard their footsteps running behind her, their voices asking what was wrong.

"I can't find Eva!" The river music was crescendoing, rising in volume, notes clashing like a horror-movie soundtrack. Panic gripped her.

Julien was taking the hillside steps three at a time, while Luc followed, checking behind cypresses.

The men kept going, while Callie paused to scan the grounds from this vantage point, searching for any sign of Eva. Peering through gaps in the oleander bushes, she noticed sunlight flash off something shiny and black in the driveway. The Peugeot convertible, with its silent, stealth engine.

Brett was here.

And Eva was gone.

# 36

# J'ACCUSE!

Callie pushed down her panic, forced herself to remain calm and focused.

Brett's car was here. Which meant he was here too. As was Eva. Anyway, he couldn't take her daughter out of France, could he?

Oh, but he could. The letter flashed through her mind.

But he didn't have Eva's passport. And she would put up a fight, punching and shouting every step of the way.

Then, the most horrifying scenario played out in her imagination: What if Brett drugged Eva? That was part of his playbook, what he'd done to Callie.

*What if, what if, what if?*

"I found her!" called Julien, from behind a stone wall on the hillside. He bent down, disappearing for a moment, then stood up, motioning to the others. In an instant, Luc was beside him, and Callie was running toward them.

She saw Eva lying on the ground, head bleeding at the temple, her knee, and her elbow. Eyelids trembling, she was clutching Julien's and Luc's hands on either side. Luc had gone into full doctor mode, gently assessing her injuries as Julien whispered soothing sounds. Chouchou had stopped barking and was now curled beside her, nuzzling her neck.

Shaking, Callie knelt down and stroked her daughter's hair. "Oh, sweet pea, what happened?"

But Eva was only whimpering, unable to form words.

Had Brett done this? Callie glanced around, silently daring him to show himself. She saw no one but heard the other dogs still barking below, near the patio gardens. Barking and growling.

"Eva's in shock," said Luc. "But it seems like she fell off the wall onto the stone steps. Hit her head and got a little scraped up. She'll need a few stitches in her forehead. Might have a mild concussion. Let's take her to the hospital."

"Okay to move her?" asked Julien.

Luc nodded. "No sign of back or neck injuries. Let's settle her on the lounge chair for a minute, calm her down, bandage her up."

Grateful for their composure, and struggling to stay calm herself, Callie nodded. The barking from Jolie and Fleur was growing louder. She suspected they were confronting Brett.

"I'll get a first aid kit and my car keys," said Julien, running toward the château.

Ever so carefully, Luc picked Eva up and carried her down the steps as Chouchou followed. She clutched him and buried her face in his chest. With paternal tenderness, he laid her on the lounge chair by the pool and knelt beside her, asking her what hurt. Her crying stopped as she nodded or shook her head—she trusted him entirely.

Knowing her daughter was in capable hands, Callie turned her attention to the dogs' escalating growls, coming from behind a cypress. Adrenaline pumping, she jogged over, now hearing a man's curses and shouts. She rounded the tree, and there was Brett.

Fleur had his pants hem in her jaws, ripping the linen.

"Get this piece of shit off me," Brett said, kicking at Fleur, just as Jolie intercepted and tore at his other pants leg.

Callie called off the dogs, petting them with gratitude, relieved they didn't appear injured. Then she shot Brett a look of iron. "What the hell are you doing here?"

"Protecting my daughter." He stammered the words, his hands shaking. "I would have helped her, but these dogs chased me away. Attacked me."

Callie strode toward him, fists clenched. "Tell me exactly what happened to my daughter."

"You let her play alone in a dangerous place, Callie. No supervision. Just like the last time. You neglected her and she nearly died. I'm the one who saved her."

Callie's head blazed with so much fury, she couldn't form words. She wished for a weapon, glanced around for a rock or stray shovel. "Were you with her when she fell? What were you doing there? Were you trying to take her?"

"Who knows how long she would've been lying there, bleeding out!"

"You saw her bleeding and didn't get me? What's wrong with you?"

He continued on his own rant. "You should be ashamed."

"If you won't give me answers, then get in your car and get the hell out of here."

But Brett went on and on. "You're negligent, and we'll have more hospital records to prove it. When I buy this place, we'll make it safer for a child."

"Get out."

"I'm not going anywhere. I'm already in the process of the purchase, just like I'm in the process of the adoption. Like it or not, I'm part of your and Eva's life. Fighting it will only make things worse."

Callie felt a fire roar within her. "Your criticism won't work anymore. And your threats are meaningless now. You have no power here. If you have anything else to say, do it through my lawyer." She gave him the name of her lawyer, then turned away and walked back toward Eva.

Back by the pool, she knelt beside Eva and kissed her head. Then she saw her daughter's eyes widen, staring over Callie's shoulder. Luc followed her gaze in alarm.

Brett was striding toward them, looking determined, as the dogs watched, baring their teeth, growling under their breaths. Before Callie could stop him, he reached out to touch Eva's shoulder.

Eva recoiled and buried her face in Luc's shirt.

Luc held her gently, and looking over her head, he murmured, "What do you want me to do, Callie? Say the word."

"I'll handle this. Just tend to Eva." Then she turned to Brett and hissed, "You're upsetting her."

Brett didn't seem to care, only shot her an accusing look. "You're letting strangers watch our daughter while you do God knows what, obsessed with your music, inflating your ego, ignoring our child."

Julien appeared and handed the first aid kit to Luc, shouldering out Brett. Callie turned her back on Brett too, blocking him from Eva's view and tuning out his rant.

"I locked the door behind me and grabbed this for you," Julien said, handing Callie her purse and keys. She touched his shoulder in gratitude.

Softly, Luc told Eva, "Listen, *ma princesse*, I'll bandage your head wound. And I'll press it gently to make the bleeding stop. *D'accord?*"

She nodded.

With a kind smile, Julien said, "You'll get to ride to the hospital in my Citroën. And afterward, we'll take you out. Three *boules de glâce*, any flavors you want."

"Chocolate, hazelnut, and cassis," she said, following their lead and ignoring Brett too.

"Sure you don't want truffle-flavored ice cream?" Luc asked, pressing gauze to her wound.

Eva made a comical face. "*Non, merci.*"

"Well then, chocolate, hazelnut, and cassis ice cream it is." Luc wrapped the bandage around her head. "Your crown, Your Highness," he said, as she gave a weak smile.

Meanwhile, Brett was rambling about Callie's negligence, trying his old tricks—but now, doubt crept into his expression. He looked disconcerted, witnessing Eva interact in French so comfortably with Julien and Luc. And he was clearly unsettled, seeing how Callie had broken out of the role he'd put her in.

At one point, Brett paused in his ranting, and Callie spoke. "Eva isn't buying your act, Brett. My friends here aren't buying your act. *No one* is buying your act."

When Brett responded with only a silent stare, Julien jangled his keys and gestured toward the driveway. "Ready, Callie?"

She nodded along with Eva and Luc, then picked up her handbag, aware of Brett from the corner of her eye.

As Luc was about to lift Eva from the lounge chair, Brett raised his voice, sounding desperate. "It's a repeat of when Eva fell out of that tree in Colorado. Almost died. Thank God I was there."

Callie could ignore this no longer. The wound was still raw.

Brett must have seen her expression change because he lowered his voice, pouring in acid. "Who knows how long she would've been lying there in the cold, unconscious?"

Luc knelt beside Eva, his hand on her shoulder in a protective gesture, at the ready to carry her to the car. He glanced at Callie, waiting for her signal, but she looked at her daughter, who seemed to have something to say.

Eva sat up and glared at Brett. In a clear voice, she said, "You're a liar." She even translated for Luc and Julien. "*Un menteur.*" She narrowed her eyes at Brett, pointing her finger at him like a sword. "*J'accuse!*"

Brett stepped back, as if struck.

The words hung in the air. This was the Emile Zola line from her open mic skit, but she wasn't joking this time, not even a smile.

"I'll tell you what really happened," Eva said. "I was walking on the wall like I do when I'm training the dogs. And then *you* jumped out of the trees and scared me. *You* made me fall. And then you acted all worried. And then the dogs chased you away. And Luc and

Julien came. They came and protected me from *you*. You would have taken me."

Eva's glare intensified, filled with righteous fury. "You would have taken me to the hospital and lied about everything, just like you did last time."

Brett said, "Eva, honey, you're making things up. You got a concussion. You don't know what you're saying. And last time you were too young to understand. You—"

"Shut up, Brett." Callie turned to Eva. "What do you mean, sweetie?" she asked, trying to control the earthquake trembling through her body.

"I remember that day," Eva said. "I was six, so everyone thinks I was too little to remember, but I do! I was climbing the tree that I always climbed, and I was good at it, and I never fell." She looked at Callie, her eyes fierce. "And, Mom, you were still a good mom. You were resting on the couch, but you were always checking on me."

Brett shook his head. "Your mom wasn't—"

"Quiet!" Eva turned back to Callie. "And then all of a sudden Brett came outside and yelled at me. 'Eva, get down from there right now!'" She imitated his voice with chilling precision. "And it scared me and I tried to come down fast so he wouldn't get angry, and that's when I fell. It was Brett's fault." She paused, letting this sink in.

Callie tried processing this revelation. He'd told her his version so many times, it had embedded inside her as the truth.

Brett said, "She's making this up—"

"No!" Eva said. "Then when I was on the ground, Brett picked me up and said he was calling an ambulance and that my own mother couldn't keep me safe, and he told everyone this, the nurses and doctor and ambulance people. And it was all lies! He was the one who wasn't safe."

Brett rolled his eyes but couldn't hide how taken aback he was.

Callie's voice emerged in a whisper. "Why didn't you tell me this before, sweet pea?"

"I did, Mom! After it happened. But you believed Brett instead of me. You were so slow and faraway."

Callie glanced at Brett, his arms folded, his expression rearranged into indignation. She kissed her daughter's head. "I'm sorry. I believe you."

"And Daddy's ghost was there too, back then. He kept me safe, and he said, 'Don't trust Brett, *mija*. Don't trust him.'"

It gave Callie a pang, how perfectly Eva imitated his voice, the slight Spanish accent.

Her daughter looked off in the distance, toward a cypress tree. "The ghost boy warned me this time. And the dogs did too. And the river. They were all protecting me from Brett." Eva clutched Callie's hand. "Don't let him do it again, Mom. He's a liar."

Brett blew out air, all condescension. "You're listening to a confused, concussed child instead of the adult who's kept her alive for the past two years."

Clearly, Brett wouldn't leave, but Eva needed a hospital, so they'd just leave him here, the would-be sorcerer with no one left to control.

"Let's go," Callie said to Luc and Julien.

Ignoring Brett, they walked to the tiny blue car, Eva cradled in Luc's arms. Callie climbed into the back seat, buckled in Eva, put her arm around her, then rolled down the window to release heat. Luc squeezed into the back seat on Eva's other side, while Julien ushered the dogs into the front passenger side, then hopped into the driver's seat.

"Don't forget about the will you made," Brett called after Callie.

*The will.* Her insides clenched. She pictured the will, tucked in the file folder in her suitcase. Of course, he'd have notarized copies of that too.

"If anything happened to you," Brett continued, "Eva would go to me." He gave her a calculated look through the open window. "Like another mental breakdown." He paused, as if considering the next words carefully. "Or death."

She shot him a fierce look. "Was that a threat?"

"It's reality. Accidents happen. Mental illness happens. Death happens." Another pause. "You're in no position to challenge me."

"I'm meeting with my lawyer," she said. "And fixing all those mistakes."

"That could take a while."

"Get out of this town, Brett. And stay away from my daughter." Callie leaned forward in the seat and said to Julien, "Let's go."

Julien stepped on the gas, and the little blue car raced away, leaving Brett in a cloud of dust.

# 37

# ENTOURAGE

As the Citroën sped past vineyards and lavender fields, Luc tended to Eva's wounds, which Chouchou—who'd scrambled into the back seat—kept trying to lick. "Your papi will be proud." Luc smiled at Eva, pointing his finger, raising the pitch of his voice. "'*J'accuse!*'"

Eva giggled and hugged Chouchou, now snug in her lap. "Did I use it right?"

"Perfectly," he said.

Julien piped in. "Let's make it four *boules de glâce*. Chocolate, hazelnut, cassis, and what else?"

"I vote for truffle," said Luc.

"Hmm," Eva said. "I think chocolate chip."

"Well, then more truffle ice cream for Luc and me," said Julien.

And on and on they bantered as Callie stroked her daughter's hair, determined to stay calm. She glanced appreciatively at Luc and Julien, who weren't trying to save them, just here for them. Lingering on Luc's profile, she tried evaluating the danger he was in. At this point, all hell had broken loose, and there was no point in pretending they didn't care about each other. Brett had witnessed the truth . . . and witnessed that Eva trusted Luc more as a father figure after a couple months than she ever did with Brett.

Callie's lawyer would have her work cut out for her, undoing so much damage. A few thousand dollars would only get her so far, especially against Brett's cadre of lawyers. The next step was clear—to contact her music manager about a new album, a new tour. The fact was, if she got brave enough to expand her world, she'd be able to pay the legal fees.

She glanced at Luc. How could she expect him to reclaim his dream of being a vet if she couldn't reclaim her own music dream?

She stroked Eva's hair, lost in thought. Up front, Fleur and Jolie had stuck their heads out the window, tongues flapping. In Eva's lap, Chouchou crossed her paws, as if to say, *This is where I belong.* The road wound along La Chanson, downstream, and Callie heard its music, cradling and comforting, like soft guitar strums around a campfire.

There was almost no traffic as they wended past hillside villages, ocher tiled roofs, dark green cypress, limestone outcroppings. Julien and Luc kept up truffle-themed repartée with Eva, distracting her from pain or fear, and in fifteen minutes, they'd arrived at the hospital. Julien parked in the shade, the windows rolled partway down, and instructed the dogs to stay. Then he and Callie hurried inside, with Luc carrying Eva.

The nurse and doctor saw her swiftly and treated her like a hero, to Callie's relief. Just as Luc predicted, Eva had a mild concussion and required a few stitches. As Callie held Eva's hand, Julien and Luc took turns making phone calls and checking on the dogs.

A half hour later, Monsieur Forêt arrived, having picked up Madame Lavigne and driven them to the hospital in his own little Citroën. Moments later, Violette and Lili and Samuel appeared, followed by Amira and Beni and Hamza.

Soon, all bandaged up and back in the waiting room, Eva stepped into a hostess role as Callie took care of the paperwork. Eva chattered to her friends about an idea for a new skit—basically, *A Hundred and One Lagotto Romagnolos,* with a devious American man replacing Cruella and the youngest pup saving the day.

Ten minutes later, the little group was crowded into the elevator, on the way to the lobby, when Monsieur Forêt asked, "What's small, green, and goes up and down?"

Eva made a thoughtful face—this was a new one.

"A sweet pea in an elevator!" He'd heard Callie's nickname for Eva, and asked about it . . . probably waiting for the opportunity to be in an elevator together. Silver linings.

"Good one, Papi!" Eva giggled, tucked her arm around his waist, and leaned her head against him, as Madame Lavigne looked on, eyes shiny.

The group stopped by the car to get the dogs, then walked to an ice cream shop downtown for treats, and Eva got her promised four *boules de glâce* in a cone. Alas, there was no truffle flavor, so Luc and Julien settled on pistachio. Callie felt a sense of contentment in the aftermath of the drama, strolling with friends through the town square as the kids' cones melted and dripped, messier by the minute.

Once the children had dropped the soggy remains into the trash, Eva spread her arms, sticky to the elbows. Thrilled at the expanse of space, she staged the new skit with her friends and the dogs, while the adults watched, amused, from nearby benches.

"Remember to take it easy!" Callie called to her daughter. The doctor had recommended only low-exertion activities for today—nearly impossible to enforce with an exuberant eight-year-old. "No running, sweetie!"

Luc was sitting beside Callie, flickering his eyes around, as if scanning the area for Brett. She, too, was aware that he might be lurking, watching them from behind a plane tree or fountain. But she would no longer hide, no longer dim herself or her truth.

She scooted closer, then picked up Luc's arm and put it around her shoulders. "If you're willing to risk it, so am I," she whispered.

Without hesitation, he nodded. "I think we blew our friends-only cover today, anyway," he said. "Brett saw how I feel about you and Eva." He gave Callie a kiss that tasted of sugar and cream and pistachio.

Lili nodded approval at their kiss, then clapped her hands and announced, "Let's make a plan to get that *con* out of our town."

Callie wasn't one for name-calling, so it took her a moment to remember this was the shortened form of the harsher insult, *connard*—but it was true. Brett was, simply put, a jerk. A *con*, pathetic and defeatable.

Now, it was her turn to play offense. Together, she and her friends made a plan to deal with him. They'd document his harassment and build a case for a restraining order. The shopkeepers would keep refusing to serve him, make life for him in La Chanson an impossibility. Madame Lavigne would continue to spy. If needed, Callie and Eva would stay in a guest room at Monsieur Forêt's *mas*.

Eva ran over, and catching the gist of the adults' conversation, announced, "Booby traps!" in English, which Callie attempted to translate through miming. After some laughter, Monsieur Forêt said, with a twinkle in his eye, "Actually, Sophie and I are experts in booby traps."

Madame Lavigne nodded. "From our Tintin days."

As Eva's grandparents shared booby trap ideas with the kids, Luc turned to Callie. "Listen, I know you have that meeting with the lawyer coming up in a couple days. Why don't I drive you? My dad can hang out with Eva in Aix while we run your errands."

"I'd love that," she said, relieved at this unexpected support.

The mention of the lawyer reminded Callie of her plan to pay for it—with her new music. She felt oddly nervous at the thought of saying her plan out loud, making it real. She looked around at her friends and cleared her throat. "I have some news," she said during a pause in the bigger group conversation.

She felt the others listening, waiting, and she forced herself to continue. "I have enough songs for a new album. I'm going to contact my manager about it."

"*Super!*" Lili said, clapping her hands.

"*Génial!*" Luc punctuated his *awesome* with a kiss on Callie's lips as cheers rose around them.

"We'll take care of Eva and Chouchou when you have gigs," said Monsieur Forêt, as the others nodded along. "You'll come home to new jokes and truffles every time."

"We'll keep Eva happy with purple *macarons*," said Violette.

"And Orangina and pool dates," added Lili.

"We can take turns being roadies," said Luc.

"Your entourage," said Madame Lavigne.

"And you can rehearse in the *salon du thé*," said Amira.

"I'll be your stylist," said Lili.

Luc said, "If you make a new album, I'll get my vet license."

To which a new round of applause ensued.

And yes, with her friends behind her, buoyed by love, Callie believed that anything was possible.

That night, Callie sang Eva her bedtime songs with such abandon that Julien and Violette applauded from the château patio. La Chanson thundered and roared and backed her up, like a muscled drummer with limbs and sweat flying in the spotlights.

After Eva fell asleep, curled up with Chouchou, Callie stared for a moment at the gauze taped to her temple. Luc had said it would heal into a barely-there line and be nearly invisible in a few years. She thought of Julien's scar, how his mother might have felt seeing it every day for decades. Maybe Madame Lavigne had done what she needed to keep her children safe.

Callie went into her room, put on her white cotton nightgown—a hand-me-down from Lili—and noticed Pepito wasn't on the bedside table. She searched the floor, hoping he hadn't fallen. Nothing. Her chest tightened as she searched the room, and then Eva's room, and the whole house. No sign of him.

Callie ran downstairs, saw the kitchen window open. There were no screens on any of the windows, making it easy for someone to climb inside. She peered outside, studied the garden in the moonlight. The rosemary and lavender were smashed, as if stepped on. She looked more closely at the windowsill, marred with dirt. Oh God, he'd climbed in through the window. She shuddered at the violation.

Most of all, she felt sick at the distinct lack of Pepito in her home. What else had Brett taken? The letters and file folders? She needed these documents to undo his damage.

Heart pounding, she hurried back upstairs, threw open the armoire doors, and unzippered the suitcase. She let out a breath of relief. Yes, the folders were there.

But she wanted Pepito back, damn it.

She wanted what he embodied—a happy family.

And Eva's heritage. Callie resolved to reach out to Nick's family in Guatemala as soon as she got a cell phone. They'd lost touch after his death—her Spanish wasn't great, and Brett had discouraged contact with them. But there was nothing stopping her now. Maybe they had some other piece of family history they could offer. This was more reason for them to visit Nick's village—which she could do once she got back into the wider world.

She resolved to go to the police station tomorrow to document the harassment and report a burglary. This time, she'd be on the offensive. From now on, she was making her own myth, weaving her own fairy tale. She would channel a Russian rusalka—one of the female river spirits, who, once hurt by men, now sought vengeance, daring a perpetrator to come close, only to entangle his feet in her hair and drown him.

She stuffed the files back into her suitcase, then went onto the balcony and played a song using the latest whisper words—*tree, sun, stone*. Tomorrow was the open mic soirée. She wouldn't cower. She would draw on her strength, use her voice.

One day later, Callie stood on the comfortable stage of the *salon du thé*, looking out at the faces of these people she loved. She saw no sign of Brett but almost wished for him to appear so he could see her true self shine. She blew bold kisses to the tourists who clearly recognized her, their phones raised and ready to record.

She spoke into the mic, first in English, then in French. "This song goes out to you, *mes amis*."

And she launched into her latest song, letting her voice fully out into the world, accompanied by La Chanson through open doors. People swayed and held hands. Eva and the kids spun in circles. Violette and Julien danced cheek to cheek.

At the table, Madame Lavigne and Monsieur Forêt leaned into each other, whispering, looking into each other's eyes, seeing, perhaps, their teenaged selves from so many decades ago, and their childhood selves beneath, tucked into each other like Russian dolls. They moved their lips together, and at that moment time lost all meaning, and they were two souls in this pocket of music—past, present, and future.

At least, that was Callie's take on it as she sang, swimming in so much love. Performing felt *right*, in the deepest way. She let the rightness of it all flow through her, the zing and the sparks that lit up her every molecule. After the final encore, she said, "*Merci*. My voice was lost for a while. It's not going away again."

Once the roar of applause faded, she walked onto the patio with Luc, bathed in light from the moon and river. Foliage and branches shifted in the breeze, and an owl hooted in the shadows. She gave Luc a long, sensuous kiss, not caring whether a certain *con* might be watching from his pool of darkness. She felt Luc sink into it, his lips soft and warm, his hands at her cheeks, trailing down the bare skin of her shoulders, her arms, sending delicious shivers through her body.

He pressed his forehead against hers, and whispered with a playful smile, "Will you be my girlfriend?"

Her laughter trilled out. "*Oui.*"

Together, they detailed their plans for Aix two days from now. She'd get a phone there too, and reconnect with the world. Soon any last threads to Brett would be cut. Soon she would really and truly be free. And she silently dared Brett to mess with her.

On the way home, walking along the river in starlight, Luc said, out of the blue, "I think my mom would have liked you."

Callie had wondered about his mother, whom she'd heard almost nothing about. It struck her as unusual, Luc's only-child status in a traditionally Catholic, small-town setting. "Tell me about her."

"She was a community nurse, from northern France, quite a bit younger than my dad—it wasn't till middle age that he got married. Now I understand that he spent his younger years heartbroken over Madame Lavigne." He released a breath. "Anyway, I only have kaleidoscope memories of my mom. Making yogurt cake together, painting pictures, planting flowers. That feeling of a mother's love."

He was quiet for a beat. "And memories of her sick and weak in bed. She died from lymphoma. I was six."

Callie squeezed his hand. "I'm so sorry."

He paused, ran his hand through his hair. "The weird thing is, I still feel guilty."

"What? Why?"

"I thought I didn't wish hard enough. I thought if I'd spent every second of every day trying to make her better, she would have lived."

La Chanson plucked a low, soft harp tune—this river had seen so much pain and joy played out over the years. All the human dramas, grand and intimate. "So you were always trying to heal others," Callie said.

"Maybe so." He gave himself a little shake. "What about your mother?"

Callie made a sound between a sharp laugh and a sarcastic smirk.

"She never wanted to be a mother. And she never wanted to have a home, or a partner, for more than three years at a time. My father was never involved, and the other men never lasted long."

It was hard to keep bitterness at bay, talking about her mom. "She did her best. Which was the bare minimum. At least I was fed and housed and clothed. She loves me, of course, but she loves herself much more."

"That sounds hard."

Callie nodded. "I always wanted a real family in a stable home in a warm community. I swore that I'd give my own kid everything I didn't have."

"And you've done it."

She thought of Brett, who'd recognized this longing and exploited it for his benefit. He'd told her he was her last chance for a real family. That if she blew it, she'd turn into her mother. Her biggest fear. "Well, there have been some bumps in the road."

"And you're getting past them. You're creating a happy life for you and Eva."

The river music shifted to wind chimes in the night breeze, and in this moment she felt the beauty of this life to her core. "I hope so."

Still, she knew the fight wasn't over yet.

That night, she had nightmares of cliffs, watching Brett push Nick off a precipice, watching him push Luc to his death too. And then there was Eva, teetering on a limestone outcropping by the river—she was playing on the edge with Chouchou, while Brett, now a black-feathered sorcerer, approached her. Callie woke up with her heart pounding, then fell asleep back into the nightmare, over and over and over.

She'd had the windows and balcony doors closed, but at three in the morning, she got out of bed and opened them wide, letting the river music in. Its melodies soothed her, and she fell asleep, now dreaming of selkies swimming free in turquoise waters, Eva and her alongside them, sparkling and splashing.

She woke up at one point, just before dawn, the sky a smear of purple-pink, and listened to the river, letting it flow through her.

*This is my own damn fairy tale.*

# 38

# RIVER GODDESS

Callie sat with Luc at a café table in her favorite square in Aix, beneath a huge plane tree by the medieval clock tower. It was mid-morning, the dappled light soft, the air crisp, blooms overflowing from the flower market booths. She tapped her feet and swayed her core, watching Eva dance with her papi to a Romani band, twirling to violin and clarinet.

Note by note, the world came to life—the ancient fountain, striped awnings, periwinkle shutters, creamy limestone, scarlet geraniums, wrought-iron balconies, and a miniature dachshund peeing on a tree trunk. In the eaves of the ancient grain hall, the carving of the Durance River goddess winked her approval in a glint of sunlight. Amid her bounty of lemons and grapes, creativity and wildness, she hung her bare foot off the edge, unbridled and overflowing. Her lover, the River Rhone, reclined beside her.

Callie smiled at Luc across the table, then returned her gaze to Eva, who was spinning, head thrown back, a pink polka-dot skirt billowing beneath a blue checkered tank, an orange scarf flying from her neck, a giant lace bow barely containing her wild hair. She looked like a Mayan eighties rock star, or a quirky echo of Callie's own self, performing right here more than a decade ago.

Her songs from that time reached through the years, and for a moment she was there, a fresh, young, yet-unknown musician, touring for fun and hatfuls of spare coins, her ten-euro-a-day diet consisting of baguettes and Brie and rosé in refillable bottles. She'd had no idea she was on the cusp of a whole mountain range of shocks and sorrows, joys and surprises . . . which had all led her back here, full circle.

She sensed the near-invisible threads unspooling from the performers in the square, silky strands reaching into forgotten places, underground labyrinths—and she felt the threads of her own music, her own self, spinning out and interlacing, inside and out, not just to family and friends but to humanity.

Eva ran up to her, breathless. This close, Callie could see the gauze pad taped to her forehead, which gave her a pang . . . but almost seemed like part of her eccentric outfit.

"Papi says it's time to meet our friends!"

"Okay, sweet pea. Luc and I have another errand later, so you all go ahead."

Callie had made plans for Eva to meet up with Nathalie and her son and their bichon frisé at the park—she'd dug out the crumpled paper with her number from her handbag, remembering this woman's kindness on the bus and her own regret that they couldn't be friends.

When Callie had called her on the landline yesterday and explained her situation, Nathalie could relate. Her great-aunt had been through something similar and had, in fact, stayed at the Château of the Lost in the eighties. That was why Nathalie had recommended it to Callie—she'd recognized a mother and child on the run. Gratitude filled Callie—people had been secretly helping her all this time.

They'd talked for an hour and made plans for a meetup in Aix, this time with Eva and her papi while Callie ran errands, but next time they'd chat over coffee on the square.

Now, looking at Luc as he sipped from his tiny cup, Callie had a pinch-me moment—she was living life in the wide world with this man she trusted with all her heart.

Well, almost. He still had secrets.

This morning, he'd accompanied her on her errands while Eva and her papi did an impromptu tour of the fountains in Aix. Callie had opened an account in a bank on the Cours Mirabeau and gotten a cell phone from a nearby shop. And this afternoon, while Eva and her papi would be at the park, Luc would come with her to the lawyer appointment—she had the folders and letters in her handbag, armed for the upcoming battle.

She took her last sip of coffee, feeling her curls long and loose over her shoulders, her eyes free of sunglasses. For a long moment, she savored the simple act of sitting here, in the bustle of Aix, without fear of being recognized.

The atmosphere was lively, and the people-watching fun, but now she couldn't help staring at Luc, trying to figure him out. He was more into dog watching than people watching, of course. His expression melted every time a dog trotted past—or was pushed along in a stroller or toted in a handbag.

Callie's mind went to the spontaneous pact he'd made with her after the hospital visit: *If you make a new album, I'll get my vet license.* His exact words, announced before family and friends, to great applause. It felt strange that he hadn't mentioned it in the two days since.

"Now that I have my own phone," she said lightly, "I'll reach out to my music manager, tell her about the new album." She arched her brow.

And he arched his in response. "Which means I'll get my license." His voice fell flat, though, no match for her enthusiasm.

She raised her shiny phone. "No time like the present." She did a quick online search, found her music manager's email address, then composed a message on her freshly made email account: *Missed you, Anita. Missed music. New album almost ready. Let's talk soon. XOXO, Callie*

Beneath her signature, she added her brand-new phone number.

She held it up for Luc to see, then pressed Send before she could change her mind. A thrill zipped through her and she looked expectantly at him. "Your turn."

When he made no move for his own phone, she chose her words carefully. "Luc, listen. Your support—it's meant everything to me. You've given me courage." She paused to study his face, which was unreadable. "Now let me do the same for you."

He gave a slight nod, which she took as encouragement to use her own phone to search for how to get a vet certificate in France. It looked pretty straightforward once the courses and internship and exams were done. Which they were. He just needed to submit his information to L'Ordre National des Vétérinaires. She passed him her phone. "*Et voilà.*"

After looking at it, he shook his head and handed it back with a pained expression.

"Luc," she said gingerly. "You were incredible with Eva after her accident. So calm under pressure. And you nursed Chouchou to health when she was a runt. You're a healer. Your dad says you even started turning part of the house into a vet clinic. You're more than good enough."

The corner of his lip turned up, but his eyes stayed melancholic. "You found your inner rock star, Callie. And my dad found his inner musketeer. And Julien, his inner poet. All of you, finding what was lost . . ." His voice drifted off.

She waited, but he stayed quiet. "I know you don't want to talk about this, Luc. And I don't want to force you. But maybe sharing it with someone who cares about you—maybe that could help." She paused. "I'm here when you're ready."

He met her gaze, took a long breath. "Seven years ago, I met a woman in vet school. Rose. We became serious, started living together. One day, three years ago, I took her for a picnic just outside of Aix—we walked far into the hills, near Mont Sainte-Victoire."

Callie nodded, picturing Cezanne's versions of this mountain, its craggy edges, the meadows of grasses and wildflowers skirting it—she'd painted the landscape in a plein air painting class during her study abroad year.

Luc's expression glazed over, his words dropping to a lower key. "I'd ordered food from a fancy restaurant, had it packed up. I was going to propose. I had the ring in my pocket."

Callie understood, from the nakedness of his voice, the quivery tremolo, that he hadn't spoken of this day for three years.

"We were on the second course when Rose started clutching her throat and gasping for air. Anaphylaxis. She had an allergy to shrimp. The chef contaminated the chicken dish." He rubbed his face. "And she'd left her EpiPen in her purse in the car."

Callie felt his pain, held his hand on the table. No wonder he'd put this off—the time would never be right to relive hell.

His chin trembled. "I called emergency services, but we were kilometers from the road. She lost consciousness. I did CPR until the paramedics arrived. But it was too late."

He lowered his eyes. "I fed her poison. And I couldn't save her."

Callie blinked back tears, her eyes stinging. "I'm so sorry, Luc."

"What right do I have to be a doctor?" He kept his gaze downcast. "To be a partner?"

"It was an accident." She squeezed his hand. "You did everything you could."

He gave a weak shrug. "I felt like my own spirit died with her. It just . . . fled. I couldn't bring myself to finish that last step for my vet license. I felt like a hollow shell. My world shrank. Just me and my dad and the dogs. I never let anyone else in."

She brought his hand to her lips, kissed his knuckles.

His gaze locked onto hers. "And then I met you," he said.

"It's time," she whispered. "You can do this."

His mouth opened, as if an excuse were about to come out. Then he closed it and nodded. She rose, walked around the table, and kissed him. As he stood up, she pressed closer, and he wrapped his arms around her waist, and she felt their selves, lost then found, wiser now, together.

After a moment, he took out his phone and opened a synced folder with his vet documentation. Within minutes, he'd submitted the application. He let out a slow breath and stretched, as if waking up from a very long nap. Then he took her hands, spun her in an impromptu dance to the violin crescendos.

As they walked toward the law office, turning onto the open, majestic avenue of the Cours Mirabeau, Callie noticed something lighter about him, a new *joie de vivre.*

Her lawyer turned out to be a whip-smart, thirty-something woman who spoke five languages and immediately prioritized her case. Throughout the appointment, tears of relief came to Callie's eyes—she was in competent and compassionate hands.

After the appointment, she checked her phone to see that her manager had sent her a barrage of texts, and within minutes she and Anita had set a phone date for the following week. Realizing she had a couple hours free before meeting back up with Monsieur Forêt and Eva, she sent him a quick check-in text, then tucked her phone into her handbag.

She grinned at Luc. "Want to wander?"

"Let's go." He led her into the oldest parts of town, the medieval labyrinth of narrow streets, like canyons between buildings. When they reached the narrowest street, Rue Esquicho Coude—Road of the Squeezed Elbows in the local Provençal—she pulled him into its cool shadows.

Alone here, she wrapped her arms around him, pulled him close, lacing her fingers through his hair. He met her lips, moving his hand over the curve of her waist, the swell of her hips, the small of her back, drawing her closer still. Part of Luc's self had been missing, she realized, but now he was here, in his entirety. And she was too, with every bit of her body and soul. "I'm glad we're together," she said.

"*Moi aussi,*" he murmured, brushing his lips along her jawline.

She sank into the pleasure, breathing in his scent of earth and forest and river, savoring every detail. Pigeons cooed from above and a slight breeze drifted over her skin, the air scented with caramelized sugar. She leaned against the ancient stone, pulled him closer, felt his heat and flesh and muscle. His stubble grazed her cheek, his lips moving from her mouth to her neck, her clavicle, the sensitive spot by her ear, then back to her lips. Being with him, with their fullest selves, was unlocking something deep and real and thrumming.

Her eyes flew open when a group of white-haired tourists turned onto the Road of the Squeezed Elbows, cell phones up, avidly taking photos, chatting with British accents, filing into the narrow space one by one. She drew back and straightened her clothes. Of course, the group probably had no overlap with her typical fan base. These tourists were retirees from the UK, most likely—but if anyone did post a photo of Callie Byrd and her boyfriend, so be it.

She exchanged amused glances with Luc, then tilted back her head and laughed, a bright, true sound, announcing her place back in the world.

Luc joined her.

At sunset, Callie and Luc meandered through the Aix visitor parking lot with their little group of humans and dogs, her sense of satisfaction running deep. The mood was as shimmery as the golden-pink glow of evening clouds.

Eva had loved her time with Nathalie's son and the bichon frisé. Monsieur Forêt had taught them dog training techniques, culminating in the bichon frisé doing a jig on his hind legs with three Lagotto Romagnolo backup dancers. Eva chattered about the pool playdate she'd planned with them, holding Callie's hand as they headed toward the little Citroën.

And that's when Callie noticed a shiny black electric Peugeot convertible with rental tags. Her mood plunged from the brightest high to the darkest low.

She only half listened to Eva, her eyes scanning the area, mind scrambling, heart thudding. Rage had fully replaced any last vestiges of fear. Rage over this violation. She pushed away the unbidden images of scythes and knives and blue bottles filling her head.

What would it take to get rid of Brett once and for all?

# 39

# A SPIDER SPINNING

Back home in La Chanson, Callie transformed her fury into productivity.

She felt like a spider spinning out threads to her touchstones in the world. She added more contacts to her phone every day and worked with her lawyer, who'd already begun untangling the knots of documents that Brett's lawyers had coerced her into signing.

First, she and her lawyer would get her rights back, void any rights for Brett, and correct the Department of Child and Family Services files, working in tandem with a Colorado-based lawyer. Once she was back on solid ground, all her legal power intact, they'd explore a criminal investigation against Brett.

During the first few days of August, Callie opened social media accounts, set up a new musician website, recorded a rough demo of her new album on her phone, and—after a deep, brave breath—sent the song files to her manager. An hour later, Anita called in a barrage of squealing, whooping, and hollering—she was too excited to wait for their phone appointment—and they proceeded to talk all afternoon.

Callie filled her in on her nightmare of the past two years, relieved to hear her support. "We've got this," Anita said.

Callie's days felt bursting at the seams, and friends pitched in to help out with Eva, who was overjoyed at her mom stepping back onto the stage of life. All these small accomplishments were edging out her anger over Brett, and Callie wondered if maybe that hadn't been his car parked near Luc's in Aix after all. Maybe he was going to leave them alone—a thought that uplifted her, even as she doubted it.

The bliss lasted three days, until Callie noticed something strange when she and Eva returned from their morning walk in the forest. Her guitar wasn't where she'd left it on the sofa—it was now by the fireplace. She never kept her guitar by a fireplace, paranoid about heat damage, even when there was no fire. An old habit.

"Hey, sweet pea," she asked Eva, who had plopped on the sofa with Chouchou, "did you move my guitar?"

"Maybe it was the ghost boy," Eva theorized.

"Hmm."

Other items mysteriously moved in her absence—the next day, her music notebook. The next, her toothpaste. She wasn't buying the ghost explanation. If this was Brett, what kind of creepy game was he playing?

Julien hadn't mentioned noticing anything strange, but he'd been gone lately, spending nights at Violette's place with Fleur and doing repairs around her house. Callie didn't ask him about it—he'd probably insist on spending more time at home, and she wanted to encourage his budding romance with Violette.

Instead, she became more diligent about locking every window and door before leaving the cottage. And resentment built as she did. The antics weren't something solid enough to call the police about, and Brett knew it. Anger welled up inside her.

One afternoon she stopped by the *cave à vins* while Eva was at the park and mentioned this development to Madame Lavigne, who mused that it could be young ghost Tristan.

"That's Eva's theory," said Callie. "But of course, it's Brett. I know it is."

"You're right." The wine witch poured Callie a glass of rosé. "And you're not alone in this." She poured herself a glass and reported that Brett continued to come in every day to refill his bottle of Burgundy.

He drank it at night, alone in his hotel room, always the same, like clockwork.

"Pathetic." Madame Lavigne felt adamant that the right wine must be sipped with the right food on the right occasion, matched with the right person in the right company.

Despite the soothing taste of rosé, Callie tensed her muscles. "You're not—you're not putting anything in his wine, are you?"

Madame Lavigne raised her chin. "I am not."

"Brett's a jerk," Callie said. "And probably a killer. But I don't want him to make me into a killer." She paused. "Let's keep a close eye on him, and enlist the police. But remember, he hasn't actually attempted any violence here."

Madame Lavigne shrugged. "He's already destroying himself."

"Is he still pressuring you to sell the château?"

"No, but Hugo's still fixated on making money from it, wants to rent it to wealthy tourists if the deal doesn't go through." Madame Lavigne sipped her rosé and, with an expression of disappointment, explained that her son had returned to Paris but was in touch with Brett daily, unable—or unwilling—to extricate himself.

Callie furrowed her brows, confused. "Why are they in such close contact?"

"Brett learned about the carnyx." Madame Lavigne sighed. "He's obsessed with adding it to his collection. Music gods, or some such nonsense. He needs Hugo's help."

Of course Brett would want the carnyx the moment he'd heard of it. A mystical, musical artifact. The challenge of an underwater treasure hunt. Irresistible to him. Briefly, it occurred to her that this could be a good thing—a new obsession to replace her and Eva.

But indignation swelled inside her. The carnyx belonged to La Chanson, both the village and river itself. It simply wasn't right that Brett felt entitled to take it. And this felt personal. The carnyx—like Pepito—was an ancient source of power in her life. It was more than an artifact—it was a treasure whose bond with her ran deep and strong.

Somehow, the carnyx had survived for millennia in the depths of a watery cave. Admittedly, she didn't fully understand how this was possible. A patina forming over the bronze, preventing rust? Something about the water chemistry? The unique geology of the limestone cave system? Or was it something more . . . magical?

She wasn't clear either, how, at certain times, when she most needed it, she heard the carnyx roar. Was it the water rushing through tunnels, angled through the six-foot-long instrument? Or was it a mythical force that brought the dragon to life, made the carnyx rumble in her bones like a battle cry?

Callie sipped her wine while considering Brett's next move. He'd probably try to dive for the carnyx himself. After all, he fancied himself the Indiana Jones of underwater archaeology. "Brett's certified in scuba diving," she said. "He's probably humble-bragged to you about Caribbean shipwrecks."

Madame Lavigne gave an amused nod. "Many times."

Callie made a face. "Well, this would be his dream dive. And knowing Brett, he'd find a way around the rules."

"Hugo and I warned him about the deaths, but that only fueled him. He's determined." Madame Lavigne went on to explain Brett's plan, her voice heavy with disapproval. First, retrieve the carnyx. Next, partner with Hugo to offer high-end tours for divers. Privatize access, charge admission to even look into the cave. Build a high-end café on the cliffs.

Callie rubbed her forehead, appalled. "What? How?"

"Brett says he'll pay Hugo to buy off the town council. To use his real estate expertise."

The thought made Callie's heart sink. The river felt like a best friend, a bandmate, even a mother. Her voice emerged in a low timbre. "We can't let this happen."

"We won't," said Madame Lavigne. "Trust me."

Usually, whenever anyone uttered those words, Callie did just the opposite, especially after Brett. But her landlady was different. Callie did, indeed, trust her, despite the woman's witchy powers, or maybe because of them.

She also, just a little, *feared* her.

Two days later, Callie was lying on a lounge chair by the pool, jotting down promo ideas in her notebook, when, in her peripherals, she caught a glint of light from the branches of a tree, a dozen yards away. And she knew in her bones that something was wrong. Thankfully, Eva was at the park with her mamie Sophie and papi and the dogs. Callie wished Julien were here, but he was at Violette's with Fleur.

She stood up and walked closer.

It was a camera lens, and it was pointed at the pool. At her.

Adrenalin surged through her body. She climbed ten feet up the tree, scraping her bare legs and arms and feet in the process, and examined the camera. Brett had to be behind it—a message to her that he'd always be watching.

Hands shaking, she tried unhooking the device, but it was locked onto the trunk. Balanced on a branch, she took off her hat, thinking she could cover the lens with it. Then, on second thought, she climbed down and ran across the patio, into the château, where she grabbed one of Julien's hammers. Then she headed back outside, toward the tree, determined.

She stuck the hammer into her waistband and climbed up the trunk, then hooked her legs around a limb for balance. With a grimace, she smashed the camera to pieces with the hammer, turning her face away as glass and plastic flew. Alone here, Callie didn't have to hide her rage—and she almost hoped Brett was witnessing this on a monitor, understanding that she, too, was dangerous.

She spent the next hours making sweep after sweep of the estate, searching for hidden cameras. She found three more, angled toward her cottage, one of them facing the balcony where she sang every night. She destroyed each one. Too late, she realized she should have snapped photos with her phone as evidence. And maybe she should have called the police first and had them check for fingerprints.

Inside the cottage, she found nothing. Brett must have resorted to cameras after she'd become more diligent about locking doors and windows when she left. It made her blood simmer to think of him watching her.

By the time Julien came home with Fleur, she'd cleaned up the mess and was washing the scrapes on her arms and legs. She ran outside to fill him in.

"We won't allow this." His jaw firmed as he took out his phone and called his brother on speaker.

"You're overreacting," Hugo said in response, claiming he'd had a handyman install the cameras for safety.

Julien and Callie exchanged glances. Hugo must have deliberately scheduled it for a time they'd been gone, knowing they wouldn't approve.

Hugo rambled on, defending his choice—after all, he was family and it was his right—this was the home he grew up in, and their mother said he was always welcome. When he learned that Callie had smashed every last camera, he said, "You're lucky I'm not pressing charges for destruction of property."

"We know Brett put you up to this." Callie fairly spit venom into the phone. "We're calling the police next. Documenting this pattern of harassment."

"Hugo, you're acting like our father." Julien's voice emerged, clear and raw. "Is that who you want to be?"

Hugo was silent for several seconds. "You're a sucker. You got taken advantage of by the Forêts. You convinced our mother to do the same. Now she's friends with the guy who killed our father. So, yes, I'd rather be like our father than a wimp like you."

"Listen, Hugo," Julien said, closing his eyes and rubbing his scar. "Monsieur Forêt didn't kill him. And our mother knows this. You need to have a real, honest talk with her."

A long, heavy quiet on the other end.

"Our father abused us," Julien said. "He was a cruel man. A weak man. I saw him leave poisoned sausage for Marguerite."

On the other end, silence, except for sniffling.

Callie stood to leave, feeling this was too personal, but Julien reached for her hand. She sat back down, realizing he needed her support.

Julien continued, tears spilling over. "The food and supplies that came every Sunday. That was from Monsieur Forêt. Despite everything, he helped our family." Julien's voice dropped to a tender place. "Listen, Hugo. He loves our mother."

"Why didn't you say something?" Hugo's words sputtered out, choppy and broken.

"My voice got lost. I finally found it."

Callie sat on the patio beside Julien, sipping chilled mint tea she'd brought out. She'd eventually left the brothers to talk privately, and their conversation had lasted two hours—hopefully, the first of many to come.

Julien drank his tea and gave her a recap of how he and Hugo had reflected on their past, their father, their mother, their troubled relationship—in a surprisingly honest way. "We talked about all the secrets, the lack of trust." He paused, emotion welling up. "We want to change that."

Callie nodded. "You can use your voice to heal the rift."

Julien gave her a meaningful look. "Listen, I told him about Brett, how he was abusive to you. Hugo was humbled. He apologized for bringing him here."

"I appreciate that," Callie said.

"But he feels powerless against Brett." Julien's expression turned grave. "Says Brett is digging up dirt on him, using it as leverage, forcing him to carry out his plans."

"Sounds like Brett." Callie sipped her cool tea, felt the mint uplift her, heard the river strum a hopeful song. "But we're all on the same team now."

Julien clinked his glass against hers. "We've got this."

"Time for booby traps," said Monsieur Forêt, tossing his arm around Madame Lavigne, who nodded enthusiastically in response. Before them, the patio table held a curious assortment of old items from the shed, from fishing line to paint cans.

Yesterday, after Julien had left to fill Violette in, Callie had called the police, then invited Eva's grandparents over today for support, knowing that Luc would be busy with truffle deliveries.

"*Oui!*" Eva sipped her last drops of *limonade,* then stood up and punched the air. "Let's make booby traps, Papi!"

As Madame Lavigne launched into details of the Tintin-inspired traps she and Philippe had set as kids, Callie realized her intention to reframe the situation to empower Eva. She appreciated this, although she doubted the actual effectiveness of the traps. Legally, of course, they couldn't use darts or blades or anything that would cause real harm. The main tactic was stringing fishing line at an adult's shoulder level—that way, Eva or the dogs couldn't accidentally set off the traps.

Over the next few hours, they strung the near-invisible lines between fruit trees by the windows and below the balconies. If Brett walked by, any number of nonlethal consequences would ensue: Empty cans would clank against each other or paint would dump onto his head.

"Mwahahaha!" Eva kept saying, relishing every second.

The best part was watching Madame Lavigne and Monsieur Forêt reminisce about long-ago adventures—you could almost see their childhood selves coming out to play. And Eva kept glancing through the trees, smiling. "The ghost boy's here. He's having fun watching us. But he's also sad. Like a merry-go-round, up and down and up and down. He's ready to get off the ride."

"Tell Tristan we forgive him," her papi said in a raw voice.

Eva did.

"And we're sorry for what happened to him," her mamie Sophie said.

Eva did.

"Tell him he can go," added her papi.

Eva did.

After a long, strange pause—silence save for cicadas and birds, and a light breeze that made her arm hairs stand up—Callie whispered, "Did he go?"

Eva shook her head. "He doesn't know how to."

Monsieur Forêt patted his hand over his chest, over the bulge in the shape of a small, silver ring box. He'd been carrying this everywhere, and when Callie had asked about it, he'd only offered a secret, sad smile. Now, he looked with longing at Madame Lavigne.

And Callie understood that before these old friends could take the next step, Tristan's ghost had to find peace.

# 40

# POISON

The next morning, something about the river music felt different, and Callie couldn't put her finger on what, exactly. There were the usual sweet strings harmonizing with robins and larks—but today it held the slightest undercurrent of wariness. As she walked into the forest with Eva, a tiny part of herself stayed vigilant, in tune with the river's strange murmur.

The deeper they walked into the woods, though, the deeper she let herself sink into the freshness of the morning and the joy of her daughter, who was over the moon to have her own *pic à truffes*. It had been Monsieur Forêt's when he was a boy and was now tucked inside a leather case on her belt.

Eva patted the sheath as she strutted around oaks. "My dog feels like a real pro now." She'd started calling Chouchou *her* dog, and so had the Forêts and everyone else in town.

Even Callie had found herself doing it. "Time to feed your dog, sweet pea. Refill your dog's water." For better or worse, this little Lagotto Romagnolo rooted them here, to this town, to this forest, to this river, to this home. To Luc.

In the week since the trip to Aix, despite her niggling worries about Brett, she'd felt more optimistic about her future, more committed to Luc, more determined to find a way to stay. Her tourist visa would run out in just three weeks, at the end of August, and she'd been exploring work visa possibilities for the future.

When Eva spotted the Forêts and their dogs through the trees, she and Chouchou ran at top speed to greet them. "Papiiiii! Luuuuc!" After the cheek kisses, Callie and Luc launched into plans for his new vet practice.

"How should we decorate the clinic?" Luc asked, swinging her hand in his, as his father and Eva walked ahead with the dogs. "I'm a fan of inspirational cat posters," Luc added, "1980s style."

"I thought you were a dog person," said Callie. "Your canine patients might revolt."

"Not to mention the *pétanque* guys," Luc admitted.

He'd been setting up his clinic—a few spare rooms in the *mas*—a task he'd begun three years earlier, then abandoned, although the furniture and equipment remained. This week he was putting on the final touches, stocking it with medications and instruments, preparing for the official opening, as soon as his license arrived.

"Hey," said Callie. "We should frame old photos of truffle hunters and their dogs."

Luc lit up. "My dad has some, and I bet the *pétanque* crew does too."

Out of the blue, Monsieur Forêt shouted. No words, just an incoherent, deep, anguished cry.

Callie's chest clenched. She scanned the forest, realized the shout was directed toward the dogs. Luc was already running toward them, and Callie following.

A few dozen yards ahead, she was relieved to see Eva safe beside her papi, but looking alarmed. All three dogs were sitting by an oak tree, staring at something and wagging their tails wildly, a strange gleam in their eyes—not normal truffle-finding behavior. Was it some type of food? They were trained not to eat anything without permission but were clearly desperate to do so, glancing at Eva and the Forêts for the go-ahead.

A shadow passed over Monsieur Forêt's face as he called the dogs to his side and told them to stay. "*Restez.*"

"What's going on?" Callie grabbed Eva's hand and followed Luc over to inspect the food—a raw sausage lying in the foliage.

He pressed his hand to his mouth and exchanged grave looks with his father.

"Take the dogs home, son." Monsieur Forêt's tone was somber. "Come back with supplies."

Luc squeezed Callie's hand. "Keep Eva close. At least until we know the sausage wasn't laced with anything."

Her chest constricted. She thought of Philippe's beloved Marguerite, killed with a poisoned sausage and buried beneath the oak. *Who the hell would do this?* Heart thudding, she watched Luc turn and run toward the house, calling for the dogs to follow.

Eva tossed an uncertain look at Callie while Monsieur Forêt poked at the meat with his walking stick, keeping a distance. He circled the area, pointing out more sausages and muttering beneath his breath. It took Callie a moment to realize that his sniffling was, in fact, crying.

Eva slid her hand into his. "What's wrong, Papi?"

He wiped his cheeks on his sleeve, opening his mouth, then closing it again, unable to speak.

Callie had the urge to scoop Eva up and take her away, but her daughter needed to understand the truth. In English, she whispered, "Someone put these sausages here, sweetie. They knew a dog might smell them and want to eat them. We're worried they might have poison in them. That could make the dogs very sick."

After a moment of shock, Eva turned to her papi. "The dogs—are they okay?"

"It's all right, *ma petite*." Monsieur Forêt gave a reassuring nod. "They're fine. That's why we train them not to eat anything without permission."

Eva chewed on her lip. "Why are you crying, Papi?"

Feeling his pain, Callie watched the tortured expression on his face as he said, "I lost my favorite dog to a poisoned sausage many years ago."

"Who did it?" Eva asked in shock.

He shook his head. "That doesn't matter anymore. We'll get rid of these sausages before any animals eat them."

"But who would want to hurt the dogs? Only a horrible, horrible person would hurt dogs," Eva pushed, hand on her truffle pick, as if she might just go after the poisoner herself.

Monsieur Forêt only shook his head sadly while Eva peppered him with questions.

Callie put an arm around him, a gesture of comfort, but he needed Madame Lavigne now. "Monsieur," she said gently, "maybe you and Eva could walk to the *cave à vins*. Then go with Madame Lavigne to the police station? I'll wait for Luc. We'll clear the forest of sausages."

"Good idea." He looked relieved to usher Eva away from the scene.

Callie stared at the first sausage they'd found. Would Brett stoop to killing animals to send her a message?

Yes. He would if he felt desperate enough. If his tactics of manipulation and bribery and threats had failed.

Hearing footsteps, she looked up to see Luc jogging through the trees, breathing hard, his vet bag looped over a shoulder.

"Hey, Callie." He drew her into a hug. "You okay?"

"Just shaken up. Your dad took Eva to town."

"Good." Kneeling down, he pulled out sealable plastic bags.

They created a system: Callie took pictures of each sausage with her phone before Luc scooped it up with a bag, sealed and labeled it, then put a rock cairn on top of each spot for the police. He wasn't willing to leave the sausages as evidence, in case any other animals stumbled across them, and Callie agreed. She scoured the area with him, praying they wouldn't encounter any victims.

They'd found nine sausages when she looked behind a pine and her heart stopped. Before them was the beautiful body of a fox lying by a stone. Its fur was a rich shade of copper, fading into white on its chest and the tip of its tail. She stepped closer, saw that its chest was still moving, thank God, but it was half conscious and limp.

"Luc!"

He ran over just in time to see the animal convulse in a seizure. Callie covered her eyes for a moment—this was almost too painful to watch.

Luc cursed, dropping to his knees beside the creature. He took out thick leather gloves and, when the seizure ended, carefully strapped a loose muzzle onto the fox. The animal seemed to sense his intentions and put up no resistance—or else it was simply too weakened.

He picked up the fox, cradled it in his arms, and jogged toward his house.

Callie grabbed his abandoned vet bag and followed him straight into the exam room, where he laid the fox on the newly sterilized metal table. "A young female," he said gravely, breathing hard. As he tended to her—pumping her stomach, giving her IV fluids, controlling her seizures—Callie did her best as an assistant, following his instructions. He worked with laser focus, wasting not a second, entirely absorbed in saving this creature.

An hour later, he moved the fox carefully onto a cushion inside a roomy kennel, observing her rhythmic breathing as she dozed, nose tucked into her bushy tail. Finally, with a deep sigh, he fell into a chair, exhausted. He watched the animal with tenderness, as if it were a sleeping child. "She's stabilized," he said softly.

Callie rubbed his back. "You saved her."

He leaned his head against her shoulder, kissed her hair, took her hand.

She sank into the peace of the moment, and then, realizing Monsieur Forêt would need an update, she texted him, along with a photo of the sleeping fox. A minute later, he sent emojis that Eva must have selected—paw prints, hearts, sad faces, angry faces, happy faces, and more hearts—followed by a text saying they'd been to the police station and were now waiting at the *cave à vins*.

"Hey, why don't you go to them," said Luc, "and I'll keep an eye on this little lady?"

Callie gave him a kiss, then headed outside into the midday sunshine. Soon, she entered the shadowy forest, on alert for any sausage they might have missed. And she encountered two local police officers already scouring the forest, the middle-aged man and young woman who were familiar with the Brett situation.

She filled them in as they took notes. There was a fierceness in her voice as she added, "Brett had motives. And I believe he's capable of this cruelty." After answering a series of follow-up questions, she texted them photos of the evidence. "You can find Luc at his clinic."

"We'll be in touch," said the woman. "And we'll keep an eye on the suspect."

When Callie thanked them, they gave her meaningful looks. They understood. They had her back too.

In the dim light of the *cave à vins,* Callie perched on a stool, damp with sweat, and recounted to Eva and her grandparents how Luc had saved the fox, downplaying how close to death the creature had been, going straight to the heart-swelling part.

"Luc is a vet hero." Eva punctuated her pronouncement with a sip of Orangina.

Madame Lavigne poured Callie a tiny glass of chilled *fleur de lavande* liqueur, claiming it would calm her nerves—it had already calmed hers and Monsieur Forêt's. "Follow me," she said, and led them into the cellar.

Unlike her first time here, Callie now felt a sense of peace, the cool air calming, the ancient stone grounding.

The wine witch gave Eva a clean rag. "Dust that far row of bottles and you'll get three bonbons as a reward, my little one."

Eva bounded away, and once she was out of earshot, Madame Lavigne told Callie, "This is what Tristan did. Put poison in the forest. Unforgivable."

Callie nodded, realizing why the wine witch had brought them into the cellar—to occupy Eva with a task, out of earshot.

Monsieur Forêt put his arm around his old friend. "That's in the past, *ma chérie*. And no dogs were hurt this time."

"The fox was." The wine witch firmed her jaw.

"Brett's capable of this." Callie wondered if he'd gotten the idea from Hugo, who might have mentioned the drama from years past. "This could be his last-ditch effort to scare us into submission."

Madame Lavigne turned to her. "Don't allow it, Callie. Never again."

"I won't." Callie's gaze landed on the blue bottles on the high shelf. Did they really contain poison? She saw the path Brett was heading down, and strangely, her rage transformed into a shadowy pool, cold and dark and sad. She understood that he'd always been pathetic, and now more than ever.

"The police will confirm the poison in the sausages." Monsieur spoke in a solemn voice. "They'll investigate. And the prime suspect is Brett. He must be stopped."

"*Oui*." Madame lifted her chin and echoed, "He must be stopped." Her voice held a strange chill, the darkness of old fairy tales, the justice of ancient myths.

Eva broke the silence that followed, galloping over and twirling the dirty rag around her head in triumphant circles. "Bonbon time!"

Over the next few days, Callie's shopkeeper spies reported that Brett looked more sickly every time they saw him. Dark circles, pale face, a profusion of sweat.

A niggling worry lodged in Callie's gut. She thought of the blue bottles and considered approaching Madame Lavigne about it. Was the wine witch poisoning his Burgundy? If so, would Callie stop her?

But maybe he really was sick. She suspected she had a cold herself after running herself ragged. She'd been caught up in the whirlwind of activity, not just from the fox incident, but from reconnecting with colleagues and putting legal actions into motion. True, she was making progress, but sacrificing sleep—and her body was protesting. Had she and Brett caught the same virus? The thought of them sharing anything, even the genetic material of invading germs, made her feel even sicker.

The morning of the open mic soirée, Callie's sore throat turned downright painful. Her sniffles had become a stubbornly clogged nose and her fatigue had transformed into utter exhaustion. Her reflection in the bathroom mirror was pitiful—nose pink and raw, eyes red-veined, skin tinged gray.

Eva was already dressed in the thrifted outfit her papi had bought her in Aix—a blue flouncy skirt, an orange striped top, a pink flowered scarf, and a purple beret. All of it thoroughly worn-in, the fabrics soft and comfy, tags long ago disintegrated. She was fairly glowing, ready to perform a dog show comedy act to her papi's cheery accordion accompaniment.

"Sweet pea." Callie braced herself for an argument. "I'm so sorry, but I have to stay home tonight."

"Good idea." Eva nodded her approval. "You look like something the cat dragged in."

Callie barked a hoarse laugh. "Thanks."

"I'll just go with Papi and Luc."

Callie blew her nose, grateful Eva had other adults to take care of her. All she wanted to do was lie on the couch and sip orange blossom tea with lots of honey.

When the Forêts appeared at the door that evening, she kept her distance, determined not to inflict this cold on anyone.

"La Troufette is fine," Luc announced. That was their nickname for the fox—Little Chocolate Truffle. "I let her go this afternoon. Now she's happily curled up in her den in the forest."

"You saved her," Eva said with pride. "All my friends say you're a hero."

Luc patted her purple beret. "Any vet would have done the same."

"A real, official vet," Callie said. "Right, Doctor?"

"Almost." He grinned, unable to hide his satisfaction—his license would arrive any day now. Eva tugged his hand, and Callie waved goodbye to her humans and dogs, then lay on the sofa, wishing for an actual TV for the first time—she could only flip through the Provence book for so long. She tried bingeing old sitcoms on her laptop, but it wasn't the same.

At nine o'clock, after napping on and off in the din of old laugh tracks, she was just shutting down her laptop and mustering energy to drag herself upstairs when something rattled outside. Her first groggy thought blamed the wind, but after a moment, she realized there was no wind. Glancing through the open windows, she saw no tree branches moving.

The hairs on her arms stood up as she remembered the booby traps, the empty cans attached to fishing wire at shoulder height.

Callie stood up and walked through the dark cottage, peering out the windows, seeing only shapes of bushes and trees, and lacy shadows of foliage in pools of lamplight. She blew her nose, tried clearing her mind, then looked around for her cell phone, just in case—112, that was the French version of 911.

She was in the kitchen scanning the countertop for her phone—which wasn't where she'd left it—when she heard the cans rattle again, coming from the trip wire beneath the balcony. She craned her head out the window, saw red paint spilled over a patch of garden. Her pulse sped. It had to be Brett. He must have set off that trip wire too.

She flicked on the kitchen light and saw footsteps of red paint like blood trailing across the terra-cotta floor.

With trepidation, she followed them into the living room, turned on the lamp, and saw them lead to the couch where she'd been sleeping.

The footsteps then led to the table with the old-fashioned phone. Her blood froze as she took in the smear of red on the handle and cord. Bending down, she registered that the cord had been snipped.

A rush of anger flooded her.

She followed the red footsteps to the front door. She considered his goal—to lure her away somewhere? Or had he just gone completely off the deep end? She forced her mind to clear. Brett had invaded her home. She was alone with no way to call for help. For a moment, she felt his presence closing in on her again. But as soon as the fear started to grip her, she shook it off, transformed it into her own power.

Hearing another sound from outside, she flung open the front door. "This is over!" she yelled in a hoarse voice. Maybe he thought she'd be more vulnerable away from the house, but he was wrong. She was on the offense now. And he was the weak one.

Grabbing the house key and flashlight from the hook, she saw Eva's truffle hunting belt hanging there with the sharp pick in its leather pouch. She buckled it around her waist, then slid on sandals. She slammed the door shut and locked it behind her.

This would end tonight.

# 41

# THE DRAGON

"Show yourself!" Callie shouted in a raspy voice, walking to the trip line by the balcony where the cans had rattled.

She heard a rustle in the leaves ahead, saw a dark figure running across the meadow and down the hillside toward the river. It had to be Brett. Intent on confronting him, she ran after him, scrambled over stones, down boulders, close on his tail. Which struck her as strange—this was a man who did 10Ks several times a week—you'd think he'd be in better shape. Even with a cold. As soon as a darker explanation crept into her consciousness, she pushed it away.

She picked up her pace, determined to end this tonight. Maybe it was her cold that made her embrace her power with such abandon—the otherworldly feel of having her head stuffed up, being yanked out of sitcom-edged dreams. Or maybe she'd just reached her limit. Her body was acting of its own accord, driven by the wild, urgent need to stop a pathetic man hell-bent on destruction. He'd stolen so much from her—two years of music, Nick, Pepito.

He would never steal from her again.

Callie skidded down the last part of the steep hillside, pebbles sliding beneath her sandals, but she managed not to fall. She hadn't been to this part of the riverbank before, about a quarter mile downstream from the turnoff to the château, in the opposite direction from town. She and Eva usually stayed upstream, on the trails, by the calm coves, or on sandy little beaches. This was an area she'd avoided, full of craggy overhangs and sketchy caves where she hadn't wanted Eva playing.

She caught her breath, gripped the truffle pick, and tuned into the soundscape. There was no sign of Brett. An eerie silence surrounded her, only cricket songs and the river music, which had turned ominous, a low viola note stretching into the night.

In a musical pause—a rest—she heard a shuffling sound from a nearby rock outcropping. She shone her flashlight over the natural stone walls, landing on the gaping mouth of a cave. Walking inside, she illuminated a pile of haphazardly stacked, sealed containers. Bizarre.

Brett wasn't here, only this odd collection of plastic bins. The nearest one looked full of packages of crackers and bottles of Perrier. Chest pounding, she poked around, finding blankets and a laptop. In another bin, she recognized Brett's clothes, high-end outdoor gear mixed in with brand-name linen. Had he been camped out here . . . spying?

With stunned curiosity, she rifled through more bins, when it occurred to her: Pepito might be here. A wave of determination swept over her. This was her chance to get him back. She *needed* to get him back, the little statue that held love and laughter and family. This was her chance to reclaim what Brett had taken from her. In her mind, Pepito shone bright, a symbol of all that she cared about, all that she hoped for.

She paused at a bin that held old takeout boxes and an empty wine bottle, drops of red liquid inside. Burgundy, she assumed. The label depicted Giulia Tofana, the seventeenth-century poisoner of abusive men, whose portrait hung in the château. Tofana water was her signature potion, wine mixed with arsenic, belladonna, and other deadly ingredients. On the label, *Eau de Tofana* was written in fancy script.

Callie let out a shaky breath, thinking of those little blue bottles in

Madame Lavigne's cellar. With a shiver, she dropped the wine bottle, then turned to the largest bin and removed the lid, revealing scuba diving equipment. *Damn it.* Here was evidence—Brett was deluded enough to attempt a deadly dive to steal the carnyx.

Furious, she unsheathed her *pic à truffes* and held it over the suit, ready to slash it to pieces. All at once, the river music rose in a dissonant crescendo that made her look over her shoulder.

She shone the flashlight beam on Brett, blocking the cave entrance, splattered with red paint like blood. She took a long, deep breath and centered herself. Then she took a step forward and aimed the sharp tip of her truffle pick at him. "Get out of my way, Brett."

"You can't demand anything of me." He attempted a cocky smile, but he looked . . . *off.* There were deep circles beneath his eyes, a deathly pallor to his sweaty face. Smelling wine on his breath, she eyed the bottle of Eau de Tofana.

Her mind couldn't avoid the connection. The fox had been poisoned last week. And now, Brett was sick. Many decades earlier, Marguerite the beloved dog was poisoned. And a week later, Madame Lavigne's husband grew sick. Callie stared at Brett. Something was very wrong with him. At the very least, he was drunk and sick. She couldn't help but think of Tristan.

"You have no power here," Brett said, swaying, as if about to collapse.

"Oh, but I do." Callie clutched the *pic à truffes* more tightly and walked toward the entrance. Her own strength flowed through her, an unstoppable river. With her shoulder, she shoved him out of the way. He stumbled to the side, banging against the rock before regaining his balance, barely able to stand.

Outside the cave, she regarded him in her flashlight beam. Pathetic through and through. Brett, the multimillionaire who appeared to have everything, actually had nothing of true value. And Callie had it all. Love, music, friends, family. Her self. Her voice. Her real, deep power. She studied his face in the shadows. "Why are you doing this?"

"I just want you and Eva." His voice wobbled. "A family."

"Never." Now that Callie had the upper hand, unexpected compassion came over her, and her voice held more pity than anger. "Go home, Brett."

He stared at her for a long moment. "But my lawyers—"

"Can do nothing. My lawyer is undoing it all. Then we'll reopen the case of Nick's death."

He looked at her with naked fear, any last droplets of strength evaporated.

"It's time for you to go, Brett."

"Fine." He deflated, and for a moment she thought he might actually leave, but then he started pulling out items from the scuba gear bin—the tank, the vest, the flippers, the gauges, the mask, the flashlight, the diver's bag. "First, I'm going to the source and getting the carnyx."

Briefly, she wondered why he hadn't stashed his gear closer to the source, then realized this cave hideout downstream was off the beaten track . . . and provided more covert access to the grounds of her home. The source was at least a twenty-minute walk away, uphill, and she doubted he could even handle walking there now—much less doing a dangerous dive.

"You'll die, Brett," she said simply.

"I've done solo scuba before." He stripped off his clothes and put on his wetsuit, swaying and off-balance.

For several minutes, she watched him struggle, considering her options. She could leave and get the police, but by then he could be dead. "Don't do this."

"It's my magnum opus." His words slurred together, sloppy. "Communing with an ancient Celtic music deity. My dad's jaw would drop."

"You're delirious, Brett."

He zipped up his wetsuit, strapped on the vest and tank, tucked his fins and mask beneath his arm, dangled the diver's bag from his hand.

She watched him stumble upstream. Again, she considered walking away, but he would die. *Damn it.* She followed him at a distance, hoping he'd just collapse before reaching the source. It surprised her that she didn't actually want him dead. She didn't *need* him dead. That was how little power he held now. She only wanted him gone from her life. Across an ocean.

Twenty minutes passed as he kept walking upstream, passing the turnoff for town, continuing up the gravel path, through wildflowers, toward the source. She followed, trying to convince him to give up, stopping short of physically restraining him. Meanwhile, the water music grew more dissonant, more furious.

The river, it seemed, was not so forgiving.

When he reached the cave that held the source, he doubled over, hands on his knees. Panting, he shone his flashlight inside the cave. No sign of the carnyx. Of course the river wouldn't show him its treasure.

"This is suicide, Brett."

"Tell Eva I love her," he said, making final adjustments to his equipment, clumsy in his movements. "And I love you."

"Don't do this." Even if he weren't drunk and sick, he wouldn't have stood a chance. Not with the river this enraged.

He held up the canvas diver's bag, meant for holding loot from shipwrecks. "Got my good luck charm here." His words slipped and slurred. "The Mayan music god. It'll guide me safely to the Celtic treasure."

Callie's brow shot up. "Pepito?" She snatched the bag easily from his hands, opened it, and found Pepito inside. *It's about time,* she imagined him saying in that nasal voice. Tears blurred her vision as she kissed his stone lips, then tucked him tenderly into her shirt pocket, close to her heart. She felt the warmth of her past life with Nick and Eva, the warmth of her future life with Luc and Eva—and their entire family of La Chanson. She felt their love.

Brett didn't try to take Pepito back. He only looked at her, and for a split second, his façade fell away, and he was just a hurt little boy, trying to prove himself. "I'm sorry."

She wasn't sure what exactly he was apologizing for—Pepito, or all of it—but it seemed sincere. Staggering and floundering, he stepped into the harness, barely managed to hook himself in. He must have rigged up a climbing rope and carabiners earlier—he'd been planning this for a while. He lowered himself down. It was painful to watch, all grunts and bangs and bashes, nothing graceful about it.

She shone her flashlight after him as he grew smaller and smaller. And she heard a splash.

For a long time she stared into the dark pool, seeing only shadows.

All at once, La Chanson let out a dragon roar, the carnyx blown with full force. Over the next minutes, the river rose and swelled and frothed.

Its music moved from chaotic rage to a funereal march, slow and somber.

Then it dissolved into a peaceful, poignant guitar melody in E minor.

And then, the outro, the coda, the finale.

It was over.

She pulled the rope up, saw the carabiner hanging loose at the end.

He was gone.

The dragon had swallowed him.

It had been Brett's choice.

And she let him go.

Through the night, the local police searched the river for Brett's body, but of course he was gone. La Chanson had taken him. He was somewhere in its cavernous depths, far underground. As expected, the police wouldn't risk sending a dive team into the source—if La Chanson swallowed a human, there was no returning. An open-and-shut case.

Luc and his father stayed all night with Eva at the cottage while

Callie talked to the officers. She showed them Brett's dive equipment at the source and brought them to his cave hideout downstream. She watched as they took photos of the pathetic mess from a man who'd clearly been unhinged.

And she tried not to show her relief when the police left the empty wine bottle in place, just noting it as a further indication that Brett had been drunk when he took his ill-advised dive. Of course, none of this was a surprise to the officers, who'd kept a running list of his suspicious behaviors. Madame Lavigne had even alerted them of his intentions to dive in the source. When Callie asked permission to clear his things from the cave sometime in the next week, they gave her the go-ahead, seeming almost grateful.

At dawn, the police offered to give her a ride home, but she declined, saying she preferred to walk and process things. Instead of going home, she found herself heading to the *cave à vins*, ringing the buzzer. Moments later, Madame Lavigne appeared, already dressed and looking alert, as if expecting her—of course, the Forêts had kept her in the loop.

After the cheek kisses, Callie asked, "Can you come with me? And bring some bags?"

"*Bien sûr*," said Madame Lavigne, grabbing shopping bags from a hook by the door. "Let's go."

Along the river path, Callie filled her in on the details of Brett's demise, then led her to his hideout. Together, she and Madame Lavigne stuffed plastic bags with Brett's trash—including butcher's paper that reeked of raw sausage. When Madame Lavigne stashed the wine bottle in a market bag, Callie met her gaze, unsure how to broach the topic. "Maybe it's time to get rid of those little blue bottles."

Madame Lavigne tilted her head. "When Julien was younger, he suspected I poisoned his father, weakened him, primed him for the accident. Such a sensitive and observant child. His imagination ran wild with the little blue bottles. But the truth is, the river took my husband. Just as it took Brett. La Chanson made its judgment."

She released a deep sigh. "I watched Tristan die from the cliffs above, not far from here. I did nothing to save him. As it turned out, my young Julien witnessed me. Recently, I told Hugo about this. And Philippe. They have all forgiven me."

"Why didn't you say something sooner?" Callie asked. "When there were rumors of murder?"

Madame Lavigne rubbed her eyes. "I worried that if the police knew of my inaction, they might have arrested me. Tristan's best friend was a local cop. If I went to jail, my sons would have been alone. I couldn't risk it."

Callie whispered, "What exactly happened that day?"

Madame Lavigne was quiet for a long moment. "Tristan was ill and intoxicated—with liquor—and said he was going fishing. I didn't stop him. I only watched. He stumbled into the water and fell and hit his head on a rock and drowned. He was ready to leave this earth. And the river knew it."

Callie reached out and touched her shoulder. She could understand the slipperiness of the situation, imagine the weight this woman had carried for decades.

Madame Lavigne let out a quivery breath. "Tristan's spirit has never been able to fully leave."

Callie gave her a long hug, and when they pulled away, her landlady's eyes brimmed with tears. "My dear," she whispered, "we must say goodbye to these ghosts, once and for all."

"Let's do it," Callie said, and together, they began to make a plan.

A few days later, Madame Lavigne hosted a dinner on the patio of the château to welcome new beginnings, as she put it. She sat at the head of a long table on the patio, built by Julien and Luc from old barn planks. She wore a silk turquoise A-line dress that skimmed her knees, accessorized with a sky-blue scarf.

Monsieur Forêt couldn't take his eyes off her as she raised the glass of rosé she'd selected from her *cave*, and announced, "We're renaming this place. The Château of the Found."

Callie and her companions raised their glasses—Eva and her papi, Violette, Julien, Lili, Samuel, Amira, Beni, and little Hamza with his sippy cup. The wine witch's gaze landed on each one of them. "We are family." Her eyes flickered to the gardens, to Tristan's favorite spot.

Callie could almost see a misty figure beneath the olive tree. According to Julien and Eva, the ghost had been making himself scarcer and scarcer lately, his form dissolving.

Eva had said, a little sadly, that her daddy's ghost had been fading too. Apparently, he'd told her she didn't need him as much now that her dog dreams had come true—which had brought a lump to Callie's throat. Her tears had spilled over when Eva had added, "And my family dreams too."

After clinking glasses, Callie sipped the pale, sunset-pink wine, savoring undercurrents of river stone, orchard fruit, ripe berries, and wild herbs. It tasted like freedom, like being lost and found, reunited with her truest song and singing it for the world to hear. Its notes were at once sweet and strong, rosemary and lavender, earth and sky, cave and source.

Luc served the apéro—thin slices of baguettes with truffle-infused honey and *chèvre* and olive oil from the label "Truffes de la Forêt." Everyone peppered him with questions about the vet clinic, and he informed them, with a modest smile, that his patient list was full.

The clinic was now decorated with old photos of truffle hunters and their beloved dogs, and Callie's favorite, a sepia photo of the Three Musketeers—a young Philippe showing off a giant black diamond truffle, a young Sophie nudging him with her elbow, an innocent Tristan holding up a feather. Callie recognized the tree behind them, the old oak where the ring had been buried, which Monsieur Forêt still carried in his pocket.

Black truffle season was approaching in a few months, and to the Forêts' delight, they had unfettered access to the entire forest. Callie's lawyer had recommended someone who specialized in ancient, confusing real estate situations. He drew up new documents, giving ownership of half the forest to the Forêts, half to the Lavignes . . . although both families wandered the entire forest together. Julien and Luc made a gap in the wall for easy passage. Now it served as two long stone benches, resting places where Papi and Mamie Sophie could sit, hand in hand, watching their granddaughter truffle hunt.

With Julien at her side, the wine witch had talked honestly with Hugo, said they planned to turn the château into a residency for poets and musicians, and that they'd welcome his advice. Little by little, Hugo was softening, opening to the perspectives of his mother and brother.

At the tail end of her three-month visa, Callie was preparing for a short trip back to Colorado the following week with Eva to arrange for a *passport talent*, a long-stay visa she qualified for as a musician, and which her trusty lawyer was facilitating. Her lawyer was also helping her figure out how to donate her inheritance from Brett to a safe house organization in Colorado. While there, Callie would pack and mail her favorite instruments and belongings, along with a box of Eva's stuff. Eva was thrilled at the thought of sharing her toys and starting school with her friends in La Chanson upon their return. This would be, in all ways, their *home*.

Samuel became Eva's assistant in dog training, and with regular pool dates, he was becoming a strong swimmer. His latest surgery from earlier this spring—the final one—had been officially deemed a success. Lili had bought a glamorous evening gown to celebrate, which she wore tonight, midnight-blue silk, with her hair in a sleek chignon. After a decade of her life revolving around surgeries, her world was expanding, her fashion-loving self peeking back out.

Lili was Callie's self-declared stylist for the Mediterranean tour her manager was arranging for next spring, around France, Italy, and Spain. Callie already had childcare lined up for Eva, their friends vying for a chance to either stay with her at the cottage or join in on a leg of the tour.

Past midnight, after the cheese soufflé and citrus endive salad and lavender crème brulée were eaten, and the dishes washed, and the guests gone, and Eva asleep, Callie sank beside Luc on her sofa, curling into him, with Chouchou and Jolie on either side.

She sipped orange blossom tea and asked playfully, "Who did you save today?"

"Let's see." He gave her a wry grin. "I dealt with a cat's stomach virus, treated a hound dog's ear infection, sewed up a gash on a poodle's leg, emptied the belly of a Pomeranian mix who swallowed grapes, and did uneventful checkups on two cats and three dogs. Oh, and a house call for a pet pig."

"The glamorous life of a country vet." Callie smiled. His license had arrived two days earlier—word had instantly spread among his informal clientele, and his schedule had filled. She leaned in and kissed him—he tasted like orange blossoms. "Stay the night?"

"Twist my arm," he said, leaning in for a kiss.

As he brushed his teeth, Callie went onto the balcony, where she sang a song with this week's whisper words—*feather, treasure, sky*—and thanked the river. It was a song of closure, for herself, for Madame Lavigne, for anyone else who needed it.

Luc came onto the balcony, saying, "I love that new song, Callie." Shirtless, he wrapped his arms around her and she breathed in the scent of mint on his breath and forest on his skin. "Sing it again?" he asked.

She picked up her guitar and sang, as La Chanson unspooled a dulcimer harmony of love and peace and forgiveness. She'd bring this feeling with her tomorrow when she and Madame Lavigne would carry out their plan in the company of their family.

In the crisp morning light, Callie walked with Luc, Julien, Eva, and her grandparents to the river. They took turns carrying an urn that had sat on the mantel in the château for decades. Tristan's ashes. It was a windless day, and the dogs trotted beside the little group, oddly subdued, as if sensing the gravity of the task. The river song wrapped around them, poignant and sorrowful, with a bittersweet edge.

The wine witch released a long breath and sprinkled the ashes into the river, then turned toward an olive tree on the embankment, where Julien and Eva were looking too. Callie let her own gaze land there, imagining a little boy wearing shorts and sandals and a beret with a feather.

Madame Lavigne and Monsieur Forêt took turns telling stories about childhood antics with Tristan, and Callie could almost hear the child's laughter mixing with the river music, which had shifted to a jaunty accordion tune. A feather rose into the air, and despite the lack of wind, it swirled upward as everyone's gazes followed. Up and up it drifted. And vanished.

"He's gone," said Eva. "And he's happy."

Callie felt the spirit of another little boy slip away with the river. Brett had made his choice, too, and she wished him well, imagining these two boy spirits floating away together. And she forgave the men they'd become. The men who were gone forever.

On the way home, in the forest, Monsieur Forêt stopped by the old oak tree and leaned his cane against the trunk. At first, Callie assumed they were taking a rest, but then he pulled the little silver case from his pocket as Eva jumped up and down in anticipation.

Looking into Madame Lavigne's eyes, he opened it, revealing the ring.

"A black diamond," she whispered.

"Sophie, I should have given you this decades ago. I've kept it safe all these years. Just in case one day you'd say yes."

She held out her hand, age-spotted and wrinkled, but for a moment in the lacy light, it was the hand of a teenage girl, fresh and smooth and hopeful. He slid the black diamond onto her left ring finger, and, like Cinderella's slipper, it fit.

"*Oui*." Madame Lavigne beamed and kissed his lips.

"You are my treasure, Sophie. Always have been. Always will be."

Callie felt the ache and hope in her throat, the tears spilling. As Eva wrapped her arms around her mamie Sophie and papi, he added, "I always knew we'd have a grandchild together one day."

Madame Lavigne leaned over to plant a kiss on Eva's head. And the embraces spread to their sons, who hugged their parents, then each other. As Callie embraced each and every one, she felt the golden threads interlinking them all.

On the way back to the Château of the Found, Sophie slipped her hand into Philippe's, and Callie slipped hers into Luc's, and Eva and Julien ran ahead with the dogs, everyone floating over countless black diamonds, so many hidden treasures waiting to be revealed.

# 42

*Next July*

On a warm Mediterranean night in Aix, Callie stood onstage in a palace courtyard tucked among seventeenth-century buildings, with more than a thousand souls before her. Feeling the springs flow beneath the city, she tapped into the source that joined them all. She plucked the first notes on her guitar, unfurled her voice like a new leaf, and sang.

She sang songs of earth and taste and secrets.

Of honey and keys and stars.

Of lemons and petals and moon.

Of tree and sun and stone.

Of dragon and spirit and fight.

Of feathers and treasures and sky.

She let herself fly, fly away with every soul there.

She moved across the stage with the grace of a selkie who'd slipped back into her skin.

And yes, maybe she shook her ass a little.

She did it again for good measure.

She blew a kiss to the audience.

"I'm Callie Byrd. And I'm back."

# EPILOGUE

Dear Callie,

Thank you and thank me.
Thank the river and the forest.
Thank the humans and the dogs.
Thank the music and the source.
Thank us all.
At the heart of it, we're one and the same.

Love,
Callie

# ACKNOWLEDGMENTS

Truly, where would I be without my writing group? Thank you, Laura Pritchett, Todd Michell, and Claire Boyles—I couldn't do this without you.

I'm enormously lucky to have landed with my wonderful agent, Kim Lionetti. Big thanks also to her fabulous assistant, Maggie Nambot, and the entire BookEnds Literary team.

I had the pleasure of working with several talented editors on this book, from the brainstorming stage with Lizzie Poteet, to the developmental stages with Laura Wheeler and Kimberly Carlton, and the copyedit stage with (French-speaking musician!) Jennifer McNeil. The whole team at Harper Muse has been a dream to work with—my gratitude to Caitlin Halstead, Sicily Axton, Hannah Harless, Lauren Kingsley, Josh deLacy, Kevin Smith, the incredible designers, and everyone else working behind-the-scenes magic.

To my consultant friends—I love you! *Gracias, merci,* and thank you to my *querida amiga* Gloria García Díaz for Spanish expertise; to *ma chère amie* Esther Vincent for French language help; to longtime friend Megan Flamant for all things French wine; to travel buddy Richele Kuhlmann for design brilliance; to Sidahmed for mint tea and fascinating conversation in Marrakech; to Nova Loverro for arranging my first Mediterranean truffle-hunting trip; to courageous friends (and strangers who became friends) over the years who've shared experiences of leaving emotionally abusive relationships—you not only helped me heal but strengthened this story, which I hope connects with others in turn.

I'm beyond grateful to readers who welcomed my first adult book into the world last year—*The Alchemy of Flowers*. It means so much to me that you spread the word, shared it with friends, read it in book clubs, reached out to me, and came to events (with friends in tow!). A special shout-out to my amazing launch team, the magnificent Kaye Publicity group, the fabulous writing/book podcasters who interviewed me, and the incredible community of Bookstagrammers and reviewers (many of whom have become friends!).

Huge thanks to the big-hearted authors who supported *The Alchemy of Flowers* by blurbing it, posting about it, being my conversation partners at events, and more: Melissa Payne, Evie Woods, Kate Khavari, Sarah Penner, Jaclyn Goldis, Nicole Hackett, Kate Shelton, Amy Rossi, Bailey Cattrell, Suzanne Nelson, Andrea Jo DeWerd, Heather Webber, Lara Payne, Aimie K. Runyan, Elizabeth Bass Parman, and the whole wonderful community of Harper Muse authors. And *merci mille fois* to the generous authors who consider endorsing this new book (whoever you may be!).

My writing journey began twenty-five years ago in the kidlit space, and I'm fortunate that this warm community has also supported my "grown-up" books. Thank you, especially, to dear writer friends Alda P. Dobbs, Melanie Crowder, Donna Cooner, Ingrid Law, Tara Dairman, Lauren Sabel, Natasha Wing, Olivia Chadha, Megan Freeman, Sheala Henke, and the whole wonderful Rocky Mountain Chapter of SCBWI. My colleagues and students in the graduate program in creative writing at Western Colorado University have also offered heaps of enthusiasm and support—I'm grateful to be in your company.

My French *maman* and *papa*, Annie and Alain Thille, offered conversations filled with laughter, love, wine, culture, gourmet meals, and so much more during my junior year living with them . . . and decades beyond. Andrea Mummert Puccini (my sister for all practical purposes), I have you to thank for those early years of letter writing and wild creativity that laid the foundation for everything.

My family has always provided a strong nest for all my creative adventures—thank you! Ian, you're the inspiration for all my love stories; Bran, you've made my world come alive with music (and offered helpful feedback on all things musical in this book!); Dad and Mike, you've supported me and my books in such unique ways; Mom, in a parallel universe, you're a world-famous book editor—and you always swoop in to save the day; Aunt Liz, in that same parallel universe, you're a world-class book publicist—I'm fortunate to have you.

Reader, thank you for spending hours of your one wild and precious life inside this story. I'm honored.

## DISCUSSION QUESTIONS

1. Callie is on a journey to reclaim her voice and herself. How does her determination to protect Eva help her do this?

2. When Callie arrives in La Chanson with Eva, she has cut off contact with family and friends. How do the people of this village help her trust others again? Which characters become part of her "found family" and why?

3. Discuss the importance of music to Callie's sense of self and how music inspires other characters in the book. Do you agree that music can affect people in deep and significant ways? If so, what has your experience been?

4. How did you feel about Callie's letters interspersed with the present-day narrative? What are some differences in the style or tone, and how do these differences reflect Callie's emotional states?

5. What role does the river, La Chanson, play in Callie's journey? Have you felt a powerful connection to something in nature? How has it helped you during emotionally challenging times in your life?

6. In her letters, Callie talks about reading ancient myths and fairy tales. How do these stories help her reflect on her reality? Joseph Campbell, Clarissa Pinkola Estés, and other writers have discussed how myths and folktales can resonate

deeply in the human psyche. Do you agree? Can you think of examples in your own life?

7. What did you think about Luc and Callie's relationship? What qualities or situations draw them together? How do they help each other grow and transform? How do you see their lives playing out in the future?

8. Discuss domestic abuse as it's portrayed in the book, in terms of Brett's and Tristan's behavior. In what ways is Brett abusive even though he never physically harmed Callie? What techniques does he use to try to control her? Compare and contrast this story's portrayal of domestic abuse to that of other books and movies.

9. Both Brett and Tristan had difficult experiences as young people. How did those experiences affect their behavior as adults? Do you think early trauma influences some people to become abusive?

10. What did you think of Eva? What personality traits drew people (and dogs) to her? How does she influence the other characters? How do her communications with ghosts (real or imagined) affect people?

Please visit Laura's website for recipes, a playlist,
and other treats: www.LauraResau.com.

# ABOUT THE AUTHOR

Photo by Tina Wood

**Laura Resau** is the author of *The River Muse, The Alchemy of Flowers,* and eleven acclaimed books for young people. Her novels won five Colorado Book Awards and appear on best-of booklists from Oprah, the American Library Association, and more. Trilingual and with a cultural anthropology background, she's lived in Provence and Oaxaca, and now teaches creative writing at Western Colorado University. You might find her writing in her cozy vintage trailer in Fort Collins, Colorado, where she lives with her rock-hound husband, musician son, wild husky, a garden of healing flowers, and a hundred houseplants.

Connect with her online at lauraresau.com
Instagram: @lauraresau